THE LOST DEMIGOD

HANNA STEELE AND THE DEMIGOD
CHRONICLES
BOOK 1

ALEX DOVE

The Lost Demigod

Book One of Hanna Steele and the Demigod Chronicles

Copyright © 2025 by Alex Dove

All rights reserved.

This is a work of fiction. Unless otherwise indicated, all the names, characters, businesses, places, events and incidents in this book are either the product of the author's imagination or used in a fictitious manner. Any resemblance to actual persons, living or dead, or actual events is purely coincidental.

Print ISBN: 979-8-218-62269-5

e-Book ISBN: 979-8-218-62270-1

For my Mom and Dad who were always there for me. My Dad never got to see this work published, but I hope he'd be proud.

REVIEWS

"This was a great read! This book captured my attention in a way that I did not expect! With exciting adventures and storyline turns, this book engages any kind of reader. 5 out of 5 stars." - Clarissa O.

CONTENTS

1

CARNIVAL TRINKETS

Hanna Steele slammed the gas driving her beat-up, red pick-up in reverse and spilled recklessly onto Cherry Blossom Lane. Her two younger sisters knocked shoulders as the front wheels missed the driveway and rocked over the curb. They sat beside her on the long bench seat, tense and panting as she fought the stick shift.

"Hold on!" Hanna ground the gears before finally jamming the truck into forward.

Ashley's head whirled to the side. "He's coming—he's coming," she shouted as their father sprinted down the long suburban driveway in his bathrobe.

"Sorry," Hanna yelled out the open window. "Gonna be late to school!"

Lexi snatched Hanna's phone from the cracked vinyl dashboard. "Watch this." She lifted it to the windshield and added, "Smile!" goading their dad with a grin as she snapped a photo.

Their father's face flushed the color of beets. He kicked off his slippers and they tumbled into the grass as he continued the chase.

"Stop!" shrieked Ashley. "This isn't funny—let him catch up."

"Wait!" he hollered. "There's something in—" but the rest of what he said never reached Hanna's ears, drowned out by the truck's backfire. It lurched out onto the road and the three sped from the front of the house. Black exhaust billowed in swirling clouds from the rusted tailpipe.

"Talk with you after school, kay? I gotta go!" Hanna yelled out the window. She tightened her hands around the wheel hoping her dad would hear.

"Go back," pleaded Ashley.

Hanna looked across Lexi. "I don't have time—"

"It's not always about you. What about him?"

"LOOK OUT!" Lexi screamed, pointing out the windshield.

Hanna's head whipped forward. Something orange and low to the ground raced in front of the truck. Jerking the wheel, she slammed her white sneakers onto the brakes. The sound of screeching rubber squealed in the morning air as the pickup spun into a wide fishtail.

"Was that Maxwell?" shouted Ashley.

Lexi twisted around to look out the back window. "He's fine, he's fine."

Ashley huffed and slumped in her seat. "Shoot, that was close."

Hanna peeked out her side mirror. The neighbor's fat feline, who looked more like a pot-belly pig than an orange house cat, waddled past a parked white Porsche. It climbed the curb and sat on the sidewalk looking in Hanna's direction.

"Turd biscuits! Was that Christopher Valentine we just passed?" Hanna's heart plummeted to somewhere below her navel. Lexi nodded. "Do you think he saw us?"

"Unless he's blind—and I don't think they'd have a blind quarterback on the football team. So, duh. He saw you."

Ashley leaned against the door. "Dad's gonna be so mad tonight. You shoulda stopped for him."

"I couldn't. If Coach Stein catches me tardy again—"

"Dad was trying to say something, but I couldn't hear."

Ashley shoved Lexi with her shoulder. "Move over! You're squishing me."

Other than some grumbling, the two fell silent until they reached the end of their street. Ashley looked around Lexi, the corner of her mouth quirked. "What do your friends think of your crush on Valentine?"

"Michael and Patrick? Uh… What do you mean?" Hanna fumbled with her crystal necklace, one hand still on the wheel.

"Duh," Lexi said again. "It's simple chemistry "Boy likes girl. Girl likes boy."

Hanna shook her head. "It's not like that. They're just my friends."

Lexi shot her the stink eye. "Boys and girls are never *just* friends. Doesn't work that way."

"Neither of them cares that I like Valentine." But Hanna almost cringed at her own words. Over the past several weeks, she'd caught glimpses of both Patrick *and* Michael staring at her in a different sort of way. She snuck a quick glance in the rearview mirror and straightened the collar of her powder-blue T-shirt.

"News flash! It ain't gonna stay that way forever." Lexi rolled her eyes. "How is it I'm a year younger than you, and I've gotta teach *you* about boys?"

The girls pulled up to the school's parking lot. Hanna steered into the circle drive at the front of Midtown Valley High School. "We made it just in time." But somewhere in the back of her mind was the nagging sensation that Ashley was right about their dad. *Should I have stopped for him?* The ten-minute warning bell shrilled and Hanna signaled to the door. "Jump out. I'll meet you here after school, okay?"

Each held up their birth-marked right hands. Hanna pressed her matching wine-stained palm to Ashley's, then Lexi's. "Sisters forever," the three said in unison.

"Grab your stuff—see you later!" She waved goodbye and watched them disappear inside the school before rolling back out onto the road. She veered up the street and into the second entrance avoiding several parked yellow buses. Stomping the gas, Hanna took a tight swerve into the parking lot faster than she wanted. A loud *thump* echoed through the cabin as her right-front tire dropped into a deep pothole.

The whole truck jerked. Both windshield visors swung down and the glove box compartment fell open with a bang. Insurance papers and gas station receipts filled the cabin. The documents flipped end-over-end like oversized confetti. Hanna slammed the brake skidding to a stop. Something hard slid from under the driver-side seat and crashed into her heel. *Ouch!*

She reached for what looked like an old cigar box. Hanna lifted the surprisingly heavy and ornately-carved wooden box to her lap. Its lid was cracked ajar, inviting her to peek inside.

"What in the—where did this thing come from?" Honking horns blared around her, but Hanna ignored them as the cars slowly passed. She tilted the box to let the morning sun caress the ribbons of honeyed caramel streaking through the grains of dark wood. She pinched her brows in concentration as she opened the lid and revealed the strangest of items. There was a folded newspaper and a slew of what appeared to be carnival trinkets.

What kind of paper is this? She unfolded the thin sleeve of bleach-white newsprint. THE KINGDOM CHRONICLE was printed in old style block lettering across the top of the page. *I've never heard of this paper before.*

Setting it on her lap, she rummaged through the chest again, peeling out a faded photograph taped to the inside lid. By the curled edges and aging in the grain of the picture, the photograph had to have been older than her. It showed two elderly people with wrinkles about their eyes sitting on thrones in a large stone room. Were those flags or banners hanging on the walls behind them?

The woman was dressed in a fancy gown, her chestnut hair done up on top of her head. The king, however, wore a golden crown and a tunic with gold-work thread. A green surcoat made of velvet or silk covered his shoulders and arms. It was fastened around the waist with what appeared to be emerald buttons. A sash of gold draped in a lazy loop across his chest. *Who are these people? Are they the king and queen of a Halloween party? They look so old.*

She tipped the box again, revealing a thick layer of strangely-shaped coins. Some were gold and circular, others were silver and square, while the rest were copper and triangular. But it wasn't the coins that interested her. It was the other trinkets that really captured her attention. Nestled in the mixture of coins was a gemstone the shape and color of a ripe pomegranate, a platinum cube the size of a Matchbox car, and a golden ring adorned with a single garnet inset into a channel of five other empty prongs.

The small metal cube shimmered aquamarine in the morning sunlight. She picked it up and found it cool to the touch. Its corners were smooth and rounded. Along the top face was a circular, beveled seam. She picked at the seam with her nail, but it didn't move. So, unable to do anything more with the strange cube, she set it back in the box.

Hanna's eyes shifted to the golden ring. There were engravings etched all along the band. She bent closer and squinted. Tiny glyphs were drawn into the band under each prong. She picked up the ring. "Ouch!" An electric spark bit her fingers. Hanna dropped it back in the box and pressed her stinging fingers against her lips.

Before she could gather her thoughts, a scorching pain flared along her right forearm. Hanna watched in horror as a slightly disfigured bird burned itself into the soft skin below the bend of her elbow. A raven? Crow? The angry, red welt, about the size of a silver dollar coin, puckered her flesh. Tears stung her eyes as her arm trembled, but the pain was over almost as soon as it started. Her desire to reach class was all but forgotten.

"Oh, God." Hanna scowled gripping her forearm just above

the scar. She looked at her branded skin and dared to delicately run a finger over the raw, raised lines. The tissue around the scar remained crimson, which juxtaposed against her milky white skin. "W-what is this? Why is this happening?"

As if the scar wasn't enough, from one erratic heartbeat to the next, a deep, gravelly voice echoed through her head. Every nerve of Hanna's body screamed at the intrusion. *"I've finally found you. It's time to come home."*

She whipped around in search of who was speaking almost hitting her head on the headrest. "What the heck?!"

Hanna screwed her eyes closed and shook her head. She tried to jostle free the intruder in her mind. Her elbow struck the wooden box, knocking the ring and cube to the floor at her feet.

"Hide if you must," the voice taunted, *"but I'll find you. The lost child will be mine."*

Her chest heaved as panic clouded her thoughts. Hanna banged the steering wheel with her fist. "GET OUT OF MY HEAD!"

"Barlow's found you, and there's no escaping me this time."

Hanna flailed her arms and legs kicking and thrusting as much as the small space in the truck allowed. A loud *thud* suddenly slammed into the driver-side door. Hanna screamed. Outside the window was a man dressed in a lab coat—but he wasn't a normal man. He was green. Hanna flung herself in a mad scramble across the squeaky bench seat pressing her back firmly against the passenger-side door.

"W-what are you?! What's wrong with your skin? Are those scales?!" He appeared as if plucked from thin air. The top-half of his body just hung next to the driver's side window, while the bottom-half seemed to disappear through some kind of disc-shaped portal the color of a cat's eye. Hanna pushed the palm of her hand against the roof of the pickup. "Are you Barlow?"

"Has the King of Thieves found you?" His wild eyes darted around the cab and then out into the parking lot. "Where is he?"

"Who is Barlow? Who are you?"

The man's white lab coat flapped about his chest and his cotton mop of hair blew in a breeze. "My name is Professor Alexander Green…come with me if you ever want to see your sisters again!"

"You're crazy!" Hanna lunged back into the driver's seat, threw the truck in gear, and stomped on the gas.

Hanna sped away, tires screeching. The man shouted after her. "Don't trust anyone—I know the truth! Everything Barlow touches ends in tragedy." She made it to the end of the parking lot when something flashed in front of her truck. *Thud*—she slammed against something heavy and stomped the brakes. A shriek peeled from under her hood. Panting, shaking, and in near hysterics, Hanna turned to peer out the narrow rear window.

Nothing was there. The green man—the lizard—was gone. The floating portal was gone too. She blinked and looked again to make sure. Her eyes felt as wide as barn doors as she searched the back lot for any sign of the strange man. But soon doubt crept into her mind as the silence around her settled in.

The brand, the voice, the strange man…could it all really be happening? And of all days, on her sixteenth birthday? The shrill whir of a police siren echoed against the school's brick-red exterior. Hanna tore her eyes from the parking lot and gazed out onto the street, her hands squeezing the steering wheel.

2

MICHAEL GRAND

Hanna sunk low in her bench seat. *Crap! I'm busted! I'm in so much—*

The red and blue lights sped out of view and away from school. As the sirens faded into the distance, the memory of the crash came screaming back into focus. Did she hit someone? She threw open the door and raced to the front of the truck. Hanna froze, her heart lodged like a chip of ice in her throat.

Lying tangled under the chipped, white paint of her fender was one of her best friends. Michael Grand lay pinned under her bumper, his bike caught under the tire. His green Minecraft T-shirt was scuffed with black, oily smears and the front pocket of his khaki shorts sported a two-inch tear.

As Hanna leaned down to inspect the damage, her hands trembled at finding a bunch of twisted metal. She stared at the crumpled bike wheel and bent handlebars. Then a sharp ringing in her ears drowned out all other sound and her thoughts drifted to an earlier time.

In her mind, she traveled ten years into the past. Hanna and Michael were both six. She guided Lexi safely down the side-walk until something else caught her attention. When she turned back around, it was already too late. Her then five-year old sister rode her tricycle into the street. A shrill scream tore from Hanna's throat as Michael darted from the sidewalk and pushed Lexi out of the way of an oncoming car. It was the bravest thing she'd ever seen—and the most ashamed of herself she'd ever been.

"You saved her! You saved her," she'd cheered before her cries of joy turned to tears of pain.

Hanna blinked slowly as she remembered Michael's lifeless body laying limp under the front bumper of the brown car. A few more blinks and her mind transported her next to Michael's mother in a hospital waiting room. Lexi and her youngest sister, Ashley, lay red-eyed and crying on mom and dad's lap nearby.

A doctor stood next to the stiff, orange plastic waiting room chairs and dropped his eyes to Hanna before addressing Ms. Grand. His voice was soft but somehow had an edge of finality. *"I'm sorry to say this, but both of your son's kidneys are damaged beyond repair. He'll have to be put on a transplant list, and there's no telling how long—"*

"I'll do it!" Hanna blurted, eyes darting from Michael's mother to the doctor.

Ms. Grand, a tall, frail bird of a woman with a thick, black afro—and who seemed to wear the same dingy mustard brown shawl day after day—leaned down and rested her slender fingers on Hanna's shoulder. *"Blimey, sweetie. Do what?"* she'd said with an English accent.

Hanna looked up into her face. The bags under the woman's eyes were swollen and puffy. The whites of her eyes were stained a dirty red from crying. Hanna took a deep breath and said, *"I'll give Michael one of my kidneys...that's what he needs, right?"*

"I'd never ask you to—"

"Michael saved my sister's life. He's my hero."

A fresh shriek shook Hanna from her memory.

"Bloody Hell!" Michael screamed from the ground, head

thrown back, eyes scanning the area. "Who's the wanker who—It's you! You bloody hit me—with a truck?!" his clipped, English accent at full strength. It was from his mother's side of the family and came out most heavily when he was angry.

"I'm sorry! I didn't even see you." Hanna rubbed her face with her hands.

Michael pushed himself to his feet. Scarlet scrapes bloomed on his elbows and knees where his skin was torn jagged and raw. His fresh sores glistened against his black skin. But he shook himself off with an indifferent shrug and then brushed back coils of dreadlocks from his eyes with his skinned hands. A droplet of blood speckled Michael's black Doc Martin's boots. "Where'd you get—"

"Oh, my God. I thought you were hurt." Hanna gave Michael a once-over.

"Hurt?" he contested. "Bollocks, Steele. Ought to know by now. A little scrape ain't gonna bugger me off."

She glanced at his mangled bicycle and cringed. "Your bike's ruined."

"It's rubbish for sure." Michael pulled his bike out from under the front of the truck as the crowd that gathered around began to thin out. One of the pedals was bent and screeched against the asphalt.

"I'll make it up to you—somehow," Hanna offered. "Jump in my truck. We can toss it in the back."

Michael's eyebrows raised and he pointed at the truck. "Bloody brilliant. When'd you get it?"

"Mom and dad gave it to me as an early birthday present last night."

He lightly patted the truck's red door and gave Hanna a small smile. "Well then, this changes everything."

Michael handed over his bike and hopped into the still idling truck. Hanna walked it to the rear, gripping the back tire with her left hand and the mangled pedal with her right. As she hoisted it into the bed, the ruined gears slipped and the pedal spun under the weight of the bike. She tried to regain control, but the heavy bike landed in the back of the truck with a clang.

Hanna's index finger slipped between the taut chain and the unforgiving steel sprocket. Pain shot up her hand searing like liquid fire. She opened her mouth wide and a speechless cry peeled from Hanna's throat. A broken toe or two from karate paled in comparison to this fresh pain.

"You alright, Steele?" Michael called back without turning around.

Heat crept into Hanna's cheeks and she bit back tears. She could see him trying to look in the side mirror. "Yeah, no problem," she lied. *I can get out of this—I can. I don't need any help.*

Her breath caught in her chest as her fingertip turned an ugly, deep purple. With only one hand to maneuver with, she raised herself on her tip-toes and bent awkwardly to her side. She slowly rotated the mangled pedal with her left hand. The chain and her pinched finger rotated around the sprocket until she was finally able to slip free.

"Oh my god!" she grunted through clenched teeth. Her forearm tingled, half with pain, half from numbness. She gripped her finger; the wavy lines of the chain's links were stamped into her skin. *How am I going to explain this? And on my birthday, of all days. How stupid—stupid—stupid!*

Hanna tucked her hand under her left armpit with an exasperated sigh. Her finger wouldn't even bend. She walked around the truck and climbed behind the wheel. Hanna threw the vehicle into gear and found the nearest parking spot and killed the motor.

Michael caressed the empty space of the cracked faux leather bench between them. "Nice wheels. There's a lot one could do in a ride like this."

Hanna picked up the box of trinkets on the floor by her feet and slid it back under her seat. "Is that so?"

Michael scooted a little closer, closing the gap between them. The seat's springs squeaked under the shift in weight. He licked his lips. She brushed her braided bangs from her face as a new flash of warmth prickled her neck. *What the—? Is he gonna try to kiss me?*

He scooted even closer. She swallowed hard. A swirl of heat rose from the pit of her stomach. For the first time, there was a flutter of something new as she stared into the deep brown eyes of her friend. Hanna folded her bottom lip between her teeth. *I can't like Michael…cause…cause…I like Valentine. Valentine's the one I'm after…right?* She raised her hand to tuck her hair behind her ear—but instead struck her injured finger against the steering wheel. Hanna squealed as a blaze of pain reignited up her hand.

"W-what's wrong?" Michael asked.

Her finger pulsed and burned, nearly bringing her to tears. She shook her head. "Nothing…nothing at all." Hanna slid her throbbing finger between her pinched knees and forced her grimace into a toothy grin. "What were you saying?"

"Well, I…I've been thinking for a while about this." Michael inched forward again.

Her heart flitted about like a hummingbird somewhere in the middle of her throat. "Oh, about what?"

"We've known each other for what—fourteen years, give or take?"

The jitters in her stomach made her words tumble out her mouth faster than she could form them. "Somethinglikethat."

Michael smiled and slid even closer without missing a beat. "Don't think I'm daft, but since it's your birthday—I could give you a present I made myself." He scooted over again, closing the small distance between them in one quick move.

3

THE NOTE

Something suddenly crashed against Michael's window. The sound echoed through the truck's small cabin. Hanna's mounting tension erupted. She leapt in her seat blurting, "Barlow!" But it wasn't some stranger. Patrick's head and shoulders popped into view. The breeze tossed his short blonde hair and wrinkled the front of his navy T-shirt.

Patrick's voice was muted as he spoke through the glass. "What are you guys doing? Oops!" He lunged for something small and white that slipped from his fingers. It blew against the side mirror. Hanna caught a quick glimpse of red writing before the folded paper fell below the window and Patrick chased after. Hanna puffed her cheeks and let out a slow breath.

"Who's Barlow?" asked Michael.

She dismissed his question with a wave of her hand. "No one."

Michael scowled and smacked the leather seat. "That's dodgy timing, Patrick. Thanks a mil," he mumbled, grabbing his backpack from the floor and scooting out of the truck.

Hanna slowly opened her door, careful not to bump into Patrick. By this time, he was on her side and on all fours digging under her vehicle. When he scooted out from under the truck,

Hanna glimpsed her name on the folded paper. *Is that for me? What could he possibly want to say to me in a note that he couldn't tell me himself?*

Patrick finally stood and stuffed the paper into his back pocket. "I was walking through the parking lot," he said turning around to face Hanna. Patrick paused and brush oily pebbles of asphalt from his bare knees. "I saw you two. Where'd the truck come from?"

"My parents. It was an early birthday gift last night."

"Magnificent!" Patrick opened his arms and leaned in for a hug. "Happy Sweet Sixteen."

A shrill bell sounded across the parking lot. "That's the two-minute warning," said Hanna. "Better get moving."

"Yeah, sure, but I've got something for you…you know, for your birthday."

Michael rounded the back of the truck and playfully thumped Patrick on the shoulder. "Mate, you've got the worst timing—*ever*."

"What'd I do?"

"Just forget it—come on."

"But her present," Patrick pleaded.

"Give it to her later. The bell rang."

"Go on ahead," said Hanna, adding a nod of encouragement. "I gotta get something. I'll meet you inside."

She waved them off before returning to the truck. Hanna searched for the ring inside the box, but it was gone. Her breakfast turned over in her stomach. She checked under the box and along the seat until she finally spotted the ring and cube under the brake pedal. Hanna snatched them from the floor and tucked the iridescent cube into her shorts pocket. The ring ended up on her right thumb after a few attempts at wearing it on one of her fingers; it was too big for any of them.

Hanna examined the etched glyphs on the ring, then the mark on her palm before returning back to the ring again. Her breath froze in her throat. One of the icons under an empty prong looked crazily similar to her birthmark.

"Naw. That's not possible," she convinced herself. "This day is getting crazier and crazier." Trying to ignore the nagging feeling in the back of her mind about the green man and the mysterious Barlow, she closed the truck door and bolted through the parking lot. *Please, let nothing else go wrong with my birthday.*

Hanna examined her injured finger as she ran. The deep purple bruise improved to something light brown. She curled it and her knuckle bent. There was some discomfort, but it moved nonetheless.

As she hurried toward the school, her mind flooded with questions. How was her finger healing? Who was that green man? Who was Barlow, and why did he want her? What was all that about not trusting anyone? Hanna held her face in her hands and mumbled, "I've got to be losing my mind. I wouldn't follow that green guy if my life depended on it."

Although she looked up when she reached the grassy, manicured lawn near the front doors, her mind remained occupied. Where'd the ring, the box, and the other stuff come from? Could they belong to Barlow? Is that why he wanted her?

"Happy Birthday, Hanna!" shouted a girl running by in a cheerleading outfit.

"O-oh," Hanna stuttered, her gaze torn from the ring. "Thanks, Olivia."

Her friend pranced past and into the school, Olivia's platinum blonde hair and her crimson and white cheerleading skirt bounced with every step. Two more friends trotted past following Olivia.

"Better hurry! Don't be late," yelled Jasmine, a black-haired cheerleader, as she crossed the threshold into school.

Hanna slipped through the front door as the second to last bell echoed in the foyer. Before she could make it two steps further, a greasy voice stopped her cold. "Late again, Steele?" A man stepped into the hall from behind the open door.

"Coach Stein?!"

"What does that make it now? Twelve, no, thirteen truancies this semester?" He *tsked* and handed her a pink slip of paper, sports whistle swaying around his neck. The corners of his mouth twisted in a curl. "Meet me in detention this Saturday."

"But I made it before the bell!"

"Are you calling me a liar?"

"No…yes—" His eyebrows raised dangerously high. "—I mean no!"

"You were late," spat the coach.

"But I made it! And Saturday's the Homecoming Dance!"

"Oh well." His sneer morphed into a smirk. "The bell rang before you were inside. I'll see you Saturday."

Hanna snatched the slip from his fingers with a glare and disappeared into the throng of students in the hallway. Dang it! So, had everything this morning been for nothing? Speeding out of the driveway? Angering dad? Michael and his bike? She finally flagged Lexi down at her locker in the upstairs hallway. "Ready for class? Got all your stuff?" she asked, grateful to have something else to think about for a moment.

"Got a test in Geometry and a quiz in English. Today's gonna suck."

"Don't fret the small stuff—just review beforehand and do the best you can. Be glad you're not taking the SAT. Now *those* suck!"

Lexi grimaced. "Just got the jitters, I guess." She glanced down at the slip in Hanna's hand. "No! You didn't!"

"Yup, I did. Detention this Saturday."

"What took you so long? We've been inside for what…ten minutes?"

"Nothing—don't worry about it. It's my problem. You worry about your test." Hanna wanted to look—dared herself to look at the scar above her elbow, mere inches from the pink slip of paper in her hand. But she didn't want to draw attention to it and force herself to look at it once again.

The final bell blared, and Lexi retreated down the hallway. "I gotta cram during homeroom. Catch you later!"

Hanna found her locker through the mass of students getting ready before the zero-hour bell, tossing her bag into her own locker with barely a glance inside. She slammed it shut and followed the rush of students toward class. She liked homeroom. It was a time she could decompress with her friends before the start of her day.

Several jocks lobbed a brown football in high arches halfway down the crowded hallway. On the near end of the corridor stood her neighbor. Valentine was nearly a head above the crowd. She followed the whip of his golden hair as he threw the ball. Her gut fluttered and twisted, an internal war between joy and terror. As a gift to herself, she was finally going to get the nerve to ask Valentine to the school dance. *If I flirt enough, maybe he'd get the hint and ask me instead?*

Her cheeks flooded with heat. She almost forgot all about her friends in class. Hanna entered homeroom and scanned the seats for Michael and Patrick. While much of the class was still on their feet, her friends were seated at their desks. She weaved through the crowd and slid in between them to her seat near the emergency exit.

"Talk about crazy days," she huffed. "Look what Stein gave me."

"Bollocks. Not on your birthday."

"Hey, yeah, speaking of birthdays…" Patrick unzipped his backpack and pulled out a thin, rectangular piece of paper. "I printed this for you." It was a four by six photograph. "I made it for your locker…it's of us in your backyard."

Hanna smiled. "Aw, it's perfect. Thank you. I know just where I'll put it, too." She eyed the photo of the two of them sitting on the floor of her backyard clubhouse together. "Thanks." Hanna leaned in and kissed him on the cheek. Patrick froze, both his cheeks flushing red.

For a few silent moments, she stared at the photo before

sliding the ring off her thumb. "My crazy birthday started with this…" She tossed the ring to Patrick, half-expecting it to burn him as it did her. But the spark never happened. Patrick merely rolled the ring between his fingers, examining the markings.

"Where did 'ya nick that from?" asked Michael looking at the ring from the other side of her.

Hanna eyed Michael. "I found it. Don't you dare snatch it. Let him get a good look at it first."

"You don't know anything about it?" asked Patrick. "Where'd you get it?"

"In a strange box in my truck. It shocked me when I picked it up."

"Shocked?" said Patrick. "What do you mean shocked?"

"Just that. I touched it and got zapped. Just the once, though. Now when I touch it I get nothing. It's fine." With a quick flick, she darted her eyes down to the inside of her arm. The puckered burn was still there. Hanna couldn't bring herself to say anything about it. What would she say? What *could* she say that would sound believable? The whole thing was insane.

"Must've been a buildup of static electricity." Patrick continued rolling the ring between his fingers. "It looks like there's a tiny picture of something etched into the metal above the setting. Something's funny here…did you notice that only a portion of the drawing is colored in blue? You see? Right there above the garnet stone. It's hard to tell what it is…maybe it's part of a tail or something? The rest of the image is missing." He frowned and scratched the engraving with his thumbnail.

Hanna shrugged. "Yeah. I saw that too, but don't know what it means. There's also some weird glyph underneath each prong where a stone is supposed to sit. Strangest ring I've ever seen."

"Mate, can I see it?" Michael stretched out his hand.

Patrick passed him the ring, but Michael jerked his arm when it touched his skin. Had that been—

"Did it shock you? It shocked you, right?" asked Hanna.

Michael sucked on the ends of his fingers. "Bloody hell…that stung!" He held the ring up to his face with his other hand. "Where are all the missing stones? Are they in the—?" Michael winced, holding his lower back in obvious pain.

"What's wrong with you?"

"Dunno." Michael grimaced and massaged his back just above his waistline. "Just started hurting. Ow—what the—" Michael grabbed his right forearm with his left hand and squeezed. Hanna's gaze dropped and she gasped as a small image burned itself into the dark flesh near his elbow. "What's happening?" he hissed through gritted teeth.

After a brief moment, the angry skin around the puckered brand lost its redness, leaving a raised scar. So, it wasn't all a hallucination?! Hanna shot out her arm showing her own matching mark.

"You've got one too?!" asked Patrick incredulously.

"It happened right after touching the ring. Just like Michael's —burned like heck."

"You ain't kidding," panted Michael. "I don't get it…w-why? How'd this happen? Why didn't *he* get one, too?" Michael jabbed a finger at Patrick. "Why didn't you warn us?"

Hanna scowled feeling somehow affronted. "How was I supposed to know?"

"You're asking the wrong questions. *How* did it happen?" corrected Patrick. He flipped his right arm around to inspect the underside. But nothing was there. He checked his left arm too, but it was also bare. Patrick stood from his seat to get a closer look. "This is insane—it just can't be real. We should see the school nurse."

"Mate, you ain't telling no one. Sit down and zip it. This thing is real. It's right here on my arm. It's as real as a heart attack and stings like a bugger. Shoot." His face darkened as if covered by a shadow. "What am I gonna tell my Mum?"

Hanna rubbed at her own scar as if it would smear away. "Why'd I get one. And why'd you and not Patrick?" She sighed and inspected Michael's arm. "Geez, I felt like I was going crazy…" Hanna rubbed her face with her hands and looked to see if the teacher was watching, but her homeroom teacher was missing. "Heck, *still* do. I felt like…like all this was happening to just me." A wave of relief washed over her and she exhaled a deep breath, slumping in her seat.

"What are you saying?" whispered Patrick. "That the brand on your arm just magically appeared because of what…that ring?"

"Yeah? You just saw what happened. That's exactly what I'm saying."

Patrick shook his head. "Magic doesn't exist. It can't. I mean, I know what I just saw. We all saw it. The scar just appeared, but I don't care. It's not scientifically possible." He looked around at the other students checking to see if anyone was listening.

Hanna raised her brows. "You saw it! Just like us. You saw it happen."

"Yeah, I saw it, but that doesn't mean I understand it."

"And you think I *do* understand?" she shot back.

Michael let go of his right elbow. "Look. I don't care if it was magic or the Easter Bunny. I just want this thing gone from my arm. Mum is gonna kill me when she finds out." Michael blew out a puff of air as he stared at his arm. When his gaze lifted, he stretched and rubbed at his back while looking around as if, like Patrick, to see if anyone else could've seen what happened.

Classmates filled the seats on the far side of them, but none showed any interest in their drama. The burn into his arm apparently went unnoticed by everyone but the three of them.

"Hey, it's gone."

Hanna furrowed her brow. "What's gone?"

"The pain in my back. It just vanished—like a kink got worked out or something." He shook his head and handed Hanna the ring. "Don't know how, but the pain just went away," he said with a grin.

Right at that moment, Coach Stein entered the room with a young blonde-haired woman Hanna didn't recognize. The pair walked to the front of the room and the woman sat a water thermos on the teacher's desk. "This is Ms. Johansen. She'll be your substitute homeroom teacher and one of our history professors for the day."

Hanna, still annoyed at Stein for her detention, ignored the coach and thought instead of how she was going to manage the growing drama between her friends. A tickle of heat crawled up Hanna's neck, threatening to fill her cheeks. She slumped in her seat and rolled the ring between the fingers of her right hand before slipping it into her pocket.

As if I need more drama, she thought to herself. *First the ring and then Barlow, now this? What am I gonna do with these two guys? After fourteen years Michael appears to finally be taking an interest in me right when I'm chasing after Valentine. And what's with Patrick? What was that note in the parking lot? What a mess I've gotten myself into.* She blinked and inhaled a deep breath. *There's no way I'm telling them I'm hearing voices. That's a one-way ticket to the nut house. Barlow—the green man—the ring. What does it all mean?*

4

COACH STEIN

Olivia and Jasmine strolled into the room walking across the back of class. They took their seats as Jasmine waved with her fingertips. Hanna returned the gesture, but as she lowered her hand, she wasn't sure if Jasmine was waving at her or Michael. She cast a glance over Olivia's shoulder and watched Coach Stein leave the room just as the final homeroom bell sounded.

Seemingly oblivious to Jasmine, Patrick sat up straight and turned in the direction of the substitute teacher who started taking attendance. He held his head up high and practically beamed with excitement. "Oh, I've been waiting to tell you all day!" He leaned over and whispered conspiratorially to Hanna. "It won't compare with your ring, but…you'll never guess what happened yesterday after getting home from school." He didn't wait for them to answer. "Do you remember how I've been taking IQ tests online to prepare for my Mensa testing?"

Hanna nodded. Michael leaned closer as if trying to hear.

"Michael Grand," called the teacher.

Michael raised his hand. "Here."

Patrick continued as Ms. Johansen rattled off more names.

"Well, last week I took my entrance exam. And I just got my acceptance letter!"

Hanna stared at him as if he asked the circumference of the moon. "What's Mensa again?"

Michael looked non-plussed.

"Guys! I've only been talking about this for months… I've been inducted into the ranks of people who have the highest IQ in the world!"

"Really?" New curls twisted up the corners of Hanna mouth. "That's great. You're better than Google!"

Michael stood reaching around Hanna and playfully slugged Patrick on the shoulder. "Nice job, mate."

"Did you get a certificate or anything? Are your parents taking you to Mensa headquarters for a photo op? Maybe to see some other members or something?"

Patrick shook his head. "Naw. It's not like that. I'm just happy to have gotten in."

Michael shot a finger toward the wall closest to the emergency exit. "Hey, Coach Stein hung up this season's try-outs for the girls' basketball team. Are you gonna try out again this year? I bet you'd make it this time. Last time is a charm, am I right?"

"Yeah, Hanna, I can't wait to see you in your uniform. Er—I mean playing on the field—court. Whatever," Patrick mumbled.

Hanna glanced left toward the poster. "I really don't think I'm cut out for it. Firstly, Coach Stein doesn't like me. Secondly, how many seasons can I try out and fail? Elementary, junior high, and my first two years of high school—every year I get turned down. Face it, I'm not good enough." She sighed and shrugged. "Sometimes, I think I'm not good enough for anything."

"Patrick O'Shea," called Ms. Johansen.

"Here."

"Hanna Steele."

"Here."

Patrick grimaced. "Don't be like that. You're better than you think."

"Nah, it's best if I don't try out for team activities. I've learned that I'm a lone wolf."

"Bugger off," said Michael. "You're so full of it sometimes."

"Doing things alone is my thing. I believe that." She shuffled in her seat and put her hands in her pocket looking for the cube. *Where was it? Oh, right. The cube was in the left one.* Hanna pulled it out and rolled it around her palm.

"What's that?" asked Patrick.

"Dunno, it's something I found with the ring. It's nothing, really." She unzipped her backpack and dropped it inside.

"It didn't look like nothing. Can I see it?" He stuck out his open hand.

She pulled it back out and handed it over. Patrick stroked the iridescent box with his thumb and tumbled it end over end. He paused to look at each surface, but stopped to more thoroughly investigate the indention carved into one side. Hanna watched for five seconds—ten—twenty. Suddenly, the combined voices in the room raised to a roar of laughter as the substitute teacher spilled her water thermos across her desk.

Patrick seemed un-phased by the new noise. "Do you know what it is?"

"No clue."

Michael rolled his eyes. "Blimey, mate. Spill your guts. Tell us what *you* think. We're waiting…"

"Hanna, can I see that ring again?"

Her stomach knotted. The day was already crazy enough without something more happening. She wasn't sure how much she could take. "Don't do anything weird."

"I promise I won't do anything with it. I just want to see something."

She flicked her eyes to her bare thumb. "Oh, right. It's in my pocket."

Hanna pulled it out and dropped the ring into his waiting

palm. The needling bees in her stomach stirred even harder. With his brows pinched, Patrick drew the ring close to the circular bevel on the side of the cube. The iridescent colors began to swirl—he pulled the ring and box apart. "Hm. I don't think this is a good idea."

From the back of her mind roared Barlow's voice. *"Come. Come. Come! Come to me."* Deep in Hanna's gut was a tug, the urge to join the ring and cube, but the shrill scream of the five-minute warning bell cut through the connection and left a trailing echo in the hall outside her homeroom class.

The intercom crackled and filled the room with a burst of static. *"Attention, students. This is Ms. Lindsey, the Assistant Principal. All juniors and seniors, at the end of homeroom please make your way into the gymnasium for a short assembly regarding the SAT this coming Fall. All sophomores, head to the library for the PSAT demonstration."*

Ms. Johansen looked to the back door and Hanna followed her gaze. Coach Stein appeared in the doorway motioning for Hanna to follow him out into the hall. When she didn't move, he approached sticking his crooked, beak-like nose into Hanna's face. "Idle minds are the devil's work, Ms. Steele." He pointed toward the doors. "A word in the hall, if you please." The coach then turned to the teacher. "Ms. Johansen, I need a moment with Hanna in the hall."

The substitute nodded and continued cleaning the sopping papers on the desk. Patrick silently mouthed the words 'good luck' and held out his hand. In his open palm was the ring and cube.

She snatched them before standing. "What about the assembly?"

"It'll wait."

5

PATRICK O'SHEA

Coach Stein walked out of the room and into the quiet hallway. On his way there, he turned around twice apparently to make sure Hanna was still following, his black, caterpillar eyebrows knitting in wooly tufts. The roar from the students quieted as the substitute teacher finally brought the class back to order. The coach stared down his long, beaked nose at Hanna.

He took a step toward her, stopping close enough for his breath to brush her face. "I've been after you all semester for a reason…given you plenty of chances to redeem yourself. But what do you do? You throw it back in my face. Always late. It's disrespectful. Your tardiness shows a lack of regard for your fellow students and the teaching staff whom are required to look after your care. It may fall on deaf ears, Steele, but the world works according to a clock. And it may be a surprise to you, but that clock isn't your private timepiece. *Tick. Tick. Tick.*"

Not meeting his eyes, Hanna fumbled with the items in her hands. As Stein continued his scathing speech, the ring tapped against the cube and the silver surface morphed into a smooth mother-of-pearl. Iridescent swirls of green and blue swam along the small sides of the cube. The dull droning of Stein's voice faded into the background as Hanna became transfixed.

"Steele! Steele!" the Coach shouted. "Are you listening to me?"

Hanna blinked and looked up at him. "Er—yeah, yeah, sure."

He pointed back down the hall to the gymnasium and toward his office near the locker rooms. "Before this year is up, I'll teach you some respect. I'll teach you not to be late. Now get back to home-room before I haul you to the principal's office for truancy myself."

Back in class, Patrick unzipped his backpack, drew out the heaviest of books—a Webster's Dictionary, 6th edition—and opened the front cover. He plucked out the folded letter with ornate stenciling. Hanna's name was written in calligraphy on the front. Her name was overlaid by a ruby red, crowned heart. He nervously bounced his foot against his chair like a jackhammer and traced Hanna's name with his finger.

Michael narrowed his eyes at Patrick. "Whatcha got there, Skippy?"

Patrick tried to hide the note on the far side of his thigh. "Nothing."

"Mate, I'm not blind. And it looks like a whole lot of some-thin'." Michael leaned closer, trying to bend around Patrick for a look. "If I didn't know any better—and usually I don't—what we have here is a genuine, grade-A, love letter."

"What? No! You're crazy."

Michael smiled a toothy, perfect grin and slapped Patrick between the shoulder blades. "You ain't foolin' me, mate! Seen the note you're hiding, num-nuts. If I know anything about girls —and I think I know a little somethin' 'bout somethin'—you've got yourself a crush."

"Er—"

"Who's the lucky gal?"

"No one." But before Patrick could tuck the note away properly, Michael tilted over and snatched it. "Hey! Give that back!"

Michael flipped it right-side-up and stared, "Gobsmacked, mate. I'm simply Gobsmacked." Patrick grappled for his letter, but Michael leaned back, arching his arm out of reach. "Let me stop you before you make a fool 'outa yourself." Michael gestured up and down the length of his own body with his index finger. "Don't you think I'm more Hanna's type?" He stroked his dreadlocks and gave his friend a once-over with his eyes. "I mean, don't get me wrong, Patrick. You're a catch, mate, for some nerdy chicks, but look at what I've got going' on. Who could turn all this down?"

"Shut up, Michael. Hanna's not like that."

"Like what? Into all this action?"

Patrick leaned toward Michael. "No. She's not into the games you play."

"Don't hate the player…hate the game." Michael smirked.

"Y-you don't like her. You're just…just…"

Michael scrunched up his face. "I'm just what, exactly?"

Patrick swung his arms as if miming his friend. "You're into every girl that walks by, that's what!"

"Am not!"

"What about Jasmine?"

"Yeah, so?"

"And Valerie. And Susan, Lisa, and…and Tara?"

Michael waved off the accusations with a flick of his wrist. "They were just—"

"They were what…pawns in your game of love? Well, that's not happening with her—not with Hanna." Patrick glanced back to the door making sure Hanna wouldn't somehow sneak in when he wasn't looking. "I-I've liked her for so long now…" Patrick eyed his note. It was still clutched in Michael's hand.

"I've known her for fourteen years, mate. Been around her longer than you. I got dibs."

"Dibs? Dibs?! There aren't any dibs—not with Hanna! You don't—you *can't* like her."

Michael raised a brow and smiled. "But I *do* like her." He smiled watching a wine-stain tinge grow up Patrick's once blanche-white neck to color his cheeks a pomegranate red.

Patrick shot to his feet and his dictionary tumbled to the floor as words spilled from his tongue before he could stop them. "YOU DON'T LIKE HER LIKE I DO!"

Kids around the room turned and stared at Patrick. A bark-like laugh came from the back of the room. Everyone was still gawking at Patrick when Hanna emerged pushing herself between them and taking her seat. An ominous 'ooooh' sounded from someone and several kids broke out in laughter.

"What did I walk into?" Patrick snatched a paper from Michael's hand. Was it the same note he fished for under her truck earlier? He bent down grabbing his dictionary and shoved it inside the top cover of the book. Hanna stared at her two friends. "Who do you like?"

The red in Patrick's cheeks reached the top of his ears. His messy weave of blond hair highlighted his now radish-like appearance.

"Yeah, Patrick," goaded Michael. "Who do you like?"

Patrick crossed his arms over his chest. "No one. No one at all." He swiveled forward avoiding everyone's stare and sulked. Kids from an aisle over snickered. Someone threw a paper ball and missed.

Michael licked his lips. "You know, we were just discussing how awesome I am."

"More like an awesome jerk," Patrick mumbled.

From the corner of Hanna's eye, a figure raced along the aisle past them. Johnny Mack, the schoolyard bully, smacked Patrick's unzipped backpack out of his hands and the contents soared through the air. Johnny's laughter faded as he sprinted through the emergency door and out of view. The substitute teacher yelled as a high-pitched shriek split the air. The alarm on the door sang in protest to it being opened. The crowd around them exploded into laughter.

Hanna bolted after Johnny. "Get back here, you bearded turd hugger!" she leapt over the sprawling mess, followed closely by Michael, but Patrick's groans made her halt and let Michael pass.

"My stuff—" cried Patrick.

"Get Johnny!" she called to Michael as he sprinted down the hallway. Hanna returned to Patrick at the edge of his seat and squat down beside him. "Johnny's a fart badger."

"Settle down!" cautioned Ms. Johansen. "Boys! Boys! Get back here this instant." But neither Johnny nor Michael apparently heard or cared about her request.

"My cell phone—it's cracked." He held it up for her to see. "My dad's gonna kill me."

She scooped a handful of papers and cradled the messy pile against her chest. "We'll fix this. It wasn't your fault. He can't blame you for that, right?" Hanna said as students crowded around them.

"Doesn't matter. He'll blame me for something. Always does." Patrick stared at the ground. "He thinks I have to be tough. That I need to stand up for myself. That I should be more like—more like Michael."

Really? What's Mr. O'Shea got against his own son? What's he see in Michael that he can't see in Patrick? If anything, why can't he see his son's heart? If only Michael had more of Patrick's emotional intelligence. Is there something here I've been ignoring?

Hanna bit her bottom lip and leaned over, stretching out over the fallen books to ruffle his blond hair. "Forget your dad. Just be yourself." She swiped her fingers across her forehead, pulling a braided weave of hair behind her right ear and looked directly into Patrick's eager eyes. "I like you just the way you are." A new smile perked the corners of his mouth.

Hanna's knee pressed against something on the floor. She leaned back and glanced down. It was a folded note—the same note she'd glimpsed in the parking lot. The front-half was stenciled in fancy script. She saw the last half of her name including a ruby red heart.

"What's this?" she asked, reaching for the note.

Patrick's face went as white as cottage cheese and he lunged forward. "It's okay. Let me get it."

"Um, okay?" She shifted back and allowed him to peel the folded paper from the floor as warmth blossomed in her cheeks. Her friend—her best friend in the world—had one of *those* notes for her?

A chill numbed her throat as if she'd swallowed a bucket of ice. It was suddenly hard to breathe as a wave of panic swirled in her gut. *Patrick likes me—I mean, he really likes me? Have I been an idiot all this time, blind to what's right in front of me?* Her head throbbed as blood rushed through her ears in a rhythmic *thrum, thrum, thrum.* But what about Michael? What about *Valentine?* Hanna tore her gaze away to find something else interesting to look at.

Patrick frantically stuffed the note into the front pocket of his jean shorts. "Thanks, I've got this now." He piled all his papers together and stacked them on top of his books before rising.

Collecting her thoughts, Hanna mumbled, "No sweat, just trying to help." She hated herself. *What a stupid thing to say!*

Patrick glanced around the room. "Er…where's Michael? He's not back?"

"He chased Mack down the hall." Right at that moment, the class bell rang for the end of homeroom. Patrick picked up his backpack and jammed his stuff inside. "Let's find Michael. We've got that assembly to get to."

As they reached the doors, the overhead speakers squelched to life. *"The PSAT prep exam will start this Saturday at 8 am before preparations for the dance."* Hanna wondered about her detention.

6

———————

BARLOW

Barlow stepped from the surface of the hot spring, water dripping from his bare skin. The wide, rocky pool, still frothing with minerals and bubbles, filled the air with the stench of rotten eggs. He padded over to the stony rim of the spring, tendrils of steam rising from his body in the crisp morning air.

The sun peeked over the Kragg Mountains and warmed the goose bumps on his skin. Barlow flicked his gaze toward two men along the edge of the pool. He caught the faintest hint of disgust fade from the tall, slender man's face. "Do my scars bother you, Rowan? Do the raised welts across my back still make your insides squirm after all this time?"

Rowan bent to one knee. The hooded cowl covering his head slipped over his eyes shadowing them in darkness. "Of course not, my lord. Forgive me?"

"Forgiveness is a luxury I can't afford." Barlow ran his nails through the scraggily, black sideburn draped across his left cheek. Droplets trickled down his long, slender fingers. Turning his right side to the light, he let the golden sun warm the rippled, scarred skin of his scalp. "Did the sight of me revolt you before scars took half of my face?"

Rowan kept his head low, his eyes diverted to the slowly bubbling pool. "Sir, I meant no—"

"Enough." Barlow raised a hand flexing his knuckles. As if pulled by an invisible string, he summoned his robe. The spider's silk garment floated from the pool's edge to Barlow's hand. The rings on his fingers clinked as he snatched the fabric from the air.

Rowan rose to his feet. Standing an inch taller than Barlow, he bowed his head, not quite meeting Barlow's eyes. His sculpted black leather suit creaked in the quiet morning calm as he stepped around the pool. "Shall I send a handmaiden to your quarters?"

"I need no slave today. The mineral bath has abated the pain for now."

Barlow turned from Rowan catching a glimpse of himself in a small pool of water at his feet no larger than a hand-mirror. As he examined himself in the reflection, he saw that the chiseled handsomeness on the left side of his face was lost against the gruesomeness of his right. The entire half of his face, neck, and skull were disfigured in a mass of gnarled, taut, pink tissue. Sinuous, angry skin stretched up his throat and across to his nose. The uneven streaks of muscle and tendon were highlighted in painful relief against the backdrop of the morning. The puckered flesh wrapped the side of his head and around the nub of his shriveled ear like bubbled caramel.

In his heart of hearts, he knew why most didn't look at him. Subservience and fear were only part of the puzzle. He was no longer stunning. He was no longer handsome, but ugly. That thought alone drove him to the brink of madness. He had once been the most handsome bachelor in the kingdom. The thought of another female being turned by his looks, even that of a slave, was enough to fuel his desire for revenge.

Barlow narrowed his eyes. "Grit."

"Yes, sir!" said the other man, standing quiet and sentinel behind Rowan.

"As Commander of the Crimson Brotherhood, I expect you to keep the ranks united."

"Yes, sir. Always strong." Grit cowed his head.

"I'll flay the backs of your hands if word reaches me again that Breakwater remains stalwart against me. The political machine in the city of Cog is already in my pocket. Turn Breakwater to our side or you'll pay for their resistance."

"I'll flay my own fingers if Breakwater doesn't fall within a fortnight." Grit's lips, though he was more wolf than man, curled into a wide grin up his snout. His silver, chainmail tunic, which stretched past his waist, wavered as he momentarily bent to one knee.

The soft skin around the left-side of Barlow's mouth curled in a smile. "I'll hold you to your word." He flexed the ringed fingers of his right hand. Two bands adorned his right hand and another two on his left. The silver ring on his forefinger was carved into the shape of a large, bulbous eye the size of a marble. A thin hood covered the eye, much like the flap of an eyelid. The second was a golden skull on his middle finger with two black pits for sockets. He polished the golden skull with the thumb of his other hand, displaying his other rings. A black band of the deepest onyx wrapped his ring finger. It was so dark that it absorbed the very light around it making it appear lost in a shadow. The fourth was a band of glass with a single diamond. Something cloudy stirred within the ring like the tumble of wind.

"I never showed an ounce of weakness when the king beat me as a child," Barlow said, more to himself than to the two around him. "Did you know that the king, my own father, whipped the flesh from my back? Did I cry? Not even once. I'd expect nothing less from you, Grit."

Barlow turned his back to the wolf and looked to the rising sun as it peeked across the land. The prince welcomed the morning with a sneer. "I'll have my father's throne, his kingdom, and all of Smaradine. I'll show the king what true power is."

He closed his eyes and drew a deep breath through his nose. Clenching his left hand into a fist, the eyelid of his silver ring opened with a snap. A solitary, blue iris stared from it. Barlow, as if reading a magical message from the ring, smiled. "Grit, prepare the witch." As the wolf-man turned and walked away, Barlow addressed the other.

"I've seen it, Rowan," Barlow added, shaking his ringed fist in the air. "The half-blood is coming, and just in time for the Summer Solstice. I can feel my mark on her, but the others—her sisters—they haven't touched the ring yet. They remain pure and untainted, their magical potential remains untapped. It was a calculated loss, losing the purity of one, but it was a necessary sacrifice. After fourteen long years, I've finally found her."

7

WEAK METAL

The class bell blared overhead. Hanna left Patrick in the growing surge of students spilling from homeroom. Hoping that Michael found and dealt with Johnny Mack, Hanna separated from Patrick and headed to her second period class. "Alright, I'll see you later. I'm off to my locker." Two minutes later she raised her hand in a wave as she passed her friend heading the other direction. "Hi, Olivia."

"Oh, hey! Happy birthday again. Gotta run to World Geography. I'm so late." Olivia reached the bottom of the stairwell. "We'll catch up at lunch, okay? Have a great day!" She smiled for a moment, then disappeared around the bend and was lost in the crowd.

Hanna climbed to the second story landing and rounded the corner. She walked into a sea of scratched, ocean blue, metal lockers lining the long hallway. A quarter of the way down, she caught sight of a colorful bouquet of balloons.

A toothy smile bloomed on her lips. Her locker was decorated with garishly-colored pink, green, and yellow crepe paper, topped with birthday ribbons and a bouquet of helium balloons. She brushed a few ribbons aside and tried her combination when a dark shadow crept across her shoulder.

"Sup, Hanna? Happy Birthday."

She would recognize that smooth, handsome voice anywhere. Hanna turned and looked straight into Christopher Valentine's eyes. "You remembered."

"What kind of friend would I be if I didn't remember my favorite neighbor's birthday?"

A nervous grin curled up Hanna's cheeks. "Is that all I am? A favorite neighbor?"

Valentine draped his arm across the top of the next locker. "I'm having a party this weekend—"

"Yes!" she blurted almost too fast. Her gut coiled like a bundle of worms. Had she answered too quickly; afraid of sounding too eager? Regardless of her desire to remain cool and collected, a fresh wave of nervous heat crawled up her face.

"Oh, cool! It starts around eleven on Saturday night, after the big dance."

Relieved that she hadn't made a fool of herself, Hanna's smile returned even wider than before. "I'll be there."

"That's a really beautiful necklace," Valentine added, bringing his face closer to hers.

"Oh, it's my favorite. I've had it forever."

He reached out a finger. "Can I touch it?"

But right at that moment, Valentine stumbled forward, thrown against Hanna as Jack Sampson, a fellow football player, crashed into his back. Valentine's hand curled around the pendant as he fell yanking both it and Hanna down with him. She thrust out her arm catching the palm of her hand on the locker door.

"Are you alright? I'm so sorry!" Valentine pleaded before pivoting to shove his teammate away. Jack didn't budge, but stared past him at something else. "What are you looking at meathead?" Valentine's voice caught in his throat as he followed Jack's eyes to Hanna's left hand. It was in the center of a basketball-sized dent in her locker.

Jack stuttered. "What the heck, Steele. You some kind of juiced-up freak?"

Hanna stared, dumbfounded. The wild chatter of students in the hall faded away. She blinked slowly as the rest of the world was lost to the ringing buzz in her ears. She couldn't tear her eyes away from what she'd done. Hanna tried to talk, but nothing came out.

"How'd you do that?" Valentine shook her shoulder, bringing her back to the moment.

Classmates crowded around, some jumping up over the shoulders of those in front to see what was going on. Hanna stared blindly at the crushed door. "I-I don't know. I didn't—I didn't do anything..." The eyes around them drilled into her. Her chest tightened and it got hard to breathe. "Y-You pushed me. You pushed me into my locker," she stammered, nervously clutching at the pendant around her neck.

Valentine pointed at her necklace. "How'd that not break? I pulled on it with all my weight."

"I don't know...I think it's from China or something..." Why'd she say that? That was stupid. She couldn't think. Everything was happening all at once.

From nowhere, Patrick spilled out from the crowd and slipped into the middle of the conversation. "What's going on?"

"Nothing, Brainiac." Valentine jabbed a finger at the dent. "I was just helping Steele before she destroyed the door. How'd she do that, smart guy?"

Hanna turned to her friend and pleaded with her eyes for help.

Patrick stared at the locker for a second and then shrugged. "Weak metal." He said it as naturally as if he were proclaiming that the sky was blue and the grass was green. "It was weak metal caused by the oxidation of the paint. Budget cuts obviously forced the school administration to buy cheap supplies. It'll happen sooner or later to all the lockers. You'll see."

Hanna blinked and exhaled a slow, relieved breath. There it

was. An answer to the craziness. Weak metal. She could've kissed Patrick right there. Students around them began looking at the other lockers. The metallic thump of someone banging on one of them echoed through the hallway.

"Weak metal, huh?" Valentine cast his eyes from Hanna to Patrick and then to the crushed door. He punched the center of the next locker and winced. "Ouch!" He shook out his hand. The locker remained un-phased. "Maybe you *are* a freak." Valentine pulled out a phone and snapped a quick photo of Hanna in front of the dent.

Ice water flooded her insides. Hanna's knees turned to jelly as her heartthrob whirled around and shoved his way through the crowd, disappearing into the sea of classmates. Everything was going wrong. Why did things have to go wrong? She couldn't believe this was happening. A hard knot formed in the back of her throat when she glanced at the remaining faces in the hall.

The hallway broke apart into a kaleidoscope of images and Hanna blinked away fresh tears. *Did he just call me a freak?* She watched the empty space that Valentine occupied only moments before and whispered to no one in particular. "It was weak metal." But in the back of her mind, she knew—she knew it wasn't true even as the words slipped from her lips. Too many weird things were happening to make such a simple answer be the truth. Hanna tugged on Patrick's arm. "Let's get out of here."

As they walked away from the lockers and the crowd, she looked down at her hands to avoid the curious gazes and frowned. Her index finger was no longer bruised. She flexed it and it felt fine—no pain. No stiffness. No indication that she pinched it in Michael's bike chain.

What's happening to me? This is the worst birthday ever. I just want this day to end.

8

MICHAEL'S SECRET

Michael slunk into his seat at the back of class as Mr. Tuner, his Geometry teacher, droned on about the obtuse vectors of triangles. He slid down so his rump nearly slipped off the end of the chair. The shaped white pine desk pressed against his belly, but it seemed to be the only position he could find that didn't add to the pain in his back.

He closed his eyes for a moment, trying to drown out the ambient sounds of the other students and the teacher. When he reopened them, his gaze fell on the unmistakable image of the bird of prey burned into the inside of his forearm. Michael tucked his arm close to his body to hide the strange brand from prying eyes. *How could this happen?*

Michael tenderly traced the puckered outline of the scar with his left index finger. He tensed initially, afraid it would hurt, but the pain was gone. The dull throbbing in his back, however, returned in full swing and it seemed to grow in intensity with each passing minute. He pushed his open textbook to the edge of the desk and let the teacher's voice fall into the background.

How is any of this happening? It can't be real. Scars and phantom pains don't mysteriously appear. But I'm not the only one with a scar.

Michael let out an exasperated huff and he closed his eyes

tight again, pinching the bridge of his nose with his fingers. A moment later, Michael lazily picked up his pencil. He doodled Hanna's name on his paper instead of working out the perimeter of a triangle like the rest of the students. He couldn't concentrate.

Nobody paid attention to him or his back pain. That was good. Because the more he thought about Hanna, the more restless he became. Michael reached into his pocket and pulled out his wallet. Opening it, he flipped through the thin, plastic flaps holding photographs. The first one was a class photo of Patrick, taken earlier that year. He wore a teal polo shirt buttoned up to the hollow of his throat. His golden hair was combed across his forehead in a thick wave. Michael flipped over the picture and read the message written on the back: *To Michael, my best friend in the whole world.*

He chuckled to himself at Patrick's cheesy grin as Mr. Turner scribbled new problems on the chalkboard. Ignoring his work, Michael turned to the second photo. Hanna beamed up through the scuffed plastic sheath. He stared at the long curls of toasted chestnut hair cascading over her smooth, white shoulders. Her white teeth and endearing smile made the corners of his mouth curl into a grin. He flipped the photo over and rolled his eyes at the message on the other side: *To the best guy a girl could ask for—friends forever.*

I ain't staying in no friend zone.

The corners of his mouth drooped as he flicked his eyes to the last photo. He stared for a moment at a man and woman in the black and white photograph. Michael traced his mom's bushy afro with the pad of his thumb as his gaze was instinctively drawn to his father. Although he knew he'd inherited his milky-black skin from his mother, he hadn't realized until then that he had his father's almond-shaped eyes. How might his life have been different if his parents had stayed in London after he was born—if he'd never come to Midtown Valley, Illinois?

Michael pulled open the pouch where he kept his money and moved past two wrinkled one-dollar bills. Tucked in behind them, he carefully pulled out an old folded note written on a thin piece of faded stationary. A black, inky grease smudge stained the top corner near a crease in the paper. Michael affectionately rolled his thumb over the smudge, soiled by his dad's greasy mechanic's hands. He lifted it to his nose and sniffed. An earthy odor mixed with the faint pungent smell of gasoline stung his nose.

Son,

I don't know how to begin to tell you how much I love you and how I long to see you grow into the strong man I know you'll be some day. While I know you won't understand the full extent of what I'm saying right now (you're still a wonderfully awesome five-year old), some day, when you're older, I hope to look you in your eyes, wrap my arms around you in a giant hug, and spend time together as father and son.

I have to leave…so you won't see me in the morning, but I'll be back for your birthday…and for Christmas. No matter how far apart I am from you, know that you're always in my heart. It's hard to explain in words that you'd understand, but your mom and I…we just don't play well together anymore.

I'm leaving for a new job in Ohio at Zuckermann's Auto Body. When you're older, stop by and see me…I'd like that…we'll catch up on all the things we missed together and share a few laughs.

Love always,
Your Dad, Jonas.

Michael rubbed his nose and sniffled. *Just because you divorced mom, didn't mean you had to divorce me, too.* He ground his teeth together in frustration. *You left ma…I get that…but why'd you abandon me?* He cupped the note closer. *You never visited for my birthday…you never came for Christmas. Or any other holiday. Wasn't*

I important? Hadn't you said so yourself? You just left and never came back…why? There has to be a reason. I'll find out some day. I'll come find you and…and we'll be together again…like you said.

He tried to sit straighter in his chair, but his back ached as if a hot poker were prodding him in the kidney.

9

OLIVIA'S SURPRISE

The final bell of the day echoed down the hallway. The corridor burst with the infectious laughter of teenagers. Hanna made her way down the hall to her locker. It was still broken. The playful crepe paper streamers were ripped into shredded fingers that dangled toward the floor. The balloons had popped, the yellow rubber lay lifeless on the floor. Her shoulders sagged as she pried open her dented locker door.

Hanna stuffed her laptop and several colored folders haphazardly into her backpack. Loose-leaf sheets stuck out the unzipped top at odd angles. Slinging her pack over her shoulders, she slammed the door shut and met Patrick at his own locker. "You ready, I need to get home. I gotta get outta this place," she said.

"Hold on a sec. I've got too much stuff in my backpack. I can't fit all my books."

Someone poked Hanna in the ribs from behind. "Did you have a good birthday?"

Hanna jumped and swiveled around. "Oh, hi, Olivia. Um, not really."

"Did your locker accident mess up your day?"

"Oh, you heard about that?"

Olivia's eyebrows rose. "The whole school heard about that."

Hanna's eyes dropped to the floor. "Oh." She felt her chest begin to tighten and pushed away the mounting urge to cry.

Olivia's cheerleading skirt wriggled as she talked. "Relax. It's not that big of a deal. How'd it happen, anyway?"

Patrick looked up from his spot on the floor. "Weak metal—a faulty door."

Hanna shrugged trying her hardest to smile. She opened her mouth to say something—anything—but a growing lump in her throat choked off her voice.

"Ah, well, don't worry," Olivia said with a smile. "It's your birthday. And we decorated your locker!"

"You did that?" Hanna said finding her voice again.

Olivia nodded. "Jasmine, Haley, and I, yeah."

"You're the best friends a girl could have *ever*!" Hanna stressed the last word and threw her arms around Olivia. She felt tears standing in her eyes. It was a tipping point like the opening of flood gates. There was no stopping them once they started. Hanna wept for the first time in a long time right there in the hallway. "My birthday is ruined." Her breath hitched in her chest as she gathered her voice. "It started out good, but then…it just…it just spiraled out of control. I don't even know how…" Hanna's voice trailed off as her breath hitched again when trying to suck in air.

Olivia pat Hanna on the back. "Perk up, okay? Did Valentine ask you to Homecoming yet?"

Hanna pulled back; eyes wide. "Yet? There's no way he's asking me after what happened today. He called me a freak. Did you know that? Right in front of everyone at my locker. He even took my picture. Is he supposed to ask me? How do you know?"

Olivia played with the pleats of her cheerleading skirt and leaned in close. "I heard from Suzie, who dates Jack Sampson, that Valentine likes you." She squeezed Hanna's shoulders. "Yeah, I heard about the photo. Suzie said that Valentine was a jerk. I think he was too. But that doesn't mean he won't ask you to the dance. I think he was just shaken up by the locker thing. It was just weird, 'ya know?"

"But he called me a freak? Why would he—"

Olivia shook her head. "I don't claim to know what goes on in boys' heads. But one thing's for sure is that he likes you…or at least he did before the locker incident."

"You think there's a chance?" Hanna said raising her voice an octave.

"Don't sweat the small stuff. Just tell Valentine what happened again. I'm sure he'll understand. I do. And if he doesn't then it's his loss, right? So, cheer up…and happy birthday, again. Feel better. Love 'ya—tootles." Olivia wiggled her fingers in farewell. "Gotta go home and *study*." She said that last word with air quotes before turning on her heels and prancing down the hall.

Once Olivia became lost in the sea of students, Hanna sighed and turned back to Patrick. "Are my eyes red? Does it look like I've been crying?"

He shook his head. "Nope. All good."

"Okay. Let's go home. The others are bound to be waiting."

The pair found Michael standing at the bottom of the stairs, and the three met up with Hanna's sisters in the circle drive. The parking lot was already half-empty by the time the five friends made their way to Hanna's beat-up truck sitting in the far back corner. All three girls jumped into the pickup's cab leaving Michael and Patrick to hop into the truck's bed. Hanna caught Lexi flashing Patrick a quick smile through the narrow, rear window and a pang of jealousy tightened in her gut. Dismissing the feeling, Hanna popped the clutch and threw the truck in gear.

They lurched forward in a rush as the clutch got stuck. The motion tossed Michael and Patrick against the broken bike. The old engine rumbled and belched a new plume of black smoke.

Cutting off a green Gremlin on the street, Hanna peeled onto Old Orchard Boulevard and stomped the gas.

Several minutes up the road, Hanna spied a girl in a red and white cheerleading outfit walking in the direction of her home. Mounting traffic behind her prevented Hanna from slowing. So, she rolled down the passenger-side window and yelled. "Olivia!" Her friend didn't reply. *I wonder if she's coming to see me at my house?* Hanna stuck her arm out the driver-side window and tossed her friend a wave as they sped by.

When they rolled up the length of the driveway, Hanna pulled the truck to a stop near the detached garage at the back of the house. She threw it in park and killed the motor. The old engine chugged for a moment before finally dying with a hiss of the radiator.

Michael jumped from the side of the truck and met up with Hanna and Ashley near the garage. Lexi stopped to help Patrick over the rear lift gate. Hanna couldn't resist slowing her pace to eavesdrop on them.

"So," Lexi said with a dramatic pause. "Are you going to the big dance this weekend?"

"Me?" asked Patrick.

"Mmm. I'd like to go," added Lexi. "But I need an upper-classman to ask me. Hanna wants Valentine to ask her. Do you think he's gonna?"

Patrick kept his eyes trained at the ground as they walked. "Dunno."

"Did you know I ordered a new dress just on the chance that someone would ask me to go?"

"Is that right?" he said clearing his throat.

"Yeah. Because I was hoping someone *would* ask me."

Hanna poked her head around the back corner of the house. "You guys coming or..." Her voice trailed as she stared at Patrick and Lexi. Lexi was standing nearly toe-to-toe with him at the front of her truck. Tightness clenched Hanna's chest. But why did it bother her? Her sister had fawned over Patrick for years, so what changed?

The longer she watched—the more a slow heat climbed up her neck. Hanna swallowed her anger as confused thoughts swirled in her head. Had everything changed because Patrick had one of *those* notes for her now?

Patrick gave Lexi an embarrassed smile and pointed toward the porch. "We, uh, gotta get inside."

Hanna pretended she hadn't been snooping as the pair rounded the porch and they stepped into the house.

They strolled into the kitchen just as the front doorbell rang. "Oh, bet that's Olivia." Hanna passed the table, snatching a thin, cottony-soft, blue school sweatshirt from the back of a chair. She checked her pockets for her smartphone and earbuds and tied her sweatshirt around her waist letting the cougar logo hang loosely behind her while she jogged to the door.

But it was just a UPS man. He handed her two tall, thin boxes and an electronic clipboard to sign. With a swift flick of her wrist, Hanna accepted the packages. The driver returned to his truck and drove away. *Humph—thought you were Olivia.* Frowning, she looked up and down the sidewalk searching for her friend, but the street was empty.

A faint girlish giggle drifted over the side hedges—

"Who's at the door?" called Ashley from the kitchen.

"A delivery driver. Just some boxes. They're addressed to Lexi."

Lexi sprinted up the hallway and snatched the packages. "My new dresses! They're here! Ashley, help me with these." In a whirlwind, the two disappeared upstairs with the parcels.

Hanna sighed and walked out onto the front porch.

"Hey, Hanna?" called Patrick. "Meet us out back. We're going to the clubhouse, okay?"

"Sure," said Hanna, still absently looking for a sign of Olivia, but the only movement came from the neighborhood cat, Maxwell. He was lurking under the front hedges.

Where'd Olivia go?

Another soft giggle from Valentine's yard floated over the hedges. Hanna froze. Stared. Then crept to the edge of her lawn and peeked through the eight-foot-high manicured bushes. Her heart nearly stopped.

Valentine's arm was draped over the shoulders of a girl in a red and white cheerleading outfit, his varsity jacket colors visible through the leaves. Nausea curdled Hanna's guts as Olivia leaned over and kissed Valentine on the lips. A heavy weight tumbled into the pit of her stomach and she almost gagged on the bile rising in her throat.

10

———————

PROFESSOR ALEXANDER GREEN

Hanna stumbled back through the kitchen and out the rear-patio door. The betrayal by Olivia, and somehow Valentine by extension, tightened the muscles in her neck. A new throb pounded in her head. She glowered over the white picket fenced-in backyards. How could she trust either of them again?

She glanced at the birthmark on her right palm and the new scar etched into the underside of her forearm. The angry, red skin around the brand already faded to a light pink outline around the puckered burn. She traced the scar with the index finger of her left hand following the bird's wing.

How is any of this possible? She flicked her eyes to her thumb. *This ring, the strange cube, my healed finger, the dent in my locker, the voices in my head, the green man in the parking lot. What does it all mean? Could I be losing my mind? Was that even possible, though? I'm not the only person the brand happened to. It happened to Michael. Patrick was a witness.*

Hanna craned her neck, searching the two-story treehouse for her friends, but the auburn-stained timber flooring and railings concealed much of her view. She stepped into the long sandbox that twisted like a brown snake around the edge of a shallow wading pool. Finely-ground sand dusted the bottom edge of her white sneakers.

She gripped a sturdy rope ladder with both hands and started to climb. The yellow nylon braid creaked as she applied weight. She squeaked her way up twenty feet in the air and pushed open the hinged door at the top. Poking her head through, Hanna finally found her friends at the far end of the spacious second story. At her approach, Michael set down a pair of binoculars. He nudged Patrick with his elbow and turned his back on Hanna. He pointed to a circular window through the trees several houses up the block.

"Mate, I think I see her."

"Who?" asked Hanna.

"Mrs. Robinson," replied Patrick. "He's been trying to peek through her windows for weeks. She always leaves her curtains—"

"Seriously!" shouted Hanna. She slugged Michael square in the shoulder. He winced and rubbed his arm but said nothing. With a huff, she turned and left the boys where they were. Hanna wouldn't be part of their pranks and prying so, she left them returning to where she entered the clubhouse. It wasn't far, but it was enough to dampen her rising frustration.

Her emotions spiraled, from hurt and angry to simply being ticked-off at the world. From across the grass, Maxwell slunk along the back edge of the fence. His heavy belly swung low like an orange watermelon as he tried to pounce on and unsuccess-fully catch a yellow butterfly. It flittered up and over the fence into Valentine's yard leaving Maxwell empty-handed and licking his paws.

Hanna flicked her eyes back to her hand and toyed with the ring around her thumb. Her mind wandered back to school, back to when Patrick brought it and the cube close together. To when she'd been in the hall with the coach and vibrant colors swirled between her fingertips. Her palms itched; she couldn't shake the impulse to try and pair them together again. *What if I did it? What if I just pressed the ring to the cube? It's mine. I can do what I want, right?*

She tapped the ring against the cube through the cloth of her pocket. *Clink. Clink. Clink.* Hanna glanced down again at Maxwell, then slid the cube from her pocket. *The boys are occupied with Mrs. Robinson. They'll never know.* She flicked her eyes back toward her friends. Patrick's warning in homeroom echoed through her mind. *I don't need their help, nor permission. It's my cube. It's my ring.*

Fingers twitching, Hanna rested the metal box on the tree-house railing. Golden rays of afternoon sun penetrated the leafy treetop. She pulled the ring off her thumb and slowly lowered it to the cube. Just as before, colors swirled across the surface as the ring drew nearer and she was starstruck. Hanna gaped in awe as she slotted it into the round groove. Hanna's eyes suddenly filled with a burst of white light. She shielded her eyes and in doing so knocked the cube off the railing. It dropped onto lawn and tumbled across the green grass below.

"What the heck did you just do?" yelled Patrick as he and Michael raced toward her.

"I-I don't know." The three bent over the railing, but the cube fell behind the base of the tree. "C'mon. Let's get down there."

Hanna was the first to reach the lawn and what greeted her stole her breath away. At the base of the tree hung an oblong-shaped window. It appeared to be cut into the fabric of space and glowed in brilliant hues of cobalt and crimson. It appeared to be just the same as in the school parking lot. Hanna took a hesitant step backward. Would the green man spring up again, too? She looked at her friends. "Am I crazy? D-do you guys see this?"

"You ain't bonkers, mate. I see it too. But what *is* it?" asked Michael.

Hanna darted forward and snatched the ring and cube from the grass before stumbling back to stand with her friends again. "I have no idea." It wasn't even a lie. She didn't know, not really. Was it just a portal? And to where? Could anyone use it or just—

Right at that moment, out stepped the same six-foot tall lizard-man Hanna saw at school. He was a marbled green chameleon walking upright like her and her friends. He wore the familiar white lab coat and a small brown satchel crossed over his chest.

"Son of a—" muttered Michael.

"It's—it's you," Hanna spat tripping over her words. "I saw you earlier!"

"Who is that?" wailed Patrick. "What do you mean you've seen him before?!"

"I thought I was seeing things in the parking lot."

Michael snapped. "And you didn't tell—"

"I don't have time to explain." The lizard pointed back to the portal. "This gateway is terribly unstable."

"Hanna Steele! Are you back there?" called a handsome voice from the front yard.

Hanna froze. "That's Valentine! Is he coming?"

"I don't know?" replied Patrick. "Who cares?"

"Has Barlow made contact again?" asked the chameleon.

"Who's Barlow?" Michael replied.

"Please," the strange man pressed. "It is important. Trust no one—he's after you. Barlow will stop at nothing to get what he wants."

"Who's Barlow?" Patrick asked, his voice rising with panic.

"I don't know!"

"I need you to listen to me very carefully. My name is Professor Alexander Green. I come from a place called Smaradine. You need to follow me there right now—we've no time to lose."

Michael pushed his way in front of Hanna. "What? You're crazy, mate. She's not going anywhere!"

Patrick stepped forward too, but he merely pointed to the window. "That's a wormhole!"

"The cube in Hanna's hand created this wormhole and it's the last of its kind," corrected Alexander. "All other dimensional rifts across Smaradine have gone dead."

"Dead?" said Hanna.

"Yes, and this portal could die at any minute, too. Now listen! You and your sisters are in grave danger."

Hanna swallowed as a panic rose in her throat. She remembered his words from the parking lot. *Come with me if you ever want to see your sisters again.* "What do you mean? What's any of this have to do with my sisters?"

The professor rubbed his face with slender, green fingers. "Barlow's been looking for you for fourteen years. I've tried to stay ahead of the prince, but this may be my only chance to save you, to save your sisters, to save everyone."

"Prince who?" asked Patrick with a growing irritation lacing his voice.

"But my sisters can't be in trouble," Hanna insisted. "They're in the house right now."

The portal flickered like an out-of-tune TV.

"Come with me, now, if you want to save them."

"Bloody hell. How do we know you're not this…this prince, bloke?"

The professor threw up his hands. "If I were Barlow, you'd already be captured. Or worse!" Hanna took a step back from the professor. Alexander raised his hands in a sign of forgiveness. "Hanna, did you touch something unusual today?"

"Y-yes. A ring. How did you know that?"

The professor stared into her eyes and replied with a dead calm. "I'm a registered Warlock. For a while, I thought I was Ni'Mago like him." Alexander pointed to Patrick.

"A what?"

"A Ni'Mago. It's what we call normal, non-magical people. This is all a shock for you, I'm sure. But we're running out of time. There was a hex on that ring. The moment you touched it—"

"Yes, yes, I know!" Hanna glanced down at the brand on her arm.

"It's more than a simple scar. That mark," the professor said pointing at it, "means that he'll know where you are. And he'll find you." Hanna stared at the band around her thumb as if it bit her. "The moment you touched it—"

"I'm getting rid of it!" Hanna cried and moved to peel it off.

"NO! Stop!" Alexander shouted, his eyes wide. "I can't believe it…That's a GodStone ring! Oh, no, no, no. Never ever take that off."

"But you said—"

"The damage has already been done. Yes, you've been hexed. And yes, Barlow can track you as he does all the Crimson Brotherhood. But the power of that ring is too great to just throw away."

"The Brotherhood?" said Michael looking at his own scar.

"It doesn't matter right now." The professor waved off his question.

"Yes, but—"

"Come. Quickly."

"What? No!" said Hanna. "We're not going anywhere until you've answered some questions." The professor wrung his hands. He glanced at the flickering portal and then back to Hanna. "What do you know about my sisters and why do you think they're in danger?"

Alexander once again glanced at the flickering portal and let out an exhausted breath. "Prince Bartholomew won't be far behind. We have to get out of here before he finds this rift."

"I said I'm not going anywhere," insisted Hanna.

Another sigh, then he set down his satchel and pulled out a foot long, spiraled stick from the narrow bag. Hanna gawked. How had such a long stick fit inside there?

"Come with me." Alexander stepped away from the portal, leading the three to the shallow wading pool. "This is a magic wand." He swirled the tip of the wand in the water and twirled it until colorful ribbons gave way to a picturesque image.

Hanna couldn't believe what she was seeing. The pool's reflective surface warped into a canvas of motion. In the mirage, Hanna was in the middle of a losing battle in an open field. She cringed as the vision of herself succumbed to the heavy blows from a scarred figure wielding a massive war hammer. The man's wicked grin coupled with the streak of bubbled flesh across his face and head made her stomach drop. The mirrored surface flickered and a new scene played out, this time depicting Ashley and Lexi being carried into the sky, gripped in the huge talons of a giant, black bird.

Hanna covered her mouth. "This can't be!" she whispered through her fingers. She spun to look toward the windows of her house—Lexi's bedroom curtains swung shut.

"The events in the pool are of an undefined time in the future. The girls won't be safe for long unless you act now to help them. Their lives are in your hands." The professor stretched out his open palm. "Now will you come with me? Your sisters don't have to die."

"Die?" squeaked Patrick.

"Yes, I'm here to save them. To save you. To save Smaradine."

"Let me understand this—" Hanna began, only to gasp and curl forward, gripping her head as a voice erupted between her ears.

"After all these years. I've finally found you. There's no more places to hide!"

Hanna fell to one knee, still cradling her head. "He's coming!"

"Barlow? Then we must act now!" yelled the professor.

"This future," Hanna said, pointing to the pool. "Can we change it?"

The professor nodded. "There's a chance to save them, but it's only a chance."

The thump of running footsteps drew Hanna's attention to

the back porch. To her relief, the back-patio door opened, and her sisters ran into the backyard. They ran over to the portal. "What's going on?" Ashley asked. "W-what's that?!"

She wasn't pointing at Alexander. Hanna whipped her head up and stared wide-eyed at the rift. A thick, coil of black smoke snaked into the yard.

The professor screamed, "It's too late—Barlow's here!"

"What is that thing?" shouted Lexi.

Hanna bounded to her feet and pushed her sisters behind her. "I don't know."

Alexander grabbed at Hanna as the coil began to circle them. "We must flee—now!" He pulled the kids toward the window and grabbed his satchel. "GO THROUGH THE PORTAL BEFORE YOU CAN'T GET THROUGH!" he screamed before leaping into the rift himself and vanishing.

"Yeah, I ain't hanging 'round here with that!" Michael followed the professor and disappeared through the portal.

"Me either," added Patrick. He snatched his backpack and leapt in.

Hanna reached out her arm, beckoning her sisters to follow. "Come. I'll keep you safe." Ashley reached out her hand and grabbed Hanna's fingertips. "LEXI, COME—NOW!" Hanna yelled as she pulled Ashley along. But just as she stepped one foot into the portal, something jerked Ashley free of her grip. Hanna slipped through the portal leaving Midtown Valley behind.

11

NOW YOU SEE ME—NOW YOU DON'T

Valentine poked his head over the white picket fence separating their two yards.

Ashley stood before a flashing, multicolor gate, staring in disbelief. "What the heck did you pull me back for?"

"Maxwell!" Lexi screamed. "I grabbed your hand cause we have to save Maxwell!"

"Forget the cat!" she yelled as the feline continued to leap after the smoky trail. "Come on! We have to follow Hanna!" Ashley dodged the billowing cloud and grabbed Lexi's hand. "Maxwell can take care of himself."

"Fine!" Lexi shoved Ashley through the portal as the inky coil dove for them again.

The rift blinked out and back in, out and back in. That's when Lexi jumped. The smoky worm followed closely on her heals. As it plunged its long snake-like head inside, Maxwell jumped and sprang pawing at the smoky tail. When the smoke vanished through, the cat leapt after as if chasing its prey.

"Son of a—" Valentine whispered heavily.

Where'd they go? He flicked a quick glance to his own front porch thinking about Olivia and then back to where Hanna and the others disappeared. *Was that man green? And what the heck was that smoke thing?*

Valentine thought for a fleeting moment about his home, the dance, his football career, and frowned. *Weak metal my keister. Nobody bends a locker like that without—without—*his thoughts trailed off. *Maybe I can, too!*

He bounded over the picket fence and sprinted like it was game day across Hanna's lawn. Valentine dove through the blinking portal. Just as he passed through the rift, it vanished entirely from Midtown Valley.

12

SMARADINE

P ellets of freezing sleet pelted Hanna's face, arms, and legs stinging like a million bees. She and her friends left the warm, springtime breeze of Midtown Valley for a new, snow-battered land. Sheets of ice and snow whipped in a biting wind. Every footstep brought a crunch under their shoes.

"Can't see a thing," shouted Hanna, her teeth chattering. "What is this place? Where are we?"

Patrick peeled off his glasses. "My eye! It's in my eye!"

"To my lab," hollered the professor. "We'll freeze if we don't get out of the storm!"

"Bollocks," Michael shouted against the wind. "Where's the lab? Can't see."

Alexander turned toward the trio. "Welcome to Smaradine! Now quickly, across the field."

"Where the heck *is* Smaradine?" Hanna looked around for her sisters. "Where's Ashley? I didn't see her come through—can anyone see Lexi?"

The words were barely out of her mouth when a blue beacon of light spread across Hanna's chest and up her neck. She held her pendant up to her face squinting against its glow. A few heartbeats later, the brilliance dimmed to a faint shine and faded completely.

"Whoa," she gasped.

"I didn't know your pendant could do that," Patrick yelled.

"Neither did I. It's the first time it's done anything—ever." Her ring clinked against the pendant and her eyes widened for a second time. The contents of her pendant, which normally sloshed in thick swells of blue liquid, spun in an angry vortex within the cylindrical crystal.

"Whoa," she repeated, dropping the pendant to her chest. She held it up again, but this time with the tips of her fingers. The pendant remained lifeless. Ignoring the wind gnawing on her unprotected skin, Hanna carefully pressed her ring against the side of the crystal again. The contents spun back to life.

"Has either Ashley or Lexi come through?" Patrick shouted, looking around, eyes shielded with his hand.

The professor walked away from the portal. "It's better this way. They're safe back home. Didn't want them here anyway. Now come on. We have to get out of the storm."

Hanna's chilled face heated with anger, defying the ice and snow still pelting them. "They're not back home! They were following me!" In a blink, Ashley tumbled through the rift, knocking over both Michael and Patrick. "Ashley!" Hanna cried. "Thank God. Where's Lexi?"

Ashley pushed herself to her knees. "She's right behind me. Where are we?" She shielded her face with her hands as the portal winked out of existence.

"LEXI!" screamed Hanna. She frantically pressed the ring to the cube again, but no window appeared. She tried again and again, pressing the ring into the beveled circle on the box over and over without success.

Ashley's cheeks bloomed velvet rashes from the cold, in juxtaposition to the professor's scaly skin, which turned a cold shade of powder blue. Hanna never gave up even as her own hands were numb and trembling. She untied her school sweat-shirt from around her waist, hoping it would help protect her sister from the biting wind and tugged it over Ashley's head.

"Where's Lexi?" Hanna looked from her sister to where the portal vanished. "Where is she?" Her eyes darted across the snow-strewn field. "LEXI—LEXI!" she shouted through the blinding ice and snow. "This is insane! I've already lost her! How did that happen?"

Ashley spun around again and squinted through the storm. "She was right behind me, I swear!"

Alexander gripped Hanna's elbow. "It's alright! It's better that Lexi is back home. The point of bringing *you* here is to try and stop Barlow from capturing *them*. The chance that Barlow is still back in your homeland is slim to none. His power is here, in Smaradine. She's probably safe for now, but we have to take shelter!"

Michael tried to stand but fell back to his knees. He grimaced, holding the small of his back.

Patrick struggled to heave Michael to his feet. "What's wrong with you?"

"Don't know—it burns. My back burns. Worse than before."

Hanna glanced at Michael, then back to the professor. "Could've warned us about the storm!"

Alexander tightened his lab coat across his chest. "I would have, but this blizzard wasn't here when I left."

Pellets the size of BBs coated Hanna's hair. Chilled to the bone, icy shivers rippled through her. She tried to think of the warmth back in Midtown Valley. As she shielded her own head with her forearm, a small tickle fingered its way from the back of her neck. A new, white light blossomed, first from the birthmark on her palm, then from her other hand. The glow intensified from a dim glimmer to that of a lighthouse beacon. A warm cushion of heat and radiance surrounded them like a dome.

"What the—" yelled Michael. The ice pellets rammed against the barrier and melted against the new heat.

"How are you doing that?" asked Patrick.

Michael threw his own hands out in front of him, as if expecting them to erupt in a fountain of light as well. Ashley mimicked Michael's attempt to cast her own glow, but her hands stayed as dark as his.

Questions flooded Hanna's mind, but the professor pleaded with them to start moving once again. So for now, she swallowed her curiosity and trudged forward through the snow. For the moment, they were protected by the warm light from her hands.

After walking for a minute or two, a large building loomed into focus. Relief washed over Hanna and the group followed Alexander through an icy door and into the safety of the lab. Snow blew across the entrance, swirling into coils like a snake about their ankles. As the warmth of the room started thawing Hanna's nerves, the intense glow of her hands dimmed. Shadows raced across the walls as her twin beacons of light faded and fell dark.

"How'd you do that?" Patrick asked again.

Hanna shrugged and stared at the henna-style birthmark on her right palm. "I-I don't know. One minute, I was freezing and the next, they blazed to life like lanterns."

Patrick mimed his head exploding. "It's not scientifically possible. This—all of this—goes against all the laws of chemistry, physics, and…and…"

She traced the mark on her palm with her opposite fingers. "Patrick, none of this makes sense."

Michael fell against the door, hunched over. "Ugh. My back. It's killing me."

"Where?" Michael twisted his arm backward and pointed a cocked-thumb at the middle of his back. Hanna frowned. "Your kidney? Where you had your transplant? How's that hurting you after all this time?" She instinctively pressed the small of her own back where she had a matching incision. "Mine doesn't hurt at all."

Michael tried to shrug, but the pain in his back seemed to steal all his remaining energy. "Dunno—it started after touching that ring."

She flicked her eyes to the professor and thought of that stick he had earlier… *A magic wand. A magic portal. My healed finger. My crushed locker. Is all this related somehow?* It had to be, right? Hanna looked at the ring around her thumb and then at the brand in the shape of a bird. *Could all this really be magic…real magic?*

"I'm worried about Lexi." Ashley mumbled, hugging herself. "I hope she's okay." Her eyes welled with tears.

"You said she was behind you, right?" asked Alexander, rubbing his knobby, green chin. "I suppose it could be possible that…"

Hanna's gut sunk. "Possible, what?"

"On the chance that she did make it into the portal…"

"What? What?! Spit it out, mate!" demanded Michael.

"Well, the portal…it was on the fritz." The professor looked from Hanna to Patrick. "It's possible that the displacement field inside it glitched. I've never seen a rift act like that." Alexander eyed Hanna's pocket where she stashed the metallic block. "That Realm Cube is the last of its kind."

"This thing?" Hanna asked, pulling it from its hiding place and holding it out to him.

"Yes—that's a Realm Cube, and it seems to have finally failed, too. Like the rest of them."

Ashley scrunched up her face and rubbed her cheeks. "What now? Can you fix it? You've got magic, don't you? You said you were a wizard or something."

"I'm half-wizard. They call me a warlock. And while I do possess limited magic, I'm afraid I lack the skills of most accomplished wizards. I focus my talents on science aided by the power of magic. Regardless, I can't fix a portal. But, as I'm sure you may have already realized, until we figure out what caused the cube to malfunction, none of you are going back home."

"So, we're stuck here?" Patrick blurted.

Michael threw his hands in the air and pursed his lips. "Mate, you brought us to the middle of nowhere!"

"And what about Lexi?!" added Hanna.

"Psst. You heard the man. She's ain't here."

Hanna glared at Michael and fumbled with the cube. She removed the ring from her thumb once again. "No! We can get her. We have to. We can open a new portal!"

"I'm sorry, but it won't work anymore," Alexander repeated. "It died out like all the others."

"NO! YOU DON'T UNDERSTAND!" Hanna screamed, pressing the ring into the circular divot again and again. "I'VE GOT TO TRY!" But nothing happened. Eyes burning and tears leaking over her lashes, Hanna slumped her shoulders. "W-where could she be?"

"We came through the portal thingy together. I was first. She followed," said Ashley.

Hanna wiped her face. "Could Barlow already have her?"

"Anything's possible, but it's doubtful," Alexander reassured. "If he got stuck in Midtown Valley, he'd have no way back here. If there's one thing to know about Barlow, he's all about greed and power. So, if Lexi stayed, my guess is the prince would've still come back regardless. But...if Lexi did escape through the portal at the moment it glitched..."

"What?" Hanna pressed.

The professor sighed. "Projection coordinates anchor the rift to a specific point in time and space, much like a physical door has a concrete location. The glitch could have caused the projection coordinates to become untethered and...scattered to a purely random location, instead."

"What?! What does that even mean?"

"It means...I'm sorry, Hanna, but Lexi could have been dumped anywhere in Smaradine, and we'd have no idea where."

She gaped, first at Alexander, then her friends. Her throat

tightened and her eyes burned all over again, but she cried herself dry. Swallowing, Hanna nodded and tried to pull herself together. Sure as sweet corn in July, sitting on the floor of a laboratory in the middle of nowhere wasn't going to help anyone, let alone Lexi. Hanna found her voice again and asked, "Just how exactly do we find her, then?"

13

CONSUMED

Lexi leapt into the portal with her right foot and landed in a new world with her left. *Where am I?* She stepped out of the flickering window and into the blazing light of a sandy, barren desert. The heat stole her breath, all thought of her cool, comfortable backyard lost behind her.

Where is everyone?

Her heart thundered in her eardrums. A low rumble, like the rattle of a motorcycle engine far away, filled the silence of the dusty landscape. Lexi's skin grew flush and clammy as the sun's rays radiated off the copper dunes in thermal waves. Fresh beads of sweat dripped off her brow.

Where are Ashley and Hanna? They were right in front of me...

She looked ahead; it was an empty expanse of rolling sands in an ever-expanding desert. Hazy ripples climbed the distant hills and distorted her view. Her still throbbing heart climbed into her throat. It sat there like a brick as she envisioned a dragon dancing in the air.

Where's Patrick?

Lexi turned and came face to face with a high butte. A black coral ridge loomed high above her head, sand-blasted into millions of razor-sharp shards. The cliff offered no reprieve from the scorching sun. She groaned and stared down at the hot dust under her boots—no shadow in sight.

Playful colors sparkled between the grains of copper. Lexi cupped a handful of glittering sand and painful stabs lanced her palm. "Ow!" she said dropping the russet powder. Tiny slivers of colored glass prickled her hand like a colorful display of quills. Lexi plucked them out with a wince. Each one stung leaving crimson droplets of blood behind.

"What the heck is this place?" she said with a sigh. "Maybe following Hanna was a bad idea." Lexi wiped her freckled palm on the front of her jean shorts staining them with little scarlet smears.

I want to go home.

But there was no home. There was no tree house. There was no annoying little sister. Nothing—nothing but the desert and the oppressive, searing heat so thick that it was hard to breathe.

She raised her hands to the sides of her mouth and yelled, "Is anyone here?" Her voice was swallowed by the barren landscape. Her eyes watered as another lump as fat as the first one clogged her throat. Lexi squeezed her lids tight and twin streams trickled down her cheeks.

I'm alone.

Hot wind buffeted her face, wicking the moisture away. She licked her lips and wondered. Was it her tears or the breeze that tasted like salt?

What's that noise?

Lexi turned left, toward what she thought was north—there was a churning, roiling cloud the color of mud. It filled the sky and stretched from one end of the horizon to the next. Thick fingers of lightning danced across the dusty air illuminating the beast from within.

"OH MY GOD," she spat. "A SANDSTORM?"

Panic flooded her gut. But it would be okay, right? She could just go back? Just hop through the portal again? Lexi spun, kicking up rooster tails of sparkling sand that stung the back of her bare legs. But her hopes of escaping back to Midtown Valley vanished. The rift was gone.

"Turd Biscuits!" she screamed, throwing her hands into the air.

The once low rumble of the distant storm grew louder. More present. Closer. She fought the urge to vomit, swallowing back the bitter bile and with it, her growing hysteria. *Get it together!* Lexi's gaze darted about, but she couldn't climb the towering bluff, nor could she enter the vast sea of dunes. So, she settled on the only real direction she had—to the right, away from the storm.

She had to run away. Lexi sprinted as fast as her legs would take her. The hot air scorched her dry throat and the strange, salty atmosphere coated her tongue and filled her nose. She huffed through the thick sand, chest heaving as she struggled to sprint across the dune when a thought struck her. *Brine! There's salt water—maybe an ocean? If only I could reach it!*

She raced along the base of the bluff that scaled above her head four times her height. The unrelenting heat robbed her of energy and the howl of the storm continued to creep closer, steadily growing louder and louder. The wind whipped sharp sand through her hair and up the back of her loose purple T-shirt. She risked a glance over her shoulder and her heart leapt in her throat for another time. Flecks of swirling grains filled the air behind her scraping her neck, arms, and legs like tiny claws.

"OH MY GOD—OH MY GOD!" she screamed. "I'M GONNA DIE!"

The black storm barreled against her back. It started to consume her. Flashes of lightening filled the roaring storm and long fingers of electricity danced in the sky above her head. The tempest swallowed everything—blotting out the sky and sun. The storm threatened to engulf the entire desert.

Ahead of her spun eddies of sand thirty feet in the air and torrents of wind grew into dust devils. The air turned thick and soupy with copper grit and needles, the once faint howl now roaring in her ears.

Run—Run—Run is all she could think, but she couldn't outrun it—she was already buried inside it.

The wind whipped and swirled about her face and she coughed on the grainy air. The dune grass along the ridge bent sideways as the storm's winds crashed against her back again and again. Lexi ran and ran and ran. Tears spilled down her face and mixed with the desert sand painting her cheeks in muddy streaks. The desert heat scorched her lungs.

"Don't look back—just run—come on—run!" she screamed, her throat now raw and painful.

The rush of adrenaline sang in her ears as the end of the world barreled down on her. She crashed to her knees and bolted back up in a panic. Pain blossomed across her hands and knees. Her hopes fled as grit and sand and glass wrapped around her like a blanket of death.

"I'm gonna die!" she cried—but just as the storm threatened to end her, something along the edge of the dune caught her eye. The towering bluff broke away, leaving a large gap in the rock wall.

It was her only hope.

Uncaring what awaited her on the other side, Lexi sprinted through the sand and the darkness, coughing and heaving. One hundred feet closer. The storm surged around her. Tears streamed down her cheeks. Fifty feet closer. The storm swallowed her entirely. Twenty feet closer. Her eyes burned, but through the pain, her hazy vision remained pinned to a way out.

She raced against the storm. Could barely see. Could barely breathe. Almost there—almost to the lip. Ten feet closer. She struggled with all her might.

Wheezing as grit coated her throat, she pushed herself further—had to make it. Five feet closer. She was there, but complete darkness consumed her world—

In the blackness, Lexi jumped.

14

THE WELL OF WISHES

Valentine fell forward and cracked his ribs on a coil of roots. "Ow," he screamed, spilling onto a slab of unforgiving rock as he fell from the portal. His right cheek and chin slammed against the cold ground and he bit through the edge of his tongue. The taste of bitter copper liquid flooded his mouth. Valentine wiped the blood from his lips with the back of his hand before flipping over onto his back, still holding his mouth. His gaze landed where the portal spit him out, but the window was gone.

"Where the—what is this place?" His voice cracked. He turned his head and spat a mouthful of red. As he inhaled, frigid air raced through his nostrils and chilled his throat. "Son of a monkey whistler!" White vapor clouds billowed from his lips with every word.

Valentine staggered to his feet, confused and disoriented. He tried to steady himself on a flat ridge along the top of what looked like a lifeless, bald mountain crest. Far below stood a breathtaking vista of colossal trees which wove a cocoon of greenery so thick, it appeared as though it were a carpet of shamrocks.

"Hanna! Where are you?" he called into the wild. His voice

echoed over the treetops, not a hide nor hair of anyone else around. A lone, low howl from somewhere beyond his line of sight was the only reply. "Hanna!" he called again, turning in search of the group he was sure must be close by.

A long set of gray and weathered stone steps slid like a great serpent down the mountainside. It wasn't the fact that the forest reclaimed most of the steps that garnered his attention. It was the sheer number of stairs descending into the distant valley. *There must be twenty thousand steps.* The call of birds in the trees and the constant hum of insects rose from the emerald canopy. A barren wall of chiseled stone pressed against his back. Everywhere but the very spot he stood seemed to buzz with life.

Several hundred feet below, the dense forest floor was choked with a thick blanket of mist. Only the tops of trees sprouted through the cold, white barrier. A mile in the distance stood a twin ridge jutting high into the afternoon sky. He hooked his thumbs inside the elastic band of his gray sweatpants, but something sharp poked his hand. Valentine withdrew a blue ink pen from his pocket. *Great—what am I gonna do with this?*

A heavy breeze tossed his sculpted, blond hair into his eyes. Millions of leaves in the treetops rustled in the gust, reminding him of the sizzle of frying bacon. Valentine turned his back to the valley and tucked the pen behind his ear, he spat red again. For the first time since arriving, he looked to the wall of granite at his back and stiffened. *What the heck is this place?*

An enormous, milky disc, which looked eerily similar to the mysterious doorway he'd leapt through in Hanna's backyard, swirled in eddies of cloudy cream that pressed flush against the mountain wall. *I'm not going in there. Not through a window that looks like that.*

Valentine brushed dirt from his jersey and varsity jacket as a wave of goose bumps prickled up his forearms. He examined a pair of chiseled columns stretching twenty feet above his head. They were carved into the bedrock of the mountain, standing sentry on either side of the colossal portal.

This place gives me the creeps. He shuddered as another howl echoed from the depths of the tree line. Searching for the source, he looked across to the next bald ridge—and spotted someone walking across its peak. *How can—how can I see that man from this far away?*

A new chill trailed up his spine. It was impossible for that to be a regular man. Valentine squinted, trying to comprehend what his eyes were telling him. "A giant—that's a giant! How can that be? Where on Earth am I?" He slapped himself in the face hard enough for his eyes to water. "Get it together! Giants aren't real!" But after blinking the moisture away, he watched in disbelief as the enormous figure disappeared into the distant trees.

From the corner of his eye, a glint of gold beyond the swirling window of fog in the portal caught his attention. Valentine knelt on his hands and knees and pressed close to the cloudy surface, his nose nearly breached the veil. He lightly touched the creamy mist with the tip of his finger, testing it before allowing the void to swallow his entire hand.

It was as if he'd plunged his hand into a bucket of ice. Cold tendrils of fog coiled around his wrist like cottony smoke. Scared, Valentine pulled back his hand. A shadow shifted in the clouds—something moved beyond the veil. The dull shine of something golden shone between cloudy tendrils beyond the threshold, but that wasn't all that was there. Something else stirred in the fog. *What was that?* Despite his trepidation, Valentine's gaze flicked nervously—greedily—back to the item again. *Maybe it's jewelry? Should I try to get it?*

His tongue moistened his dry lips and with a sudden burst, like snapping off the perfect, crisp pass to a wide receiver, he shot his hand through the icy portal once more. Ignoring the chill, Valentine stretched up to his armpit, careful not to put too much of himself through so not to fall inside, and groped for the object. His cheek, still raw and stinging from scraping it on the ground, was inches from the cold veil. He patted the ground frantically searching for the jewelry. Finally, his fingers grazed the wiry rim of something thin and cold.

"There it is!" he exclaimed. Valentine pulled, but the object barely moved. He pulled harder. Still no give. More shadowed movements swirled in the mist, but he ignored them and tugged with all his might. *Snap*. The object broke free.

"I got it!" he hollered, falling backward against the rough stone. He shook the bite of frost from his arm and withdrew from the mist. Clutched between his frigid fingers was a bleach-white, skeletal arm. "What the—" he screamed, dropping the bones and scrambling back like a crab.

The arm shattered like clay. Chunks and splinters of dried cartilage scattered across the rocks. He leaned his back against the nearest stone column, breathing hard, but the shock wasn't enough to keep his eyes off his treasure. Around the back of the brittle, boney hand and draped up its wrist was a jeweled cuff made of worn leather and gold lattice. Green and crimson gems speckled the leather like small stars. *That's so cool…it reminds me of that medieval video game back home.*

Inching forward again, Valentine ran his fingers over the bumpy, golden mesh. From one breath to the next, he put his favorite console game to the back of his mind and shook the remaining bones to the ground, freeing the cuff. The ancient band was encrusted with a sliver of gray stone. The stone chip, which was no larger than a Matchbox car, had a strange, black glyph burned into its surface. Gossamer strings of golden lattice were strapped on the ends with beaver-brown leather.

Admiring his find, Valentine slid his right hand through the honeyed-gold metal and cinched the leather straps tight around his wrist. It fit perfectly. Suddenly, something cold snaked around his ankle. Frowning, he glanced down—and screamed. A long, muscled tentacle the color of a purple bruise slipped through the portal where his foot still perforated the veil.

"What the—" Valentine tried to bolt up, but the tentacle jerked him back. He stumbled and smashed the back of his head against the granite floor. For a moment, his eyes rolled and blinding pain surged through his skull, but the dull scrape of his scalp against the unforgiving stone rattled him back to his senses. It was trying to pull him in! "NO—NO!"

He clawed against the hard rock but continued to slide toward the abyss. His sneakers disappeared beyond the veil. The doorway was filled with a single gigantic eye. Frantic, Valentine searched for something—anything—to stab with, but nothing was in reach. Then he remembered the pen!

Valentine grabbed it from behind his ear and drove the metal tip deep into the tentacle. A spray of purple blood arched into the air along with a ground-shaking roar. The tentacle immediately detached and uncoiled from his leg.

"Get away!" he screamed, kicking at the flailing limb.

Valentine scrambled back as more tentacles reached out from the portal and instinctively he crossed his arms over his face—but nothing grabbed him. Shaking and confused, he lowered his arms and pried his eyes open. Time nearly stopped.

A soft, blue light illuminated the stone in the cuff and washed over the area around him. The tentacles, which were only inches from his face, simply hung in mid-air. Valentine scrambled away from the portal and bolted to his feet. He paused a few paces back to examine the new jewelry strapped to his wrist and reached out a hesitant finger, brushing it over the stone. Time slowly sped up again. The corners of Valentine's mouth quirked. *I can control time.*

Without looking back at the portal, he sprinted faster than his legs had ever carried him on the football field. His feet seemed to barely touch the ground as he raced as fast as a hundred horses. He sprinted down the winding, granite steps and disappeared into the mysterious countryside below.

15

THE DIMENSIONAL BAG

The ice pelting the outside of the lab lessened to a light tinkle and then soon to nothing. Hanna finally peeled open the door and rushed outside, just in case somehow Lexi was out there. As she ran into the snow-covered field, Hanna stopped dead in her tracks. Her mouth hung open as rays of sunshine shot through patchy, white clouds and bathed her in a blanket of warmth.

"Blimey," said Michael, pushing past her.

Patrick raised his arms wide. "How's this weather possible?"

Alexander pointed across the open field. "Look against the horizon. Those are the Kragg Mountains. They isolate our land from the Ice Kingdom of Ba'Noor to the north."

"There are other kingdoms?" asked Ashley.

"Smaradine is broken into several. Over there," he pointed off to the northwest, "is the elven kingdom of Ka'Thia, and the surrounding waters of Smaradine make up the ocean kingdom of Ka'More. Right now, you're in Manna, the largest of Smaradine's four kingdoms. Every so often, the northern winds blow the high frigid air from the Kragg Mountains into the low valleys. Although we have little warning, we take comfort in that the storms are brief and usually do little harm—except for those in the Fire Sands."

"What are the Fire Sands?" asked Ashley, pushing the melting snow around with her shoe.

The professor pointed west. "They're that way. The Kragg winds cause deadly sandstorms in the desert. They'd peel the skin from nearly any living creature—except dragons."

"Now I've heard it all." exclaimed Michael. "You didn't just say what I thought you said."

"He said they have dragons," Patrick repeated, though his expression proved he was just as astonished.

Trying to ignore the growing hysteria of her friends, Hanna shifted her gaze past her other sister to the rolling hills of the eastern meadows. Her eyes followed the land until they reached the dark point on the far horizon. "What's over on that shadowed ridge topped with the circle of clouds?

"That's Blunder Mountain, home to Barlow and the Crimson Brotherhood."

Michael shook his head. "Mate, this is one messed up place. You've got dragons and gangs. Hanna's hands glow, and you have dimensional portals."

Ashley chewed her bottom lip and stared down at her own hands. "Why *did* Hanna's hands glow?"

"Why didn't *mine* glow?" Michael cut in. "I don't want to be Ni'Mago."

Hanna grimaced at her own palms. "Good question. How *did* they glow?" She looked at the professor, but Alexander seemed to purposely avoid her gaze.

"Was it you?" Michael said accusingly. "Did you hex us—put some kind of curse on us? Fix it!" He grabbed the lapels of the professor's coat. "Fix my back! It's killing' me!"

"L-let go of me!" Alexander staggered back, his scales shifting red. "I did nothing to any of you."

"What are you *not* telling us, then?" barked Michael.

"Why were you searching for me in the first place?" added

Hanna. "How do you even know anything about me? You said you knew the truth…so what of it?"

"Look…please. Save these questions for later. We've got to get to Hemlock Castle." At her frustrated growl, the professor continued. "I told you I know the truth, and it's true. I do. Please trust me and you'll have all your answers in time."

"Why in time? Why not now?"

"Because we're on a time crunch, remember? We're searching for your sister?"

"You don't have to remind me of Lexi!"

Ashley scrunched up her face. "What if she's not back home, though? What if Lexi's lost somewhere out here? Or stuck in between worlds?" Her shoulders slumped. "We left the house with no note or anything. Our parents have no idea where we are or when we're coming back."

Hanna's gut tied itself in more knots. "She's out there, alone and terrified. I just know it. We have each other," she glanced from Michael to Patrick and Ashley, "but she's got no one."

Michael winced and pressed a hand to his back again. "What's Hemlock Castle, anyway? And why are we going there?"

"It's up that way." Alexander pointed to the north. "It sits along the northern rim in the royal city of Castletown and is home to Manna's royal family."

"Royal family, huh?" Michael sneered. "Well, how are they gonna—"

"Find my sister?" Ashley finished.

"If you think it's our best chance at finding her…" Hanna placed a placating hand on Ashley's shoulder, "then it makes the most sense. Please, just answer this, and I'll save my other questions for later—what's the deal with Barlow? Why does he want me and my sisters?"

"The one question you ask is the one I cannot answer. I'm sorry."

"Why not?"

The professor sighed. "I don't know why he's after you. Power, I presume, but how to get it from the three of you is beyond me. And it's not like we can just waltz up and ask him."

Hanna thought back to her dented locker, her near-broken finger, her glowing hands—and had a nagging suspicion that somehow she wasn't Ni'Mago. She looked to her sister. Ashley was trying desperately to cling to whatever normal she could. Even Hanna herself struggled with this new world of magic, and she was apparently capable of wielding it.

She stared at her hands. *It's got to be magic that I have, but how? How do I possess powers at all? Was it the ring that caused all this? Is it the same magic that Barlow has? How else could he have talked to me in my head?*

Hanna flicked her eyes toward Michael and Patrick. *Should I tell them about the prince speaking to me?* She bit her bottom lip and quickly squashed the idea. *They wouldn't understand—heck, I don't understand.*

"What if Barlow's taken Lexi already?" asked Ashley.

"I have an idea," added Alexander, patting Ashley on the back and then ushering the kids back inside. "We'll find her. Somehow. But for now, though, come with me."

The professor led the group back through the lab and down a corridor opening into a vast room filled with shelves of gadgets, toy-like devices, and holographic displays. The room clicked and hummed. Across the way, several spinning globes hovered in mid-air as if suspended by an invisible string. Other oddities like moving mobiles made of a liquid metal were strung together like silver water. They sat on a table in the middle of the room, turning back and forth, pendulum-like.

Alexander moved toward a long desk upon which a wide white parchment lay unraveled. The thick paper was drawn with a series of glowing lines crisscrossing the entire map. The word S.P.A.R.K. was stamped along the bottom corner. "I've charted a grid of coordinates along Smaradine's Ley Lines."

Hanna fidgeted nervously with her fingers. "What are Ley Lines?"

He pointed to one of the glowing stripes on the map. "Ley Lines are magical pathways through which energy flows throughout Smaradine. Most major towns are built upon them, and each city has a portal bound to the strongest of those lines." He pointed to some of the cities: Breakwater in the west, Cog in the center, Winter's Edge along the northern border of Manna, Castletown nearing the east, and Thule on the far eastern edge of the map. "Minor townships and some outlying areas are susceptible to portal activity, but more likely than not, Lexi's gate would open on a major coordinate—the magic's simply stronger there."

Patrick pointed to the northern ridge of mountains high above Castletown. "What's this area?"

"That's the Kingdom of Ba'Noor —it's forbidden. Although Ley Lines extend beyond the northern border of Manna, by royal law, you're not allowed to venture past the Kragg Mountains."

Ashley hesitantly raised her hand as if back in school. "So, if the Ley Lines go all the way up there, then magic's everywhere?"

"Everywhere, yes, but not within everyone. Most people in Smaradine are Ni'Mago—normal people without magical abilities. And all witches and wizards—and yes, Warlocks—in Manna require a permit from the king to practice magic. I just hope your sister's portal opened inside our kingdom," Alexander added, smoothing out the wrinkles in the map. Ashley's eyes widened as she scanned over the expanse of the new land they'd tumbled into. The professor picked up the map a moment later and handed it to Hanna. "Take this and put it someplace safe."

"Where are we now?" asked Hanna in a cracked voice.

He leaned in unfurling the paper in her hands and jabbed a finger near the bottom of the map. "We're here at the southern end of Manna. As you can see, there's a lot of land to be covered in order to find your sister. We need to get you in front of the princess. She might have an idea of what to do."

"Is this the only map?" asked Patrick.

Alexander waived his hand dismissively. "A basic map can be found at any one of Marty's General Stores, but I've added the Ley Lines to this one myself. You won't find this anywhere else."

Hanna nodded, then rubbed the back of her shaky hand across her nose and leaned toward Michael. "Do you see this map?! It's H-U-G-E. I don't know how we're ever going to find Lexi."

"We'll find her," Michael reassured her as he pushed himself away from the desk. "I promise you that."

But the weight on Hanna's chest grew heavier the longer they stood doing nothing. "I hope so." She rolled the map and folded it in half before stuffing it into her back pocket. It barely fit. As she did so, a large blue hippo wearing a matching white lab coat to that of the professor emerged from the other end of the room.

Hanna's jaw fell agape as she took in the sheer size of the creature. She had to crane her neck just to look at his face. Two bulbous white teeth popped out of his bottom jaw like plump marshmallows. His mouth was so large that the thought of him swallowing her whole made her take a tentative step back toward Michael.

"Hanna, I'd like you to meet my assistant, Hugo."

"'Ello," Hugo said in a deep, slow drawl. A smile curled the corners of his lips and Hugo turned his head taking in each of them one at a time.

Ashley, who stood furthest from Hugo, waved eagerly. Hanna swallowed her fear and held out her hand. Hugo reached out and wrapped her pale hand in a warm handshake. He bent forward so they could look one another in the eyes. "A pleasure to finally meet you." He had a silky voice that reminded her of a southern gentleman. Her anxiety melted away the more she listened to his friendly drawl. "The professor's been searching for you for an awfully long time." Her eyes widened and she turned to look at the professor.

"Really?" probed Ashley before Hanna could reply.

"Sure." Hugo frowned, seemingly confused. "He's been scouring the six realms for fourteen years for all of 'ya, hoping you'd be with the king."

"The king? Why...would we be with the king?" asked Hanna.

Hugo's thick black eyebrows creased even more. "W-well," he stuttered, "He and the queen went—well, I mean, I'd assumed...I'd hoped that—"

"All of this can be sorted out later, Hugo." Alexander waved his hands irritably. "We've got more pressing matters in finding her sister. Lexi didn't come back through with the rest."

"That's good, though, right? You didn't want 'em here anyway, and—" he stopped short as his eyes fell on Hanna's expression. "Oh, that's bad...I see."

"The portal glitched when we came through," Hanna clarified, glancing at her friends for a moment before returning her gaze to Hugo. "Lexi's out there alone. We've got to find her."

"Oh, well...er—I'm truly sorry about your sister." His big bulbous eyes flicked toward the professor and then back to Hanna. "But I need to be in Breakwater this—"

"Hugo, why the rush?" interrupted Alexander. "We need your help finding Lexi."

Hugo's mouth hung open for a moment as if he didn't know what to say. "Er—I need to collect Wayfairy grass from the Lazy Lagoon. We're almost out. I need it to complete the new dragon bite salve."

"Can't that wait?"

"Pestle and Potions School of Apothecary is out so I have to pick my own." He glanced at Ashley and Hanna in turn. "I have a plan. Tell me what she looks like and I'll post signs about Lexi in Breakwater before getting the Wayfairy grass."

"Good...good." The professor nodded, then eyeballed

Patrick's backpack. "And it gives me an idea." He pat Patrick on the shoulder on his way over to his desk. Alexander scribbled something on a small piece of paper, folded it in half, and handed it to Hugo. "Get a messenger to the court wizard about this before you go to Breakwater. Kids, wait here. I want to show you something."

"Er…sure, yeah. But first, can I get that description?" Hugo asked Hanna. "I gotta get the grass and return before the recipe spoils."

Hanna grabbed the same pencil the professor used and a new sheet of paper from the desk. She quickly sketched Lexi's clothes and face and jotted down the best description she could think of.

"Great, thanks. It'll be okay…you'll see. We'll get your sister back." Hugo accepted the second piece of paper with chubby fingers as thick as sausages. "I'll see you all later, yeah?" He waved goodbye and exited the room without hesitation.

As they waited for whatever Alexander wanted to show them, Hanna found a lonely stool. She plopped down onto it far from the lab equipment and tables. Although her gaze fell Ashley from across the room, Hanna's mind wandered.

How am I supposed to save my sisters if I can't even keep the girls from getting lost? I mean, really, who's this Prince Barlow anyway? And these voices in my head are driving me crazy. What makes anyone think I can beat this guy or even remotely help? I can't even make the basketball team!

The professor's return startled Hanna from her thoughts. "I've got something for you." he said, pointing to Patrick. Curious, everyone shuffled over to his desk where he held a small, black disc by its rim. It had the familiar shape of a pancake. "This is a portal of singularity," he announced. "Also known as a dimensional bag."

"Can we use it to go home?" asked Ashley.

"No, it's not that type of portal. This singular one doesn't take you anywhere at all, actually."

"I don't understand," replied Hanna.

"It works like this." Alexander held the disc steady and plunged his free hand deep into the belly of it. His arm disappeared up to his elbow. "See?" he said. "If anyone or anything were to touch the inside of the disc I'm about to put at the bottom of that canvas bag, they'd be inside the dimensional portal. Think of it like an invisible bottomless sack. Either drop a marble or an anvil inside, you'll find that they'll both fit and more."

"Whoa," gasped Patrick, his eyes swelling to the size of gumdrops.

"Unlike a physical bag, which has walls like the canvas of Patrick's backpack," the professor continued, "the dimensional bag can hold practically anything."

"That's amazing!" said Ashley.

"Indeed. And, I'd like you to have it." He withdrew his arm and nodded to Patrick. "Pass me your backpack." The moment it was in his hand, Alexander unceremoniously emptied Patrick's entire bag onto his desk, its contents littering the already cluttered surface with knickknacks, half-engineered models of electronic gadgets, and crumpled papers of old design sketches. Seemingly satisfied, he then reached inside the pack and stuck the dimensional bag to the bottom. "Alright. All done. Now, put your stuff back inside," he encouraged, gesturing to the mess on his desk.

"Sure," said Patrick re-filling the pack with his trinkets. With everything back inside, he slung it over his shoulders and wrinkled his face in confusion. "Whoa! It weighs like, nothing."

"That's a side effect of the dimensional bag."

Patrick pumped his fist in the air. "Aw, man! Thank you so much! It's the best thing ever!"

Offering a small smile, the professor nodded before opening his desk drawer and pulled out a leather pouch bound with a tight draw string. He handed it to Hanna. "Here, this should be enough. Keep it somewhere safe."

"What is it?" Hanna asked while already stuffing the small but weighty pouch into her front pocket.

"It's gold kaura, silver tara, and copper kobbers." Hanna frowned as she tried to make sense of what she just heard. "Money," Alexander clarified, another smile taking over his scaly face. "It's a bag of money."

Hanna's lips shaped a silent O.

Before sliding the drawer closed, he removed a thin blank tablet with a type of carabiner looped through a small hole near its top. The professor hooked the carabiner through a buttonhole in his lab coat and placed his three-fingered hand on Hanna's shoulder. "And now, it's time to go to Castletown and introduce you to the royal family."

16

KNUMBSKULL CAVE

Lexi landed hard, sliding on her back and barrel-rolling down a steep dune. The thick, choking wind blew in torrents over her head as gritty sand filled her mouth and nose. She tumbled down the incline as the tempest's throaty howl continued to flood her ears like the bellow of a deafening horn. A coughing fit overtook her as she tried to expel the sand from her throat.

Her heart pounded spastic and fast against her chest, threatening to burst free. She spit sand from her mouth and wiped her tongue with the shoulder of her T-shirt. Lexi hacked up mucus-like phlegm which was speckled in gritty sand and colored glass. "I'm alive—I'm alive!" Her voice was raw and as dry as the desert engulfing her, but she survived, and that's all that mattered.

Lexi stole a glance back up the dune, but her vision was blurred and hazy. She pinched her eyes tight for several moments trying to make them water and rinse away the debris, but no relief came. The continued roar made her open her eyes in fear from the storm—afraid that it chased her down the dune.

The black winds, however, remained above her tearing across the rocky opening. Still wheezing up grit, she scrambled for a hiding spot and scurried into a hollowed nook at the backside of the rocky cliff. The thick face of the butte pressed firmly against her back as she strained to gulp fresh, clean air from the relative safety in the cove. Above the dune, the roaring storm blotted out the sky. Thin eddies of air curled around her and pulled the ends of her sand-filled hair against her face.

The back of her neck pressed against the face of the butte and she winced lurching forward. She gently probed the nape of her neck with her fingers and found that the skin there was tender to the touch—maybe even rubbed raw. "I can't—" she panted, trying to catch her breath. "Where is everyone?" But her cracked voice was lost in the howl of the tempest. Lexi dug her hand in the dune and threw a fistful of sand careful not to get more grit in her already irritated eyes. "Where's Hanna? Where's Ashley? Patrick? Where is everyone?!"

The growing lump in her throat threatened the onset of more tears, but they wouldn't flow. She'd used them all. They couldn't come because she had no more water in her eyes than she had in her dry scratchy throat. The desert stole it all—sucked it out of her in the race for her life.

Her shoulders began to shake as sobs quickly dissolved into wails of relief. She was alive. Her sudden joy mixed with the horrible realization that she was completely alone. Lexi's shoulders trembled in spasms as she cried, unable to touch the prickly glass shards which stuck from her skin like tiny colored quills.

"I can't believe it—I'm alive!" She sniffled and absently rubbed at her cheeks as a spasm of pain blossomed where she touched the slivers of glass.

Her eyes slowly climbed the length of her arm from her hand to her elbow. Her limbs were covered in a blanket of small needles. Lexi tentatively tried to pluck one out from the back of her hand, but the moment her finger grazed a shard, she jerked her hand back from the piercing pain. It was like pulling a barb from her flesh. The soft pliable skin on the back of her hand rose with each attempt to pull the glass out. This wasn't going to work.

Lexi couldn't bring herself to do it. It was too much like pulling a Band-Aid. She was covered in needles. There was no way, Lexi realized, that she was going to be able to pluck one let alone all of them out by herself. She leaned against the cold shadowed butte and closed her eyes. Something hard dug against her thigh from inside her pocket.

She was sitting on something. Lexi lifted her hips and fished in her back pocket careful not to graze the prickles on the back of her hand. "Oh, crap!" she exclaimed with glee when she pulled out her cell phone.

Her excitement brought on another bout of coughing. When she calmed herself, she held the phone in her hand for a moment and stared, unable to digest the sight of it. Would it even work out here in the desert? Was she even still on Earth?

Lexi pressed the power button and the screen bloomed to life. "I can't believe it still tuns on. Hanna—I can call Hanna!" She thumbed through her contacts and tapped on her sister's name followed by the green call button.

It rang…and rang…and rang.

Lexi pulled the phone away from her head and stared at the screen. Maybe it didn't work out here after all? But then, why had it rung? She shrugged at not having an answer, but Lexi didn't really care as long as it worked. A recorded message echoed through the speaker.

"Voicemail?" she yelled. "I don't want stupid voicemail!"

She hung up and redialed again and again. Twelve more calls resulted in the same outcome. She tried Ashley. And Michael. Then cycled through both of her parents until finally landing on Patrick. Nothing, but empty rings and more voicemails. Exhausted, Lexi shoved the phone back into her pocket and stared at her scraped, glass-abused lap. When was the last time she'd seen Patrick's face? It seemed like a lifetime.

What am I gonna do now? I had all this time, and I never told him.

I'm such a cross-eyed earwax bandit. She thumped herself on the forehead with a flat, sand-dusted palm. *Why hadn't I told him I loved him? What was my problem? And now I'm lost. Alone. In some strange place. He'll never know how I feel. If I find him — no, when I find him — I'm gonna tell him. He's got to feel the same about me, right? I know he does. Then we'll never be apart.*

Lexi pinched her eyes tight and inhaled a deep, slow breath which made her cough again before finally gazing around and taking in the soft, white sand. Wait, white? She glanced down at her boots. They were buried ankle-deep in fine grains that didn't cut.

Down the dune, above a windy sea, floated a colossal wall of huge gray clouds pressing across the sky like a dam, cutting off the whirling, deadly sands. The storm rolled along the edge of the sky overtop the butte but never pushed out to the water. But it wasn't the wall of sky fluff or the dune that stole her breath away.

"Holy crab-nuggets!"

A pirate ship rocked in waves of ocean blue not more than a few hundred feet away. Docked against a set of wooden piers that jut out into the surf, it was as if the ship were ripped from storybooks. High rounded sidewalls encased a row of black cannons along its flank, and atop the central mast flew a black flag painted with the infamous skull and cross bones.

Lexi struggled to her feet, careful not to brush against any of the painful needles still stuck in her skin. She half-waddled, half-sprinted down the pearl-white knoll, thoughts of imminent death were replaced by the need to dunk herself in the crisp ocean waves. As she left the dune and hobbled to the smooth, wet sand near the surf, tiny red crabs scurried from her path.

Cautiously, she moved toward the crashing waves until her boots were wet. *Not too deep. Don't get pulled in by the drag.* Lexi inched in until the water climbed to her shins and filled her boots. White-capped waves sprayed clouds of salty mist in her face and the cool relief pulled a sigh from her throat. It felt good, at first, until the salt bit into her wounds igniting them with a thousand pricks of pain.

Lexi grit her teeth against the sharp sting as the cold water chilled her hot skin. Holding strong, she became numb to the pain and squatted low to play with the waves. She danced her fingers through the knee-deep tide. A few more steps and her knobby knees were below the surface of the water. Lexi's breath caught in her chest as she lifted her gaze. Thick, ash colored clouds swam overhead. The ocean rose as the tide thrashed in the wind. She straightened and then edged closer to shore. *Not too deep.*

The desert tempest roared like an old train behind her while new shadows above her head blanketed the beach. A gust brought a new, unusual chill in the air and nipped at her wet skin. She looked up as a bolt of lightning forked between the smoky clouds. Lexi turned her gaze to the billowing sails of the ship. The seaward wind picked up, and the scent of seaweed and stale fish assaulted her nose. Her tangled, sand-laced hair whipped around her face in a near-perfect imitation of the ship's flag.

"I've got to find a place to hide. If it's not one storm, it's another."

She scanned the beach for a reprieve. As she did, the wind half-blinded Lexi pasting her hair against her cheeks like ropes of licorice. She shielded her eyes with her hands and spotted some caves to the left of the dunes, but they had an unsettling likeness to the face of a skull. Squinting against the assault, Lexi scanned the area for a better choice. A small shed, maybe the size of a large doghouse, stood in relief against the blowing green dune grass. The name Daisy was written in letters above the door. She started for the doghouse, but a soft voice almost lost to the wind called from somewhere near the caves. "Little girl…little girl…"

Lexi whipped her head around. A gray-haired woman stood across the beach. She waved her arms, beckoning Lexi over.

Droplets of rain the size of marbles began to fall. They sprinkled lightly, at first, but then came in heavy sheets pockmarking the white sand in dark, round divots.

"I'm coming!"

As Lexi hobbled through the rain, she eyed the strange woman through the steadily thickening downpour. Maybe it was a trick of the droplets in her eyes or the ragged, patch-filled, denim dress the lady wore, but the old woman looked green. Either way, Lexi welcomed the invitation of shelter and conversation.

"Yes, yes. Come to me. Come to Paula!" the old lady shouted. "Come! Come get out of da squall."

Lexi reached the craggy overhang and stood at the mouth of the cave. She stared at the deep wrinkles creasing the woman's cheeks. The grooves in her face stretched up to the corners of her eyes where her skin was stamped with heavy crow's feet. Behind her, the rain swallowed her boot prints and washed away any trace of Lexi from the sand.

The woman dangled a blue towel and opened it in an invitation to wrap Lexi in its cotton folds. Lexi hesitantly stepped forward and accepted, allowing the stranger's arms to envelope her until a blossom of pain prickled up her bare arms. Lexi suddenly jerked away from the woman's touch.

"Ole' Paula ain't gonna hurt you none. Wadda cute little girl doing on my beach in da rain?" The woman parted her lips in a near toothless grin. "Ya almost caught ya death in the sandstorm, I see. Don't you worry none. We git ya inside and pick dem nasty needles from ya, kay?"

The patchwork denim outfit fit the woman more like a curtain than a dress. It draped off her like a sail. Lexi stitched her eyebrows together and took a tentative step backward into the pounding rain. It hadn't been a mistake of her eyes; Paula wasn't human.

The woman frowned. "What in da six realms 'ye doin' in da

squall?" Lexi scrunched up her face in confusion. "You not from round des parts?"

"No. I'm not. I'm from Midtown Valley. Do you know where that is?"

"'Fraid not, dearie. I know every bit of Smaradine, and I done never heard no place like dat."

"Smaradine? W-what's Smaradine?"

"It's where 'ye is, dearie." Paula stretched her arms out to encompass everything.

"Have you seen my friends—my sisters?"

"I ain't seen nobody but you, dearie…"

Lexi's gut dropped like the cascading rain. "I followed my two sisters and our friends here through some door thingy…a portal—"

"Kambo's mercy!" exclaimed Paula cutting across her. "Ain't been no portals between worlds in don't know how long." She scratched her green chin which shifted the kerchief tied around her head. "You tellin' da troof? Don't be pullin' no pranks on ole' Paula."

"No, no! It's the truth," Lexi insisted. The woman seemed to relax, and Lexi glanced around, peering through the downpour and into the cave. "This place…it's so strange." Her gaze fell back on Paula. "And you're green."

A long smile slid up the woman's thin lips. "I know."

Lexi's clothes were soaked and her hair was matted to her head. She glanced up the dune to where the churning wind still whipped across the gap in the butte and pointed, words failing her for the moment.

"I know, dearie. Got yous caught in da sandstorm, alright."

A new wave of tears welled up in Lexi's eyes as the weight of the crushing realities started to finally settle in. She tried to push them away, but fresh tears fell in streams down her already wet cheeks. Lexi dropped her eyes to the door mat near her host's feet.

Paula opened up her arms and waved her forward with a

twitch of her four-fingered hands. "Come now. Come inside from da rain. We'll chat a bit and git dem prickles off ya."

Lexi gave one last parting glance toward the tempest and then again out to sea where a new storm rolled across choppy waves. "Er...okay." A heavy weight, as if tied to a balloon, lifted from her shoulders as she stepped out of the rain. Paula opened a wooden door which was knotted together with bands of rope. The woman led Lexi from the cold rain to the warm confines of her home.

17

———————

A DIFFERENT KIND OF PORTAL

Hanna stood on an old, wooden train platform in the middle of a large meadow. She leaned against a weathered post not far from where the portal that brought them to Smaradine once stood. As she scanned the open meadow, Hanna grimaced at the thought of Lexi being out there alone. "Where do you think she's at?" Hanna asked Michael.

He shrugged. "Dunno. Bet she's found some cozy nook to hole up." The corners of his mouth drooped as he turned to face her. "Bloody hell, you're white as a sheet."

"I think I need to sit down. I don't feel good." Hanna held her stomach as she sat on the platform. The splintered wood bit into the bare underside of her thighs. "Ugh. I don't know if she's here or back home. I don't know if she's safe or in danger. The naked truth is that I don't know if she's alive or…" But Hanna's voice trailed off unable to complete her sentence. "What a lousy big sister I turned out to be."

"Rubbish." Michael knelt beside her rubbing her back. "Don't be like that. You're smashing. Anyone would kill to have you as a big sister."

Hanna ignored his choice of words. "I should've gone last! I should've waited for both of them. I should've protected her.

Alexander said Barlow was after them. He said they were in danger. What'd I do about it? Nothing but give 'em a better chance to grab her."

Michael slid his arm around Hanna's shoulders, pulling her close. "That's bollocks. Then maybe you'd be lost and not her." He pressed his face close to hers.

"Would that be such a bad thing? I'd rather it was that way so—" From the corner of her eyes, she saw his lips pucker into a kiss. An icy coldness trickled down Hanna's throat. "W-what are you doing?"

Michael jerked away with an awkward expression that somehow matched how she felt. "I just—"

"You just what?"

He tried to fix his expression into something more confident, but just came across more and more like he got caught putting his hand in the cookie jar. "I was just trying to—you know."

"No, I don't know. I'm worried about my sister and you come in with all the right moves?"

"No—that's not—aw, forget it." Michael pulled himself to his feet and stormed off into the field toward where Patrick stood talking with the professor.

Somehow, instead of feeling vindicated, Hanna felt even worse than ever.

Ashley strode over from the far side of the platform and sat beside her. "I didn't see that explosion coming."

"Eh, you saw?"

"Er, yeah. You'd think he'd be more consoling instead of…" she shrugged, "whatever that was."

Hanna threw her hands onto her lap and sighed. "Maybe I was too…I don't know…harsh. But…but I can't believe him! Of all the times to try that. Maybe if things were different…if Lexi wasn't lost…"

Ashley breathed a heavy sigh. "Yeah, I get it. But you shouldn't be so hard on him." Her gaze flicked to Michael as he joined Patrick and the professor. "People handle grief in different ways. He's stuck in this mess with us, too. Cut him a break."

"Yeah, I know," Hanna replied sheepishly. "I should probably apologize."

Ashley grabbed her hand and they stared in silence at a set of old, rusty train tracks. The worn rails disappeared into the tall savannah grass beyond the professor's northern border. "I'm worried about her, too."

"I just don't know what to do. How do we find her?"

"I think we'll have to put our faith in him." Ashley jerked her head at the professor. Hanna glanced up; Alexander was flagging them down.

As they joined the group at the edge of the field, Hanna reached for Michael's hand, but he ducked away and stepped just out of her grasp. She gaped and caught Patrick's eyes as Michael moved to the other side of a small, raised, circular platform. Alexander rested his green foot against the edge of the short stone plinth. The flat, old rock had smooth rounded edges that looked to be worn by time and weather. The heavy block sat an inch above the grass and was as wide as a bathtub. A familiar symbol which Hanna had seen her entire life was etched into the face of the stone.

She glanced at the palm of her right hand, which bore the same design. Beside her, Ashley's eyes broadened as wide as quarters as she, too, must've made the same realization. What could it mean? How could a birthmark she and her sisters shared since birth end up on a stone pedestal in the middle of a field on some distant corner of wherever they were?

"We're using a portal to get to the royal palace," Alexander announced.

"Thought you said they were all broken, mate?"

"The ones connecting the six realms are broken, but these portals," he pointed to the stone slab beneath his foot, "these allow free travel within Smaradine."

Ashley looked back to the wooden platform. "What about those train tracks?"

"That's an old railway. It's used only for freight now." Alexander offered a half-smile. "I have to say, even without magic, your kind sure know how to create some fantastic machinery."

Hanna frowned. "What do you mean?"

"It was from your world that I took the idea."

"What idea?"

"For the train. It's true—it was made a long time ago before our portals were closed. I was young then and there are loads of fancy gadgets in your world. I've been trying to pull Manna into a new age, like your home, for as long as I can remember. You see, not all of Smaradine—or the other realms for that matter— lives in old castles and citadels. Dank hovels are a thing of a bygone era." The professor cast a glance toward the tracks. "I digress. We'll be traveling by portal."

Michael scrunched up his face. "You've been to Earth before?"

"You mean Havendale."

"What's Havendale."

"That's what we call your Earth."

"Hold on," Patrick said. "You're telling me that we're not the first people to visit Smaradine?"

The professor stifled a chuckle. "Goodness, no. People have come from Havendale for eons. It's where our population of your people came from. But Havendale is not the only other-worldly place."

Hanna blinked. "There's more?"

Alexander gave a slow, long nod. "Oh, yes. There are six realms of which Havendale is but one. But Smaradine and Havendale are bound together like Siamese twins. Our worlds are parallel to each other. We surprisingly share a single realm, bound together by the same godly magic. Although travel to

Havendale was restricted, we were free to move to and from other realms freely before the old pathways failed."

"Why was travel to Earth—Havendale, or whatever—why was it restricted?" asked Ashley.

"Let's just say that Havendale is young. Most of its people are delicate."

"I ain't delicate," snapped Michael.

The professor sighed. "Some have a long lineage here, like the royal family, but most humans traveled to Smaradine by accident. They've done so for a millennium. They'd mistakenly enter a gate and end up here. They'd lose their way back and become stuck."

Patrick counted his fingers and muttered, "I knew there had to be life outside our own planet, but I never expected six worlds bound together."

Michael threw his hands in the air. "Wait a minute! Is there a way for this Barlow guy to travel to Earth—I mean Havendale— or whatever. Can he get through one of these old pathways, too?"

"He already found a way through this morning. Duh," snapped Ashley. "Remember that big, swirling, black cloud that snaked into our backyard?"

Michael glared. "I know that! I was there, remember?"

"Well, you said it, not me."

"Arg! What I meant was, can this guy find his way back again?"

"Anything is possible, but unlikely." Alexander shrugged. "The magic ring, a Black Cat ring if I remember, which was used to find and manipulate the old portals, as well as generate new ones, has been lost for generations. Plus," he added with a slight huff, "you must remember that all rifts, except on Smaradine, are broken. I don't even know how Barlow got to Midtown Valley through yours. Dark Magic, I suppose. If he could have beforehand, though, he'd already have done it."

"Why couldn't Barlow use a cube like we did?" asked Patrick.

"Unless he steals hers," the professor pointed to Hanna, "she has the only one."

Patrick frowned. "And what if he finds the ring that opens the old ways? What did you say it was…a Black Cat?"

Alexander opened his mouth to reply, but Michael spoke over him. "Wait, wait, wait a second. There're two magic items that open windows to new worlds?"

"Yes, but they're different in significant ways. While her cube and the lost ring were forged from the same magic, they serve separate purposes. The ring can only open portals between your world and Smaradine, while the Realm Cube controls access to all of them."

Michael rubbed the small of his back before leaning toward Patrick. He tugged up his green T-shirt, pooling it at the nape of his neck. "Hey, does my back look different or anything? It really hurts."

As Patrick examined Michael, Hanna stole a glance and flinched. There were angry red lines streaking outward from the middle of his back. A deep bruise the color of plums stained his dark skin at the site of his transplanted kidney. Hanna absently rubbed at her own back at the same spot, but there was no pain there at all. So why was Michael suffering?

Ashley bit her fingernails. "Did I do that when I bowled you over coming through the portal?"

Michael shook his head. "Naw, it started after touching Hanna's ring."

The professor offered a sympathetic look before focusing instead on the position of the sun. "We should get moving." He waved his hand at waist-level over the stone plinth and a black doorway six feet tall and three feet wide flickered into existence. Ashley staggered backward, Hanna, however, just stared. It resembled the one that appeared in their backyard. Alexander picked up the small, rectangular tablet dangling from the front of his lab coat and pressed his fingers to the blank slate. Its surface glimmered to life in an array of numbers and shapes.

"This is a Portal Dial," he said, holding up the tablet in the palm of one hand. "You need one to travel through rifts. If you don't punch in the coordinates of where you wish to go, there's no telling where you'd end up. The portal could spit you out anywhere in Smaradine." He flicked his eyes toward Hanna and added, "you'd be as lost as Lexi. Or worse."

The word 'lost' sparked something in Hanna's brain. Barlow. When he first made contact, back in the school parking lot, he said she was lost, too. Even though she didn't feel very lost at the time.

"Hanna," The professor cut across her thoughts. "Are you ready?"

"Hm? Oh, yeah. I'm ready," Hanna said with a hint of apprehension.

Alexander's fingers danced across the Portal Dial. "Alright, we're set to go to Castletown's seaport first. Check the coordinates on the map if you need to. I think it's important you get a better understanding of the world you've walked into before we meet the royal family." Hanna frowned—her concern about the timely return of her sister must have been written plainly across her face. "Don't worry," the professor added. "It won't take long to walk from the Wharf to the palace."

Hanna's face relaxed as she looked from the portal to her sister and back to the professor. "We'll go together," she said, grabbing Ashley's hand. They'd already lost one sibling. She wasn't going to make that mistake a second time.

"When you arrive at the Wharf, just move out of the way so the others can come through without crashing into you, okay?"

Hanna nodded and squeezed her sister's hand. "Are you ready," She got a nod in return and the two stepped from the meadow in tandem into the inky, black portal. The rich grassy aroma of the meadow disappeared and her nose was assaulted by the pungent odor of saltwater.

Hanna blinked several times, trying to get her bearings, her hand still gripped tightly around Ashley's. The green field of purple flowers was replaced by a gray cobblestone street lined with stout, buildings. To their right, curling, white-capped waves licked the surface of an ocean harbor. Skiffs and ships rocked near long, wooden piers.

Almost forgetting to step off the pedestal, Hanna pulled her sister to the side of the stone platform. Ashley stepped away just in time to avoid Patrick striding out of the portal. As the others joined them, Hanna's gaze dropped. The platform they now stood on also bore the same uncanny emblem as their birthmarks. With Michael and Alexander through the portal, the rift flicked and winked out of existence leaving them clustered together along the side of the street.

18

CRIMSON BROTHERHOOD

The heavy, seaward wind whipped Hanna's long hair into a mess. Her ponytail brushed the sensitive nape of her neck while the two solitary braids about her temples flapped wildly against her cheeks. A dusting of ocean water blew from the harbor's crashing waves covering the group in a fine coat of dewy mist.

"What is this place?" she asked.

The professor stretched out his arms. "This is Salthouse Wharf."

Ashley wrinkled her nose. "It stinks."

Hanna didn't even need to sniff the air for her lips to curl in disgust. The odor was so thick that she could taste it on her tongue. "What is it…dead fish?"

"Blimey. Smells worse than my locker. Is it like this everywhere?"

Alexander shook his head and wrinkled his small nose. "No, but as an industry seaport, the Wharf the second-best place for salted fish in the kingdom."

Hanna slowly spun, soaking in the activity of the harbor. Sailors unloaded pallets of bags, barrels, and boxes. They carried them from big ships and small skiffs which rocked next to the docks in the choppy waves.

The Wharf was filled with people just like the professor. Cat people, dog people, and humans dotted the busy streets of the harbor. Every animal breed Hanna could think of was walking and talking just as they were. Nearly everyone was a bipedal, talking animal except for a few oxen and pack mules pulling carts. And just like on Earth, the people here came in all shapes and sizes. Hanna blinked. *Never in my wildest dreams would I've thought this place existed.*

The darkened shadow of a flock of pigeons crossed over their heads. They fluttered noisily, landing in the gutter up the street. Pecking at something unseen in the uneven bricks of the road, the birds clustered in front of a building with a sign that read, *The Sandpiper Inn.*

Michael stepped near a large brown, dust-covered oxen tied to a post outside the inn. As he drew even with the animal, the birds burst into the sky in a wild frenzy. He looked the oxen in its bulbous black eye and said, "What's your name? Mine's Michael." The beast of burden replied by sticking its long, wet tongue up one of its nostrils and shook its head, dislodging a fly from its eyebrow. Michael stared at the animal as it stomped its front hoof on the cobbled stone street.

Alexander cupped his hands to his mouth and shouted. "Don't be silly, that's just an animal."

Michael flicked a confused look to the professor as he stepped away from the creature. "Huh?"

"Not all creatures have the capacity for higher intelligence. That one just pulls wagons."

Hanna led the group away from the plinth, stepping toward The Sandpiper Inn. Ashley, who followed right behind her sister, asked Alexander, "How can you tell the difference?"

The professor chuckled. "If it walks upright on two legs, and if it's dressed in clothing, best bet they will talk like us. We're humble people, much like you in Havendale."

Hanna slugged Michael's shoulder and said under her breath, "Idiot."

The corners of his mouth curled upward. "Bollocks? How was I supposed to know?"

"Right then, this way everyone." Alexander weaved through the group and led them up a tiny hill. "Follow that other wagon and we'll dry from the sea mist as we walk."

Hanna followed the cobblestone road with her eyes traveling up the lazy curve of the ridge. The damp stone was peppered in a fine ocean spray that seemed to cover everything in the wharf. "Where are we headed?"

The professor removed his coat and shook off the water with several snappy flicks. "We're headed through the heart of the royal city. That will take us through the town square. We'll finish the last leg of our journey in the Emerald District before entering the royal grounds." He slid both arms back into his white lab coat.

Once over the crest of the hill, they left the busy port behind. The muted grays of the harbor shops were replaced by bright whites, crisp yellows, and vibrant blues of new storefronts and street vendors. Salthouse Wharf was not completely unlike Midtown Valley. The industrial sector of Castletown was reminiscent of the street where Hanna's dad worked on Printer's Row in the city. The brilliantly painted buildings of the mom n' pop shops offered a quaint and cozy appeal.

Hanna leaned over and whispered in Ashley's ear, "This place is amazing!"

"Right? I know!"

"It's like we stepped out of a story book and jumped back in time two hundred years."

As they walked into town, it became a struggle for the group to stick together. Standing clusters of people and vendors blocked their path on either side of the street.

"What are all the decorations?" Patrick asked, pointing to the garnished light posts.

Workers stretched high on tall ladders dressing light posts made of polished, black steel in lazy loops of crimson garland and cherry blossoms.

"They're preparing for the Summer Solstice festival. It starts in a few days and lasts several weeks. The celebration ends on the day of the Summer Solstice—a day of great magic and jubilation for everyone."

Continuing up the sidewalk, they skirted around the edge of a large crowd packed around a parked wagon. A pair of red, velvet curtains on the back of the covered caravan swished open. Four wooden, hand puppets popped into view. The bustle and noise of the crowd dropped to a low murmur as a street show began.

One puppet was dressed in all black and painted like a clown. He was surrounded by two other puppets wearing devilish, crimson masks. The fourth puppet was a plump baker whose white jacket was so swollen, it spread the buttons at the belly.

"Oh, no!" cried the baker, "it's B-B-Barlow! Don't hurt me, puh-puh-please!"

The clown pointed a wand at the baker. "You didn't pay me my ransom for your kidnapped daughter. Your insult will make everyone suffer!"

"But Barlow, I have no coin left. Your Crimson Brotherhood has already bled me dry."

"I care nothing for your excuses," shouted puppet Barlow. "Your daughter will be a slave to the Brotherhood, and I'll turn you into a rat."

The piercing cry of a baby with long honey gold locks carried across the crowd. As she watched the baby's mother carry her from the masses, Hanna's mind drifted to her own parents. Neither she, nor her sisters, said good-bye before leaving Midtown Valley. It wouldn't be long, she was sure, that their mom and dad would start worrying...

A small puff of smoke on the stage brought Hanna back from

her thoughts. The baker disappeared and was replaced with a poorly colored cardboard cut-out of a rat. An angry mob of stick puppets chased the prince and his two goons off the stage. The throng around the traveling show erupted in a wave of cheers. Many threw small, triangular copper coins onto the stage. Alexander reached into his own pocket and tossed up several kobbers.

Hanna stared at the empty stage. "Is that what Barlow's like?"

Alexander took a deep breath and rubbed his forehead. "Everyone loves to mock him, but the reality is that the whole kingdom lives in fear of the King of Thieves."

A dirty man dressed in a ragged, brown coat and a sweat-stained shirt crashed into Michael. The two collapsed in a heap and the man's oily black hair fell across Michael's face. Even from where Hanna stood, the pungent stench of cheap beer and vomit wafted from the man's mouth as he spoke.

The stranger on top of Michael babbled incoherent gibberish as he tried to push himself up but fell clumsily back onto Michael three more times. Strings of spittle flew from the man's lips. Michael recoiled as the droplets stuck to his shocked face.

"It's mine I tell you! It was *always* mine," the drunk shouted in a heavy slur, his words finally somewhat clear for a moment.

Michael struggled to push the man away. "What are—get off —ugh—you're bonkers, mate!"

"They found me—they, they found me," he stuttered, "'twas hiding on the Sailor's Wench, but they'll never get me." He cackled a coarse bark-of-a-laugh. "The Brotherhood may know 'bout da medallion, *hick*," his shoulders shuddered with a hiccup.

"Shove off, 'ye crazy git." Michael kept pushing the heavy man's face away. The drunk slumped atop him. Hanna bent down to pull the guy off, but caught the full stench of him as he belched in her face. She gasped, and Michael kicked again, trying to free himself, but even with Hanna's help, the man was simply too heavy.

"They can't have it—don't tell em'," the sailor protested in a sudden wave of slurs. His eyes rolled one direction, then the next, never really focusing on either of them. "It was never Barlow's coin—I won it fair and square." The drunk pressed the crusty tip of his dirty index finger into the plump flesh of Michael's lips. "Shh—they'll never find it now." He puffed out his cheeks like twin balloons and belched again.

Michael visibly gagged as the man rolled back, finally setting him free. "Find what? Get yer hands off— 'ya dirty bloke!"

The sailor staggered to his feet and cast a worried glance over his shoulder in the direction of the harbor. Then he limped away breaking through the small crowd. The twin tails of his long coat flapped behind him as he staggered careening his shoulder along the stone wall of an alley and disappeared.

"What the heck was that all about?" Hanna said, hoisting Michael up.

He coughed and brushed dirt from his clothes. "Guy's a nutter."

Hanna nodded. "I think he's on the run from someone. Acted real jittery. Hm…he seemed scared, didn't he? See how he kept looking over his shoulder?"

No sooner had she finished her sentence when a lone man rushed into the area from behind the traveling stage. As soon as he entered, the mood of the audience turned cold. It was as if everyone had something else better to do as the figure scanned the faces in the crowd.

Hanna inched her eyes up the new stranger's tight physique. He was dressed in dark boots and black, leather pants. Along the outside of his thighs were strapped a series of slender throwing knives. He wore a sleeveless crimson jacket with dirty, silver buckles across his chest. Even from a distance, the ripped muscles of his arms flexed as he curled his fingers into fists. The man's head was concealed by a heavy, black cowl pulled over his brow, darkening his face in shadows.

He turned, rotating counterclockwise, revealing a pair of long rapiers strapped in an 'X' against his back. The gilded, slender blades shimmered in the late afternoon sun. He continued flexing his fingers and absently rubbed the inside of his right arm. Hanna studied him as he shook his arm loose—it was the same way she did when her own scar hurt!

Hanna's jaw fell slack. Burned into the inside of the man's forearm was the same raven brand. What did that mean? Who was this man? He turned, looking over his shoulder and then, silent as a whisper, sprinted down the shadowed alleyway.

She looked from Michael to Patrick. "Who was that guy?"

The professor rubbed his temples. "His name is Rowan. He's an elite among the Crimson Brotherhood; he's half of Barlow's personal muscle."

"Half?" Hanna asked, a brow raised.

"Yup. There's another. A Dire Wolf named Wesley Grit. The two do Barlow's bidding and hold a tight rein on Smaradine. Grit, from what I hear, leads the Crimson Brotherhood—the criminal underbelly of Smaradine. Rowan heads the Legion—Barlow's personal guard. He's as mean as Grit is nasty. The two make the perfect pair. One's the anvil and the other's the hammer."

A crisp clippity-clop echoed off the buildings. Hanna turned, mouth agape, as three brilliantly white unicorns with tall, slender, spiraled horns paraded through the intersection and down the street toward the wharf. Each unicorn, boasting a bushy mane of silver, was tethered by a long leather leash clasped in the hands of three extremely tiny creatures. She swallowed hard, trying to comprehend what she was seeing. There were no other words to describe the creatures—they were colorfully dressed yard gnomes with pointy red hats.

Mouth still half-open, Hanna turned to Michael and Patrick. "Did you guys see that? Were those—"

"Yeah," said Patrick. "Those were unicorns."

"Being led by a pack of gnomes," finished Michael.

The professor leaned in and cleared his throat. "Gnomes are the keepers of the unicorns."

"I can't believe I just saw that. Unicorns, of all things…" added a visibly stunned Ashley.

Alexander nodded his head and watched with the others as the procession disappeared down the street. The clippity-clop of their hooves against the cobblestone faded into the background of the city. "Believe it or not, unicorn spit is a highly valued ingredient at apothecaries across Smaradine."

"Spit?" said Hanna incredulously.

"Saliva, actually. Incredible healing properties. The gnomes guard their herds violently, if needed. In fact—" but the group didn't get to hear the rest. Alexander stopped short and stared out into the intersection. Hanna followed his gaze.

A reddish-brown bat-eared fox with large, cup-shaped ears crossed the now empty intersection carrying a frosty mug. The woman walked from a tavern on the opposite side of the street. She flattened her ears against her head and gripped a round tray in one hand, balancing the frothy glass full of dark, creamy liquid in the other.

"Ya'll shouldn't be talking like this out in the open. I could hear you way over yonder." She pointed back to the saloon. "You'll get yourself in a heap of trouble. The Crimson Brotherhood is all over the wharf—no telling who's listening." Hanna passed a sheepish glance to her friends. "I'm a bar maid at the Twisted Tavern." The fox jerked her thumb over her shoulder. "See these ears? I hear everything."

She upended her drink, finishing it in a single, long chug and wiped the white froth from her lips with the back of her arm, smearing the suds into her matted fur. "Look there," she said with a nod of her chin. The bar maid pointed down the same alley the drunk and Rowan disappeared into. "See that tag on the alley wall—that's how I know the Brotherhood is around. They leave their mark."

Hanna turned and peered into the dim alleyway. Painted at eye-level on the corner was a smudged, circular, crimson tag. The graffiti was the size of a dinner plate and displayed a crude picture of a raven in flight. Its wings curved upward to complete a circle. On the bottom were a pair of clawed feet extended into menacing talons. It was identical to the brand on the inside of her arm. It itched, and Hanna grimaced, hiding her scar behind her back.

What does this mean? How can that symbol be on the wall and also on Rowan's and both my and Michael's arms? Are we a part of the Brotherhood now, too? I don't want to be part of any Brotherhood!

"If you see that crimson tag anywhere, then Kauras-to-crème puffs the Crimson Brotherhood ain't far off. They recruit all across Smaradine. There's nowhere they ain't already spread their finger of filth," the bar maid spat with unveiled venom.

"How do you know so much?" asked Hanna.

Patrick took a step backward. "You're not with them, are you?"

The fox stepped closer and shook her empty mug. Froth and bits of dribble flew from the lip of the glass and peppered the cobblestones with dime-sized stains. "With 'em? I hate 'em! They took my little brother—brainwashed 'em. Haven't seen him in years. Don't know if he's even alive."

She pulled a dirty hand towel from a pocket in her apron and dabbed at the growing pools that threatened to overflow her eyes. The bar maid sniffled, then spat on the ground nearly hitting Michael's shoe. "The princess—that rotten whelp—is worthless. She's just like the rest of 'em. Just as bad as the lot on Blunder Mountain. She won't do nothin' to stop the Crimson Brotherhood—won't stop her brother. Barlow's gonna destroy this kingdom one day. Mark my words."

Patrick threw his hands in the air, turning from her to the professor. "Wait. Just hold on. Barlow's the guy after Hanna and her sisters, right? You're saying that he's also the kingpin for the largest gang influence in the kingdom? On top of all that, Barlow's also a prince of Manna?"

The professor pursed his thin, green lips and nodded. "I'm afraid so."

The bar maid jabbed a finger at Hanna. "Did he say Barlow's after one of you?"

"Yes, and my—"

"You're a dead girl walking," the fox said in a deadpanned voice.

Hanna nervously tucked a braid behind her ear. "I'll be okay. I know I will. He's never getting me or my sisters—*never*," she said defiantly. "What's your brother's name?"

"Parker—his name is Parker. He's got beautiful, green eyes." She cast her own to the ground. "But—but, I ain't ever gonna see them again," she hissed through gritted teeth and slammed her glass goblet into the gutter, smashing it to pieces. Her face purpled in rage, vibrantly enough to show through the fur coating her cheeks as she looked into Hanna's blue eyes. "If Barlow's after you, there ain't nowhere in the six realms you can hide."

A wave of anxiety churned in Hanna's stomach. "Right. Well, we really need to get moving."

The professor leaned in close. "Remember what I said—"

Trust no one. A new knot tied in her stomach.

The group finally left the bar maid behind and followed Alexander the next few blocks in silence. A noise that Hanna had mistaken for horses and wagons grew louder. It rose to a low roar, more like the steady rumble of cheering. But her thoughts drifted back to the bar maid's somber words. Was there really no hope? Were her sisters destined to be Barlow's as predicted?

19

ANCIENT RUNES

They passed pubs, bakeries, and restaurants that filled the air with the delicious scent of meat pies and spicy, giblet fritters. Hanna's stomach grumbled, joining the steadily building ruckus that became their backdrop. She hardly noticed that the sun tipped to the other side of the sky.

As they reached the end of the block, the professor stopped near the corner of an intersection outside of a small shop and waved to someone across the street. A thin woman in a white dress with blue frill crossed to greet them. She hustled past a slow-moving mule-driven wagon and stepped up onto the curb. Hanna noticed when she was closer that the professor's friend had an inch or two on her. Maybe it was the way she wore her hair.

"What a pleasant surprise to see you, professor." She tucked her fiery, red hair back under her powder-blue bonnet.

Alexander smiled and waved Hanna closer. "Hanna, come. I'd like to introduce you to Ms. Zoe Beauparlant, head nurse to the royal family."

Hanna stuck out her hand in offer as she turned to look beside her. "This is my youngest sister, Ashley." She placed a hand on Ashley's shoulder, then pointed near the doorway of the nearest store. "Those two are my friends, Michael and Patrick. We're looking for my other sister, Lexi. She's gotten herself lost."

"Oh, dear." Ms. Beauparlant gasped and covered her mouth with her hand. "Now's not the time to get lost with the rise in Brotherhood activity. If there's anything I can do, please just let me know?"

"Thanks, but…" Hanna gave an empty shrug. "I-I'm not sure what to do myself."

"You just find me in the hospital wing of Hemlock Castle. Any friend of the professor is a friend of mine," she said with a dainty smile. "I'm off to Haag's Herbs & Organic Apothecary, right now, though. I need to replenish my supply of bone marrow, tea leaves, and slug slime."

"Bone marrow? Slug slime?" Ashley whispered.

Hanna stepped on her sister's toes and forced a smile. "Shut —up, sis," she hissed from the side of her mouth before turning back to Ms. Beauparlant. "It was nice meeting you." The royal nurse returned the smile and nodded before walking past them into the heart of the wharf.

"Come inside," said the professor, stepping past Michael and Patrick and through the nearest doorway. "I've got something to purchase I think you'd be interested in."

Hanna glanced up to the wooden sign hanging above the doorway as a cool breeze caught her hair. "Golinveaux's Emporium…" She frowned and followed the professor across the threshold of the store.

The narrow spaces between the tables afforded little room to move as Hanna was nudged forward by her friends trudging inside behind her. She sidestepped a table filled with trinkets to make enough room for the five of them to fit comfortably. She moved to the back of the store and stood next to Alexander with her fingertips resting on the low front counter. A solitary silver bell sat alone on the counter. The professor rang it once. The high-pitched *ding* echoed through the store.

Like her friends, Hanna gazed around the high-ceilinged room. Trinkets were everywhere. The store was lined with wooden shelves that stretched from floor to ceiling. The place was filled with thick, colorfully bound books and tomes and rolled scrolls of bleach-white parchment. A batch of light-blue orbs, like magical fireflies the size of bocce balls, hung in an invisible line from the ceiling. They floated in a random pattern in mid-air, six feet above their heads.

Arranged on a few small tables not far from the front counter sat an array of strange gadgets of which Hanna recognized only one. Her eyes were drawn to the collection of long, thin sticks set on foot-tall pedestals. "Are those…" Hanna pointed to the gnarled shafts of dark-grained wood.

Alexander nodded. "Golinveaux's Emporium is full of magical items—even wizarding wands. The owner of this shop is the grandson of the great Golinveaux, who started the Golinveaux School of Magic and Enchantments in Cog."

Hanna took a long moment to gaze about the room. There were tall walking sticks with dried, shrunken heads of various creatures spiked onto the tops in the corner near the door. Rolls of delicate and intricately colored fabrics were folded into neatly lined stacks on the bottom row of shelves below a thin line of books. Hanna had to do a double-take to make sure the fabric hadn't just wiggled on its own. Thick rolls of multi-color threaded carpet were stacked on end near the shelf.

"Look at this," said Ashley from across the room.

Hanna stared at a low table next to where her sister was standing. A variety of small objects were strewn across the top of a dark oaken dresser along the far wall. Next to the clutter of jars of what looked like oddly colored glitter and clear tubes of black jelly was a collection of gem-studded rings and gilded bracelets. As she stepped closer, her brow knit together in confusion.

Among the half-dozen rings sat a petite silver watch. Adhered to its back were colorful peacock feathers. Was this a broach? The strange thing about it was that the hands of the watch ticked slowly backward. Hanna bent forward, reaching out to stroke the multi-colored plumage when Alexander caught her wrist.

"I wouldn't touch that if I were you," he warned in a calm even voice. "In fact, don't touch anything—especially that. Without knowing how to work it, you've no idea where in time you'd end up."

Hanna's eyes widened and she pulled back her hand. Time travel was real, too?! Gasps of amazement flitted across the room from where Michael and Patrick stood. Their backs were to the front window and they peered at a near translucent-white crystal geode.

"I thought I knew weird, but this place takes the cake," Ashley said in low tones so that only her sister could hear.

Hanna nodded in agreement when a squeaking noise, as if from a rusty chain, echoed from somewhere behind the rows of shelving in the back. She turned to face the front counter and searched the shadows for the source. Something dark and low to the ground shifted from the recesses of the store. It came between the narrow space of two tall shelves filled with dusty artifacts. A form appeared through the gloom—a man in a wheelchair.

The large wheels squealed as he pushed himself out of the shadows and into the opening beside the front counter. The light from the nearby window revealed that he wasn't really a man at all. Although he sat upright in his chair like a human, tiny, pointed ears and long whiskers extended from the base of his auburn nose.

"Good afternoon, Mr. Golinveaux." Alexander bowed his head slightly.

Hanna took in the entire figure of Mr. Golinveaux. His face and hands were covered in short brown-marbled fur. The hair appeared to melt into creamy ribbons the color of golden butter. He was dressed in a button-down, off-white Oxford with crisp, pressed sleeves ending in a pair of cufflinks at his wrists. A light hazelnut vest covered his torso. It stretched down to his matching pressed slacks and polished shoes.

Mr. Golinveaux looked up from his seat and purred in a soft, silky voice, "What pleasures bring you into my shop today, professor?"

Alexander smiled. "I've come to purchase a Portal Dial."

"Oh, I think I have what you need right here." The shopkeeper turned his chair and rolled close to the front window. He stopped just shy of knocking over the walking sticks with shrunken heads. "And how many will you be needing today?"

The professor glanced at Hanna. "How many do you think? One, two, at most?"

She looked to her friends and sister and ticked off numbers on her fingers. "One, two, three, four…and with Lexi, that makes five. Hm, but I guess we could share a couple…"

"That'll do it then." Alexander nodded at the shopkeeper. "'Suppose we'll take an even pair."

From across the room, Mr. Golinveaux pointed a wand toward the top of the shelves. *"Trage Locomotis,"* he mumbled, and a blue light shot from the end of his wand. Two small tablets floated down into his free hand.

"Where do I get me one of those things?" Michael said with a smile that spread from ear to ear.

"A hundred golden kaura will buy you a wand." The shopkeeper spun his chair around and wheeled himself back toward the front counter. "Magic must be in your blood, however, for it to be of any use. If you're a Ni'Mago, the wand will simply be an expensive stick."

As Mr. Golinveaux rolled past the low-slung counter, stopping at the register, Michael rested his arm on a tall dresser. "No offense or anything, but if I had magic like you, and I was stuck in some dumb wheelchair, the first thing I'd have done was fixed myself."

"Michael!" snapped Hanna.

Mr. Golinveaux knit his brow. "You must be new to magic,"

he responded with a curt change in tone. "Or you'd know there are some things magic simply cannot correct."

The professor cleared his throat uncomfortably. "The boy, I'm sure, meant no harm."

"Perhaps. But he'll need to learn about magic and social etiquette if he's going to survive out here. Whether he's using it or avoiding it, whatever his proclivity." Mr. Golinveaux eyed Michael as he opened the register. "He's a bit old to be discovering magic for the first time, so my inclination is the boy is the latter." He then picked up a Portal Dial and glanced at the price tag. "That'll be thirty kaura, five tara, and two kobbers for the set of Portal Dials."

Alexander opened his money pouch and spilled a handful of colorfully shaped coins across the counter. He pushed a small pile toward the register and picked up their purchases turning toward the group. "Here, put this somewhere it won't get lost." He handed a Portal Dial to Hanna. She eyed the stone-gray tablet before sliding it into her back pocket. It fit perfectly. Then, Hanna froze, her gut dropping.

"What is it? What's wrong," asked Ashley.

Hanna pat down the front and back pockets of her shorts. "Where is it? Where's my phone and ear buds?" Her hands again flying from one pocket to the other and back again. "Crap! I've lost it!" she moaned.

"You sure you had it?" asked Patrick.

"Yeah, I'm sure. I stuffed it into my back pocket before leaving the house."

"Come on," called the professor, a few paces away already and with a tone of indifference.

Hanna pat down her pockets one last time before giving up and dejectedly followed Patrick, Michael, and Ashley out of the front door. As they reached the sidewalk, Alexander passed Patrick the second Dial. Behind them, Michael's face showed that he probably wanted to hold it.

Hanna slugged him on the shoulder. "Come on, cheer up. You can help me use—"

Searing pain tore through the brand on her arm and rippled up to her head. It was as if a red, hot poker was pressed against the inside of her skull. She screwed her eyes tight and fell to both knees, crying out and clutching her forehead in the middle of the sidewalk.

"HANNA! HANNA!" A strong grip took hold of her and tried to pull her to her feet.

Creases rippled across her forehead and Patrick's voice was drowned out by Barlow's voice ringing through her mind. *"Bring me your sisters. Spare them the misery of your poor choices. I know you're in Smaradine. I can feel you're close."* As quickly as it started, Barlow's voice, the stabbing pain across the inside of her arm, and the violent throbs inside her head vanished. Vaguely aware of Patrick's grip around her arm, Hanna shakily rose to her feet.

Michael stepped in front of Patrick. "Are you okay? What was that about?"

Patrick glared. "I've got—"

"What happened? What can I do?" Michael pressed.

"Voices," she replied, her head still swimming.

Michael twisted his face in confusion. "What do you mean, voices?"

"Um." Hanna bit her lip. "I've been hearing voices since… since this morning. I didn't want to worry either of you. It sounded silly to say out loud. I was still trying to make sense of it all myself, but things just snowballed."

"Voices?" Alexander asked. "Who is it? Do you know?"

Hanna avoided everyone's gaze, but over the next half hour, she explained her mental encounters with Barlow as they left the Salthouse Wharf behind. The shops melded into a blur of landscape as they eventually wandered into the town square. The background buzz of applause and cheers grew clearer.

"Do you guys hear that?," asked Hanna.

Patrick put his ear to the air. "Sounds like…like cheering…maybe…"

Michael shrugged. "Don't know what that is, but I hear something."

As they approached town square, something pulled Hanna's attention from the cheers. Burned into the cobblestone was a large circular diagram about six feet in diameter. The emblem, which took up nearly the entire center of the circle, was the same as on her hand. Hanna's mind was made up—it was unmistakable. She had to say something. This was more than a coincidence.

"How's this possible?" The group's eyes turned to her as Hanna pointed to the emblem. "The drawing on the street and our birthmarks are the same."

Patrick rushed to stand beside Ashley and squint at the mark. "What are you talking about? That's cra—" He stopped short, head swiveling between the emblem and Ashley's hand, his mouth dropping open.

"What's going on?" Hanna insisted. Her frustration bubbled over feeling more and more that she was being left out of something important. "What—is—going—on?"

The professor cleared his throat and pointed at the ground. "That's a magical rune."

Hanna gaped. "What's it mean?" Alexander inhaled a deep breath. "Look," she added as her face scrunched up in irritation. "I'm not going any farther until you tell me what's really going on here. You've been stringing me and my friends along without telling us much of anything. I know you're keeping something from us. From me, specifically. So, spill! You said you knew the truth and that's what I want. RIGHT. NOW!"

Alexander closed his eyes for a moment, and when he opened them again, they were filled with tears. "I wanted to wait to tell you—"

"WAIT FOR WHAT?" Hanna yelled. "I'm tired of this. I'm right here—tell me now!"

"It's been so long," he whispered.

"What's been so long?"

"I wanted to wait until you'd met the court wizard, as I know you'd have questions only he could answer!"

"I thought *you* knew the truth?"

"I do! But this isn't only about the truth…the devil is in the details…" The professor wrung his hands avoiding her gaze.

"What details? What are you talking about?"

"The magical details…I told you I'm a warlock, not a full wizard, yes? So who better to teach you what you really need to know than the best wizard of them all?"

Hanna swallowed her anger like a bitter, chalky pill. She pointed down to the rune on the ground. "Fine. But when we get to the court wizard, and not a moment after, you and he will tell me e-v-e-r-y-t-h-i-n-g." She hissed her words slowly annunciating each letter.

Patrick placed his hand on her shoulder. "Hanna, relax. He'll fill us in when we get there, I'm sure. Just wait. You'll see."

"I…I know. I'm just stressed about Lexi." Hanna rubbed her face in her hands.

Michael pointed to the rune etched into the stone at their feet. "Is this another portal?"

"Yes. An old and broken one. It connects to the other realms, but as I said before, these rifts stopped working a long time ago —no one knows why. The only portals that continue to work are the ones that connect across Smaradine."

"How many of them are there?" asked Hanna.

"If you're speaking of the local ones, there are countless dozens around Smaradine." The professor gestured back to the rune beneath them. "But these…these portals that connect the realms, they are much rarer. Only one per major city."

Hanna stared at the large design carved into the stone. "My sisters and I," she began, "have the same rune on our hands. How's that possible?" Alexander opened his mouth, but a tremor shook the ground. Hanna shot a glance to the professor, then to her sister, whose eyes were the size of teacups. "Did you feel that?"

Ashley nodded, panic washing across her whitened face. A low, slow baritone *thud, thud, thud* echoed off the buildings nearby. It seemed to rumble through the earth as much as it did the air.

Patrick's eyes darted around the square. "Is that a quake?"

Ashley pointed over the rooftops.

"Bloody hell! What in the—" Michael's mouth fell open.

Rising fifty feet above the tallest buildings lumbered a creature draped in massive chains. Although several blocks away, Hanna could make out the gnarled and dirty, gray-green skin of something being pulled forward by shackles around its neck.

"What is that thing?" asked Patrick as he backed away a few steps.

Without needing to turn and look, the professor replied, "That's a Hoarfrost Giant."

Michael gripped his forehead with both hands. "You've got to be winding me up."

"W-why is it in the middle of the city?" Ashley asked, her arm still outstretched and pointing to the creature.

Hanna couldn't take her eyes off the creature. The matte of greasy hair on top of its head hung as limply as its long, lanky arms. A mess of tattered, blackened hide was draped over its body like a tunic, and a bundled, dirty loin cloth covered its waist. Ringlets of massive chains looped from its wrists to the shackled collar around the giant's neck. Huge reptilian birds, like real life pterodactyls, flew in swooping dives around its boulder-sized head.

"Shut-the-front-door!" shouted Michael, now pointing to the half-a-dozen flying lizards in the air. "Are those people? That can't be—it really looks like people are riding those things!"

Alexander jerked his chin toward the giant. "Security is escorting it to the arena."

"What arena?" cried Ashley. "What are they doing with it?"

"They're taking it to the Curmudgeon Games."

The booming *thud* of footsteps continued to shake the ground even as the Hoarfrost Giant became lost among the buildings on the other side of town. For what seemed like forever, Hanna was sure she could still feel the tremors through her shoes.

"We'd better get to Hemlock Castle," said the professor, turning away.

"That's it?" barked Michael. "We see *that thing*—a bloody giant—and that's all you're gonna say about it?"

"Yes. What more do you want?"

Michael mimicked his head exploding. "Mate, you act like this is an everyday thing."

"You don't seem to understand the magnitude of the situation." Alexander glanced back at them and frowned. "I don't have time to fill you in on all the little differences between Havendale and Smaradine. And Lexi doesn't have the luxury of time for me to hold your hand whenever you find something out of the ordinary. I'll tell you *what* I can *when* I can. The rest will have to wait."

"That's bonkers, mate. You're a piece of work," quipped Michael before he shook his head. "Come on, mates. Let's go."

The day had grown late since leaving the roar of the stadium behind. Soon the landscape opened before them as the sky on the horizon began to grow dark. The narrow roads and cramped buildings gave way to spacious meadows filled with flowering trees and the luxurious homes of the wealthy and influential.

The buildings finally withdrew, revealing a wide-open prairie lined by row after row of pink and white cherry blossom trees in full bloom. The air was alive with the aroma of their sweet nectar, and soon, a castle climbed into view. The group made their way toward a great gate nearly reaching the safety of the castle's outer walls.

20

MORGANA

Tall, white castle walls shot high into the early evening sky. On top of steepled ramparts, green and white checkered flags flapped in the wind. Cylindrical towers stretched like fingers to touch the clouds. Overhanging canopies with blue-peaked roofs poked their necks above the sun-bleached facade. Hemlock Castle glittered green in what light remained from the sun as if dusted with a fine coat of emerald sugar. High over the ramparts, circling above the tallest towers, flew a flock of large, black birds.

Michael squeezed next to the professor. "What's the plan?"

"Simple," said the professor. "I'll ask the princess for asylum."

Patrick clasped his fingers around Hanna's hand. "How are you feeling?"

She blinked and tried to steady her voice as a lump knotted in her throat. "It's rough. Truth be told, I'm terrified. I just don't know how we're going to find her."

"I can't imagine what you must be feeling. I'm worried, too, but you must be out of your gourd. Nightfall is coming soon and we're no closer to finding her now than when we started. She has to be safe though…she just has to."

Hanna attempted to raise her cheeks to a smile. "Thanks for being such a good friend."

Patrick released her hand. "I, uh. Yeah. Of course. Anytime. I'd do anything for you." He mumbled his words and dropped his eyes avoiding her gaze. "Lexi means the world to me, too. Together forever—isn't that what you say with them?"

Hanna nodded. "Yeah. We kind of got into the habit from my dad." She rubbed her pendant as a pang of guilt knotted below her navel. "He's drilled it in us since we were little."

"I can see that." Patrick nodded along.

"He always said that no matter what we did in life, we'd always have each other. That family is family," she finally grinned. "I got the itch. Been looking out for my sisters ever since."

"Does anyone else have asylum?" Ashley asked from the rear of the group.

"Some," replied Alexander.

Hanna perked her ears at Ashley's question. "What?"

"Obviously everyone doesn't get asylum. It's royal protection, you see. Golinveaux sits on the king's council. Helps him with advice."

"Golinveaux," Michael repeated, a brow raised. "The guy from the shop?"

Alexander shook his head. "No, a different Golinveaux, but they're related. As you could see for yourself, the man from the shop was part feline. His grandfather, the court wizard, however, as you'll soon see, is quite human like yourselves. It doesn't happen often, but some humans are blessed with the gift of magic. Golinveaux certainly was." He pointed to the left-most tower which was covered in a thick blanket of green ivy. "Do you see there? That's where the court wizard lives. He's the greatest wizard of our age."

"Is that the wizard you wanted me to see?" asked Hanna.

"The very one."

They reached a wide moat around the castle and walked

through a high, gabled archway into a busy courtyard. Several ravens took flight from the ground to the high ramparts as they passed. The courtyard was crammed with colored tents and wooden shacks of all shapes and sizes, the place a flurry of activity. Tradesmen buzzed like bees while laborers carted goods in and out of the castle. Hanna's mouth watered at the scent of sweet breads, braised meats, and roasted chicken.

"O.M.G.," moaned Ashley. "It's as if I can taste the air." As they continued, the delicious aromas mixed with the sour stench of tanning leather and bitter wood lacquer. Ashley scrunched her nose as they neared the blacksmith. "What is this place?"

"These shops belong to the Guild de Triumph—an elite worker's union specializing in food, furniture, and weapons unlike any other. They fetch a high coin for their work."

The group followed the professor through the bustle of the stadium-sized courtyard until finally stopping at a guard post. Three dozen polished, granite steps rose from the courtyard floor to stop before a set of tall, arched, teakwood doors.

A guard stepped through a recessed doorway concealed by an overhang of green ivy. "State your business."

"I'm here to bring important guests before the royal family," said Alexander.

The guard's eyes fell across the faces of each of Hanna's friends. "Who are they?" he asked after a moment's pause. His hand waited to jot down the information in a journal between his fingers.

"I've brought Hanna Steele and her sisters."

The guard perked an eyebrow. "And how does that warrant an audience with—"

"Hold on," barked a booming voice.

Hanna's eyes widened as the largest man she'd ever seen squeezed through the shadowed six-foot wide, ivy-encrusted doorway. She wasn't sure if he was really a man at all. His height was too big. His shoulders were too wide. The hunched figure was so large that he had to inch himself sideways through the recessed door.

He stood at least eight feet tall and had hands the size of Christmas hams. Blond hair was tossed about his head like a nest. From the sides of his skull above his ears, thick, boney horns jut outward and bent upward before abruptly stopping. The horns didn't end in deadly points, but were sheared off. The tips ended in gilded, flat caps. A closely shaven beard covered his cheeks in twin lamb chops. His bare, bald chin and upper lip remained exposed. A pair of thick lips revealed a wide mouth of teeth under his bulbous, doorknob-sized nose.

"I'll see to them," said the gargantuan figure, who looked to be some mixture of man and oxen.

"Yes, Captain." The guard saluted before retreating back through the doorway.

Alexander leaned in to whisper in Hanna's ear. "You'll find the royal guard more familiar, except for the captain. The royal family employs only human—or in his case, half-human—guards to protect the castle."

Hanna frowned in mild frustration. "Isn't that discrimination or something?"

"That's the way it's been since the Slavenguard Uprising eighty years—"

"What's your business?" barked the captain, scratching his chest. The silver weave of his body armor glinted in the remaining sun.

Hanna did a double-take as she stared at the captain's form-fitted protective suit. She was sure an iridescent shimmer in the fabric rippled over his tight abs. Although he was as thick as a tree, his armor reminded her of a swimmer's neoprene uniform. It stretched from the top of his body to cover everything including his arms and legs. The long handle of some powerful-looking weapon stuck out over his shoulder.

Alexander cleared his throat. "I've brought these children to seek asylum with—"

"Asylum from what?" he thundered, crossing his arms over a crimson emblem on his chest plate.

"Barlow," Hanna spat before she could think better of it.

"The King of Thieves?" The captain scratched his thick sideburns and swung one of his massive arms toward the great doors of the castle. "Why didn't you say so?"

As they climbed the steps, the half-human took them four at a time. He passed everyone up as they climbed. An exquisite silver war hammer strapped across his back came into full view.

"Crowthorn," he suddenly said.

"Excuse me?" replied Hanna, a bit startled.

"Wallace Crowthorn's my name." He paused at the top of the steps for them to catch up.

Hanna couldn't help but examine the walls. The castle looked like it was built from blocks of solid marble, each encrusted with flakes of emerald crystals. "What are those green chips in the rock?"

Crowthorn reached for the door. "Hemlock emeralds—the second rarest of all magical crystals."

He peeled open the towering double doors surprised to have a young woman step out. "Princess Morgana."

She was no more than two or three years older than Hanna and just as tall. Her black dress clung to her slender sides. The woman's straight, ebony hair was parted so it divided her head in equal parts, falling to either side of her face. Hanna couldn't help but notice that the woman was beautiful.

"On the eve of my big day, you bring strangers to my inauguration?" She rolled her eyes over Hanna until reaching Hanna's arm. Did she spot the brand? Maybe not. So, Hanna folded her arms tightly over her chest concealing the raven scar from view.

"Who's this?" the woman demanded. "More Crimson Brotherhood from my filthy brother?" Hanna's heart plummeted through the floor in her stomach. The princess had seen… The captain opened his mouth, but before he could utter a reply, the woman turned to Alexander. "I never liked you, professor—you always favored my father's rule over mine. By the start of the Summer Solstice celebration in a few days' time, when I finally take the crown, you'll learn what kind of ruler I'll really be."

Hanna stepped forward and opened her mouth, but Crowthorn held her back with an outstretched arm.

The professor's jaw fell slack. "You're assuming the throne in your father's absence? B-but he'll return eventually—I'm sure of it!"

"They've been gone for too long, and Manna needs a strong ruler now more than ever."

"Yes, Princess Morgana, but if you'd reconsider and give your father more time—"

"Who are you to advise me? They've had fourteen years to return! I'm done waiting. I should've taken the throne when they left." Morgana sneered before whirling around and striding back inside, the great door slamming closed behind her.

Hanna's face scrunched. She leaned around Crowthorn's barreled chest to Michael and Patrick, then turned back to the professor. "What was that about?"

"Yeah, who does she think she is?" snapped Michael.

"Bite your tongue," snapped Crowthorn, casting sharp eyes at him. "That's Morgana, the king's daughter, and the next heir to the throne!"

Crowthorn's over-sized head pressed so near Michael's face that Michael stepped back a step or two. "S-sorry, mate. Didn't really mean nothin' by it."

The captain mumbled something under his breath before opening the great doors again. Hanna followed him through the entrance trailed by everyone else, Alexander at the rear.

A reptilian man dressed in a shabby brown tunic and ragged pants caught Hanna's eye as he sprinted through the busy court- yard. He stopped and panted at the guard post. "Professor! Professor, please! I have a courier message for you. It's urgent— it's from Hugo!"

All eyes turned back to the professor as bright torches lit

aflame across the ramparts. Shadows scurried from the grounds as the castle yard was bathed in an unnatural white light.

"Excuse me. I'll meet you inside." He stepped back through the massive entrance doors and down the great steps toward the courier.

Hanna glanced back over her shoulder. What was more important than finding Lexi? Something tugged her fingers. It was Ashley pulling her by the hand into the castle.

She followed her sister behind Crowthorn until the great doors shut behind them and a new unease unsettled her stomach. Hanna was bathed by ribbons of colored light which danced through stained-glass windows. Higher windows were cut farther up into the arched, marble ceiling presumably for ambient daylight to stream through. Streaks of colored light streamed like candied rays into the long hallway. Tiny dust motes caught in eddies of air floated in the glow. And the corridor was covered with floor-to-ceiling murals down the entire length of the hallway. Who was missing was the princess. There was no sign of Morgana.

So, they left Alexander behind. Although they followed Crowthorn, Hanna eventually became lost in the series of twists and turns. Every hallway looked the same as they blindly followed the captain down one hallway and up another.

This is all so much to take in. Who do I trust? Who to believe? The corners of her mouth drooped. *And will I find Lexi out there in a world I know nothing about? Finding her before dark was certainly out of the question. Would Lexi remain safe before they found her? That was the nagging question.*

"Hold up," said Ashley, peering down a deserted side-hall-way. "Is that—it couldn't be, but—"

Hanna double-backed to where her sister stood transfixed. "What are you talking about?"

The two stared at the tail end of an overweight, orange cat strutting away in the opposite direction. They shared a glance and whispered in unison, "Maxwell?"

Crowthorn peered down the hallway. "Humph, I'll have the guards kill the flea bag and—"

"No!" Ashley half-shouted. The captain's eyebrows rose toward the ceiling. "I-I mean, please don't. We know him. Don't hurt him. It's nice to have a friend here. Even if it is just a cat."

With his hands on his hips, Patrick snorted, "What, are we chopped liver?"

"Maxwell! Maxwell!" called Ashley, ignoring the boys and stooping over, half-crawling toward the sauntering feline. "Come here, Max…come back and—"

"C'mon now. Not much farther," Crowthorn snapped, continuing to lead them away from the cat. "Your fightin' an uphill battle already."

"How so?" asked Hanna, trailing behind him, taking several steps for each one of his.

"Having Morgana see you with the professor put you at odds with her. Gotta convince her you mean no harm—I'm sure you can do that, though. You seem harmless enough."

"Bye, Max," called Ashley and raced after her friends down the corridor.

A few minutes later, Crowthorn came to a stop at a set of ornate, wooden doors that towered high above his head. A set of four guards, two on each side, stood sentry protecting them. Each guard was dressed in a thin coat of green whose golden sleeves slid down to their wrists. Emerald pants covered their legs, ending in a pair of black, shiny boots. A golden sash fastened at the shoulders and hip draped across their stiff chests like a thin ribbon of honor. As if carved from stone, each stood immobile with twin silver swords held at angles over their chests.

Fastened to the wall, just beyond the furthest guard, was a bronze placard. Hanna examined the three-foot tall crest. The tarnished placard, now more dirty brown than a shiny finish, formed the shape of a long shield divided into four, equal segments. The top-left quadrant showed an emblem of a rearing unicorn; the top-right held the bonze relief of a dire wolf; the bottom-left and bottom-right showed the images of a raven and a mermaid, respectively.

Hanna flicked her eyes from the crest on the wall to Crowthorn's chest. He, too, wore a matching crimson raven. "What's this?" she asked, pointing to the design on the wall.

Crowthorn strode to Hanna's side and placed a weighted hand on her shoulder. It was so heavy that it buckled her knees. "That's the royal sigils of the four kingdoms of Smaradine— drawn up hundreds of years ago. That treaty's 'bout worthless now as we're on the brink of war."

"War?" Hanna said wincing under the pressure of his heavy hand.

He scratched his burly sideburn. "Yup. Makes us all a bit jumpy." As Crowthorn stepped toward the closed doors, excited shouts echoed through the gilded wood.

"You're back!" said a familiar female voice. "H-how's that possible? Where'd you come from? W-where'd you go all these years?"

The Captain of the Guard tapped his bald chin with the tip of his finger. "That's Morgana I hear. But who's she talkin' to?"

"Aren't you glad to see us?" said a deep voice. "Come here, give me a hug. You've grown up tall and beautiful."

"Well, yes, of course—I mean—but I was to have my coronation at the Summer Solstice… Wait. Who was that? Who were you talking to?"

"No one. Doesn't matter. Let him leave," replied the stranger's voice.

"What in blazes would stop Morgana from becoming queen?" Crowthorn asked more to himself than anyone else. "Hm, don't know that we should intrude on whatever's goin' on in there."

Hanna's breath caught in her throat as a swift breeze whooshed by brushing her hair to one side. She looked around but saw nothing. "D-did you guys feel that?"

"Feel what?" The captain stepped forward and reached out a ham-sized hand toward the door handle. "Didn't feel a—" The massive doors suddenly burst open. Crowthorn recoiled with a snap and stumbled back. "What in Kambo's name?"

A slender man with pointed ears and skin the color of wilted kale barged through the gap. Without a word, the stranger gripped the captain's bare forearm and charged through the group with surprising strength. His force sent Hanna tumbling into the nearest guard. Ashley was knocked to the ground. In the next moment, a shriek of agony cut through the hallway.

"Guards!" Crowthorn yelled to the soldiers flanking the doors, "Throw him from the castle."

"Take your hands off me! Do you know who I am?" the man shouted as he was swarmed and dragged roughly down the hall.

Ashley groaned from the floor—she lay flat on her back. "Ashley!" Hanna screamed. She fell to her knees by her sister's side. "Not you, too. No, no, no...not you..." Ashley's arm was stained scarlet and a silver sword lay on the floor next to her, the blade tainted in her blood.

"W-what happened?!" cried Hanna.

From the corner of her eye, Michael glared after the stranger being dragged away. "That bloke did it. H-he bloody hell just plowed into that soldier, and...and his weapon just fell."

"Put pressure on the wound," boomed the captain. "Stop the bleeding. Apply pressure, I say!"

Ashley's face was as white as cottage cheese. Her voice quivered as she stared slack-jawed at her arm. "Hanna?" she whispered. The gash was a bloody line stretching from her elbow to her wrist.

Crowthorn bent and scooped Ashley off the floor and pinched the gaping wound closed. "We've got to get her to the hospital wing. Ms. Beauparlant will know what to do."

Hanna racked her brain trying to remember why that name seemed familiar. But in the thralls of panic, she couldn't think. "Who?"

"Ms. Beauparlant—the head nurse." The captain wasted no time and strode briskly down the corridor.

Then it dawned on Hanna who Ms. Beauparlant was. "No," she screamed, stopping Crowthorn halfway down the hall. "We can't take her to the hospital wing. Ms. Beauparlant isn't there!" She raced after him with Michael and Patrick at her heels. "We saw her in town earlier this afternoon. She was on her way to buy supplies."

Crowthorn crumpled his face in thought as a long groan escaped Ashley's parted lips. "By Kambo's will—Hagadorn! We can take her to Hagadorn. He'll know what to do."

21

HAGADORN

The door to Hagadorn's dungeon office flew open with a loud crack and the splintering of wood. Crowthorn pulled his bucket-sized boot from the door and crossed into the lab with Ashley in his arms. His hands, arms, and vest were smeared scarlet. Hanna, Michael, and Patrick trailed into the room at his heels.

"Alchemist. Where are 'ye? Alchemist," the captain's deep voice boomed.

A man whose face was draped in curtains of long, black hair peeled back a cloth screen hanging from the ceiling at the far end of the room. "What in the six realms is all the—"

"Come 'ere, Hagadorn. Quickly. She's been hurt." Crowthorn laid Ashley down on one of many long, granite tables that patterned the dungeon in rows.

"Oww! Stop—STOP!" Ashley cried as tears streamed down her cheeks.

"What's happened? Who is this? Who are these people?" Hagadorn demanded while pulling scrolls of parchment and spell books from beneath Ashley's back. "My work—you're ruining my work!" His eyes darted around before resting on the blood coating Crowthorn's chest. "What's going on?"

"My sister—she's been hurt," Hanna blurted as Ashley's sobbing cries filled the lab.

Hagadorn flicked his beady, black eyes at Hanna, then back to the wound stretching up Ashley's forearm. "Obviously, I can see that for myself," he snarled. "Step back—STEP BACK," he snapped, still yanking papers out from under Ashley. "Do you have any idea of the kind of work you're ruining?" He huffed again and pushed all the remaining scrolls to the side before shoving his way between Hanna and the captain.

"Let me get a closer look…Why not take her to the hospital wing? Why bring her here?" He slipped his hand into the crease of his dark cloak and drew out what looked like a straight, white, slender animal horn from his pocket.

Hanna opened her mouth but struggled to get the words out. "Ms. Beauparlant isn't there. She's—she's out in town. We—"

"I thought that you'd be the best person to help," Crowthorn cut across her.

"You're right." Hagadorn huffed and tossed a glance across his table of stained and ruined work. "No matter, she's here now." Hanna's eyes widened as he waved the long, ivory object like a wand just above Ashley's arm. With a quick twitch of his wrist and a muttering of words Hanna didn't catch, the blood spilling from her sister's arm slowed to a trickle, then stopped altogether. Hagadorn stroked the tip of his wand lightly against the length of the wound and it sealed together as if stitched or glued. As Ashley's cries quieted, Hanna breathed a sigh of relief. It was as if Hanna's panic became as weightless as a feather. It lifted off her shoulders and blew away.

"T-that was amazing," stuttered Patrick from the far side of the table.

"This isn't show-and-tell, boy," sneered the alchemist.

"Come on over 'ere and give 'em some space to work," said Crowthorn.

Hanna backed away near a long bank of shelves and cast a nervous glance at her sister's arm. A fresh, angry line bubbled and puckered Ashley's flesh. Hanna wiped her blood-stained hands on the front of her jean shorts, streaking them with stripes of scarlet. With the danger averted, Hanna relaxed and examined the wall behind her.

The room was unlike anything she'd ever seen. Two of the walls were lined from floor to ceiling with shelves of clear jars in every size and shape. Some contained weird, fleshy objects floating in colored liquid. Others held only dried leaves or sticks. Hanna paced the length of the wall whispering the names of each container as she passed: Wolfsbane, milkweed root, Curdling Dust, frosted blood berries, boomslang venom, dried cockroaches, spider eggs.

A noise brought her attention back to the others. Looking over her shoulder, Hanna caught the captain corralling her friends into the hallway. "We're not leaving, are we?" she asked, frowning. "I can't leave her like this."

"Leave 'em to his work. There ain't no better alchemist in Manna," said Crowthorn.

"What? No! I'm not going anywhere without my sister. I've lost one already today. I'm not gonna let *her* out of my sight, too!"

"Get out of my lab," barked Hagadorn. "Do you want her arm to scar?"

Hanna flinched and reflexively rubbed the raven brand burned into her own arm. "No, of course not."

The alchemist's voice turned angry. "Then listen to Crowthorn. Let me to my task. Take everyone with you."

"Come on. I'll take 'ye back to the Royal Hall," said Crowthorn ushering the group into the hallway. Once they were all outside the lab, he closed the now broken door behind them.

"You guys go on up," Michael said, jerking his head toward the stairwell. "I'm gonna stay put right here. Gotta make sure she's safe."

Hanna paused, but the captain tugged her arm. "Morgana's gotta see you."

Hanna's lips twisted into a frown. "Morgana? Do we *have* to see her again?"

Crowthorn nodded. "It's the only way. She's the only royal blood left in the castle."

She sighed and looked back to Michael for a moment. "Thank you," she mouthed silently.

"Nothing needed," he replied, waving her off. "Ashley's family."

Hanna gave a look back to Michael wanting more than anything to get a look at her sister one last time. But she did as she was told and walked behind Crowthorn, her head slung toward the ground. Hanna didn't want to look at Patrick. She didn't want to do anything. She failed her sisters, both of them. Lexi was lost. Ashley was wounded. *What would dad say if he saw me now? "You're supposed to protect your sisters, keep 'em safe not let 'em get lost and hurt under your watch." That's what he'd say.*

She sighed. Thinking of her father sparked the last memory she had of him when Hanna sped from the driveway with him chasing after. That was the last time she'd seen him. *What a fool I am. I should've stopped—got a detention slip regardless. He was calling something after me...what could it have been about? I may never know.*

She wasn't living up to the kind of person he taught her to be and she knew it. 'Sisters forever' is what he taught her—taught them. Wouldn't that same bond go for mom and dad, too? Sure, it would. Her heart hung heavily in her chest. She couldn't have messed up more if she tried. Hanna wanted to talk—needed to talk with her dad. To find out what to do. To just...to just have him wrap his arms around her and give her a hug. To tell her that everything would be alright. To let her know that things would be okay. But that was just it...things weren't okay. They were far from okay. Things had gone terribly sideways and she didn't know how to get them back on track.

One thing Hanna wished she could've done differently is brought her mother and father with her to Smaradine. Dad would know what to do. He always knew the right thing. But he wasn't there to protect them, to guide them, to steer her in the right direction. Hanna was alone. She felt more lost than she ever had in her life. She'd have to find out by herself how to navigate this new world alone. In a whisper, just soft enough for her to hear it herself, she said, "I love you, dad."

Michael's friends disappeared down the hall and up the stairs. He scooted toward the wall so his back was at the edge of the door jamb. He pressed his ear to the gaping hole made by Crowthorn's massive foot and listened to the conversation in the room.

Something in his pocket pressed against his thigh. He reached into his shorts and pulled out a golden medallion no larger than a silver dollar. "Where'd this come from?" he asked the empty hallway. At the coin's center rested a thin, red ruby no larger than a penny. Michael flipped the medallion between his fingers, inspecting both sides. It seemed identical except for a thin strip of writing etched into the surface of either side.

Something furry brushed against his arm. Michael glanced down. "Maxwell, ye' dodgy cat! What are you doing here?" He bent and stroked the length of the cat, curling his fingertips along the large rolls of fat and fluff. "How'd you get here? You must be daft to follow us. Did you miss us that much?" Maxwell purred, arched his back, and rubbed his whiskers against Michael's side.

"Ow, Max," Michael winced, pushing the affectionate cat away. "Bollocks! Don't push so hard on my side. It hurts." Maxwell turned in a circle and continued purring. "Something ain't right with me," Michael mumbled. He pulled up his shirt and tried to examine himself.

Angry red lines spilled around his side, staining his already dark skin. His ribs were tender under his fingers as he prodded them. Maxwell came close again and sniffed, only to turn his nose away with a quick jerk. Michael tried to pet him again, but the feline sauntered away and sat just out of reach. The sound of Hagadorn's voice through the broken door pulled Michael's attention from Max and back to his friend.

Michael turned from the cat and quietly pushed open the crushed door, scooting into the room unnoticed. He positioned himself so he could easily peer around the nearest table from his angle on the floor. The alchemist picked up a pestle and mortar from a nearby stand and placed it with a heavy *clunk* near Ashley's arm.

"Don't move," Hagadorn said gruffly before stepping away from Ashley to rummage through some shelves. He returned moments later. Michael caught a glimpse of a green leaf and what seemed like several tadpole-shaped objects. They dropped from Hagadorn's outstretched hand into the stone bowl.

"This is how alchemy *should* be practiced. Even with the royal laws and the regulation of magic—the kingdom's run amuck with untrained wizards. It's a travesty." Hagadorn ground the ingredients harder and harder. "A complete misuse of magic. There are laws for a reason. It just makes me sick." he seemed to mutter to himself rather than to Ashley.

With a shaky voice, she replied, "I thought alchemists worked with metals and stuff."

"I do." He jabbed a finger toward a row of shelves behind him. "See those wooden bins along the wall? They're filled with minerals and ores."

"So, you do magic and alchemy?"

Hagadorn pointed to her arm. "Obviously, yes." His voice dripped with contempt. "I am a wizard, but I'm also trained to transmute one metal into another." He looked directly into Ashley's eyes for the first time and lifted her outstretched arm into the air a foot or two above the table. Hagadorn held up his other hand, showing that his fingers were covered in a greenish paste. "I'm going to apply this salve to your wound. You'll feel a faint burn. That's the medicine healing your arm. Should only take a moment."

The alchemist pulled her arm closer and began to apply the paste near her wrist. A hint of a smile parted Ashley's lips as the scent of mint wafted through the air. Then a grimace contorted her face. "Oh—that—that does burn." Michael could see the obvious discomfort on her face. As he watched, the raised scar turned from an angry crimson to a soft, fleshy pink.

Hagadorn worked more of the paste around her wound. As Ashley's hand opened and closed and then opened again, the alchemist froze. His eyes were pinned to her bare palm. "Who— are—you?" he asked slowly. "What is this mark on your hand?"

Ashley cocked her head, visibly confused. "What do you mean?"

"It's simple English, girl. Who—are—you?" he repeated, gripping her wrist.

"My name's Ashley—Ashley Steele."

"Where are you from," he demanded, a hint of malice threading his voice.

"You're—you're hurting me." Hagadorn dropped her hand. "I'm from Midtown Valley."

"That's no place from around here."

"I'm from Earth," Ashley added, staring at her arm for a moment. "Havendale, I mean."

"Are you sure?"

"Yes, why? What kind of question is that?"

Hagadorn turned to a cupboard and grabbed a glass beaker and some kind of liquid which was the bright shade of alabaster. "Extend your arm."

"W-what are you going to do?"

Michael slowly and silently got to his feet, though he remained at the end of the table for now, his gaze was locked onto Ashley and the alchemist. The strange medallion remained forgotten in his palm. He stroked it absently with the side of his thumb.

Hagadorn seized Ashley's arm in a fluid motion with one hand and pulled out his wand with the other. He mumbled something under his breath that sounded something like 'Levitatum' while waving his wand over her newly healed arm. Droplets of blood seeped from the tips of Ashley's fingers. "Departe Locomotis," Hagadorn said curtly, and in a twirl and flick of his wrist, the crimson beads rushed through the air and into the beaker of fluid.

Before Michael could think to cover his eyes, the beaker erupted in a blaze of white, hot light. The silhouette of Hagadorn and Ashley's bodies were outlined in the flash. The glow disappeared and as the spots of light faded from Michael's vision, Hagadorn's face contorted into a sneer.

"You shouldn't be here. Get out of my lab!"

Ashley recoiled, and Michael sprinted out from his hiding spot. "What's your problem?"

"Get this girl out of my lab immediately." The alchemist didn't even seem upset at Michael's presence, too caught in whatever angered him about Ashley instead. "Go to Ba'Noor—go north and see the Ice Queen. Leave this kingdom!"

With the mysterious coin still clutched between his fingers, Michael looked down at the angry skin under the salve on Ashley's arm and back to Hagadorn. "What about her injury? Ain't you gonna finish fixing it?"

"I care for nothing more but to get this liar out of my lab!"

Michael creased his eyebrows and stepped toward the alchemist, hissing through gritted teeth, "You're gonna fix her arm and you're gonna do it right now."

A white, foggy film coated Hagadorn's eyes, as if he'd lost focus—and the alchemist parroted Michael's words. "I'm gonna fix her arm and I'm gonna do it right now."

Before Michael could react, Hagadorn pushed his way past him to Ashley and finished applying the salve to her arm. With a flurry of his ivory wand and another muttering of words, the pinkness faded completely from her skin. The once angry, raised tissue receded back into smooth, unblemished flesh.

Michael flicked his eyes back to Hagadorn's. The white cobwebs faded from the alchemist's eyes and a sneer replaced the placid expression across his face.

"Didn't you hear what I said? I said leave," he snapped, as if the previous sixty seconds hadn't occurred.

Michael grabbed Ashley and swept her from the room for the safety of the hallway.

22

PIRATES

Lexi shuffled past the old woman baring a toothless smile and stepped inside her home. The floorboard under the entrance mat groaned in protest to her weight. She squinted into the foyer, her eyes adjusting to the dim lighting. Tall shelving stacked with dusty books lined the walls. A ship's broken steering wheel sat canted to one side like an oversized bookend. Shadows danced between cobwebs wrapped around pegs in the wheel.

"Kambo's mercy," said Paula. "Let's get you into da kitchen. First, we get you all clean. Den, I make you a pot of da best spiced tea in da six realms, kay?"

Lexi sucked in a slow breath as she followed the woman. She didn't think about her safety…her feet just moved on their own. "Yeah, sure. Sounds good. These needles sting a lot."

She slowly hobbled down a murky corridor, eyes as wide as hubcaps. The walls were coated with dangling strips of peeling wallpaper. Where the ceiling met the wall, several ribbons of crimson paper hung in tattered fingers. Near her feet was a small, shadowed hole gnawed into the chestnut running board, and piles of wood shavings and mouse droppings speckled the floor. As Lexi let the strange woman slip slowly ahead, a single thought slammed into her brain. *Is that a tail poking out from behind her dress?!*

The short corridor came to a sudden end, splitting off to the left and right. Hung directly in front of her on the chipped plaster wall was a black and white photograph framed in tarnished brass. The bottom corner of the photo curled in the humid, sea air. It was a bust shot of a lizard in a captain's hat standing on what looked like the bow of a big wooden ship. *I wonder if that's the same ship docked outside?*

Soft music on the radio was almost drowned out by the rising storm. Howls of wind rattled a nearby window as thunder ka-boomed overhead. Lexi peeked to her right and found a large family room filled with bandaged furniture. Behind her came the high-pitched squeal of chair legs. She turned—Paula was pulling a seat out from the kitchen table.

"Come, dearie. Sit while da squall finishes outside. Da rain will be done soon, and I got me some shopping ta do at da market. Let me boil some water for da tea."

"The market? What about the sandstorm?"

"Oh, don't you worry 'bout dat. It'll be gone soon 'nuff. It won't reach da market. Never does." Paula stood and moved to the stove throwing some tea leaves into a pot. She added water, a pinch of spice, a cinnamon stick, and an entire orange, and turned on the flame. "Now let's get ta dem needles." She joined Lexi at the table, the woman's old knees cracked like broken celery as she sat.

Lexi couldn't help but goggle at Paula. She pulled her cell phone from her back pocket with two fingers and placed it on the table.

"My mama taught me twasn't nice ta stare," mumbled Paula. Her voice was soft but firm as she grabbed another empty saucepan and hauled it close.

"Sorry."

"Don't worry none." She smiled and picked up a pair of

tweezers from the middle of the table. "I do dis for me boys all da time—don't you worry."

"You do?" Lexi scrunched up her nose and Paula plucked the first sliver of glass from her arm. She tried to ignore the tugging and sting as each needle was pulled from her skin. The small slivers clinked like pennies as they were dropped into the metal skillet.

Trying not to squirm, Lexi looked absently about the room. There was a fridge nearby. A collage of art and pictures were taped to the door. The ocean storm beat against the kitchen sill and Lexi cast nervous glances at the rattling window frame. Lexi felt as jittery as a long-tailed cat in a room full of rocking chairs. She brooded about where she was. She wondered how she got here and where her sisters were. More than that, she worried how to find them. The storm kept her frantic thoughts company. The booming thunder did little to keep her calm.

"Dearie, yous got ta settle down," Paula said patting her now clean arm.

Lexi tried to soak in Paula's words. How could she be calm? At the same time, how could she push away the worry of the raging storm twisting inside her? She picked up her phone and stared at the display. *Three bars.* She silently mouthed, "Where are you, Hanna?"

Lexi dialed her sister.

Nothing.

She tried again and again and again. Each time there was no answer. Frustrated and exhausted, she finally left a lengthy story on Hanna's voicemail. Giving up for the moment, Lexi pointed to a few life-like colored pencil sketches on the refrigerator. "Are those your kids?"

"Yup—I got two boys—day're a spat older dan you. Wonderful boys dae is." The drawings were of two green, scaly men wearing ragged T-shirts and cut-off shorts with black boots. One man was short and fat—the other tall and lanky.

Lexi held her breath, then released it in a whir of words. "Are you an iguana? Cause I've never seen a talking iguana before."

"You're as inside-out as a dirty pair of skivvies. Where did yous say you was from again'?"

"I'm from Midtown Valley, Illinois."

"Nope, never did hear of no place like dat in Smaradine—lived here all my life."

"Smaradine—where's Smaradine?" Lexi asked, scrunching up her forehead in confusion.

She turned from the woman to stare out the clouded window. *I've lost my home. I've lost my family. I'm lost in some strange place—I've lost the chance to go to the big dance with Patrick.* As hope drained out of her, the pressure inside Lexi's head mounted. She wanted to forget about the desert. She wanted to forget about the rain. She wanted to forget about the pain. She wanted her sisters. She wanted Patrick. She wanted her life back.

When Lexi looked back at Paula, all the glass needles were plucked clean. She slowly ran her open palm over her now smooth thighs. The prickles were gone. The stabbing pain diminished to phantom aches. Her scarlet-stained skin was washed clean as Paula dabbed her with a damp dish rag. The hint of a smile played around the corners of Lexi's lips as she inhaled a deep breath, only to frown again in a heartbeat.

She'd lost Hanna. Lost Ashley. Lost Patrick. She sat across from a strange, green woman who looked like something out of a movie. Lexi was alone, removed from everything and everyone she knew. Her mind burned as if it were on fire as nagging thoughts replayed in her head.

This has to be a nightmare. Sandstorms of glass, talking lizards, pirate ships, and was that really a dragon I saw in the desert? This can't be happening. It just can't. I want to go home.

The loud claps of thunder and heavy wind finally died away. Paula stood from the table and turned off the stove. She poured a roasted, auburn liquid into two ceramic mugs and placed them on the table. Reaching into the pantry, she handed several dried biscuits to Lexi and grabbed one for herself. Lexi's stomach gurgled and she tore into the biscuits, muttering a muffled "thank you," as an afterthought.

Paula looked up from the steam which swirled above her mug. "Da answer to 'yer question earlier is no. I'm ain't an iguana—I never did hear an iguana talk. I'm a gecko." She pointed across the table to the fridge. "Dem two boys on da fridge are my pride and joy—da chubby one's name is Pete and his brother's name is Pete. I find it easy to remember der names dat way. Some call my tall boy RePete cause of da way he talks. I don't mind dat none."

Lexi's eyes drifted from the refrigerator to the yellowed, torn newspaper clippings at the center of the table. She picked up the top one.

This month's farmer's market features baked good, meats, and fruit and veggies from around Smaradine. Frosted blood berries from Winter's Edge are one tara a carton. Special deliveries from the Crow's Nest brings the best fish in the six plains. Enjoy crates of smoked salmon, jerked trout, pickled herring, and turtle stew. Featured from the far reaches of Thole past the outskirts of Rumjic Peninsula is a limited quantity of six barrels of honeyed mead.

She leafed through a few more and stopped on one with black, charcoal circles.

Marty's General Store at Breakwater's annual Peasant Moon Festival is offering a free bottle of Marty's-Mug-O'-Mojo to the first fifty guests. Music and dancing by the Lazy Lagoon until dawn. Come to the magnificent bonfire where we burn the king & princess in effigy. S'mores and wiener roasts for the kids 'till ten o'clock.

• • •

Lexi looked to Paula with a frown. "Why is Breakwater gonna burn the king and princess?"

Paula tapped the yellowed article with her green knuckle and chuckled. "Don't you worry none 'bout dat. Da Tavern Telegraph is just saying dat Breakwater is havin' sum fun—just burning some stuffed dolls dat looks like da royals. Dats what dat means."

"Tavern Telegraph?" asked Lexi.

Paula tapped the cut-out squares of paper. "Dem articles you reading 'bout. Dere from da regular paper, da Tavern Telegraph."

"Oh, but why would Breakwater want to burn dolls of the king and princess. Are they bad?

Paula shook her head. "Don't matter if dey is or if dey ain't. Perception's is whut matters. Breakwater ain't no friend of da king or da princess. Da king abandoned da kingdom years ago—his daughter, Morgana, ain't much better. Spouts dat she hates Barlow and da Crimson Brotherhood but don't seem ta do nuttin' 'bout it. Breakwater jus caught between da king and da Brotherhood."

"Who's Barlow, and what's the Crimson Brotherhood?"

"Don't you worry none 'bout Barlow," Paula interrupted. "We'll go together—have us a good time at da market together."

How can I have a good time? That's the last thing on my mind. I just want out of this place. Why'd I come here? Why'd I follow Hanna and Ashley? A mounting panic gripped Lexi by the throat. *I don't know this woman. Why is she green? How can geckos talk?*

"Who are you?" Lexi chirped, her voice cracking.

A new, sour gust of wind burst the window open. Salty air flooded the kitchen blowing the newspaper clippings to the floor. The window pane swung wide and cracked with a loud bang against the wall as rain soaked the floor.

Lexi leapt to her feet as if catapulted by a spring and backed away from Paula. She pushed off from the table knocking over everything behind her, her voice rising in panic and volume. "W-what is this place? This—this Smaradine? I want to go home! I want my sisters, and I want to go home!"

"Don't git all worked up. Paula can help," she said almost in a whisper as she stood and stepped toward her.

Lexi pulled at her hair. "You can't talk. Lizards just don't talk! This has to be a nightmare or something." She backed into the stove.

Paula inched closer. "Ain't no nightmare, dearie. Paula can help. Let me help?"

Lexi shuffled away from the stove—cracked her head against the open window. She winced and pressed a palm to her skull. Tears welled up in her eyes and Paula broke into two, then four, and then the room was a kaleidoscope.

Paula closed the gap and grabbed her about the shoulders. "Tis alright, dearie. Paula's here." She wrapped her green arms around Lexi squeezing her tight. "Paula's got you now," she almost hummed and pulled Lexi close to her bosom.

Everything that'd happened built up like a dam of emotion and spilled from her eyes. Her shoulders heaved against Paula's apron. "This just—this just—doesn't—make sense," she choked through broken gulps of air. "I almost d-died. The storm—so huge. Everything—was black. And t-the needles—they stung— so badly. I almost died," she repeated, burying her face against the woman's chest.

She pat Lexi's back. "Let it out, dearie. Gonna be kay now. Paula's here to make it better." Seconds turned into minutes, until finally, Lexi's tears dried up. "You sit tight and let me check on dat rain." Paula helped guide her back to her seat at the table before leaving the kitchen without another word. The front door squeaked open. Then clicked closed. "Tis all done," she shouted from the entryway. "Da sky's a clearin'." In a few breaths, Paula was back in the kitchen. "Tip 'yer cup and finish 'yer tea. Shopping havta wait till morn. Night will be here soon 'en a mess 'o clouds still comin in from da sea."

Lexi stood from the table furrowing her eyebrows. "Stay? Tonight? But what about my sisters? Finding my friends?"

"'Taint going no where t'night. What you think you gonna find in da dark? I ain't going ta Breakwater with da weather upside down." Paula pointed off to the worn-down couch. "Hunker down over 'dere. I get you sum blankets ta keep off da chill."

Lexi opened her mouth to protest once again, that she wanted to—no, *needed* to find her sisters. But Paula already did so much for her. She set her mug on the table with a *clunk.* "Thanks."

"We'll go shoppin in da market at first light. You'll see. "

"Is it far?" asked Lexi.

"Oh, walkin' would take hours for sure. But we'll take da dingy round da backside of da sound—slip into Breakwater's Lazy Lagoon, we will, cause it got an entrance from da ocean. Won't take but two shakes of da oars. Easy work for a pirate's mum."

"Your boys, the ones on the fridge, they're pirates? Real pirates?"

"Born and raised since I and Pappy first hatched 'em"

"Who's Pappy? Is he with the boys?"

"Oh, goodness, no. Pappy's my late husband. He done been dead for some stretch, but dem boys are out fishing in da squall."

"Pappy's dead?"

"Don't you worry 'bout it none, dearie. 'Tis done and gone a long time ago. He went off on one o' dem fool errands—chasin' dem dag gum Totem Stones he so crazy 'bout. He never came home."

"So, he might actually still be alive?"

"If he ain't dead, I'll kill 'em meself fur leavin' us like he done did." Paula nodded curtly and pulled off her apron laying it across the back of one of the chairs.

"What's a Totem Stone?" Lexi asked while swirling the bottom dregs of her tea with her spoon.

"Some crazy relic of 'ole island magic dat I don't none believe in." Paula left the kitchen once again and walked back up the hallway. "Don't matter none now," she called back. "Listen now. First light. Get up 'en let's shoo on out in da morn. Gotta make da tide before it's too late. Never missed da tide yet—don't plan on missing it now."

Paula left and returned a moment later with a lime-green sheet, a heavier blanket, and a pillow. She set them on the couch. Lexi followed her with her eyes and then after a minute followed her into the living room. It looked like a well-loved room. As she took a seat next to the blankets, Paula patted the leather back of the couch with her hand. "Got sum knittin ta do. Leave ya to yurself out here. Find me in da first bedroom up da hall if ya need." When Lexi next turned around, Paula was gone.

Lexi remained on the couch, a piece of old tape holding the leather together stuck to the underside of her thigh. Not knowing what to do with herself, she stood and walked toward the kitchen and examined the photo of Pappy. Lexi wondered if he was safe like she. Where had he gone? Why hadn't he returned? And what exactly were Totem Stones? It was a blessing that she found this place, a godsend that Paula took her in. Would she have made it out in the wild without the woman's help? She thought not.

Something tugged at her mind pulling Lexi into the kitchen. She rinsed and placed her mug in the sink and went to examine the sketch of Paula's two boys on the fridge. The fat one looked rather comical next to his tall lanky brother. Could they really be twins? A sudden yawn overcame her and she turned to look out the kitchen window. Paula was right. It was getting dark and the clouds over the water still looked ugly and brooding. She wanted to put an end to this crazy day. Hopefully she'd wake up in her own bed in Midtown Valley. Maybe this whole horrible experience was an elaborate dream.

Lexi threw herself onto the couch and straightened the sheets, it was too hot for any type of blanket. As she laid on the pillow staring up at the ceiling, the pull of sleep tugged at her consciousness. Before she knew it, the world around her turned black as she drifted off to slumber.

23

HURRY UP AND WAIT

Hanna and Patrick hustled to keep up with Crowthorn as he took the winding staircase from the dungeon four steps at a time. When he reached the top landing, Hanna huffed with exhaustion, still half a flight behind.

"Come on, you two." The captain waited by rubbing something off one of his blunted horns and flicking it to the ground.

"Do you really think Ashley will be okay?" Hanna asked, finally arriving at the top step.

"J-just a minute," Patrick panted, holding a stitch in his side and wincing. "That was a lot of stairs. Gimme…gimme a minute, okay?"

"Like I said on the way up 'ere, I'd have rather taken her to Ms. Beauparlant, but Hagadorn will fix Ashley. She'll be okay. Let's get you to the Royal Hall to formally meet Morgana."

"Why do we *have* to see Morgana again? Why not the king?" Hanna looked around the castle stairwell. "You *do* have a king, right?"

"'Twas an incident some years back involving the king and queen and—" Crowthorn stopped short as if he couldn't say more. He turned, visibly frustrated at having to wait, and continued down the hall.

"Did they die?" interrupted Patrick.

"No one knows for sure. Morgana's parents vanished n' left their daughter behind."

Hanna struggled for breath as they rushed to keep pace beside Crowthorn. "That's horrible?"

"'Twas Dark Magic that took 'em, some say. In all the confusion and turmoil surrounding Kambo's death, they just went missing. Some suggest that Fe'Mal had her hand in the mix. Others say Barlow was in the mess of it. Don't know what's true anymore."

Hanna cocked her head. "Kambo? Who's that?"

"Gods save me," the captain exclaimed. "How do you not know the God of Light?" She raised her brows and shrugged. "Well, never you mind, We're here already."

Hanna looked up. They were face to face with the same great doors to the Royal Hall where Ashley was injured. A dark scarlet stain smeared the gray cobbled stone floor where Ashley fell. Hanna looked to the four guards posted at the sides of the entrance.

Crowthorn stepped forward and pressed his ear to the massive wooden doors. "Can hear voices inside, but no telling from who."

"Sir," said one of the guards posted to the right of the door. "The royal gates will be closing soon for the night."

"Closing for the night? 'Tis that late already?" Crowthorn turned to Hanna and Patrick. "Your meeting with Morgana will have to wait. I've business with the guards that needs attending." He then turned to the first guard. "Take these kids to guest quarters. Find 'em bedding for the night. Keep a guard at the door 'til I return for 'em in the morning."

"For the night? We can't wait that long!" said Hanna. "We need to see Morgana tonight."

Crowthorn raised his brows. "Don't know where yur from, lass, but you don't get to make the rules round here. Mind yur place. You're a guest 'en the only reason that's so is 'cause yur with the professor."

Hanna continued as if she wasn't just scolded. "What about my sister? She could be anywhere out there. We have to find her. That's why we came here…for Morgana's help."

He huffed. "It'll havta wait 'till morning. All there is to it." And just like that, Crowthorn turned to the guard with a nod and walked off down the hall from which they'd originally come.

Hanna turned to Patrick with a sigh. "I can't believe this. We've come all this way…"

"Look on the bright side. We found help. Let's assume that Lexi did too," said Patrick.

The guard moved past the two friends and started down a different hall past the spiral staircase. "Follow me."

With reluctance, Hanna followed with Patrick in tow. "What about my other sister, Ashley? The one who got hurt. She and Michael are with Hagadorn in the dungeon."

Without inflection in his voice, the guard replied, "I'll have your friends brought to your quarters." After several twists and turns down one hallway and up the next, the guard brought them before a slender wooden door. "Stay in your room tonight. No wandering the halls. A guard will be posted throughout the night."

A frown pulled at the corners of her mouth. Hanna opened the door to find a room not much larger than a broom cupboard. Several beds lined the small room, enough for the four of them, she thought. They were ushered inside and the guard closed the door behind them. She turned to Patrick. "I feel more like a prisoner than a guest."

She flopped onto the bed. The springs gave a squeaky protest to her weight. Hanna stared up at the ceiling for maybe ten minutes or more until the door opened again. Ashley and Michael were framed in the entrance. The four of them were together again.

"How's your arm?" Hanna asked. Without waiting for a response, she rushed to her sister and gently grabbed her injured arm. "It's all healed?"

Ashley smiled. "Good as new."

Patrick shook his head. "This is a strange place. Very, very strange. If we only had that kind of medicine or magic or whatever it's called back in Midtown Valley."

"So, you believe in magic now?" Michael said holding out his arm to show the puckered scar just below his elbow. "My scar wasn't good enough?"

Patrick simply looked at him. "What do you want me to say?"

Michael shook his head and stared at the four beds. "Blimey, this room is small. So, what's the game plan? Are we gonna talk to Morgana? Are we gonna find your sister or just hang around what they call guest quarters all night?"

Hanna felt her heart sink like a weight at the mention of Lexi. "We're stuck here for the night—"

"Bollocks!"

"No, seriously," said Patrick. "We've got to stay in this room. Crowthorn posted a guard until he comes for us in the morning."

"I ain't a prisoner."

"We're prisoners?" asked Ashley.

"Nobody said anything about being a prisoner," replied Hanna trying to reassure her sister and convince herself at the same time.

"So, what's that mean for your sister? Leave Lexi out there in the wilderness all night long with nothing and nobody? Mate, that's a load of rubbish. We get beds and what does she get?"

A pull from somewhere inside Hanna tugged at her guts. How could she stay in this castle while her sister was somewhere…anywhere but safe with her? "What choice do we have? We're captive guests." She added air quotes around the last word.

Michael turned back to the closed door and wrenched it open. Not one but two fully armed guards stood sentry. "You were told to remain in the room," one said snapping around to look down at Michael. "Any breech would be considered an act of aggression against the crown. You're guests, but that could change to something completely different if you continue. Leave the door closed until you're summoned in the morning."

The guard pulled the door shut with a dull *thunk* against the frame. Michael turned, his jaw fell slack, and he looked back at the others. "That guard's a right git." Michael paced away from the door and sat on an open bed. He rested his elbows on his knees and covered his eyes with his open palms.

Patrick stood and moved next to Hanna. "Look. Morgana's gonna help us tomorrow. The professor said as much." He took her hands in his own. "We'll find your sister. You'll see."

She just grunted a "thanks" and fell back onto her pillow. She rolled away from the group to stare at the gray stone wall. Hanna didn't even get under the covers of her bed. The creaky squeak of springs and the rustle of covers made her turn to see the rest of her friends bedding down for the night. A torch hung on the wall above them illuminating the room in a dull white light. There was no way for them to turn it off so, Hanna simply rolled over and closed her eyes.

Hanna couldn't believe how she'd come to this place. The day started rough. She raced away from her dad in the driveway for school. And ended with her lost in some crazy world of wizards and gods. Hanna wanted to pinch her eyes closed and forget it all. She wanted to open them in the morning and find that it was all a bad dream.

But she knew better. Somehow. Someway. Hanna knew better. Lexi was out there somewhere in Smaradine and Hanna was determined to find her. The soft pillow beneath her head seemed to blend her thoughts into a fog. The effort and anxiety of the day slipped away. Soon, the relaxing tug of sleep pulled at her thoughts, unraveling her worries until she finally pondered them no more.

24

———————

THE LAZY LAGOON

A noise somewhere behind Lexi woke her from her dreams. She shot her eyes open hoping against hope that yesterday's nightmare was just exactly that. When she sat bolt upright in the strange living room, the tape again sticking to the underside of her thigh, she knew she wasn't in Midtown Valley anymore. Roused from bed, she gathered herself, and soon followed the green woman out the front door. Lexi didn't collect a thing to bring along except the bedsheets bundled around her from the night before.

Lexi and Paula left the cave before the rays of the morning sun warmed the beach. She was finally thankful for the warm blanket. Even though the sky was clear and blue, Lexi could see her breath cascade in wispy puffs as she trudged through the sand. She pulled her blanket more tightly around her shoulders. Lexi winced as it scraped against the tender nape of her neck where needles once protruded like a quill of spines. A new chill ran up her bare legs as they reached the length of beach where the sand turned wet from the surf.

The sky to the east began to brighten as the sun crested the tops of the desert dunes. The horrible storm was all but a memory. She turned back to the water as they neared a thin, wooden pier reaching out into the white-capped waves. The dock was as crooked as a dog's hind leg. The air all around was filled with the sounds of rough waves beating the shoreline as seagulls squawked their high-pitched calls overhead. The relative quiet after the storm was a welcome relief.

She turned and looked up the large dune she'd tumbled down. The tempest was gone. And with it, no remnants of the sandstorm that almost killed her. Paula ushered Lexi to a small rowboat tied near shore. Choppy waves battered the sides of the dingy, spraying cool, salted mist into the air. Lexi stared into the depths of the ocean. She couldn't see the bottom. The water under the dock looked cold, dark, and deep.

"Here, dearie, climb into da boat."

Lexi pinched her eyes closed. *Don't fall in. Don't fall in. Don't fall in!* She imagined sinking in the water. Images swam through her mind of her clawing upward toward the surface where the darkness couldn't grip her feet.

"Whatcha waiting for," cried Paula, nudging Lexi forward. "Climb into da dingy."

The rowboat bobbed in the unrelenting waves. They sent the small, wooden craft, which looked as if it would tip over at any minute, crashing into the dock. Lexi knew that she had to climb inside. What other choice did she have? Lexi took a tentative step forward and placed an unsteady foot on the front seat. Her weight shifted the boat. Lexi screamed and fell into the hollow bow between the seats with a thud.

"Whatcha afraid of, dearie? Ain't 'ya never been in a dingy before?"

Lexi shook her head as the boat bucked against the moored rope that anchored it to the dock. "I-I can't swim," she confessed, her stomach knotting into cramps.

Paula made a noise that Lexi didn't know if it was a cough or a laugh as she climbed inside. She untied the dingy and shoved off the dock. Lexi's fingers gripped the side rails as she peeked over the edge and into the choppy water. Too petrified to watch her new friend row, Lexi listened to Paula wrench the oars back and forth, pushing the dingy away from everything she knew and through the open, heavy waves.

Forever and a day seemed to pass before the boat rounded the southern face of the island. Lexi craned her neck to see the top of a coral cliff that rose hundreds of feet above the dingy. As they rounded the corner, a city high on the edge of the cliffs took shape.

"How do we get in? Do we climb or something?"

Paula shook her head. "No dearie. Breakwater's da most protected city of da kingdom. No way up, no how. Dat city sits up high in dem cliffs, but 'ole Paula know. 'Ole Paula know a way in, sure I do. We gots ta hurry. Ain't never arrived dis late before. Da squall pushed us back—gonna miss da tidal window."

"Window? What window?"

"Gotta hurry or da water might get too high."

"Too high for what?" Lexi asked, shooting to her feet. The boat rocked violently to one side and she nearly toppled out.

"Sit! Sit! Sit!" Paula screamed.

Lexi threw herself back down to the bottom of the boat, her heart pounding. Paula guided the dingy toward a small, half-submerged cave. Lexi pointed to where the sea water sucked into the black, lightless hole. "We are NOT gonna go in there!" she barked, eyes wide, a clear tremble wavering through her voice. "No way, no how. We're *not* going in that cave."

"Have some faith, dearie."

"It's dark in there—we can't. Wait—I don't wanna go!"

"Sit down. Stay low. Here we go," Paula cut across her. "Hold on tight. 'Tis gonna get bumpy."

"Wait—wait—just wait a sec—" Lexi panicked. "Has anyone died going through here?"

"Sure, but not me."

Lexi barely had time to grip her seat before the shadow of the cave crossed six feet above her head, swallowing the bow. The small boat lurched forward as it was caught in the swift, tidal currents. Fear gripped Lexi's chest as they were quickly consumed by darkness.

The dingy jostled from side to side in the turbulent current. It banged its edges against the damp cave walls. The tidal currents gurgled and dragged them forward. The cave smelled stale and musty with the pungent odors of seaweed and brine. It robbed her of both sight and sanity.

"H-how far is it?" stammered Lexi.

"Not to worry none. Da light at da end of da cave will git here soon."

Lexi crouched in her seat trying to stay still and small and calm. It was a trifecta of impossibilities. The darkness was disorienting—confusing. Terrifying images swirled through her mind as she envisioned herself drowning in the pitch blackness. She held her hand up but couldn't see an inch from her face. The rowboat slammed into the side of the tunnel again, this time throwing Lexi to the bottom of the dingy.

"I'm gonna die—I'm gonna die—I'm gonna die!" Lexi cried. She shot to her feet once more and cracked her skull against the coral ceiling. She collapsed, her knees folded like a paper doll. "Ow!" A warm trickle of blood fingered its way down her temple. The ceiling was no longer six feet above; the water levels had risen several feet. "It's closing in—the ceiling—we're gonna get stuck against the ceiling!"

"Stay seated," shouted Paula. "Or yur gonna fall in or tip us both over!"

"But the tide's rising!"

"Don't panic," Paula repeated as the dingy rocked from side to side.

Half-slouching, Lexi raised her hands to the ceiling once again. Her stomach clenched. She could only stand half as tall as before. Forced to sit from lack of room alone, Lexi landed with a thump onto something hard.

"What the—?" she said, her voice rising in pitch. In the blackness, Lexi reached in her back pocket and pulled out her phone. Not knowing who to call for help, or what they could do for her once they arrived, she dialed the first number that came to mind. Hanna.

Lexi pressed the power button and her face was bathed in the soft, white light of the screen. Her momentary cheer fell through the bottom of the dingy when she saw for the first time just how little room they had left. She turned the phone's illumination on Paula and the remaining hope she'd held drained away. The old woman sat bent in half just to pull the oars. The roof of the cave loomed only inches above their heads. The dingy bounced off the side of the cave again, and Lexi spun forward, losing her grip on the phone. She lurched to her feet to catch it, once again cracking her head on the low rocks.

"Git down," yelled Paula.

The boat continued to wildly rock back and forth and the phone hit the bow and bounced. Lexi's eyes widened in the near darkness as it tumbled and fell overboard. She lunged for the phone, this time cracking her ribs against the side of the boat. She managed to barely catch the phone with the tips of her fingers before it fell in.

"OH, CRAP, that was close!".

"Git low in da dingy—yur gonna tip us over," shouted Paula. "Ugh. Girl. Sit down!"

Lexi pressed her phone to her chest and crouched again, struggling to inhale. She tried to swallow, but a lump was lodged in her throat. The spit in her mouth was gone, leaving her tongue dry and tacky, her breathing rapid and erratic. The only other thing racing through her mind besides trying to survive was the burning desire to talk to someone—anyone. She didn't want to die alone and afraid with no one she knew.

"I gotta call Hanna—I gotta call Hanna!"

"Ain't nobody gonna help!" screamed Paula. "Put dat ting down! We got in dis mess—and we git out."

"Gotta tell Hanna where I am," Lexi repeated, ignoring

Paula, and dialed her sister. No answer. She tried again. Still nothing. She dialed Ashley. She dialed her dad, her mom, Patrick, and even Michael. Each call ended in a mountain of frustration. She threw her head back and screamed into the darkness. Echoes of her frustration rippled through the cramped darkness.

Lexi held up her hands and pressed them against the cold, wet stone. She dragged her dirty fingers across the rough surface of the ceiling. Tears began to stream down her face. *This is it. I'm going to die in this cave, alone, with a woman I don't even know. I never should've followed Hanna.* Her heart sank like an anchor.

The boat bumped against the wall of the cave and they turned around a bend. A small dot of light in the distance formed out of the darkness. Lexi stared at it, squinting. It was the end of the tunnel!

Lexi frantically dialed Hanna's number again. Still nothing— the spot of light grew larger. A hint of fresh air tickled her nose. The boat slammed against the wall once more. The rough grating of wood scraping along the sharp coral permeated the darkness. Lexi imagined the rails of the dingy shredding like soft cheese.

"Help push! Help push!" barked Paula.

Panicking, Lexi ignored Paula and tried the phone again. Nothing. The current gurgled against the bottom of the skiff. The remaining space between her head and the roof of the cave shrunk with each passing breath. The relentless tide seemed to squeeze the life out of the cave.

Lexi finally plunged her free hand over the side, trying to paddle them closer to the exit as she continued to try and reach anyone on the phone. She had to make contact—the signal *had* to get through. They were close to the exit, so close, she could make out shapes in the light out the other end. Her hair grazed the ceiling as they inched still closer to freedom

"Da end is near! Da end is near!" Paula was bent so low, her knees pressed against her chest. "Told 'ya I git us through."

The soft glow from the phone's screen cast a somber light

against what little space remained. The top rim of the boat bumped and grated against the coral ceiling as the wash of tide stole what remaining room was left. Lexi couldn't even sit. Her back was pressed firmly into the bottom of the boat.

Then it happened. The boat banged to a halt. It jammed in place against the ceiling.

"Oh my god!" Lexi shouted, kneeling against the floorboards. "We're stuck—we're stuck!"

"Push—push with da oars! We're almost there!"

New streams of tears blanketed Lexi's cheeks. "All I wanted was to find my sisters," she sobbed holding her face in her hands.

Like an unforgiving piston, the tide rose and swelled up the sides of the dingy. The boat's frame groaned against the pressure. Several boards popped from their moorings as the wooden dingy began to splinter.

One of the oars burst from its casting and struck Paula in the face. She let out a piercing scream. Lexi tried to yell, but lost her breath as icy, salt water spilled over the rim of the boat. She gathered what strength she had as the cold water sunk its teeth into her skin. What little air that Lexi exhaled came out in a timid cry. "OH MY GOD! OH MY GOD!"

Icy cold knives prickled her legs, her waist, her chest. The freezing water chilled her to her core. She held the phone above the waves and pressed dial one last time.

A *click* through the speaker.

Someone picked up! It worked! It finally worked!

"Hanna—Hanna!" Lexi screamed into the phone as stale brine water flooded her mouth and garbled her voice. The cold stabbed her body like icy daggers.

"Ello? Where are you?" a deep, unfamiliar voice echoed through the phone.

Lexi spit out mouthfuls of water. "I don't know!" she sobbed. "I'm in a cave. Paula—Paula—where—where are we?"

But Paula was already swallowed by the swelling tide.

25

GOLINVEAUX

A rough banging startled Hanna awake. She sat upright in bed. Her heart raced before her feet touched the floor. The others sat up startled as the door to their guest room slammed open.

Crowthorn ducked through the opening, his sawed-off horns barely fitting through the space. "Get up! Get up outta bed. It's time to see Morgana."

Hanna was on her feet before any of the others. "Have you heard any news? Has anyone found my sister?"

Crowthorn scoffed. "Yea don't know what you're talking 'bout. Yea don't know how big Smaradine is. If she's lost out there like yea say, word of her hasn't reached anyone let alone Morgana herself."

"It feels early. What time is it?" asked Michael.

"Bout an hour after sunrise."

Patrick's eyebrows shot up to his hairline. "Morgana sees people this early?"

Crowthorn shook his head. "Nope. Wanted to make sure you got something to eat in the Grand Hall before you met the princess. Being as yur guests 'en all, should treat 'ya like it, right?"

Hanna scoffed at the comment and then blanched, glancing over toward Crowthorn to see if he heard. Although they left right away, it was a few minute's walk until they reached a massive room with tall wooden doors. The room was larger than Hanna's whole house back in Midtown Valley. Long wooden tables were lined in rows. Plates, cups, and silverware were neatly stacked at the ends of each of the tables. What looked like servants or servers brought platters of food and pitchers of drink to a table of soldiers on the far side of the room.

"Grab a seat. Eat quickly," said Crowthorn. "Don't want to get stuck behind a slow crowd. Plenty of others come to gather to see Morgana."

Hanna nodded and everyone took a seat at the nearest table. Ashley took a seat to Hanna's right while Patrick and Michael took seats across from them on the other side of the table. Before long, servers set plates and silverware before them. Platters of eggs and bacon, biscuits and hash browns, and a dark rich drink were placed within arm's reach.

Crowthorn reached between the sisters and acted like a wedge between them. As Hanna and Ashley bent out of his way, he grabbed a tall cup and the pitcher of drink. "I love Spiced Meade in the morning." He put the cup to his lips and tipped his head back downing the drink in two long gulps.

Hanna's stomach growled, but she wasn't in the mood for food. Not when her sister was still out there and they were no closer to finding her. As Michael and Patrick loaded their plates with food, the only thing she wanted was a glass of Spiced Meade. She winced licking her lips at the somehow sweet, yet savory taste that lingered on her tongue.

"C'mon, now," said Crowthorn. "Why don't I take yea to see the princess while yur friends eat their meal."

Patrick leapt to his feet, his wooden chair screeching on the stone floor. "I'll come."

Michael looked up; his plate still covered in scrambled eggs. "What about us?"

"Come when you're done," said Patrick.

"No, I mean how do we find you?"

"The Royal Hall is down to yur right. Follow the noise of people 'en you'll be sure to get there. When you see posted guards, that's the place."

Michael shrugged and shoveled a forkful of eggs into his mouth. Hanna gave one last look back to Ashley before Crowthorn swept her and Patrick from the Grand Hall and into the corridor. The way to the Royal Hall wasn't as simple as the captain implied. They turned one way and another before finally coming to the tall ornate wooden doors secured by two sets of posted guards.

No one gathered outside the Royal Hall. Crowthorn, Hanna and Patrick were the first ones to the door. "What now?" she asked.

Let's take a look inside." He grabbed the heavy handle and swung a single door open.

Hanna and Patrick followed through the threshold. They were bathed in colorful bands of light that crisscrossed the floor. Rays from the sun flooded through stained-glass windows making a patchwork of color across a solitary strip of red carpet. Her eyes naturally followed which led to a raised dais at the far end of the room.

The corners of Hanna's mouth curled in anticipation. Finally, she'd get some answers. But would Morgana cooperate? Or, better yet, would she even know what to do?

Excited voices carried across the near empty hall. They weren't from any of the guards posted along the inside walls. The voices came from an elderly couple arguing with someone near raised thrones at the end of the long red carpet. It was Morgana.

Crowthorn gasped. "May the Gods protect 'em—they've returned!"

"What do you mean? Who's returned?" Hanna whispered.

As they approached the three figures, the captain bent down

on one knee. "My king. My queen. You've returned! I am yours to command."

A scowl flashed across Morgana's face. A sudden movement from her right caught Hanna's eye and she turned to look. In the shadow of a tall pillar stood two figures. They huddled close to the column as if afraid to be seen. The argument between royalty continued unabated by their approach up the red carpet.

The king wore crimson robes of silk and linen which draped to the floor. Heavy streaks of white robbed his short, black hair of its youth, and his tightly trimmed beard lost any pretense of remaining young. The queen's braided, white hair was curled in a thick cable which fell across the silks of her frosted blue dress. They were everything Hanna dreamed a king and queen might look like.

The captain pushed himself to his feet. "How is it that you've come back after all this time?"

"This was *my* time," snapped Morgana, her gaze going from Crowthorn to the king. "The sun was rising on my time. MY TIME!"

"This isn't what we planned," said the king. "It was never our...you must understand—"

"Understand what, exactly?" Morgana threw her hands in the air. "After all these years, you finally return to reclaim the throne you abandoned? Where were you when I was a girl? Where were you when I needed my parents? Hm? I didn't want some whelp—some stupid nursemaid. I wanted you. But you left. You were gone. YOU WERE GONE!" For a moment, Hanna thought Morgana was going to cry, but then she pulled herself together standing to her full height and continued. "For my whole childhood, I've grown on my own. And now...now that I'm a woman...now that I'm at the pinnacle of *my* time...when *my* ascension to the throne is in two days, you strip *me* of *my* right!"

The queen stepped toward their daughter. "We've always loved you."

"Love? Love?! I can't believe this. Love wouldn't abandon a child—to have her grow up alone!"

"We left you in good hands," added the king. "Golinveaux, I'm sure mentored you well."

The queen opened her arms as if to offer Morgana a hug. "But we're back now. Let us show you—"

"NO! I don't need you to show me anything! Who do you think's been ruling this kingdom while you were away? By the gods of the six realms, it's taken me years to muster the courage to take your place—to put my mourning behind me. I thought you dead. The whole kingdom thought you dead. Now we find the truth. Now we find that you abandoned us? ABANDONED ME! For what? Can't you even tell me that?"

The king stood quiet. Morgana, obviously taking her father's silence for rejection, spun on her heels and marched for the door. She waived her hand in a flurry. Two teenage figures emerged from the shadows of nearby pillars. Hanna had to nearly jump out of the way so not to be trampled. Slack-jawed, she gaped as Morgana and the two young men stormed from the Royal Hall.

As the doors closed behind them, Morgana yelled through the crack. "You may be back, but my day in the sun will come!"

Hanna leaned toward Patrick and whispered, "Do you think the king and queen were trapped somewhere? Held captive, maybe? Could've been Barlow…"

The king raised his eyes to Hanna, as if seeing her for the first time. "Crowthorn, my loyal Captain of the Guard. Who have you brought before me?"

"King James," said Crowthorn with his head slightly bowed. "I bare new guests to Smaradine—to Manna. This is Hanna Steele. She and her friends seek asylum."

The king cleared his throat and held up a hand beckoning the group forward with a twitch of his fingers. "How is it that they've come to the Kingdom of Manna?"

Hanna stood before them and reached into her pocket pulling

out the metallic cube. "We're from Havendale, sir. We came here because of this."

"You have a Realm Cube?!"

The heavy hall doors reopened and Hanna prepared herself for another argument with Morgana. But it wasn't her.

"What a glorious day, my king," said a slow, deep-throated voice. "Your return was foretold—I've seen it in the fortunes of my tea leaves." The man spoke in a smooth, calm tone.

The king smiled. "I would expect nothing less from the court's wizard."

"I've found some people wandering the hallways I thought that this young lady should see."

Hanna turned—Ashley and Michael were standing next to a tall man. The newcomer held a long staff and was dressed in flowing, velvet robes of dark, emerald green. Wire-rimmed glasses bridged his nose. His head was topped with a cottony bush of salt n' pepper hair. Below his wrinkled face was the longest, silver beard she'd ever seen.

"My name is Golinveaux," he said. "I've been expecting you." The corners of his mustache twitched into what she took as a smile.

Hanna pressed her finger to her chest. "Me—you've been expecting me?"

The wizard pursed his lips. "I've a lot to tell you and time's running out."

She pulled Ashley close and passed a glance from her friends back to Golinveaux. "I need to ask the king about Lexi. My other sister is lost alone in Smaradine."

"With the King's favor," Golinveaux said. "Follow me if you want to save your family."

The professor's prophecy stirred to the surface of her mind. The vision of her being struck down in battle and then her sisters being taken flashed behind her eyes. Hanna's gut churned into knots.

The king pounded the end of a golden staff on the floor. The wide room echoed with a dull *thwack, thwack, thwack.* "What about the Realm Cube?"

Golinveaux turned to the king. "King James, the Cube is moot—"

"How could she travel between realms when the remainder of Manna—all of the six realms, for that matter—have been denied passage? How has *her* Cube worked when all other attempts have failed?"

Hanna's eyes widened. "I tried to go back. The portal was gone. I tried the Cube again. It wouldn't work. It's just a stupid chunk of metal now."

"Could it be," the king looked to Golinveaux again, "that with the Cube broken and all travel between realms impassable once more that we're still safe from the Dark Queen?"

The wizard lowered his gaze. "If only it were so simple, my lord. With the God of Light gone, there's no one to stop her. There's no one to stand in his sister's way. But the Pillars de Luz and the Well of Wishes should continue to hold her at bay...for now."

The king sighed and shifted his eyes to Hanna. "Why do you seek asylum?"

"Barlow," she blurted. "He drove us from our home. He forced us from Havendale!"

"I believe he intends to harm or even kill them, your grace," added Golinveaux.

Hanna froze stiff feeling as if a bucket of ice tumbled down her throat.

"If the darkness takes over, all the realms will be lost," the king said without inflection.

"My king, the children are here—*his* children," said Golinveaux. "They're asking for help."

What? Whose children is he talking about?

"They may be the key to everything."

"What have your fortunes told you about Fe'Mal?" asked the king.

The wizard pursed his lips, as if collecting his thoughts. "She will come. I've seen it. But when, I cannot tell. The future is shrouded in darkness and uncertainty."

The king seemed to consider Golinveaux's words. "I see," he said after a pause. "For now, I cannot stop the Dark Queen, but I may be able to do something about Barlow. Like a cancerous tumor, our son, Barlow, has a way of seeping into every crevice of Manna—and beyond. Although the darkness threatens us, I can do nothing against it at the moment. It's obvious that the clear and present danger right now is our son.

"I'll grant you asylum and quarters in the north tower. Leave me. My guards will take you there. The queen and I have much to discuss." The king's eyes shifted toward the wizard. "Golinveaux, return right away. I'll need your council. And as for you, Crowthorn. Make preparations for a grand festival for our return at the beginning of the Summer Solstice. All of Castletown—all of Manna will be ripe for celebration."

Golinveaux nodded and ushered Hanna, Ashley, and their friends out of the Royal Hall. The massive twin doors closed behind them with a dull thud. A lanky man with curly red hair and thick, ginger sideburns approached from down the hall. He stepped to the wizard's side and reached into the front of his brown, leather vest. The man pulled a white, satin handkerchief from somewhere beneath the folds of his scorch-marked clothes.

"Golinveaux, sir," he said holding out the cloth.

"Thank you, Archibald." He accepted the hanky dabbing his own forehead.

Michael raised a hand as if still in school. "Golinveaux, sir? I know you're busy and have a billion things to do, but do you think you can help me find my dad?" Hanna slid her arm around Michael's shoulders and squeezed him in a half-hug. Michael returned her gesture with a smile. "I know we're trying to find Lexi right now, but when she's back and things have settled…do you think you can help me?"

"Another time, my boy." He pat Michael on the cheek. "Reuniting Hanna with her sister is of paramount importance."

"Right, I know, I know…"

With a half-smile, Golinveaux nodded at Michael and turned to Archibald. He placed a hand on his companion's boney shoulder. "This is Archie—my loyal apprentice."

Patrick stepped forward. "He's learning to be a wizard?"

"In time, a powerful one, yes. It takes time to truly come into your powers. But with the right training and guidance, a budding wizard could become great. He's already completed his training at Golinveaux's School of Magic and Enchantment."

"Sounds lucky. What about the rest who don't get training?" asked Michael.

Golinveaux raised his bushy, white eyebrows and gave a weary expression. "Barlow is a prime example of a good wizard gone bad. He's but one in a sea of examples. We're in a quiet war."

Hanna frowned. "A war?"

"Not the war between the kingdoms, but a silent and deadly one between wizards. There are those in the magical world who would rather rule over the weak and dominate the defenseless."

Patrick mumbled Johnny Mack's name under his breath.

"Some wizards, like Barlow, are a prime example of the cruelty and misuse of magic by wielding it over the Ni'Mago. At our school, we teach new wizards from a young age in hopes they'll learn by good example to treat everyone as equals."

26

UNEXPECTED LESSONS

"I've foreseen your coming," Golinveaux added looking into Hanna's eyes and drawing out a long, white wand with a single ribbon of gold spiraling up its shaft. "I would guess that by now you've experienced some semblance of magic on Smaradine?" He lightly tapped Hanna's chest with the tips of his fingers. "It comes from within here regardless of its form. Wands may harness the power and play an important role for some, but it is the skillful witch or wizard who must properly wield it."

He drew a series of tight swirls in the air and golden sparks shot from the tip of his wand. Leaning in close, he spoke softly in Hanna's ear. "Unicorn horns make the best wands, but I think you'll have no need of one yourself." Golinveaux slipped his own back under his robes.

Hanna glanced at her sister, then down to her hands. She turned the ring around her thumb. "Sir? This has—this *all* has been so strange." Golinveaux nodded in agreement and simply smiled behind his long white beard. "The professor said he knew the truth. He said that you could—you could fill in the missing pieces. I've got so many questions, but he wanted me to talk with you first. Do you know what he's talking about?"

She looked down at her hands. "I don't have a wand," Hanna said tentatively, "but I've had a *lot* of strange things happen today."

"It would seem so."

"My locker was destroyed, then Barlow, and when I first arrived in Smaradine, my hands glowed with a bright light." She looked inquisitively into the wizard's cool, blue eyes. "I never had a wand at that time and it sure seemed like magic. How come—"

"That's because you and your sisters are very special people. None of you *needs* a wand. You've got something unique already inside you."

"What does that mean? If I have magic, why don't I need a wand? What's inside me?" she asked hesitantly. "And about the professor, what is the truth?"

Golinveaux furrowed his unwieldy, white brows. "It's vitally important for *your* safety, the safety of your *sisters*, and maybe even the future of *Smaradine* that we talk."

He turned his back to the group and leaned down once more to whisper into Hanna's ear. "You and your family are in grave peril, that much I'm sure you already know. I can only presume to know how you arrived in Smaradine, though. Can I see the ring?" There was a hint of excitement in his voice.

Hanna reached for it, but before she slid it from her thumb, Golinveaux grabbed her wrist. "Wait! Never, *ever* take it off," he said sternly. "Not for your sisters. Not for anyone. Not even for me. "

"But you asked— Okay, why?" she whispered in return.

"This is a GodStone ring. There's only one in existence, and *you* have it. It's a coveted treasure and you'll come by many trials against many foes who'll wish to strip you of your prize."

There was that word again. GodStone. But that still didn't explain anything. Not really. "W-what's it do?"

"Havendale and Smaradine share the same realm, thus they share the same GodStone."

"You mean this," she said, pointing to the reddish rust-colored gem in the ring.

"Yes. Fe'Mal is coming—and you'll need to complete this ring to defeat her."

Hanna felt her pulse begin to race, her heart actually thundering as she listened to the wizard's words. A gnawing ache formed in her gut just below her navel. A slew of questions rose up almost faster than her tongue could speak them. "Who's Fe'Mal? Complete the ring? What about Barlow?"

"Barlow is a problem in his own right, but there is a larger end-game we need to worry about. You may have heard me say it to the king. I think that you're key to everything."

Hanna swallowed. "Me? What can I do? I don't know anything. I just got here. I don't know anyone."

"You won't be alone. The whole world of Smaradine will be at your back. We'll do everything to help you fight the darkness —to stop Fe'Mal."

Something was off—Hanna felt she wasn't getting the full picture. She was just a girl from a small town in Illinois. "B-but why me? Why my sisters? I-I'm not a—"

"Your father was very special," Golinveaux cut across her. "Because of him, you and your sisters each hold a glimmer of hope in defeating the darkness that threatens us all."

Flustered, she glanced back to Ashley and then at Golinveaux. "What can I possibly do?" Hanna asked again.

"You hold a natural power. As for the ring and the stones, in time you'll need to collect them all. There are six realms and six stones."

Hanna flicked her eyes to the five empty prongs in the channeled groove of the ring. "Six realms? I-I don't know anything about realms and stones. I feel so lost." Her mind whirled thinking of the tasks set before her, the most important of which was finding Lexi.

"I know it seems daunting, but it can be done—*must* be done. This single stone is from this realm—of Havendale and Smaradine," continued Golinveaux pointing to the only gem in her ring. "With it, you may control the soil and stone."

Hanna eyed the band around her thumb as she tried to absorb the new information. The image of her destroyed locker flashed in her mind. "What about metal?"

The wizard nodded. "Metal is an element from the very soil that gives birth to this power. Learn to bend it to your will and soon you'll learn to master the elements."

"What about the other empty prongs?"

Golinveaux smiled behind his beard. "Most of the other GodStones are locked in other realms."

"Most?"

"Some stones have already been collected. That's one of the reasons Barlow is so dangerous."

"He has a GodStone?"

"You must find them all and eventually master their power too. Right now, however, you must use what you have to find your sister and keep your family safe from Barlow."

Hanna stared at her hands. "When I first arrived, my necklace came to life. It glowed blue. And my hands shined white hot."

"That's the natural magic you were born with—your sisters too. It's unmatched by any in Smaradine."

"Born with? I was born with magic?" Hanna's head was spinning. She had magic. Real magic. All of the events of the day seemed to fall into place with this news. Hanna thought about her hands in the meadow—how they glowed. The spark of excitement and the trickle of fear mixed into a jumble of emotion inside her head. "So, I have magic—a magic that I was born with, but know nothing about, right?"

Golinveaux nodded.

"I can make light? And heat—I melted the snow, didn't I? And with my ring I can control the earth below my feet?" She studied Golinveaux's eyes as she spoke. They revealed no trace of joke or prank or even hesitation. Hanna thought about the words spilling from her mouth. A thrill of excitement lanced through her, but a lingering trail of doubt remained. "But how do I use it?"

"You'll need to sense it—feel it flow within you. Draw it out and guide the magic from your core. Use your senses to master it. Don't let your emotions overtake you."

"You mean, I just think it and it happens?"

"Something like that, but with more control and finesse." The corner of Golinveaux's mouth curled. "The magic, whether from yourself, a ring, or other magical artifact, comes from within and learning to manage and harness it is the key to everything." He leaned in and pressed his thumb to her forehead and then touched his other hand to her breast bone. "Magic comes from here and here. For most, its channeled through the use of a wand or magical artifact. As I said, for you and your sisters though, there's no need for wands, but the delivery is all the same. Believe in yourself like I do, Hanna. Trust in yourself."

She didn't trust anything about whatever magic that was supposed to be within her. If truth be told, Hanna felt more frightened than anything. How could he expect her to wield magic when she didn't know the first thing about it.

"What about my sisters? You said there's power in each of us, right? So, they can do magic too?"

Golinveaux tipped his head toward Ashley. "They can, yes, but they've not yet unlocked their inherent abilities. They need Smaradite to do that. Yours was in this ring."

Hanna reached for the band around her thumb again. "I can let Ashley touch it now, then? That way she'll have magic, too."

"No." The wizard placed a firm hand on Hanna's shoulder not letting her walk away. "Your tasks will become exponentially more complicated right now if you share your newfound gift. It's not that I want to keep them from their magical rights. It will only distract you from the immediate goal. Right now, you must remain focused on finding your sister and keeping them both safe."

"Wouldn't it be easier if we all had magic?"

"Teaching and training three new mages is a daunting task—especially for one so new to Smaradine. Don't worry. In due time, I'll have new rings forged for your sisters." He paused and pointed at the scar on the inside of Hanna's arm. "New rings that won't come with the extra burden of Dark Magic."

She rubbed at the brand. "Er, right. I wouldn't want them exposed to—*him*. Do you think it's possible to beat him, though? To beat Barlow?"

"With the power of your father—"

"Where there's a wizard, there's a way," Archie cut in, pointing to Hanna and the rest of her friends with a smile. "You can do anything you set your mind to."

As they talked, the alchemist came into view from a stairwell. Hagadorn marched straight toward them sliding a knobby, spiraled, ivory wand into his pocket. Now was her chance to thank Hagadorn for healing Ashley! It was the least she could do.

Without even a sideways glance, however, the alchemist barged between Hanna and Golinveaux. "Don't believe such foolish tripe," Hagadorn said to Archie. "I heard the apprentice. That's foolish advice from a foolhardy boy." Blossoms of heat grew up Hanna's cheeks. A flash of anger threatened to spill out. "Not only is the boy's advice worthless garbage, it's bound to get you all into trouble!"

"Sounds like good advice to me, mate," interrupted Michael.

Hagadorn rounded on him. "It leads to an overactive imagination."

Archie opened his mouth, closed it. Then opened it again and said, "Well, I think—"

"Since when is an apprentice allowed to think?"

"That will be enough, Hagadorn," interrupted Golinveaux. "I'll scold my own apprentice, if you please." He turned from the alchemist back to Archie. "Why don't you run back to the tower."

"But—but I thought—"

The wizard cleared his throat. Archie's shoulders slumped which gave the appearance of a deflating balloon. He turned and disappeared down the hallway.

Hanna side-stepped Hagadorn. "Excuse me, but—"

The alchemist whirled on her. "Mind your place, girl. Just because I saved your sister, doesn't give you any special favor. I have business to discuss." His piercing gaze shifted to Ashley. "I see you're still here. You should take my advice and flee. Put this kingdom behind you."

"Flee?" Hanna frowned. "Wait, why would you tell her that?"

Golinveaux held up a placating hand and raised his brows above the rims of his glasses. "There will be no fleeing today." He spoke with a patience that had disappeared from Hanna the moment they'd been interrupted. "Yes, Hagadorn? How may I help you?"

The alchemist turned back to the old wizard and whispered into Golinveaux's ear. Hanna caught bits and pieces. *Divination —Breakwater—Barlow.* When the whispers ended, without even a glance at the others, Hagadorn spun on his heels and retreated. The back of his patched, black robes flowed in his wake as he rounded the stairwell. Much like Archie, the alchemist disappeared from view. Before she could ask about what happened, new clomps of hurried footsteps carried up the hallway behind them.

"Hanna—Hanna," echoed Alexander's voice from halfway down the corridor. "It's your sister! Lexi's—she's been found!"

"Wait, really?!" Ashley squealed, clinging to Hanna's arm.

Finally reaching them from down the corridor, Alexander doubled over, gripping an obvious stitch in his side. "She—she's okay." He stood and inhaled a deep breath wincing through the pain. "Don't know...all details...yet." He stood, holding his chest. "Hugo found her. She's at the Lazy—"

"Come on!" Michael gripped Hanna's elbow and tugged. "Let's get her."

Hanna was torn. She wanted to get Lexi—wanted to see that she was safe, but at the same time wanted to talk with Golinveaux. Both seemed equally important now that Lexi was safe. "But Golinveaux said—"

Michael grasped her by the shoulders. "What's more important? Your sister," he said, flicking a quick glance at the wizard, "or talking to that old man?"

Golinveaux stepped forward and grasped Hanna's hand. He bent close to whisper into her ear. "Similar to others before him, I fear that Barlow's searching—like Gilgamesh and Nicholas Flamel—for eternal life. Don't give him the chance to steal any of your precious aura. May Kambo's light serve you well and always remember that the way forward is found within."

My what—aura? She peered up into his icy, blue eyes as they parted. Michael tugged at her hand and she was pulled toward her friends. "There's so much I want to ask, but—"

Ashley yanked on Hanna's other arm. "Come on! They found Lexi!"

"Use your time well," Golinveaux called with a wave. "Like family—time is invaluable to have, but once gone, you'll never get it back."

Hanna trailed behind her friends as they finally ran out of the castle and into the courtyard. With the professor in the lead, they wound their way to a local portal in the open yard.

"Bollocks, mate. Why'd we go to the Wharf if there was a rift 'ere?" asked Michael.

The professor either didn't hear Michael or ignored him altogether. He lifted his Portal Dial and showed Hanna and Patrick how to punch in the coordinates. Alexander first pointed to his Dial before gesturing for Patrick to walk through the gate. Michael followed closely behind, then the professor also vanished from view. Hanna dialed the coordinates for Breakwater and waited for her sister to step through before following closely behind.

27

MORALS IN QUESTION

Christopher Valentine was exhausted, hungry, and scared as he slowly approached the outskirts of a rural farming village. Having left the thick cover of mountain trees miles behind, he dragged his heels up a lone dirt road bordered by lush fields of corn and beans. Valentine walked off the adrenaline rush throughout the night. He was exhausted by the time the first farm came into view. A light breeze rustled the green stalks in the field. It felt good and cooled the sweat which clung to his skin.

He curled his upper lip at a new smell. The pungent scent of swine dung wafted through the late morning heat. A wooden barn sat in the distance and, as he approached, mule or cattle pens became clearer. The prospect of meeting someone was exciting, but Valentine still pulled the sleeve of his varsity jacket down over the new cuff on his wrist. *Don't want to draw attention to my treasure.*

Valentine stared for a moment at the arms of his jacket and then down to his football jersey. The wrinkled and dirty shirt stretched untucked past his waist. Would his stained sports clothes mark him as a stranger? Probably. Would that matter?

What do the people look like here? Is everyone a giant or have tenta-

cles? He shuddered. *If not, then what do normal people wear? Would I blend in? And if not, how do I get new clothes? I don't have any money.*

He patted down the pockets of his sweatpants and the outer pouches of his jacket—nothing. But he had another pocket inside his jacket. Valentine slipped his hand into the shallow chest pocket and touched something thin and papery. "Booyah!" he exclaimed as he pulled out a crumpled twenty-dollar bill wadded in his fingers. Surely, that would be enough for something, right? But what if his money wasn't accepted here? Then what?

His sense of isolation and loneliness began to lift as he neared some semblance of civilization. The concept of home and just how far away it probably was began to scare him. His confidence and bravado ebbed away the farther the sun shifted in the sky. *Where exactly am I? And what were those creatures back on the mountain?*

He tossed ideas back and forth, but he just didn't have a clue. Maybe he could ask someone, but truth be told, he wasn't sure he really wanted to know. Going home sounded better and better the more he thought of it. Was following Hanna the best choice?

Speaking of home, what would Olivia say when he didn't come back to the porch? His heart fell in his chest. *What about my parents?* The revelation that he so quickly abandoned them and his whole life in Midtown Valley dropped like a lead football onto his conscience. What were they going to think when he didn't return? But it wasn't only him missing. There were a lot more than that. Ugh. The need for sleep tugged at his eyelids. He wanted sleep—needed sleep—he'd need someplace to stay.

Valentine jogged off the dirt road and into the strip of green crab grass that lined its edge. He surveyed the open expanse of the farm. Behind him stretched miles of cultivated fields, but up near the buildings the fields came to an abrupt end. A collection of structures showed signs of intelligent life.

There was a tall grain silo made of weathered wood. Next to it was a livery stable with a large open door showing a horse and a mule or two inside. An acre or two behind sat a two-story house peeking from behind the stables. A barn a quarter-mile away sat in the shade of some large trees waiting to be explored. Chickens and pigs milled about their pens making his stomach growl. There had to be something to eat around here. He just hoped he could convince whoever owned the property to share. Maybe his twenty-dollar bill could help?

It took him several minutes to cross the field and enter the tall shade of the barn. Finally out of the sun, Valentine gave a sigh of relief. He was sweltering in his jacket but was too anxious to take it off. Valentine didn't want someone noticing the cuff. Above the wide barn doors was a name: LaRoux's Farm. The tall brown wooden letters stood out in stark contrast against the barn's faded red paint.

"Hello?" he called into the barn. "Is anyone there?"

A rustle of hay and the stirring of feet beaconed him into the dimly lit space. His eyes had to adjust to the low light. There were several cows, a horse, and something else he didn't recognize standing in wooden stalls lining either side of the barn. The floor was covered in a thick blanket of hay. Clumps and splatters of something-or-other, maybe poop, coated the main entrance like giant cocoa-bombs.

Valentine could tell just by looking around the area that it was a well-used farm. Rakes and shovels stood in jumbled heaps in the corner. They were covered in dried mud and broken strands of hay. Ropes, shanks, rings, and other harnesses hung in neat rows along the walls. A stack of gray metal buckets sat on a wooden table near the cows.

Several sets of clothes were hung on wires draped between crooked, rusty nails. Dingy brown shirts hung limp and drying. Two were wearable and relatively clean, the third appeared only recently washed. Below the shirts and next to the buckets perched a short stack of brown pants folded neatly on the table.

A round canteen sat propped against a small sack of mixed vegetables. He licked his dried lips and rushed forward, snatching it up. Unscrewing the cap, he lifted the container to his nose and sniffed. It had no smell, but when he jiggled it, something wet sloshed inside.

Valentine took a tentative swig. It was wonderful. It was warm. It tasted like tin, but it was water all the same. He took another long tug on the canteen and sighed. He couldn't remember the last time he had something to drink. With his thirst quenched, he called out a second time, but again, no one answered. He looked around the barn once more. A spilled sack of dirty carrots, a few apples, and other veggies on the table caught his eye. *Were those for the animals? Taking a swig of water is one thing, but stealing food is another.*

His stomach growled as he looked out the far end of the barn through the open set of wide double doors. Not a single person was in sight. Valentine took a deep breath and glanced at a red apple peeking out from between what could be two potatoes. *It's just some veggies. And this is a farm. No one would miss a sack of animal food on a farm, right? What's the harm?*

He wrestled with the thought of stealing for a moment before pangs of hunger made up his mind for him. Valentine snatched the small brown burlap sack of unwashed fruit and vegetables and walked into the nearest vacant stall. Like the rest of the barn, the floor was covered with hay. It was empty except for a stool and metal bucket. He pressed his back against the wooden wall and slid to the ground. Diving his hand into the sack, he pulled out the fattest apple he'd ever seen. Valentine was halfway through the sack of food when a renewed thought struck him.

What if I don't fit in here? He didn't want to be a magnet for attention, if he could help it. Leaving the burlap sack in the hay, Valentine stripped the wires clean of the dry shirts on the wall. Taking the pants for good measure, he returned to the empty stall and held the clothes up to his body to gage which ones fit best when voices floated his way. He froze, crouched down in the stall so that he was hidden from view, and waited.

A soft-spoken female voice said, "I don't think you should do it. Not with what they said last time."

"I care nothing for the Brotherhood," a deep, gritty voice replied. "Their band of vagabonds and thieves hold no sway on my farm."

"You speak with bravado now, but when your farm, your houses, our jobs and everything you own is burned to the ground, then what? What will all that bravado do for you then?"

"Look, Shalini, I built this farm from nothing. If I give in to the Brotherhood's demands, then I've given up everything I stand for and everything I believe in."

The voices grew louder. Closer. Valentine peeked around the corner of the stall, but the strangers were still blocked from view.

"Is it really worth it?" asked Shalini. "All the other farms in the valley have surrendered their livestock to them. Is selling the horses to the city of Thole rather than giving them to the Brotherhood really worth that much to you?"

The voices were so loud now that they had to be inside the barn.

"If I give in, it'll make them that much stronger. It will embolden them to continue their reign of—"

"Who cares?" interrupted Shalini. "They're just horses."

"It's more than the money. I'd be giving up part of myself if I cowed to them."

"You might just lose everything in your gamble."

Valentine poked his head around the edge of the stall, but their faces were out of view.

"The Brotherhood may end up taking my horses, my farm, but they can't take my soul. If I went belly up and gave them everything, that's what I'd be doing. I'd be giving them my soul and I can't do that."

"If they have a SoulStone, they may take that too, LaRoux. If you don't bend to the Brotherhood, it may be the end of everything for you. And everyone here. You've heard how they are—you know the rumors. Everyone on this farm is counting on you to make the right decision!"

Valentine reflexively crumpled one of the pairs of pants and shirt in his hand as they stepped into view. His jaw fell slack as his eyes opened wide. A ringing filled his ears as a sense of panic robbed him of thought. He tried to move, but his legs wouldn't budge. Valentine felt as if he were walking on stilts.

Before him, not a dozen feet away at the entrance to the barn, was a six-foot tall marbled tabby cat. He was dressed in a wide-brimmed cowboy hat, a midnight-blue T-shirt partially covered by a leather vest, and a pair of chestnut chaps ending just above what looked like alligator-skin boots. Valentine flicked his gaze from the cowboy to the girl. She, too, was far from human. Her skin was covered in a sheet of green scales. A white spaghetti-strap sun dress with a ring of red flowers ending just above her knees covered much of her body, but there was no question that she was reptilian. She reminded him of that other strange man in Hanna's backyard.

H-how can animals talk? And walk like…like humans? Valentine gulped. Regaining movement of his limbs again, he blindly stepped backward and stumbled into something. Tripping over the bucket and stool, he tumbled wildly onto the ground with a clatter of metal and wood.

"What's that—is someone there?" called Shalini.

Valentine stroked his cuff and with a whir of wind, he sprung up from the hay-covered floor and sprinted from the stall. The barn was illuminated in a blue hue. Time around him slowed to almost a crawl. He hoped that as he passed the cowboy and girl he would only be a blur in their vision. By the time he stopped running, the farm was far behind him. His chest heaved and a stitch bit into his side. His lungs burned. Valentine struggled to gather his thoughts as he panted with exhaustion. He tapped his cuff and slowed to a walk.

Could it be true—walking, talking animals? What kind of place is this? He looked behind him just to be sure that he wasn't followed. LaRoux's farm was nowhere to be found—probably miles away by now. Valentine was alone again. Suddenly, something brushed his leg. He looked down to find that it was just the bundle of clothes from the barn. The pants and shirt were still clutched in his fist. In the end, he took more than intended.

Valentine stood in the middle of the country road not having a clue of where to go next. He collected his thoughts and tried to control his breathing. It was hard to do, he thought, because his heart still raced like a herd of stallions. It was funny that he thought of that particular simile given his feelings about the talking animals. They were strange…weird even…and he didn't like them. He wasn't sure why. Was he afraid? Hm. If he was honest with himself, that may have had something to do with it.

Up the dirt road, not fifty feet away, stood a sign at an open intersection. Directions were posted to someplace new. Maybe there was someplace he could stay. A wooden placard hung off one arm pointing to a place called the Crow's Nest. It was in the same direction he'd been traveling since the farm. The sign indicated the nearest place was only five miles away.

A second arm, pointing toward the shifting sun, showed that Castletown was forty miles away. And a third arm pointed to a place called Thole. It was back in the opposite direction. He remembered a conversation from the barn. The cowboy cat, maybe that was LaRoux, wanted to sell his horses to the city of Thole.

Valentine looked to the sky. He would only have several hours of morning remaining. If things progressed as they had, he'd need lodging before the heat of the day was at its highest. Using the power of his magical cuff, Valentine reached the outskirts of the Crow's Nest in a matter of minutes.

A large wooden bridge spanned a wide river running adjacent to town. The bubbling rush of water split the otherwise quiet of the countryside. Following the river with his eyes, Valentine found a series of buildings dotting the shoreline closer to town. Tall water wheels rotated in the flow of the river. Valentine figured they were granaries or mills of some sort.

Beyond the mills, he could see straight up through the main thoroughfare of town. The view was magnificent. Steep, high cliffs cupped each side of the Crow's Nest. Mountain ridges grew from the farmland like blades of stone. The salty tang of sea water stung his tongue the closer to town he walked. The road, which was once dirty and dusty near the bridge, was now paved with cobbled stone leading into the city.

Over the town, a half-a-dozen white albatrosses soared high on thermal drafts. The glint of sunlight glimmered off the seawater in the fjord beyond the Crow's Nest. It drew Valentine's attention to a shadowy high tower standing like a slender, crooked finger at the far edge of town.

The first sign of people sent a tingle of anxiety down his stomach. Would there be more strange people here, too? Walking up the center of the town's main street, Valentine stared wide-eyed at everyone. His breath caught in his throat. Valentine's worst fears were realized. Walking, talking animals were everywhere. Dog people, cat people, more lizards, and even some sort of bovine.

In some twist of irony, he stared for a moment at two little children running through the street after their pet. A small, mangy mutt raced across the cobbled street followed by a boy and girl—except they weren't normal, not in his way of thinking. The boy's floppy ears flapped over his shoulder as he chased the dog. His brown coat and long snout gave Valentine the impression of a Cocker Spaniel. The boy, dressed in pressed black pants and an ironed shirt, was followed by a smaller poodle-like girl. Her knee-length sun dress, which was the color of golden Marigolds, swished behind her as she chased the real puppy to the opposite sidewalk.

The deeper he walked into the center of town, the more his gut clenched. Although strangers mingled along storefronts minding their own business or j-walking away from him across the street, with every new person, his chest tightened until he struggled to breathe. His mind was caught in a fog—he couldn't think straight. The only thing he wanted to do was flee, but his legs again betrayed him.

Valentine stumbled to the edge of the stony street and gripped a wooden pillar holding up the front awning to a store. Looking up to the sign above the door, he read: Marty's General Store. He tried to force his legs to move. Valentine wanted to escape the busy sidewalk and enter the safety of the building, but there was nowhere to go. A man covered in a burnt auburn fur coat and wearing deep blue overalls blocked his way inside. The man stared back at him and made a move toward Valentine as if to touch his shoulder. Startled by the gesture, Valentine reflexively pulled back. "Don't touch me."

He turned from the porch toward the open street and passed a woman pushing a baby stroller. His eyes swelled as she walked by. Both she and the baby were covered in a fine downy coat of marbled brown feathers. The woman hustled past, looking back over her shoulder. Staggering on his feet, Valentine dodged out of view into an alley along the side of Marty's storefront. *This can't be happening! Animals don't dress up like this!*

Valentine stumbled down the alley clutching his jersey. His chest heaved in spastic spurts as he tried to regain some sense of normalcy. His cheeks grew hot as a rush of heat splashed up his neck. He fell and thumped his back against the dirty alley wall. Panting, he slid down it and rested his butt on the hard ground. Safe from view, Valentine remained nestled between several tall wooden barrels and a stack of discarded boxes.

Catch your breath. Just breathe—breathe. His wave of anxiety slowly ebbed away. He closed his eyes and pinched the bridge of his nose trying to force himself to relax. *In through the nose and out through the mouth. Breathe. Breathe.* Pinching his eyes shut, Valentine pushed all thought of walking, talking animals from his mind and drew in calm, even breaths until something startled him.

"Oomph!" came a sudden grunt from somewhere behind the alley.

"Thought you could get away with not paying your protection fees?" came a gruff voice.

"No, no! It's not like that! Oomph!"

"Oy, mate. Are 'ye deaf? Did 'ye not hear what we said?" snapped a third voice.

Valentine sat frozen for a moment, then shifted turning toward the voices. Through a slender gap between the barrels, he spied two figures. One big guy and a smaller person hovering over a third. The last one was cowering on the ground. The two standing up wore some sort of leather jerkin and armored pads down their legs. Valentine squinted to get a better look and then his eyes widened in excitement. On the ground, not twenty feet from him, was a man—a normal-looking man. Valentine's head buzzed. He wasn't alone in this place! There were more like him.

"We came for payment yesterday and you left the Brotherhood high and dry," said the big figure with horns.

"I-I—It's not like that," said the man on the ground. He held out his arm as if it could protect his face. "It was my day off." He cringed almost expecting another blow. "I didn't work—I didn't work yesterday!" The smaller thug, who had what looked like a thick, whip-like tail, kicked the man in the gut. "Oomph!"

"Pay day is pay day, mate! We don't give a hoot when you is or ain't workin'."

Valentine's fear slowly bubbled into anger. *What is going on here? What exactly am I seeing?*

"Wait…please…" pleaded the man on the ground as he struggled to get to his feet.

"We ain't got no patience for this." The smaller one looked at his partner. "Break his arm."

"No, no! No, please, no!" The guy scrambled back on his hands and feet as if he were a crab. "I've got your money! I'VE GOT IT—I'VE GOT IT!" He crawled across the cobbled, back-alley pavement just out of Valentine's view. "H-here, take it!"

The *clink* of coins echoed off the walls and the smaller man reached forward. He disappeared out of Valentine's view for a moment before straightening back up with a small sack in his hand—it was a shakedown. The two thugs turned away laughing to each other. The man cowered alone in the shadows. As the thugs strode past Valentine's hiding spot, he gulped. The larger of the two was part bull. The second, mottled with brown and red scales, was like Shalini—some sort of a bearded lizard.

He couldn't let this happen. This was wrong. Animals don't beat up people. Valentine had to do something. But the question was, what? Before the thugs reached the mouth of the alley, he sprung to his feet. With a quick flick of his cuff, the air about the cramped space changed—a blue hue infused the light of day and everything slowed to a crawl. Everything except him.

In a blur of motion, Valentine bum-rushed the Brotherhood from behind. He clipped the bull's knees and sent the lizard flying into the alley wall. As he passed their falling bodies, Valentine stripped the sack from the lizard's grasp. Before they hit the ground, Valentine zipped away, disappearing up the busy street.

He slipped into a shop and ducked behind some curtains. From his hiding spot, Valentine peered out the front window. *I did it! I can't believe I did it! Are they following?* He searched the busy street for any sign of them. A few heartbeats later, the bull and lizard skulked up the busy sidewalk scanning the faces of people as they went. Valentine ducked low so only his eyes peeked over the lip of the window. His gaze followed the Brotherhood as they searched the streets for him. *They'll never find me and certainly never catch me.*

When they walked past his hiding spot, Valentine let out a trapped breath. "Oh my god—that was awesome," he whispered. His heart pounded like a percussion drum. Switching to the other side of the windowpane, he watched the thug's backs disappear up the road and fade into the crowd.

Valentine exited the store and strolled with almost a cocky

stride back down the block to Marty's General Store. On the other side of the alley, stood a saloon pouring loud music out its front doors. The name stamped into a wooden sign above the place read: Marty's Place. *Marty's got a saloon and a store?*

He glanced over his shoulder ensuring the coast was clear. No problems in sight. Valentine walked to the rear of the store. He found the man on the back porch with his chin resting in his hands. "Are you okay?" It looked as if the man was lost in a daze. Valentine held out the small burlap sack. "I got this for you."

The man, whose hair was in a tousled mess, looked up at him dumbfounded. His close-shaven black beard was smeared with streaks of blood which dribbled from his lip onto his white cottony shirt. "W-what—what did you say?"

"I got this for you. I saw what happened. I saw what they did. And—"

"Y-you shouldn't've done that!" His voice grew angry. "That's not yours to take."

Surprised, Valentine tossed the sack down onto the porch with a metallic *clink*. "Whatever, dude. I just wanted to help."

The man frowned, at first, and then pulled the bag closer. "They'll be looking for you."

Valentine shrugged. "Doesn't matter." The man eyed him as if he'd just said the stupidest thing or maybe because Valentine looked like a complete hobo. Valentine looked at his own clothes and wiped dirt from his chest and belly.

"The name's Devereaux—Gilles Devereaux." The guy stood on unsteady feet and offered his hand. "Look, it's not that I'm not glad to have my money back. I-it's just…these guys…the Brotherhood, they'll be back and more angry than before."

"I just saved that—"

"No good deed is left unpunished," Gilles cut across him. "It's not that I'm not thankful—"

"Shugh, yeah, it sure seems that way," Valentine snapped. "Should've kept the money for myself, if this is the thanks I get."

"Is there anything I can do for you? These guys are bound to be back looking for their tribute."

"They're long gone. I saw them leave toward the other end of town." Valentine licked his lips and cast a sideways glance into the back room of the shop. "I am starving, though. And I'm looking for a place to stay for the night. Maybe longer?"

"I run Marty's General Store in the Crow's Nest. Let me set you up with some food, at least. Plus, I own a hunting cottage not far from here." Gilles pointed over Valentine's shoulder. "It's out of town on the way toward Thole, near Mermaid Bay. You can stay there for a while. I'm not using it right now."

"That sounds great."

"Step inside. I'll draw you a map and grab some food. You're going to need to lay low for a while, though. There's bound to be a price on your head, so you can't stay here—they're sure to return."

Valentine shook his head as he stepped through the back door of the shop. He was sure the thugs were long gone, but he wasn't in the mood to repeat himself.

The torches along the storage room walls flickered in the breeze from the open door. Gilles grabbed glass canisters of raisin & date custard, boxes of spiced cakes, and jars of bread and butter pudding. He stuffed them into a burlap sack. "You look horrible. When was the last time you ate?"

Valentine shrugged. "This morning…" and then he remembered that he'd walked all night long and the fruit and vegetables from the farm really didn't count as a meal as far as he was concerned. "Yesterday sometime," he corrected himself. "Maybe an early lunch, but that seems like ages ago."

"How about some dried mutton or canisters of jellied eels?"

"Ah…I've never tried eel…"

"Hm…okay. How about some jerky, then? I've got strips of marinated venison and snipe."

"Jerky sounds great, thanks."

After hastily packing the bag of food, Gilles scribbled a hand-drawn map and handed them both to Valentine. "Thanks again, but you'd better be off before more trouble comes looking for you."

"No prob," he replied straightening his varsity jacket. As he did so, Gilles's eyes flicked to his wrist. Valentine glanced down. The cuff was poking out from under his sleeve. "Well," he said taking the sack and stuffing the map into his sweatpants pocket. "Thanks for the food and the cottage."

As he turned to leave, a large shadow fell over him. A bull with horns wider than the doorway blocked his passage.

28

A TIME FOR CELEBRATION

Hanna stepped out of the portal with her friends and into a sand-covered furnace. People of all shapes, sizes, and species milled about a street fair. A blanched city made of sun-caked mud and stone stretched to the west as far as she could see. Unlike the Salthouse Wharf, Breakwater was filled with the raucous laughter of playing children. Several large unlit bonfires were built not far off. They sat like oversized matchstick teepees.

Ashley cupped her hands to her mouth and shouted over the roar of entertainment. She pointed in amazement to a throng of musicians, performers, and acrobats dancing in the streets. Men on stilts were dressed in flamboyant pink outfits. Animal trainers paraded a line of dwarf ponies down the middle of the street stopping every now and then to give another child a ride. A man led a miniature dragon past a group of children. Gouts of flame erupted from the creature's mouth into the late morning sky.

The professor smiled wide and spread out his arms. "This is the Peasant's Moon Festi—"

"Hey! 'Ya smell that?" Michael asked.

Hanna lifted her nose in the air and sniffed the sweet

fragrance of grilled meats. "We can eat later—still gotta get to my sister."

"Follow me." Alexander stepped in front of the group giving Michael a pointed look. "Lexi's not far away." He led Hanna and her friends through the market's main square.

"What are the bonfires for?" asked Patrick.

The professor turned as he passed a fourteen-foot-tall grouping of logs steepled together. "They launch this evening's celebrations with a bang. Small powder kegs and hand-held fireworks are a rampant display of entertainment during the Peasant's Moon Festival."

"Wait, I thought I heard someone say that gunpowder was outlawed because of some treaty or ordinance or something?"

"That's right, but many people don't follow the king's ordinances—not during the festival. It's their one time of the year to express their happiness and displeasure in such a public forum."

"Displeasure? Why would they be unhappy?" asked Ashley.

"Many of the people across Manna are frustrated with the royal family and the absence of the king."

"So, that can change? The people can be happy again now that he's back?"

"What? Who's back?" Alexander frowned, his gaze dancing from Ashley to the others.

Ashley smiled. "He's back. And the queen, too. We saw them in Hemlock Castle."

"Kambo's Mercy! That's great news!" he exclaimed throwing his hands up high into the air.

Hanna told the professor what he missed in the throne room. As they continued to the far side of the square, the vendor stalls selling meat pies and fried fritters finally thinned out. They gave way to rows of bungalows and small cottages about the time where the sand covered the road. Alexander pointed through a gap in the homes toward the beach. "My friends live in the last two houses on the shore. Lexi's with Hugo, so look for the blue one."

Hanna kicked up sand from her heels as she raced through the last rows of cottages. "Lexi!" she shouted. "Are you there?"

"Hanna?" came a muffled shout from inside a bungalow at the end. "Hanna, is that you?!"

Hanna burst through the bamboo door and wrapped her arms around Lexi in a tight hug. "Oh my—You're really here! You're alive! Are you alright?" She held Lexi at arm's length to give her sister a good look.

"Yeah, I'm okay." Lexi wriggled free as the others reached the porch. She pulled away from Hanna and lunged for Patrick, her arms open wide as he cleared the top step. Lexi folded her arms around him and pressed her cheek against his neck.

"Thought we'd never find you," Patrick whispered flicking his eyes toward Hanna.

Another tinge of jealously wriggled in Hanna's gut. But she pushed away the sour feelings in favor of seeing her sister alive and happy. She glanced toward the porch's door and her eyes widened. A familiar tall, blue hippo—now wearing a white T-shirt and a pair of bright orange shorts spotted with white flowers—strode through the door. Hugo draped his thick arm over Lexi's shoulders creating a natural wedge between her and Patrick.

"You found her?" Hanna asked. "I can't believe it! How?!"

Hugo nodded solemnly and pointed over his shoulder across the lagoon. Right as he opened his mouth to say something, a second hippo stepped through the door. This one was light pink wearing a matching white polka-dotted dress. As the newcomer stepped to the side of Hugo, a flash of movement caught Hanna's attention. Peeking out from behind the pink hippo was a green lizard wearing an old, patched, denim dress.

Hugo smiled a wide two-toothed grin. "This is my little sister, Kimberly. And that," he pointed to the older woman, "is our friend, Paula."

The professor waved. "Hanna, you and your sisters owe Hugo a great thanks."

She fumbled nervously with the ring around her thumb and pressed out a smile. Hanna wanted to hug Hugo, but everyone was in the way. "Thank you so much. How *did* you find Lexi, though? I mean, it's just incredible!"

"It was cause of this." Hugo stretched out his hand. "I realized after finding Lexi that this must've been yours."

"My phone?!" Hanna gasped. "Where—how'd you get that?"

"Is that what this is called—a phone? Fascinating device. Your sister's a lucky girl that I found that thing. It was in the lawn in front of the professor's lab. It saved Lexi's life."

"What? How?"

"When I picked it up, I didn't know what it was, or whose it was, for that matter. I'd never seen one before. But when it rang, I figured out how to answer it, and your sister's panicked voice was on the other end."

Hanna finally wrapped her arms around Hugo's wide belly in spite of the others. "Thank you so much!"

"Hey, yeah. I couldn't not help, you know? I left the lab through the portal and sprinted all the way through the market to the bayou—found your sister and Paula in Devil's Grotto on the far side of the lagoon."

"Devil's Grotto?!" spat Lexi. "You took me through a cave called the Devil's Grotto?"

Paula smirked sheepishly. "Well, we done made it out."

"Hugo arrived not a moment too late, I might add," said the professor. "We all got very lucky."

Hanna stepped toward to Lexi. "How'd you know where to look?"

"It was the only place I could think of where there'd be a dangerous cave near Paula. And she's the only Paula I know. I took a gamble and it paid off."

"It was an amazing rescue," added Alexander.

Hanna's head spun in his direction as her face crumpled in a look of confusion. "Rescue? What do you mean? I thought you just found her? What happened?"

"Nothing…really," Lexi said with a shrug.

"Ya almost died, dats what," said Paula.

Lexi scrunched up her face. "Naw, it was nothing like that."

Paula looked at Lexi over her wide nose. "Dat ain't da story I saw. Firstly 'ya almost died in dat sandstorm 'ya done did."

"What?!" spat Hanna. "What sandstorm?"

Paula ignored their questions. "Secondly, 'ya almost died in dat cave. Of course, twas mostly my fault, but still."

Hanna threw her arms up in disbelief. "You almost died *twice?!*" Lexi let out a huff, but Hanna wasn't having it. "When you didn't come through the portal from Midtown Valley, I was scared to death. Seriously, what happened to you when you didn't come after us?"

Lexi inhaled a deep breath. "When I followed you through the portal—you weren't there. One second I was following Ashley and then the next I was in the middle of a stupid desert."

"Is that when—" Hanna pointed to Paula. "That's when she saved you?"

Paula shook her head. "Da girl saved herself from da storm, but I did a little of dis and dat along the way. 'Ole Paula's happy ta help. You be safe out dare now, kay? Paula be watching you." She winked at Lexi before turning and striding off the porch. "Twas nice meeting ya'll, but 'ole Paula's got ta go to da market. Seems I got ta buy me a new boat."

A hurt look crossed Lexi's face. "You're not leaving already? Not when my friends just got here."

"Sorry luv. I'll see 'ya round. Manna may seem big at first. We rub elbows again. I's sure of it." Before Paula could take two steps off the patio steps, Lexi raced across the deck wrapping her arms tightly around the green woman's waist. The patchwork dress wrinkled with her hug. "You's a good girl. Paula know what I know." The woman looked to Hanna with a toothless grin. "Keep dis one outta trouble, kay?" She peeled Lexi's hands from around her waist and with a wave soon disappeared between the colorful rows of cottages.

When Lexi talked next, a tremor threaded her voice. "Did you know—" She cleared her throat. "Did you know she's a pirate? Whole family is—they even have a ship, too!"

"That's bloody awesome." quipped Michael.

Kimberly sucked air through her oversized teeth. "Her kids aren't the sharpest crayons in the box, though. Don't get me wrong," she added quickly, "Paula's nice, but...you can't trust her kids."

"I don't care! She helped me when I had no one else." Kim threw her hands up in mock surrender. "Paula took me in. Healed me from the storm."

Hanna creased her brow. "What do you mean healed you?"

Lexi held out her arm. "See the little pricks? Kind of like freckles, but not. Those tiny marks are from little slivers of glass."

Hanna looked in the direction Paula left through the cottages. "She did that? Paula removed the glass?"

Lexi nodded. "That's where I stayed the night, too. With Paula. She has a home on the beach. Don't know what I would've done without her. All I know is I wouldn't be standing here if it weren't for Paula, that's for sure."

A finger of guilt wormed its way through Hanna's gut. "If I'd have known, I would've said more...thanked her...or something..."

Lexi looked from Hanna to Patrick and then Michael. "What happened to you guys? Where'd you go when you stepped through the door-thingy?"

Hanna pointed to Alexander. "We went with the professor. Saw his laboratory—"

"We stayed in a castle!" interrupted Patrick. "They have castles here. Met a princess and was introduced to a court wizard."

"A castle?" Lexi surveyed the group as if trying to gauge whether Patrick was fibbing. "You all stayed in a castle last night?"

Ashley grabbed Patrick's arm and squeezed. "They have magic here. Real magic." She pointed to her arm where she was sliced with the sword. "A wizard healed my arm with only a magic wand."

"Shut-the-front-door!" cried Lexi.

Hugo chuckled. "Wadda 'ya say we swap stories over a Mug-O-Mojo, huh? Anyone game? You guys can tell each other your whole adventures then."

Patrick arched an eyebrow. "What's a Mug-O-Mojo?"

"It's only the best soda in the kingdom! We've got one of Marty's micro-breweries right here in Breakwater."

"I'm game," said Hanna.

"Can we spend some time at the carnival?" asked Lexi. Hanna nodded. "I hear they're getting ready for some kind of Summer Solstice party. Hugo told me that the celebration goes for like a few weeks or something. Is that right?"

"Yup," Hugo said. "Everybody loves a party. Goes for three full weeks and ends at nightfall on the Summer Solstice. It's the most magical night of the year for Smaradine. Do you have a Summer Solstice where you come from?"

Patrick shook his head. "Never heard of it before. We have Christmas and Easter and St. Patrick's Day. Those are based on magical creatures." He widened his eyes. "You're not suggesting…"

Hugo slapped Patrick on the back nearly sending him tumbling forward. "Let's go drown our stories in drink. Marty's got like a million flavors. First round's on me."

The group made their way across the beach and back to the market. They came upon a place where laughter spilled from of a set of swinging, wooden doors. Hanna looked up at the dirty sign dangling above the entrance: Marty's Place. A grin spread across her cheeks as she and the group followed Hugo through the saloon doors. Playful ragtime piano music filled the tavern. Hanna was soon shoulder-to-shoulder with more people than she could count.

Hugo strolled toward the main lounge filled with tables and chairs. "Grab a seat—I'm gonna get a round of suds." As he stepped away to the bar, he pushed himself through the crowded saloon without issue. He was so large, Hugo's whole head was above the rest of the crowd.

"Hey, over there," called Patrick, pointing across the room. "That group is leaving. Quick, before someone else grabs it!"

Ashley made a dash for a large, circular table near a window. She claimed rights to it before anyone else could sit down. The others shuffled about the edge of the newspaper-strewn table to join her grabbing stools for themselves.

Unable to hear her friends over the noise surrounding them, Hanna snagged a yellowed newsprint the color of sawdust and the texture of fine sandpaper. "What's the *Tavern Telegraph*?" she asked, pointing to the thick, black letters titling the page.

The professor grabbed another copy from the center of the table and flipped it open. "It's a back-alley print—has a good readership among the locals."

"Poppycock," snapped Kim. "It's not a back-alley paper—it's *real* news, unlike that made-up stuff in *The Kingdom Chronicle*."

Hanna froze stiff as if splashed by cold water. She'd heard that name before. But where? Where did she hear of the Kingdom Chronicle? She thought about it and after a moment it came to her. It was in the parking lot of her high school. A bleach-white newsprint with the same title spilled from the wooden chest in her truck. How did all that stuff end up where she'd found it? Hanna opened the paper and leafed through several yellowed pages. Reading a few columns, she began to nod her head in agreement. It seemed the town loved their calendar celebrations.

She read an article at the bottom of page three:

The Breakwater Inn is hosting its annual Peasant's Moon barbecue. The year's largest carnival opens at Overlook Park at dawn. Enjoy free libations and half-priced pork sandwiches for all guests who arrive before dusk. A greased pig race is scheduled for all kids under twelve—winner keeps the pig (grease and all). Come for the fireworks display starting at nine o'clock, rain or shine.

She continued on to another clip from the top of page five, but the vibe about the next article was haunting:

The Crimson Brotherhood continues to make inroads into our towns. Their grip is strongest in the towns outside local protection. Reliable sources say politicians at the highest levels are paid off for their silence. Where's the king? Where's the law and order? Why can't the royal family stop one of their own? Do they even want to stop Barlow?

"Who's ready for some suds?" Hugo asked, breaking Hanna's concentration.

Scooting behind her chair, he carried a dozen mugs of Marty's Mug-O-Mojo. They were all lined up on a long, two-by-four plank of wood. He rested the makeshift tray on the table and everyone snatched up the nearest glass of frothy drink.

"This is delicious," said Hanna, wiping a foamy mustache from her upper lip.

Hugo raised his own mug in the air. "To our new friends—I salute you!"

As they raised their arms in unison, a scent wafted through the air and the corner of Hanna's mouth curled. "What's that smell?"

The whole table paused and sniffed.

Hugo licked his lips and stood. "Oh, I know where that's coming from! Let's get some chow."

"We're leaving already?" said Ashley. "But we just got here."

"Ain't you hungry?" replied Michael. "Surprised you couldn't hear my stomach growl."

He drank the rest of his Mojo and followed it up with the most enormous belch Hanna ever heard. The crowd around them erupted in cheers. Everyone at the table downed their own before following Hugo to the front porch.

29

THE PENDANT'S SECRET

Hanna exited the saloon doors and stood next to her sisters on the porch of Marty's Place. The glow of the sign in the window illuminated her back in a bright pink hue. With Lexi at her side once again, she stood next to both her sisters and was happier than she'd been in a long while. "Is that grilled pork I smell?"

"That's Dutch's barbecue," corrected Hugo. "The best butcher this side of Cog." He swiped his large tongue across his lips and stepped into the unpaved street. "Follow me."

"Wanna know a secret?" asked Kim, bending toward the girls. "Dutch's wife runs the local apothecary—waddaya think of that?"

Ashley shared a quick glance with her sisters. She then looked back to Kim as they passed several storefronts along the block. "What's an apothecary?"

"It's a store of medicines. But I think it's really a front for a black market underground herbal trade."

"Don't listen to her," Hugo cut in apparently having overheard. He waved off his sister's accusations. "Kim went vegan a few years ago and has something to say about meat-eaters everywhere she goes. So what if his wife dabbles in magical herbs?"

A few more paces and they stopped outside a local greasy spoon. A big sign over their heads said: The Dutch Touch. "The hard fact is magic is a pretty special thing—not everyone has it. You can't just go popping off spells hither and dale. Gotta have a permit. Issued by the royal family. Otherwise, it's illegal. It's a serious offense since Barlow went bad."

Hanna licked her lips at the scent of spiced, meat pies and fried fritters. Her stomach rumbled. With all the excitement, food had been the last thing on her mind. It'd been hours since her last meal and she left breakfast early to follow Crowthorn to the Royal Hall. A man leaned out a window to the street. His long, handlebar mustache hung nearly to the counter.

"Hey, Dutch," said Hugo with a wave. "We'll take two dozen fritters and a spiced pie for each of my new friends."

"That'll be six tara and three kobbers," replied the mustachioed man with a tip of his cowboy hat.

Hugo tossed seven silver coins on the counter. "Keep the change."

The group sat at some outdoor tables near The Dutch Touch and close enough to the center of the square to see the fair. Hanna hadn't realized how hungry she was until her meat pie was already half gone. She licked the juice from her left hand and watched the others. Her friends and sisters were all together again and, in her opinion, it was a moment to celebrate.

Before Hugo finished his eighth fritter, a thunderous rumble rolled across the heavens. Hanna swallowed her last bite of spiced pie. She glanced up at the sky as a bank of muddy clouds crept from the northeast blotting out the remaining blue above Breakwater. In the distance over the desert, flashes of lightning lit the clouds. The crack and roll of thunder echoed against the tall coral cliffs around the lagoon. A small, dirty smudge appeared low on the northern horizon.

"Is that a plane—or something?" asked Hanna.

Patrick scrunched up his brows and held a hand over the

ridge of his eyes staring out over the desert. "I don't think they have airplanes here. That…that's something else entirely."

Hanna frowned wincing and grabbing her new scar. A knot twisted in the pit of her stomach as her raven brand burned as if freshly made. Her heart thumped wildly against her sternum. She knew who was coming even before a shriek echoed through the market. "Barlow!"

The place erupted into a frenzy. People scattered everywhere. They fled in every direction. Food and drink splattered the cobbled streets. The portal spawned to life in the middle of the square. A gout of men of all different species spilled from the rift. It was a parade of ramshackle brutes dressed in jerkins of boiled leather and plates of padded greaves. At least two dozen creatures—some of which included a bull, a pack of wolves, and several humans—raced into the market. Their swords were drawn and they surrounded whomever remained.

"Barlow and the Brotherhood," whispered Alexander. "This…this isn't good."

They were cornered. The man who needed no introduction floated from the sky to the center of the square. His wavy curls of ebony hair blew across his forehead as he defied gravity. The King of Thieves levitated twelve feet off the ground. Barlow was dressed in a jumpsuit of ivory-white silk with a flowing crimson cape. Even from a distance, he was a handsome man—until he turned in their direction.

The left-half of his face was covered in a thick lamb chop sideburn. The right-half, however, was a scarred mess of bright pink skin. Most of his jet-black hair above his right ear was burned to the scalp. The entire side of his head and face looked like a wrinkled slab of ham; scarred peaks and puckered valleys made by intense heat. And a deep cleft in his face stretched from the boney ridge above his right eye to the middle of his ruined cheek.

Cries carried across the market. Townsfolk huddled in clusters of three and four. It was a fruitless effort to protect themselves by sheer numbers alone. Barlow's henchmen strode freely amongst them.

"So that's where Elvis went," whispered Lexi.

"Shut-up," Hanna hissed through clenched teeth.

A team of four horsemen stood sentinel behind Barlow. The riders were shrouded in thick, black capes that draped their bodies like weathered wool ponchos. Each of their faces was hidden under the shadow of a long cowl. Their steeds ran the gambit from healthy to horrible. The first figure rode a massive beast whose muscles rippled under its pearl-white coat. The next two were nothing special aside from one boasting a shiny coat of burnt crimson and the other one of midnight black.

The last horse, however—if you could even call it one—was the sickly, pale color of curdled milk. The creature's ribs pressed against its skin like the bent teeth of an old comb. Its skin hung loose as if it were draped over them like a bone hanger. Its rider bowed the beast's back as the creature's belly sagged toward the ground.

Barlow held up a hand with several fingers coated in rings. The square went stone quiet. That was the moment Hanna knew they were on their own. Nobody was coming to save them. Hanna's stomach curdled and the pungent taste of bile crept up the back of her throat.

"I am Prince Bartholomew," he announced. A wicked grin spread up one side of his mouth. "But you may call me Barlow. I'm sure most of Breakwater already knows me. Today I'm addressing our new guests. I welcome them to our kingdom— *my* kingdom. Let me introduce you to them."

I know you're here. Barlow's burly voice echoed through Hanna's head.

He scanned the crowd. Had he not noticed her yet? Hanna peeked over her shoulder and down the alleyway next to Dutch's place for an exit. The raven-shaped scar on her arm prickled with heat. She bit back a hiss as she frantically searched for a way out. Hanna couldn't help notice everyone's fear. It rolled off them thick enough to almost touch. Many were cowed by Barlow's presence. Most stared at the ground or shielded the faces of their children. But a select few stared defiantly at the prince instead.

Two dozen feet away, on the other side of the square, a wolf larger than any canine she'd ever seen walked upright amongst the crowd. He was dressed in chainmail and boiled leather. Without notice, he thrust a wooden staff into a man's gut. The man buckled over holding an infant to his chest. The baby's cry split the muffled quiet of the square as the man fell to his knees. The wolf's mouth moved, but Hanna was too far away to hear his words.

That's got to be Grit. One's the anvil and the other's the hammer. So, where's the other one?

It'll be better if you just come forward before things turn ugly, purred the voice in her head.

Barlow's Brotherhood continued to weave themselves into the crowd. Hanna's breathing quickened as she watched the bravery of a young woman erode into a trembling panic. The henchmen expanded through the crowd like a dense fog. They pulled back the sleeves of every young woman in the crowd examining their right arm. She glanced at the brand below her elbow and tucked her arm behind her back.

An elephant picked up an entire food stall and pitched it across the square. The cart crashed into another stall directly behind them. Smashed fruits and ruined vegetables flew everywhere. A tiny piglet in a yellow sun dress scurried through the crowd crying and disappeared behind a familiar toothless, green gecko in a patchwork denim dress.

"Ah," Barlow sighed from behind Hanna. "I've finally found you."

Hanna whirled and stared up at Barlow's half-disfigured face. "Leave us alone!" she hissed through gritted teeth.

"It's so nice for you to have brought the whole family." He pointed to Lexi and Ashley.

"When the king finds out that—"

"The king is gone," snarled Barlow.

"He's back! The king is back. I've seen him with my own eyes! And when—"

"Even if what you say is true, the king can do nothing to stop me!"

"Leave us alone! We've never done anything to you…"

"No, but your father has!" Barlow's face grew red as the veins in his neck stood out like cords.

"That's impossible!" Hanna yelled back. "YOU DON'T KNOW WHAT YOU'RE TALKING ABOUT!"

"He should've finished me off when he had the chance!" Spittle flew from Barlow's lips, his face a deep shade of pomegranate. "You and your sisters will be mine and soon I'll rule Smaradine!"

"What do you want from us?" Ashley asked cowering behind Hanna.

"What do I want?" he repeated. Barlow feigned a look of surprise and lowered his voice. "It's so nice of you to ask. I only want the cooperation of the Princesses of Ba'Noor."

Hanna creased her eyebrows together. "What are you talking about? You're not making sense."

"I want your whole family, of course. Your father—"

"My father has nothing to do with his! I already told you that."

"Oh, but your father has *everything* to do with this. Your father and I go way back—"

"YOU KNOW NOTHING OF MY FATHER!"

Barlow stroked his single mutton-chop sideburn with the back of his knuckles. "Au contraire—I know everything, my dear. It is *you* who know nothing." The scarred side of his face remained taught and rigid. As he spoke, the right side of his mouth barely opened causing him to sound as if he had cotton stuffed in his cheeks.

He spread his arms wide in a gesture to accompany everything around him. "These fine people can attest to my knowing your father—The God of Light." Barlow scrunched up his face. "Kambo was a God, but your mother, not so much. That still makes you and your sisters powerful in your own rights. A power that I will take for my own."

"WHAT ARE YOU TALKING ABOUT?" she screamed. A God? What is he saying? That couldn't be true. But the conversation she'd had with Golinveaux tugged on her brain. She thought of all the miraculous things that've happened to her today, and like a puzzle piece, everything clicked into place. God of Light. But if that were true, why didn't her father ever tell any of them?

Barlow snickered. "It's laughable that you've never realized what or who you are."

Hanna looked to her sisters. She then passed a slow glance to the people in the square. Every one of them stared back as murmurs flittered through the crowd.

Despite her confusion, a swell of courage and confidence bubbled in her chest. "A demigod," she whispered under her breath. "I'm a demigod?" Hanna glanced at the ring wrapped around her thumb and studied the strange, foreign glyphs stamped upon the band. Images and events swam in her memory. Her metal locker door crumbling under her weight; the birthmark on her right palm; the bright, white glow from her hands in the snow storm; her finger miraculously healing after being crushed in Michael's bike chain.

Barlow descended to the ground and stood a few feet from her face. "Why don't we stop playing games and start by having you hand over *my* ring, hm?"

Hanna's gut curled. *His* ring? Of course, he knew about the ring. He'd cursed it after all, branded her, and used it to track her to this very market. She instinctively covered the scar with her other hand. Hanna touched her scar and rubbed it with her thumb as if trying to scrub away a smudge of dirt. Michael flicked his eyes to his own scarred arm and covered his matching brand. Hanna then absentmindedly clutched her blue, crystal pendant.

"It took fourteen long years for you to finally invoke the curse I put on it. But the time has finally—" Barlow halted his speech and followed her hand with his eyes. "What's that around your neck?" He stretched out his arm and beckoned with his hand. "Come to me, girl." Against her will, she was swept up in a cushion of air and pulled toward the prince. Hanna struggled against the current, but nothing stopped her from landing exactly where Barlow wanted her. "This…this amulet. I can feel a power radiate within me." Hanna curled her lip. "I thought it was lost forever, but you've had it all this time?" Barlow reached for the pendant with a lopsided grin. "You have no idea of the power you hold, child."

The moment Barlow's fingers grazed Hanna's neck, her mind drowned in a flood of images. That moment seemed to stretch for hours. She became lost in a cloud of memories that were not her own. A towering, cobalt-blue figure was locked in a magical battle with Barlow. The man was larger than Crowthorn or anyone else she had ever seen.

"*If I die,*" said the enormous man, "*there will be no saving the six realms from Fe'Mal. My sister will devastate Smaradine and each of the realms in my absence. The Dark Queen will consume everything!*"

In her mind's eye, Barlow raised a ringed hand. "*I'll take care of her the same way I'll finish you. Your children are being rounded up and killed as we speak.*"

The images faded and when Hanna came to, she lay on her back in the middle of the street. Faded echoes of Barlow's voice remained in her head like an oily smear.

"GET AWAY FROM ME!" she screamed. Hanna clutched her forehead and rose up on shaky feet.

"Did you see that?!" shouted someone from the crowd.

"He touched her and they were blown apart. She *is* Kambo's daughter!"

"They're back! They're back! Kambo's daughters are back!" hollered another voice.

Across the square, Barlow lay sprawled in the sand. The prince pushed himself up on one arm and knelt on shaky knees. He brushed his fingers over the scar that smeared half his face. "I need that crystal," he sneered. "I'll peel that ring and pendant from your dead body—I've divined it!"

At that moment, some villagers fled the square. They slipped away while the Brotherhood was distracted. But most remained. She wasn't sure if it was out of fear or for the excitement of a sideshow attraction.

Suddenly, a pair of crimson eyes glowed like tiny embers from a skull ring wrapped around one of Barlow's fingers. A beam of rusty crimson light shot out from the band. The glow swirled, snaking across the ground and wrapped around Lexi and Ashley like a physical cocoon.

"No more games!" Barlow boomed. "You've got five seconds to decide which of your sisters dies."

"LEAVE THEM ALONE!" Hanna shouted.

"Five. Four. Three—" Before he reached the count of two, her sisters screamed.

Ashley buckled to the ground as a strange aura swirled around them. Something flowed from her and Lexi and into Barlow. It was as if he were siphoning something from them.

"Stop it! Stop it!" Hanna cried.

A grim smirk crept up the soft half of Barlow's face. "You failed to choose, so I'll kill them both."

Hanna's head throbbed. It took all she could to focus. Double vision swam in her eyes. She pressed the heels of her hands to her face and strained to stitch the images into one. A fiery warmth spread from the pit of her stomach—a new rage roiled within her.

"NOBODY HURTS MY SISTERS!" she screamed. Hanna focused all her anger, all her guilt, all her fear at Barlow. She balled up her fists, her fingernails biting four crescent moons into the meaty flesh of both palms.

The prince cackled and levitated the girls five feet into the air. "I've waited a long, long time for this day. The day I finally rule Smara—"

Hanna shrieked at the top of her lungs, "LET THEM GO!" The hair on the back of her neck stood on end as a bundle of nerves tickled the nape. The sensation bolted down her arm leaving an odd trail of goose bumps. A tingling like butterflies settled in her fingers.

The ground below Barlow's feet rumbled. The sandy road split and large stone spires thrust upward from the earth like pistons of thick, marbled granite. The prince rocketed backward trying to dodge the assault, and tumbled instead across the gaping ground.

Hanna creased her brows in confusion when Michael mimicked her hand motions. *What is he doing?* She unclenched her fists and wiped at the sweat trickling down her temples. Her gaze traveled from the shafts of rock, which stood like monuments of triumph, to the ring around her thumb.

Patrick's mouth dropped open. Michael stared in awe at the columns of stone. "Bloody hell. I wanna do that!"

The next Hanna looked, Ashley and Lexi dropped to the ground. They lay huddled together not far from where she stood. She rushed to their side taking her arm to cover a cut on Lexi's shoulder.

Barlow climbed back to his feet. "No one leaves here alive!" Turning to the sickest of his four horsemen, he yelled, "Death Bringer—ride and deliver pestilence!"

Before anyone could respond, the eyes of the horse who's back bowed like warm licorice blazed with a fiery glow. He galloped into the gasping crowd. The Death Bringer swung a makeshift morning star from the end of a long chain above his head in great sweeping circles. An ugly, green fog leaked from holes and spread across the open market.

The crippled horse carried its dark rider with ease through the village square. The wind carried the green haze and engulfed everything in sight. It filled the plaza and choked the beachfront homes. The square erupted in pandemonium. The onlookers lining the streets tried to escape in droves.

A small, milky-white creature, no larger than the gnomes Hanna saw in the Wharf, darted into the market's clearing on a pair of translucent, turquoise wings. "Quick—come to me!" she said to Hanna. The fairy-like creature spread her small arms. She twirled a magic wand casting a sky-blue, translucent dome that draped over her and Hanna's friends. The smoke soon choked all visibility outside the shield as unbridled chaos unfolded around them. Panicked screams and chortled gasps erupted across every inch of the market.

"What's happening?" asked Lexi, pressing her face against the magical barrier.

"Is it poison?" yelled Michael.

"It's the *Curdling*," replied the fairy.

Hanna looked to Lexi and then to her other sister—but instead of finding Ashley by their side, Ashley was nowhere to be found. Hanna's heart lurched in her chest. "W-where's Ashley?" Her head whipped around in search of her, but Ashley wasn't with them in the safety of the dome. Where had she gone? How could she have left them? As the thick cloud of smoke dissipated, figures slowly became visible. People fell where they stood. They gasped for breath lying disfigured in the street, on the sidewalk, and even in the alleys.

"Where is she?" Hanna pleaded, panic half-choking her voice.

"Where was she last?" asked the professor.

She pulled at her braids. "She was right here. Right here with us a minute ago."

"There!" shouted Hugo, pointing to the ruined fruit cart. "She's under there!"

"How did she get over there?!" screamed Hanna. Ashley lay

on her back. A lingering blanket of green fog clung to her distorting her features. "I've got to get her!"

The remaining haze drifted like dust bunnies in a breeze. They clumped together in sickly green curtains and then were whisked away in a puff. The severity of the situation was made clear as Ashley's skin peeled away before their eyes. What was left of her once beautiful skin was covered in purple stains. The blotches swelled into angry ulcers marring her pale skin.

Hugo grasped Hanna by the arm holding her tight. "You can't go out there! There's nothing you can do for her right now."

Above them, Barlow levitated high over the choking smog, his shadow creeping over them like a blight all of its own. "Maybe that'll make you think twice before crossing me again!" A new wind blew in from the desert and pushed the fog into the lagoon. "You and your sisters will be mine before the end of the Summer Solstice. It's been foretold!" As his voice echoed through the barren streets, the prince turned tail and flew back over the nearby sands as his men escaped the market into the safety of the portal.

What was it that the professor said?

Everything Barlow touches ends in tragedy.

The fairy dissolved her protective bubble. As soon as it was down, Hanna scrambled to Ashley's limp body. She shoved away smashed fruit and bits of broken wood and stretched her sister out flat. "It's gonna be okay," Hanna whispered. "It's *got* to be okay."

Hanna couldn't peel the fleeting thoughts of the last time she let her family down. Thoughts of Lexi's five-year-old body laying crumpled in the street were superimposed over Ashley's body. "Why can't I ever save my sisters? Why am I never good enough?" Ashley's chest heaved in quick, spastic spurts as she brokenly gasped for breath. "What can I do?" Hanna pleaded with tears in her eyes.

The fairy shook her head. "I'm sorry, but there's nothing—"

"There's one thing you can do," a stranger from the far side of the street called.

A short creature which resembled a walking tree came toward them through the plaza. It stepped around and over the fallen bodies as it made its way toward Hanna. The figure, no taller than the fairy, had dark, gnarled skin and a collection of leaves that sprouted from his limbs. It had no visible hair but appeared to be covered in a skin of bark.

"My name is Gob, and I may know how to save her. Possibly, how to save everyone." He spread his arms wide as if that would give them all the answers they needed.

"How?" pleaded Hanna.

"But I need your help—she needs your help." Gob pointed to Ashley. "It will be dangerous, but the lives of everyone here depend on it."

Hanna looked in the direction of Blunder Mountain, her gaze chasing the faint image of Barlow in the distance. "I don't care. Just tell me. I'll do anything!"

The creature nodded. "As you can see, I'm unaffected by the Curdling—a benefit of being a Wood Troll."

At the second mention of the Curdling, Hanna rifled through her memory. She'd seen that name before. Then it dawned on her. It was in Hagadorn's lab—in a glass jar labeled Curdling Dust.

Alexander's head shot up. "The sheriff. The sheriff! Someone's got to inform the sheriff. A messenger—I need a messenger. Who will take a message to Spur City? We need help and to quarantine the lagoon."

Two disheveled men dressed in dirt-covered clothes rushed up to the professor. "We can do it," one announced, glancing to the other and then back to Alexander. "We know how to find the Sheriff."

"Good! Leave now. Tell her what's happened. And bring help, too!"

The second of the two men pulled a small Portal Dial from

his pocket. The two men disappeared through the mass of people darting off in the direction of the portal.

The wood troll pointed toward Barlow against the darkening horizon. "I live outside of Neverwander Swamp. I see the effects of the Curdling more often than I'd like and have discovered that a demon in the bog oozes similar compounds."

"What?" asked Hanna. "What demon?"

"It's a cursed and dangerous creature that dwells in the swamp," said Gob. "I've created a remedy—but I've got to warn you, it's never been tested on anything larger than a tree rat."

"This is the first I've heard of a possible cure," said the fairy.

"The Curdling is no way to die. It's a long, slow, painful death."

The fairy fluttered closer to Gob. "How? How is it possible?"

"It depends on the severity of the—"

"We have to try!" cried Hanna. "I'll go right now. Tell me where?"

New voices cut through the groans of the crowd. Two figures emerged from around the back row of tents that lined the market's edge.

"Mum? Mum? Can ye hear me, mum?" called a high-pitched voice.

"Aaargh! Where is 'ye mum?" hollered another in low, raspy tones.

From up the sandy path walked two figures shadowed by a row of bungalows. A tall, lean figure jerked his head one direction and then another as it leaned over one body and then the next. The lanky fellow was followed by a shorter, fatter one. The two emerged from the shadows crossing the street in the bright mid-day sun.

The tall, lanky, green creature was dressed in a red skullcap and a tattered, dirty, white T-shirt under a brown, leather vest. He wore a pair of torn, khaki pants that barely covered his knees. The lizard's bare feet were as long as canoes and were covered in a scaly patterned skin. The only protection he wore from the hot sand was a pair of mossy-green flip-flops.

The short, squat man wore a wide-brimmed, black captain's hat. His shirt was stained and wrinkled, and the laces of his V-neck were undone and dangled down his chest. The worn, leather belt of his cut-offs was barely visible under the darkness of a heavy, green belly. It jiggled from beneath the rolled-up hem of his shirt. Unlike the other, his tiny feet were covered by black buckled boots.

"Aaargh! What happened here?" said the shorter one.

The professor curled his lip. "It's the pirates. Come to loot the dead?"

The lanky one turned to Alexander. "Why would 'ye say such a thing? Why would 'ye say such a thing?"

"Aaargh! 'Ye no good fool—we're not here fur none of dat!"

"It was Barlow. He did this to everyone," replied Kimberly.

"Hey, I know you guys," said Lexi as the two neared. "Let me see—" She fingered her chin in thought pointing to the fat one. "You're Pete," and you're RePete, right?" she added, pointing to the other.

"Aaargh! Lass we've never met." Pete took off his captain's cap.

"No, but your mother helped me. I've seen your pictures on her fridge."

"She knows our mum? She knows our mum!" replied RePete. "Have you seen her?" he asked, continuing to survey the surroundings. "Have you seen my mum?"

Lexi turned and pointed across the street. "Over there. Saw her just before the attack."

The two geckos crossed the road in the other direction. "Thanks, lass."

Lexi looked back to her sister. "Do you think Ashley will be okay?"

Hanna knelt and stroked the sweat-stained hair from Ashley's forehead. "I don't know if anyone will ever be okay."

30

THE CURDLING

Hanna stared at the overturned crates, smashed stalls, and at all the injured people spread out like trash on the ground in the ruined square. She tried licking her parched lips, but her mouth was as dry as the Fire Sands. A clatter of footsteps in the cliffs above the lagoon drew her eyes to the main city of Breakwater which overlooked the once happy paradise.

Alexander swung his arm in an arc toward the littered market. "We've got to get everyone to safety. We need to make a triage center."

"This is a real cock-up, innit? How'd you suggest that?" Michael said with a tinge of attitude and anger. "Make it from broken bits of splintered wood?" He threw his hands in the air. "Look at this place. How are we gonna—" He grimaced mid-sentence and grabbed at his lower back, falling to his knees.

"Michael!" Patrick gripped him by the shoulder.

"Don't touch me!" shouted Michael, swatting his friend's hand away. "It hurts—everything hurts!"

"What's wrong?" Hanna gasped. "Are you sick from the Curdling?"

Michael pinched his eyes and winced, still holding his lower back. "No…No, just leave me be," he spat. "It's my back, dang-it —it comes and goes. When it comes, it hits me like a truck. Go. Go fix your sister."

From somewhere behind Marty's Place, a wave of guards rifled into the square from Breakwater. New townspeople swarmed between and around them. Some folk helped the sick, while others gathered into an angry mob.

"I've had it with the royal palace," hollered a voice from the crowd. "The King abandoned us!"

"Morgana does nothing to stop her brother," called another. "Barlow runs free while the kingdom pays the price."

The professor walked forward confronting the growing crowd. "I know you're mad, but if you want to complain, do it somewhere else. If you want to help, then start by creating a medical tent for the injured." He pointed to the stalls spread throughout the market. "Take down the tents and move all the carts and wagons to the far side of the plaza. Setup makeshift housing on the other side so they stretch out together in one long string. We need to separate the injured from the dying."

Hanna turned around and knelt, pressing her forehead to her sister's. Ashley's skin was hot against her own. She was burning up with fever. *I'm not gonna let you die.* "It's gonna be okay," she whispered to herself as much as to Ashley. "I'll get you better, I promise. And I won't let Barlow hurt you anymore."

I can do this. I'm good enough—I'm strong enough. I won't let her down. I'll make her better. But as Hanna made promises to herself, an ashen grayness replaced the once youthful color of her sister's skin. Crimson welts as thick as ticks sprouted on top of the purple stains. They festered into angry blisters which quickly burst open leaking a yellowish puss.

Hanna choked back a half-sob. *Is it true what Barlow said about dad being a god? It'd make sense with what Golinveaux said about me having powers without the use of a wand.* Images of Midtown Valley and their father flashed through her mind. Thoughts of her dad chasing after her and her sisters up the driveway in his bath robe.

If I am a demigod, what else can I do? She thought a moment. Hadn't she healed her own finger before they'd tumbled through the portal? *Could I heal Ashley, too?*

Hanna held her open hands above her sister's fevered arm. She was close enough to feel the heat radiating from Ashley's discolored skin. Hanna pinched her eyes closed and concentrated—pushing thoughts of healing her sister. She thought of fixing Ashley's blistered skin. She strained and willed herself to cure the sickness…but nothing happened. Nothing at all.

Why wasn't anything happening? Hadn't Golinveaux told me to search my feelings—use my thoughts to spark my magic? Hanna thought back to her injured hand and realized something she'd missed. She didn't do anything for her finger. It healed all on its own. Then the thought of Golinveaux's Emporium rose to the top of her mind. Hadn't the crippled shopkeeper said there were some things that magic simply couldn't fix?

Alexander's voice pulled her from her failed attempts. "You need to get a group of people to bring every last bed and mattress from each cottage. If you can bring the bed frame, do it. If not, just bring the mattress," he said to the nearest villagers. "Line them up under the tents. Don't skimp on bedding either. We'll use every sheet, pillow, and blanket available."

The pirate brothers reappeared and shuffled toward the professor. Pete laid a sick Paula on the ground next to Ashley. "Aaargh! We found our mum, but we ain't doing nothin' but watching out for our own!"

Hanna combed her fingers through Ashley's hair. Her sister whimpered in a way that tugged at her heart. She was careful not to touch the festered blisters that were now the size of dark, plump raisins. Pinching her eyes closed, Hanna held Ashley's fingers in her other hand and thought of Gob. *Don't trust anyone,* floated from the hazy recesses of her mind.

The moans and sobs from nearby tents swept the once busy

market into a cacophony of misery. Hanna flopped next to Lexi and sighed into her hands, aggravated at her helplessness. "I've got to get the antidote from Neverwander Swamp."

"The recipe for the elixir is in my cabin," said Gob. "You need the raw ingredients." He spread his short, wooden arms to encompass everyone under the tents. "Act fast. These people's lives depend on it. The young and old will die first. The rest will linger on in agony—maybe for weeks before succumbing to the sickness. In the end, they all will die without it—if it works at all."

"Tell me where it is and I'll get it," Hanna blurted. "I'll go alone. I'm faster that way."

Gob scowled. "That's a fool's errand."

"You can't go on your own," stamped Lexi. "You're not leaving me here!"

"Seriously, Hanna," added Patrick. "We've barely arrived in this place and you want to go running off on your own? How do you think that'll work?"

"Cause…cause I can," she snapped. "I'm faster—"

"Just stop it, okay?" Michael cut across her. "Bloody hell, 'ya can't do everything alone. 'Specially now, geesh."

"You'll need help—listen to your friends. You've gotta hike into the swamp to complete the recipe," said Gob. "Most of the ingredients can be found inside the herbal humidor in my cabin, but you'll need to retrieve the main component from the bog."

Alexander turned a shade of lemon and shuffled closer to Ashley's bed. "You can't be serious," he whispered to the troll. "You'll have these kids go into the swamp?"

"Right now, these kids are all that stands between life and death for these people."

Hanna turned toward Gob. "How long do they have? My sister—how long will she live?"

Gob seemed to study Ashley. "It's hard to tell. Like I said before, some die within days. For others it takes longer—sometimes weeks. The lucky ones die quickly. Suffering is no way to go. The unfortunate ones live longer and it's a painful end. You must understand that until now everyone eventually succumbs to the Curdling. My recipe might not work, but…there's a chance. A very slim chance."

A few villagers from the market carried several beds over and lined them up next to Ashley and Paula. Slowly, carefully, Hanna and Patrick lifted Ashley onto one of the beds while the pirate twins did the same with their mother.

"What in the name of the six gods would they need to get in the swamp?" spat Alexander as a fifth and sixth bed was lined up in a long row.

Gob leaned his hands against the footboard of Ashley's bed. "A horned Calypso mushroom."

"Those are poisonous."

"Poisonous or not, we need them. *They* need them. The horned Calypso mushroom grows in the heart of the swamp. And with this many infected, we'll need more than a few. How many can you carry…we only need the stems?" he asked, eyeing the growing number of beds around them.

Hanna's eyes flicked to Patrick's new backpack.

Hugo buried his face in his hands and groaned. "I don't know about this plan. You saw what happened here. Barlow. The Brotherhood. His men are going to be a problem in the swamp."

"We don't have a choice," shouted Hanna. "I'll go alone if I have to."

"We've been through this, Hanna," snapped Michael. "You can't. Don't be daft."

"Okay, let's just settle down." Alexander raised his hands in a placating gesture. "Who's gonna go?"

"I'll go," said a new voice.

The professor turned as the tent flaps parted and a donkey in a cowboy hat, vest, and chaps strolled in.

"Deputy Dan! Thanks for coming."

"Yup, and I brought half the town of Spur City to help out."

"Huzzah! That's great news," Alexander hollered. "Let me

introduce you; Hanna, Lexi, Ashley and their friends Michael and Patrick. Everyone, this is Dan." He then pointed to the blue fairy hovering at the edge of the tent. "And we can't forget Felicity and her part in saving everyone in this group."

Hanna's eyes momentarily locked with Felicity's as she mouthed a 'thank you' across the tent.

"So, who's going on this maniacal mushroom mission?" the deputy asked.

"I'm going, of course," Hanna quickly replied.

"Me too," said Lexi.

"You're not going within a mile of that swamp."

"If you're going, I'm going."

Hanna groaned. "I'm not letting you get hurt—or lost—again."

"I'm going and that's that!" Lexi stomped her foot into the sand. "Ashley's my sister, too."

Hanna rolled her eyes and sighed, not knowing how to beat that argument.

"We're going too," added Michael slapping Patrick on the back.

"You're gonna need some help, then. Can't have all you kids wandering around Smaradine alone on some goose chase," Hugo interjected. "My sister and I will go, too."

"What about you, professor? You coming?" asked Lexi.

"Oh, no. I've got to remain here and help the sick."

Hanna looked to Gob. "And what about you? Are you going to take us?"

The Wood Troll shook his head. "Can't—like the professor said, I need to tend to the sick, too."

How was this going to work without his help, though? Hanna started to respond, but Michael cut in before she could speak. "That's nice 'n all, but don't you think we could use *your* help at *your* cabin?"

Hanna turned for a moment holding onto the steel bed frame

with one hand and dabbing sweat from Ashley's forehead with the other. "Gob, how are you going to help?"

"I can't cure the Curdling on my own. But I can heal them some. My sap is a health serum of sorts."

"This is bonkers, mate! We're asking for trouble going out there without Gob."

"What do you want us to do, then?" asked Hanna, jerking a thumb toward Ashley. "We're out of options! And there's no way I'm letting Ashley stay here in Breakwater far away from me, so she's coming with."

The professor raised his eyebrows in surprise. "What?!"

"If we're going out there for the serum, wherever *there* is at, then my sister's best chances for survival is to be with me. We'll find this mushroom—this horned Calypso thing—and make the cure. We'll give it to Ashley there in Neverwander Swamp. Test it on her first."

"In the swamp?" asked Patrick, a wave of doubt crossing his face.

"You won't be alone out there. There are creatures that dwell in Neverwander Swamp," said the professor.

"I'm not taking Ashley *into* the swamp. She'll stay in Gob's cabin."

"It still sounds reckless. Your sister should stay here with the others," said Alexander.

"Hear me out," said Hanna. "It's not reckless. Like I just said, she stays at Gob's cabin. We get the mushroom and make the cure in the safety of his home. Once we know it works then we rush the remainder of the serum back here to Breakwater."

Alexander looked as if he was considering the plan.

Hanna gently stroked Ashley's head with her right hand. "After what I've been through with my sisters since arriving, I'm not letting them from my sight. Gob said it himself. He can't cure anyone—not now—not without this mushroom. So, if she's here in Breakwater or out there in the cabin by the swamp, what's the difference? Out there with me she'll be closer to the cure."

The professor looked as if he were giving up the fight.

Gob's eyes followed the inside curve of Hanna's scarred arm. "That's a nasty mark you have."

She tried to hide the mark, but he'd already seen. "Yeah, I suppose it is."

The Wood Troll pursed his lips. "I hear it comes with baggage." He tapped his forehead with a finger.

Hanna's eyes widened. "You know about the voices?"

"Only through campfire stories and bar room talk. No brands on me. I can't speak about it myself, but there's plenty of murmurings in Smaradine to sort out the truth."

"The voices are killing me," Hanna said through gritted teeth. She pressed several fingers to her temples. "I never know when Barlow's gonna pop into my head."

"Boil some milkweed roots, then throw out the water and put a single root under your tongue," he whispered. "Not much— it's poisonous, but it should help."

"Poisonous how?" Why was everything he recommended dangerous?

"It'll make you go blind if you drink the juice of the milkweed. It's the fibrous root you're after."

"Ah…Thanks, I'll remember that."

"Where do they go to find your cabin?" Alexander asked, steering the conversation back on track. "Neverwander Swamp is a big place."

Gob bent low and did something that made Hanna question everything she knew. His arm grew. Tiny branches and coils of sinuous twig sprouted as Gob extended his right hand toward the dirty, sandy floor. He snapped off a new twig and started drawing a box in the sand ignoring the gasps from Lexi and Patrick.

"This square is Rumjic Junction where the group of you will portal into the area." He continued to rake through the sand, making a line extend out from Rumjic Junction. "There's a trail leading off to toward the swamp. It's a hike—maybe two hours or more depending on if you run into any trouble along the way. Pulling the bed will make your journey that much slower. If you find it getting dark before you arrive, don't dawdle. Get there as fast as you can. Find my cabin in the glen and stay the night. Set off for the horned Calypso mushroom at first light."

"You need to go soon," the professor added. "Hugo, Kim, Dan—keep these kids safe."

As Hugo and Kim turned to leave, Gob said, "You'll find beds for the night and food in my fridge, but stay out of my back study. There's a map to the horned Calypso mushrooms tacked to my wall near my desk." The Wood Troll then bent down and picked up a stray white tin cup from the ground. He blew dirt from the inside before extracting a blade from within the folds of his branches. Gob slit a gash along the palm of his hand.

Hanna gasped. "What are you doing?"

"If you're so intent on taking this sick girl with you, you'll need this." He dripped sap from the slit in his hand into the cup. "Have her drink it every half hour until she falls asleep. I fear with your sister in tow the trip will be much longer than expected."

A voice from behind the group made Hanna jump. "Aaargh! If 'ye is leavin' fur a cure, don't 'spect us to hang 'round en let me Mum die of dis blasted Curdling."

"Great," she said, throwing her hands in the air. "Now what? How's this supposed to work? Is everyone coming?"

"Me mum is sick. Me mum is sick," replied RePete.

"Ain't no way we're letting the lot of 'ya to grab dis serum fer yerselves," said Pete.

Hanna sighed. She took the cup from Gob and peered into its shallow depths.

"You'll have to share that between the two of 'em." The Wood Troll pointed to Ashley and Paula.

"Will this be enough?"

"It'll have to do. I can't spare any more. I've got to save enough for this whole tent."

"Sure, of course." A tingle of shame trickled through her for even asking. "Thanks for this."

Michael stepped beside Hanna and reached for the cup. "And just how do you expect to get Paula there? Ashley's small enough, we can manage her. But Paula's a whole lot heavier than my friend."

"Aaargh! Same as you lot, I 'spect. And how's you gonna do dat?"

From the corner of her eye, Hanna spied Paula's scaly hand snatch the hem of Lexi's T-shirt and tug her down toward the mattress. Her throaty voice rattled in her chest as she spoke. Lexi bent to listen as Paula's other hand gripped the nape of her neck. She pulled Lexi so close that the tips of her dry, cracked lips scraped against Lexi's ear. In a few heartbeats, she released Lexi's neck and wheezed a final time before her hand fell, exhausted on the bed.

"I'll take care of that problem," Felicity said, floating between Michael and Patrick. She stopped near the end of both Ashley and Paula's beds. "Levitatum." With a flick of her wand, their mattresses rose and hovered a foot off the ground.

A light groan seeped from Ashley's lips as her bed tottered in mid-air. Hanna blinked in wonderment. Smaradine just kept getting even stranger.

"How do we get them down?" asked Patrick.

"Oh, I'll take care of that," replied the professor.

Hanna's brows lifted. "You're going with us? I thought you were staying with Gob?"

"I don't have a choice, now do I? Who else is going to get them down?" Alexander turned to the Wood Troll and sighed. "Do what you can for the rest of them, okay?" Pulling his wand from his pocket, he strode to the tent entrance. "Trage Locomotis." Both beds moved as if pulled by an invisible cord and floated along behind Alexander as he stepped outside.

Michael, Patrick, Hugo, Dan, Kimberly, and the pirate twins followed close behind. Hanna turned and exited through the cloth flaps into the cool breeze leaving Lexi alone with the other sick patients in the tent.

"Hanna," came a soft voice from the shadows of the tent.

Felicity fluttered after her. "You have a tough road to travel."

"To be honest," Hanna said, not taking her eyes from the sand, "I don't even know what's going on. I'm so confused. I mean, everything's so—so different." She tried to choke back the rising lump in her throat. "How do I deal with all of this? This morning I was just a regular kid. Midtown Valley didn't have any of this." Hanna waved her hands all around. "There were no talking animals. No dragons. No Barlow. And no magic."

Felicity placed a delicate hand on her shoulder. "Find a way to deal with your new reality. You're not in Midtown Valley anymore. You're in Smaradine. Danger lurks around every corner."

Hanna nodded and tucked her bottom lip between her teeth. "I mean, really," she threw her hands down to her sides, "I don't even know what to think of what happened in the square. Barlow said my father's a god—is that true?" Even if it were, a part of her resisted the gnawing fact about what she was. She tried to latch onto the fragments of magic-free life she'd known up till now.

"If what Barlow says is true—and Kambo *is* your father—then you are indeed a demigod."

A twisted thrill of both dread and excitement ran down Hanna's spine. "How do I know what powers I have?"

"Presuming that your father is Kambo, the God of Light, I'd say your powers would manifest from there. *Feel* the magic within you—it will obey. Have you done anything special you can't explain yet?"

Hanna didn't reply, but her mind raced back to the handful of unexplainable events she'd been over again and again. "How do I wrap my head around this?"

"You'll have to figure it out in order to save your sister."

Felicity pointed to Hanna's thumb. "That ring, it looks like it has a GodStone, but it couldn't be."

"It is. Golinveaux said as much."

"Oh, well, with what's inside you combined with the added power of that ring, you've got a lot of magic to wield. You just need to learn to harness it. That band is quite the catch for someone so new to Smaradine. Where'd you get it?"

"I found it," Hanna half lied.

"Quite a find. I might just start questioning *how* you found it."

"Who says I want this power?"

"I think you'll need it if Barlow's got anything to say about the matter. He's declared your death and your sisters as his property."

"There's no way that's gonna happen."

"I hope not." Felicity held out her palm and passed her wand over it. Two goldenrod crystal pendants on leather straps materialized. "Take these."

Hanna opened her mouth to ask about them when Lexi threw open the flaps to the tent and barged her way into their conversation. "What are those?" Hanna took the necklaces by their woven cords before Lexi could grab them.

"These pendants should help you on your quest. They're Invisibility Stones."

"Invisible?" asked Hanna incredulously.

Felicity nodded. "Just touch the crystal and the effects are immediate."

Hanna smiled and thanked the fairy while dropping the pendants into her pocket. Then she and Lexi turned and followed the rest of the group to the portal.

On their way, they passed a winding line of people which stretched through the market and all the way back to the rift. Each carried crates of blankets and clothes and boxes of bandages and gauze.

Hanna scanned the endless line of people who'd come to

help. *Do they hate Barlow, too? And maybe the king as well? Manna—Smaradine—this world doesn't seem to be a place to be feared. Yeah, the Brotherhood is a serious problem and Barlow needs to be stopped, but everyone else...all the people we've encountered seem genuinely real.*

A new sense of confidence bubbled up from somewhere inside her filling Hanna with purpose. *I can do this. I can save my sister—save everyone.* She gave a final glance over her shoulder at the rows of medical tents constructed in the center of the market square. Hanna then turned her eyes toward Blunder Mountain. *I can do this,* Hanna thought, and she followed the rest of the group to the portal.

31

THE GINGERBREAD HOUSE

The wooden shack that Gob talked about sat on the far side of a meadow just like he described. For a moment, Hanna thought about the map the Wood Troll drew in the sand and realized that the way toward Neverwander Swamp wasn't as clear in her mind as she thought. The meadow to the right was filled with yellow flowers and the tree line in the distance appeared full and green—a forest ripe with life. She looked left and saw a decidedly marked trail up through the meadow toward a row of dead and fallen trees.

"I think we need to go this way," Hanna said pointing off to the left. "Look at the trail. Gob said there'd be a trail."

"Um, I'm not so sure...," replied the Deputy. "Hugo, Kim, professor?"

The professor eyed one way and then the other. "Neverwander Swamp is an enormous ecosystem stretching across miles of bog. I've never been to Gob's home. Honestly, I've only been to the swamp once and that was when I was young. It was nowhere near Rumjic Junction either. Dan, your guess is as good as mine."

Hanna pointed off toward the dying trees to the left. "Look at those trees out that way. Doesn't that look like a swamp?"

"Turd biscuits," exclaimed Lexi. "Now I don't know which way to go. I thought he said go this other way, but Hanna's right. Look at the trees in that direction. Those look like they're from a swamp."

Hanna looked to Hugo and Kim who both returned a shrug. "Okay. Let's go to the left and if it looks like we're headed in the wrong direction then we'll turn around."

The group made their way up the worn trail following the path of the sun. It baked the back of their necks for what seemed an eternity. The walk was slow as the professor had to pull both beds while Hugo and Kim shielded Paula and Ashley from the dying heat of the day. The further Hanna walked the more a gnawing in her gut told her something was wrong.

Now that they were past the first of the dead trees, the place looked something closer to Christopher Robin's Hundred-Acre Woods than where they needed to be. Although she had never been to a bog, the trees, the forest, and everything around them didn't seem like what a bog would look like. What made matters worse was they were already hours in the wrong direction. Maybe pulling Ashley and Paula along wasn't the best choice after all?

"I think we've gone the wrong way," said the professor. "This way is getting no better. No closer to the swamp. The forest here is vibrant. It's full of life. There's no sign of standing water."

Hanna's heart sunk realizing the professor was right.

Dan clucked his tongue against the roof of his mouth. "I have to agree with the professor. I think we've made an error. We need to turn around and head back the other direction."

Lexi grunted her dissatisfaction. "Ugh. We should've turned back sooner. How much time did we waste?"

The sun tipped to the other side of the afternoon sky. As the group trudged back in the direction they came, Hanna was thankful at least that the heavy heat softened giving way to a new coolness. A refreshing breeze rustled the leaves up the trail and kissed their sun-baked skin.

By this time, Hanna knew they lost hours. What was worse was that she knew it was her fault. She suggested they go in that direction. There was no way to make up for lost time. Pulling the beds and caring for her sister and Paula made time slip between their fingers. Daylight quickly drained away forming the long shadows of late afternoon. It wouldn't be long before they lost the light completely. Twilight loomed around the corner. Then what would they do?

Because of Hanna, the group lost the advantage of daylight. A crispness in the air swept away the heat from their skin as the sun tucked itself far to the opposite side of the sky. Just as the sun fell from view, the wooden shack in the meadow appeared in the distance. By the time they pulled near, the sun was completely gone. The Peasant's Moon, which crept up the eastern horizon, was cloaked in a finger of clouds.

She couldn't have felt more stupid than she did in that moment. Hanna sighed and peered into the meadow where they started. A layer of thick, cottony fog blanketed the ground threatening to choke what remaining light they had. How could the day have escaped so quickly? She couldn't believe so much time passed.

If they'd only gone the right direction from the start, they'd be at Gob's cabin by now. She squinted through the haze at a grassy knoll of clover. Thin blades of moonlight slipped through slender gaps in the cover of night. A tingling chill crept up her arms as a wave of goose bumps coated her skin like a sheet of freckles.

The night was much cooler here, and for an instant, Hanna longed for the warmth of the desert. She, Lexi, Michael, Patrick, Hugo, Kim, Dan, the professor—still trailed by the two beds—and the pirate twins stood alone in the chilly dusk. The wooden shack was no bigger than an oversized outhouse. It was barely visible at the end of the field. Hanna stepped across a set of barren railroad tracks and made her way toward the abandoned building.

A single torch cast a dim glow next to the shack. Shadows danced in the flickering light. An oaken placard dangled precariously from a wooden signpost. It hung like a crooked cat dangling from a single paw. It creaked in the wind as it swung on its solitary metal hinge. Hanna squinted and silently mouthed the words written in oversized lettering: Rumjic Junction.

"Yuck." Lexi pinched her nose. "I don't like this place," she grumbled in a funny, nasal voice.

"Blimey—what's that stank?" Michael snapped.

Patrick wrinkled his brows. "Do you guys smell rotten eggs? Was that smell here before?"

Michael shook his head. "I would've noticed."

"What you're smelling is Neverwander Swamp," Kim said.

Patrick blew a finger of chilled vapor from his mouth. "How can we be there already?"

"We're not," corrected the deputy. "It's the wind. It sometimes pushes the *scent* of the swamp southward."

"Give it time. You'll get used to it," mumbled Hugo.

"Aaargh! 'Ye meaty hippo. Does ye know the way ta go? I'm done standin' in da cold."

Hugo scowled and pointed at the faint outline of another path farther across the meadow. "The way must be over there."

Hanna hated herself for missing that path the first time.

Kim squinted through the darkness. "How are we supposed to make it to Gob's place? You heard what he said. Never dawdle in the dark. We aren't alone out here...other things live in the swamp."

A nervous knot formed in Hanna's stomach. Could she make her hands glow again? She swallowed hard.

Hugo waved everyone forward. "We'll manage. Come on. We'd better get moving. It's getting late, and it's only bound to get even dar—"

The crack of a stick split the dark. The group froze. Hanna

stared blindly into the dimly lit meadow. "What was that?" she whispered, searching the area for the source.

"Who knows what's out in these woods," Kimberly murmured.

Ashley groaned and twisted like a worm under her blanket. Her hoarse voice, low and cracked, seemed to come from someone else. "Hanna, where are we? I'm cold. So…so cold."

"We've moved. We're getting help. Something to make you better." Hanna shifted closer and wiped the fevered sweat from her sister's forehead with the edge of the dirty bedsheet.

A muffled noise like the slow pace of something moving their way crept from the fog. The clink and rattle of metal pierced the quiet. Hanna whipped her head around and peered into the mist, but it was no use. She couldn't make anything out in the darkness. "Isn't there something we can do to keep them warm?" she asked the professor.

Alexander nodded from the foot of the beds and strode down the middle splitting the pair side-by-side. He lofted his wand above Ashley's chest making sure to keep its tip pointed into the fog. "Pyrokora," he mumbled, and an orange gout of flame one foot long erupted from the end his wand.

In the new bloom of light, a shadowy cluster swam into view at the edge of Hanna's sight. The continued clink of metal grew ever louder. A group of people, led by a monstrous figure, spilled from the darkness. As they stepped into the light, Hanna sighed with relief. "Crowthorn, what are you doing here?"

"About ta ask you the same thing," he replied, yanking a heavy chain in his hand. The captain pulled four ragged men in shackles and torn clothing forward. "'Tis not safe in these parts." He gestured to the men he led by the ankles and wrists. "The Crimson Brotherhood are as thick as thieves in these hills and…" He paused as his eyes fell on the pirate twins. "What are *they* doing with you? How did you get mixed up with the likes of *them*?"

"Aaargh! The likes of whom, 'ye yellow-bellied land—"

"Watch your tongue, lizard, before 'ye find yourself strung up at the end of this chain."

"Did you hear about what happened to us?" interrupted Lexi, as if the open threat wasn't lingering in the air. "Our sister's sick. Barlow poisoned her—he poisoned the whole lagoon."

Crowthorn nodded and held up a placating hand. "I know, I know. Near everyone's heard 'bout what he did in Breakwater. News travels fast."

Hanna pointed up the path behind him. "We're after a cure. There's a cottage—"

"There ain't no cure for the Curdling," cackled the lead man in chains. Spittle flew from his mouth and caught in his shaggy beard. "They's all dead. Dead I tell 'ya—oomph!"

The captain jerked the heavy shackle looped about the prisoner's neck. The ragged man flew off his feet and sprawled face down on the dirty path. "Shut yur hole, maggot!"

Hanna took a hesitant step back as the man shakily pushed himself to his feet. With eyes as wide as eggs, Lexi stumbled back too. "Gob said he had a cure."

Paula gurgled something soft as a whisper. "Don't trust 'em."

RePete bent down with his ear to his mother's face. "Don't trust who, mum? Don't trust who?"

Crowthorn slumped his shoulders and avoided Hanna's eyes. "Don't know much about the Curdling, really. Hagadorn's the one you should be speaking with 'bout that." She frowned. Hagadorn's lab was where she'd first heard of the poison. "Cause," the captain continued, shrugging, "everyone knows 'bout the alchemist. Well, er—except you guys, 'suppose." He pursed his lips. "It's his pet project—a manufactured poison."

Hanna stumbled a step or two backward, bumping into Ashley's mattress. "My sister could die cause Hagadorn had to have his pet project?!"

"Now wait a minute—I didn't say that. Least, not in them words," corrected Crowthorn. Hanna pinched her eyes tight and choked back a sob. She stepped back, this time bumping into Lexi, who stumbled in turn toward the shack. "Hold on there!" The captain lunged for Lexi and caught her by the shoulder. "You need to watch where you're stepping." He pointed at the ground behind her.

Lexi stood inches from a shimmery, wooden sign that glowed with a dark iridescent sheen. Sitting two feet high in the shadow of the shack was a dark, round disk. It was carved from a solid piece of mahogany. There was no mistaking the giant, black raven carved into its face. Several coils of poison ivy sprouted around its base and twined themselves up the wooden post.

"What is that?" asked Lexi, jerking back.

"Go on, touch it," shouted the first prisoner again. "You'll see —you'll see."

Dan shook his head. "Don't. Don't get anywhere near those."

Lexi sneered at it. "Those? There's more of whatever that is?"

"Those are shrines to the Crimson Brotherhood," replied Dan.

"Don't be scared little girl—touch it," spat the prisoner as the others in the chains jeered him on.

Crowthorn yanked the chain again, pulling all four prisoners to the ground. "I said shut it!" He stomped on a hand and mashed the first prisoner's fingers into the grass with the heel of his boot.

"Aaagh!" came an anguished cry as the guy tried to free his broken fingers.

Ignoring him, the captain turned back to Lexi. "Touch that shrine and you'll be branded with the same raven sigil."

Hanna stared at the wooden bird, not needing to look at her own arm to understand what he meant. "He uses them for recruiting?"

Crowthorn hefted a war hammer in his free hand. "Them shrines is cursed with evil magic. So, yeah. A powerful jinx I wouldn't wish on anyone."

"Go on, the Brotherhood awaits." Despite clutching his crippled fingers, the prisoner didn't seem to know when to stop. He held out his trembling right arm and exposed a darkened brand of a raven just below the inside of his elbow. "Go on then, touch it, and you can be like us," he cackled. "We all have 'em. Join our family. Its bigger than you could ever imagine."

Hanna curled her lip. "That's sick!" She pulled her sister even further away from the shrine.

"They're all over Manna, positioned in outlying cities favorable to his influence," said Crowthorn. "We destroy 'em when we can."

"Right, well, let's get out of here." Hanna tugged Lexi by the arm and marched around the prisoners and up the shadowed path.

"Be careful," the captain warned as he pulled the prisoners to their feet with another jerk of the chain.

"We'll be waiting," came a cackle from behind as Hanna led her group away, leaving Crowthorn and the prisoners alone in the mist. She spared a lingering glance back over her shoulder; the pirate twins trailed their group and Crowthorn smashed the shrine with the war hammer.

The Peasant's Moon was higher in the black sky and peaked over the crest of Blunder Mountain. They used the looming silhouette of Blunder Mountain as their compass. How could they not? It stuck high above the darkened tree line. While they marched, the moon slowly arched up the cold, night sky.

Hanna dropped back behind the professor to the other side of the beds from the twins. RePete held the cup of elixir to Paula's mouth with a shaky hand. Some of the liquid dribbled down her shadowed chin. With a tremor in her arm, Paula pointed and said something Hanna couldn't quite understand. So, she bent down with her ear to the woman's lips. It was difficult to keep her face close enough to listen while they walked.

"Da girl…give da cup to da girl." She weakly pushed RePete's hand from her mouth.

Hanna motioned for him to listen in; she didn't want to argue the point with the twins.

The scrawny lizard traded places with her and put his ear close to Paula's lips. After a moment, he stood up with his eyes wide. "But mum…but mum," he said with a quiver. RePete tried one last time to make her drink, but Paula again waived off the cup pointing toward Ashley.

Nearly spilling the elixir in his anger, RePete shoved the cup into Hanna's hands. "Take dis," he said. "Take dis. Me mum don't want no more of it. It's all hers. It's all hers."

Hanna looked into the cup. "But—"

RePete held up his hands palms-out warding it away as if it was a disease instead of medicine. "Don't matter none. 'Tis what she wants. 'Tis what she wants."

Her heart warmed at the same time as her gut tightened. Hanna lightly stroked Paula's dry scaly forehead. "Thank you." Then she turned toward her sister and tipped the elixir between Ashley's parted, dry lips.

"Aaargh! How much farther is dis forsaken place?" asked Pete as they trampled through a patch of dried elephant grass.

"Not far, I'm guessing," answered the professor. He repositioned the flame to cover more of Ashley. "We've been at this for a long time already."

"Oi, keep me mum warm before I lose me temper and—"

A flutter of something above drew Hanna's attention to the shrouded sky. Another noise from behind and something snapped a branch somewhere in the dark.

"What was that?" interrupted Lexi, a nervous crack in her voice.

"Dunno." Michael shrugged. "Can't see in the dark."

"It sounded big…"

"Maybe it's Crowthorn again? Mate, hold up your wand so I can see farther."

Alexander shook his head. "Won't do any good. The flame's

not that bright. It's better if I keep a chill from settling in on these two."

A knot balled in the pit of Hanna's stomach. "Let's keep moving." She peered over her shoulder, glancing to her sick sister, then into the darkness as they continued up the path. The source of the strange noise remained hidden from view. *How long have we been in the woods? Seems like forever.*

Even with the Peasant's Moon high overhead and the extra light from Alexander's wand, she couldn't see more than a dozen feet in any direction. The night air was crisp and a new wave of goose bumps crawled up Hanna's bare arms. She untied her sweatshirt from around her waist and started to pull it over her head. Stopping halfway, however, she pulled the sweatshirt back off and laid it overtop Ashley's chest.

Another crack sounded in the darkness, closer than the last.

"I don't like those noises," said Lexi.

A third and then fourth snap pierced the night. Whatever was out there was getting closer.

Lexi groped for Patrick's arm in the darkness. "Something's following us."

Hanna peered behind her and something stirred in the night. A gray, shadowy outline split the darkness—a saddled rider on a twelve-foot dragon drew itself up and unfurled a pair of scaly wings.

"What are you doing in the swamps in the dead of night," asked Morgana. "Something's not right about you arriving the same time as my father—I'm going to get to the bottom on this!"

Hanna balled her fists. "I don't have a clue what you're talking about. Today's the first time I ever met your—"

A new pair of dragons cantered up behind Morgana's mount. Riding them were the pair of teenagers from the Royal Hall.

"Felonious, Hannibal," Morgana gestured to her colleagues, "say hello to Hanna Steele, dead girl walking."

"Is that a threat?"

"Hm…if you plan to continue into Neverwander Swamp, it'll

be the last anyone sees of you. And if not, well, I might see to it myself."

"Why are you threatening me? Why are you following us?" Hanna barked. "I've not done anything to you."

"I wanted to catch you red-handed—and I did," Morgana sneered as her dragon snapped at fireflies in the air. "You're headed back to my brother. I've seen the scar on your arm."

Hanna stalked forward. "If you had your finger on the pulse of Manna like I suspect you think you do, you'd have known that Barlow poisoned my—"

"How dare you! I know everything that goes on in Manna!" Morgana screeched. "How do you think I knew you were here?"

"I don't really care," quipped Lexi. "I've never met you before. I just want to get moving."

"My time as Queen was at hand!" Morgana yelled. "Go ahead and get yourselves killed. I couldn't care less, but I'll get to the bottom of this. Somehow, you're tied up with my father returning and me losing my throne. I just know it!"

"That makes NO sense at all!" Hanna yelled back, this time advancing toward Morgana.

The princess's dragon lunged forward, snapping its jaws at her with an audible clap. Hanna jerked backward. She stumbled out of reach and fell on the ground. Patrick snatched Hanna by the arm and hauled her back to her feet.

"Aaargh! Thought da king wasn't much good when he was around. You're still not half da ruler of yur fa—"

"I'M TWICE THE RULER MY FATHER WAS!" Morgana screeched.

"In da time yur father's been gone, da kingdom's fallen in ta ruin cuz a yur brother—yur stinkin' brother. Barlow has run da kingdom into da ground," barked Pete. "What have *you* done about it? Nothing, dat's what."

"I'll have your head on a pike, pirate!"

"You ain't queen yet. You ain't queen yet," murmured RePete in a sing song voice.

Patrick held up his hands. "Okay. Let's just settle down."

"We'll be watching you," came the hoarse voice of Hannibal.

Patrick turned to leave but stopped. "Where did you get those things you're riding?"

Morgana sneered at him. "You *must* be thick. Don't you know what a Dwarf Dragon is?"

From behind the princess rose a chuckle. "Next they'll be saying they don't know what the Curmudgeon Games are," snickered Hannibal.

Morgana gave a dry, hollow laugh. "Dwarf Dragons are bred for the games."

"So, how'd you get one?" asked Lexi. "Do you play in the games?"

"You don't get it, do you? I do *whatever* I want."

Hugo tugged on Hanna's elbow. "Come on. Nothing good's gonna come of this."

Morgana pulled the reins of her dragon and swung around. "Let's take off boys. It stinks around here, and it's got nothing to do with the swamp." She whipped her reins and her dragon shoved off the ground with a push of its powerful back legs. It was in the air with a few beats of its leathery wings. Coils of fog spun in swirls around Hanna's feet. Hannibal and Felonious took off just as quickly and followed the princess into the night sky. The trio were soon swallowed by the darkness.

"That chick's a sock sniffing turd magnet," snapped Lexi.

Hanna smiled a little and tussled her sister's already messy hair. "That's funny." She wrapped her arm around Lexi's shoulder and let out a chuckle.

The group continued up the overgrown path in near silence. The moon already shifted high in the night sky and Hanna's shoes wore heavy on her feet. Another twig snapped to their rear —Hanna let out an exasperated sigh and turned around. "Guess who's back?"

But nobody was there. Nothing but the cold, inky blackness of night. No sooner had they started to walk again when a new crack split the air. Something small raced unseen through the brush.

"Morgana?" Hanna called into the darkness. She wrapped her arm around Lexi again drawing her closer as she stepped toward Ashley's bed. A sickening curl twisted in the pit of Hanna's stomach. She balled her hands into fists.

Something was out there. Something was waiting in the dark. *I won't let my sisters down again. Not this time—never again.* Hanna frowned at her hands. *This is crazy, but if my dad is really the God of Light...*she concentrated on her hands. *Come on—do something*! She screwed her eyes tight for a moment and forced with all her might for something to happen.

A flutter tickled the back of her neck and a faint glow outlined the mark on her right palm. The light grew in intensity and Hanna's breath caught in her chest. Her eyes widened as the new glow swallowed her hands and soon bathed the whole group in a blanket of white. Her light dwarfed the dim flame from Alexander's wand. Everyone turned toward Hanna. Ashley wriggled under the sweatshirt and groaned.

"How'd you do that?" Lexi asked, gaping at her sister.

"I don't know. It started with a tickle behind my head...I remembered the same feeling when I was fighting Barlow. I just tried to recreate it, but instead of making rock come up from the ground, I thought of light and warmth...and it worked."

Hanna's glow washed over the meadow casting the area into bright focus. At the very edge, where the darkness still swallowed all visibility, a shadowed figure lurked. Someone finally stepped into view and a familiar oily voice broke the silence.

"That's a nice trick."

"Hagadorn—is that you?" asked Hanna.

"Douse the light," the alchemist barked. "Thought I told you and your sister to flee north—away from Manna. This certainly isn't far enough away."

Lexi almost growled. "We don't answer to you—"

Hagadorn pointed a finger from under his grimy sleeve. "You're frightening my quarry. Kill the light."

Hanna dimmed one hand by thought alone. "Why are you following us?"

The alchemist pulled back his cowl exposing his face. His disheveled hair shone greasy in the light. "I wasn't following you. I'm collecting specimens," he snapped with an icy glare. "You kids are asking for trouble coming this close to Never-wander Swamp." He flicked his eyes toward the tall peak over the treetops. "It's dangerous to lurk in the shadow of Blunder Mountain."

"Listen, bloke, you've been following us for the past ten minutes."

"Here to spread more of your Curdling on us?" barked Lexi.

Hagadorn scowled. "What are you getting at? You don't have a clue of what you speak."

"The Curdling," Lexi growled, pointing at their bedridden sister. "This is your fault, admit it!"

"That was no more my fault than the truth about me following you out here. I'm sorry about your loss—"

"Aaargh! Loss, 'ye stupid alchemist. De ain't gone yet."

"There's no cure for the Curdling. Their time will come soon enough. Say your goodbyes before it's too late and let me get about my business in peace. I've got quarry to catch."

"So, you *have* been following us. Why?" shouted Lexi. "Haven't you done enough?"

"Bah," Hagadorn barked. "I'm here for fire mice—an ingredient for a potion I'm working on. They're night hunters. Now, no more questions!" He huffed and threw his hands into the air. A pouch was twined around the fingers of his left hand. It waffled back and forth dangling from a short cord. "The potion is for the king."

"The king?" asked Dan. He cocked his head to the side and reached for the bag.

"Don't touch! These little vermin pack a nasty bite and a lingering burn."

Michael crossed his arms. "Prove you weren't following us."

The alchemist waved his hands with an air of impatience. "I've no time for games—get on your way."

Hanna's glance lingered on him a few moments longer until she finally turned to her sister. "Come on, guys. We gotta get going."

"Wait," urged Hagadorn and he stepped toward the bed's metal headboards. With a wave of his wand and a muttering under his breath, the old rusty metal frames transformed into a shiny silver. "This should make for easier traveling."

"What did you do?" asked Hanna running her fingers along the now smooth metal surface.

"I transmuted the old heavy iron into a lighter aluminum. They won't be so heavy to pull."

Hanna glanced into Hagadorn's beady, black eyes. "Thanks, I guess."

"Hmpft. Be on your way, then. I've got work to do." Hagadorn snapped before disappearing back into the darkness.

With the help of Hanna's illuminated hands, Hugo navigated the remainder of the trip with ease. Before long, an open glen peeled out of the night that stretched out under the moonlight. The field encircled an out-of-the-ordinary cabin from which the faint hint of warm ginger and apple cider filled the air. The smell was a welcomed reprieve from the rotten stink of the swamp. The group broke into a run.

"This is it! This has to be Gob's cottage!" Hanna shouted, dousing her palms.

"I'm so knackered," droned Michael. "All I want is sleep."

"Is this real?" asked Patrick, stretching out his own hand to stroke the side of the cabin.

Hanna shrugged. "I've never seen anything like it. Could this really be a gingerbread house?"

"Don't be ridiculous," chided the deputy. "Who lives in a house made of cookies and candy?"

The dainty home was dotted with colorful gumdrops and dollops of marshmallow fluff. White frosting in the shape of icicles dripped over lips of candy canes that edged the graham cracker roof. The gingerbread door was outlined in ribbons of red licorice and swirled taffy. The sugar-glass windows held the faint reflection of the moon.

Gob's cottage looked more like a carnival attraction than a home. Nonetheless, they had no choice but to enter. They knew it wasn't safe to linger in the dark. Hanna grabbed the swirly pop knob and pushed the door open. A warm glow stretched across the taffy doormat as it swung ajar. A heavy scent of mint mixed with tobacco, oregano, and thyme hit them as they stepped inside.

Lexi's jaw dropped open. "O.M.G!"

The inside wasn't anything like Hanna expected. The furniture wasn't crafted from candy, but rather from dark, polished mahogany. In the far corner, near the orange radiance of the hearth, sat a double bed with its sheets neatly folded. A heavy chest sat on the old, wooden floor at the foot of the bed. And near a pair of closed doors along the leftmost wall sat two recliners.

His home was a wide open space except for two thick timbers which stretched from the floor to the ceiling near the center of the cottage. The only interior wall wasn't really a wall at all but a giant, smooth pane of sugar-glass that separated the back of the house from the front. A small, maple door was cut into the glass.

Even in the dim light from the fireplace, Hanna could make out the dried leaves that hung in the space beyond. A slender crack of light shone under a misshapen door to the right of the kitchen. Crimson flickers slipped through the door's edges and licked the floor. Was that Gob's study?

"What do we do now?" asked Lexi.

With a flick of his wand, the professor doused his flame. "Let's get inside and get warm."

"Aaargh! Da sun will be up in no time."

"Pete's right," said Hanna. "We're gonna be no good to anyone if we wake-up tired."

Hugo rubbed his large eyes and yawned. "Why don't you girls take the bed in the far corner."

"I've got the sofa chair," called Michael.

"I've got the other one," cried Patrick.

Dan walked over to the set of doors and opened them one-by-one. "Two bedrooms over here."

"I'll take a room with my sister," said Hugo.

"Aaargh! Me brother 'n I will take de other."

"Well, I guess that leaves the floor by the fireplace for the rest of us," the deputy said frowning.

Alexander pressed his way between Hugo and Kim and pulled the beds through the door. "Departe Locomotis." With a wave of his wand, the beds floated past Dan and Hanna, the glint of the fire reflecting off the new aluminum frames. Once they were wrapped within the warm glow of the hearth, the professor swirled his wand in the air again and said, "Anti-Levitatum." The beds descended slowly until they rested flat on the floor.

Hanna slid onto Gob's straw-covered mattress and swung her arm across Lexi's chest. She stared momentarily at their sick sister lying in the orange glow of the hearth. The flames flickered and danced like a normal fire, but this wasn't a normal fireplace. There was no smoke rising through the flue. Magical flames fluttered within the stone alcove and floated several inches above the brick flooring.

"I've been meaning to ask," Hanna whispered to Lexi, "what did Paula say to you before we left the lagoon?"

Lexi turned to look at her. "She said 'Beware of gobbonbog'—or something like that."

"Gobbonbog? What does that mean?"

Lexi shrugged and rolled over, pulling the covers up over her shoulders. "It was something like that. I dunno, it was hard to tell. Her voice was so quiet and raspy."

"I wonder if it was important?"

"Maybe. I'm tired," she grunted. "Sleep now. Talk later."

Hanna lay awake, her mind turning over Paula's words. Eventually her thoughts drifted to what the professor first said before she came to Smaradine. *Why can't I trust anyone? And who exactly should I not trust—Alexander, Paula, Morgana? Alexander said he knows the truth—but the truth about what, exactly? Should I not trust Hagadorn? That seems as obvious as the nose on my face. He's up to something, but I can't figure what he's playing at. Why doesn't he like us? Why's he always slinking around in the shadows? Something's up with him.* The inside of her arm prickled. She pulled it from under the covers and examined the raised brand. *Barlow—of course not. Ugh, it's too much to think about right now.*

Hanna rolled onto her back and something hard pressed into her buttocks. She arched her hips and wriggled her phone out from her back pocket. "I completely forgot about this," she mumbled.

With the press of a button, her face was bathed in a small rectangle of light. A picture of herself with her family in their backyard by the clubhouse stared solemnly back at her from her phone's wallpaper. Pangs of homesickness gripped her gut.

Hanna tapped the camera icon on her phone and she glanced at the last picture. It was the photo of their dad in their driveway that Lexi snapped. *Could it really have been this morning that this picture was taken? It seemed so long ago.* She stared at the way his arms and legs were frozen in mid-stride. The bath robe opened up and came loose exposing his chest as he ran toward her truck. Hanna absently rubbed the tip of her thumb over his tousled, wet hair as if trying to fix his messy head. *Was he really a god? And why didn't he ever tell us any of this? What was he waiting for? And why is everyone calling him Kambo?*

She leaned closer to the screen. Hanna studied the picture,

examining the features on her dad's face. His mouth was wide open, preserved in a yell. "What was he saying?" Hanna stared at the image, trying to rack her brain at the last words she'd heard their dad say. She vaguely remembered him saying something—but what?

Her eyes flicked to the ring wrapped around her thumb, then back to the photo. *Could he have been yelling about the box of trinkets? Was he afraid I was going to find it and learn about Smaradine? No—can't be.*

She swiped her thumb across the phone's screen, and although she scrolled through image after image of her friends, eventually Hanna returned to the last photo on her phone from that morning. She traced her finger over their father's angry face.

What am I going to tell him when I see him next? How am I even going to get back to tell them anything? How am I going to explain that I know he's a god and...and that I've learned what I am? Her eyelids grew heavy as she rummaged through her memories. The one that came to mind wasn't even her own.

Who was the big, blue man she'd seen in that vision when Barlow touched her? He seemed so strong—so powerful. And why did those visions flood her when the prince came close? What did it all mean? Hanna tossed those thoughts around in her mind until sleep finally overtook her.

32

A WOLF IN SHEEP'S CLOTHING

In the heart of the night, movement stirred in the cabin. Michael tossed the throw blanket aside and it slid to the floor. A new pain in the scar along his arm throbbed like never before. He first rubbed at the brand, then the sleep from his eyes as he quietly climbed out of his brown, leather recliner. He tip-toed across the worn, burnt-orange floorboards in the glow of the fireplace. Every creak from loose boards gave him pause.

Gob's words played through Michael's head like a recording: "Find bedding for the night and food in my fridge, but stay out of my back study." The Wood Troll's secrecy drew him one foot-step at a time, lured by an unknown urge toward the oddly-shaped door across the kitchen. What was he hiding?

It's not fair how Hanna's got this magic n' stuff. I should have it. I deserve it, too. If my dad could see me now...I'd show him how great I really am—magical or not. Michael stared for a moment at the bird-shaped scar on the inside of his forearm before tracing the outline with his left hand. *This scar makes Hanna and I even closer —more the same. Will she finally like me now?*

A fresh wave of pain pulsed through his lower back. He stretched and rubbed the area of his transplanted kidney. *Naw, man,* he thought, still looking at the raven brand, *this is my badge of honor. Why, though?* He paused in the kitchen. *Why did I get this scar if Barlow cursed the ring for Hanna? What does that mean?*

Michael continued across the kitchen until his bare toes were bathed in crimson light from the crack under the door. As the light kissed his feet, his brand burned in a searing pain. He couldn't shake the hot prickling even as he flexed his hand trying to rid himself of the sensation. What bothered him even more than the scar was the pain in his back. He tried to ignore the throb, but he couldn't dislodge the nagging ache. It was a consuming ever-present discomfort.

Michael inhaled a deep breath and knelt on the floor. He placed his eye to the study keyhole. A sudden voice slammed into his consciousness catching his breath in his throat. Stumbling backward from the keyhole, he fell and sprawled onto the floor with a *thunk.* He gripped the sides of his head and bit back the urge to scream.

"Who are you?" croaked a voice in his head.

"What!?" Michael almost said aloud.

"Are you a wolf in sheep's clothing?"

"I DON'T KNOW WHAT YOU'RE TALKING ABOUT!" Michael mentally screamed.

"I don't know how you've obtained your powers—just know that there's no hope for you."

Barlow's voice cut off in Michael's mind as quickly as it came. Michael rolled upright, his palms pressed firmly against his forehead. As the burning sensation in his arm began to ease, the corners of his mouth twisted upward.

Did he say powers?

33

CAPTURED

Valentine's head throbbed as a sickening wave of nausea washed over him. The idea of even opening his eyes ached behind his sockets. Something was dangerously wrong. A pulsating pain on the side of his head thrummed with every beat of his heart. As he tried to raise his hand to rub at the spot, his hand wouldn't move.

His eyes flashed open. He bit through the ache adjusting to his new dark surroundings. A fuzzy orange light swam across his vision. Valentine didn't know where he was, but he knew one thing. He was in deep trouble. That thought chilled him more than the evening air. He wasn't in the Crow's Nest anymore. Gilles Devereaux, the shopkeeper, was nowhere to be found. His wrists were bound by a tightly knotted rope. When he looked at his hands, the elevator in his stomach plummeted to the basement. His new magical cuff was gone. *W-why am I tied? What's going on?*

He struggled, looking wildly around as the crisp night air bit into his skin. Two shadowy figures, not far by their sounds, laughed over top of each other near a dancing light. A campfire. It flickered close by. The crackle and snap of the logs, the musk of smoke, and the heated pine was unmistakable.

Valentine rolled his stiff neck and the round crisp image of the full moon came into focus. A million stars bloomed before his eyes. It was as if they were drawn by a long stroke of a brush and painted in a thick belt of molten color. He stared up into a vast canvas of twinkling lights. The open expanse of the sky stretched on forever. The light freckled the midnight backdrop like diamond dust.

Chills trickled down his throat as if a pitcher of ice tumbled into his belly. *I'm such an idiot! Why'd I have to be so cocky?* He shook his head at the magnitude of his carelessness.

He was propped up against something. Without making a sound, he twisted around; he was leaning against a wooden wagon wheel. A horse nearby stomped its foot and whinnied in the darkness. Valentine craned his head toward the voices and stared into the night through a finger of smoke. The dark silhouettes of the bull and his smaller lizard companion swam into view.

Yup, I'm in deep sh—

"What you gonna do with that bracelet?" asked a oily voice across the campfire.

Valentine froze.

"Dunno," replied a low, gruff voice. Valentine peered through the campfire smoke. He saw the bull twirling something on his finger. It glinted gold in the firelight. "Gonna sell it—trade it fur somedin' useful. Won't fit round my wrist."

"Give it to me. I'll make it fit."

"I ain't givin' it ta you. Told 'ya I'm tinkin' on trading it fur somedin' useful."

"Like what?"

"Dunno," he said again. "Maybe a new helmet. Hey, throw me another can of that pudding."

The golden webbing and leather straps flipped around and around the bull's finger. Valentine struggled against his restraints, but the twine binding his wrists and ankles bit into his skin with every move. The lizard stepped away from his companion and rummaged through a brown burlap sack until pulling out a can and tossing it to the bull.

They don't know. They still don't know what the cuff does…

The bull set down the cuff, resting it on top of the fallen tree on which he was leaning. He peeled open the lid to his food and scooped out bread and butter pudding with thick sausage-like fingers.

I've got to get it back. It's the only way I'll get out of here alive.

The lizard was head down in the bag of food. His squeaky voice rolled out muffled and broken. "Oy! When der fin meedup wiff da ceerava?"

"What? Git yur bloody head out of da bag."

"When do 'ya tink we'd meetup with da rest of da caravan?" he replied again, pulling his head from the gunny sack with a fist full of jerky.

"In da morning. Thole. Somewhere near Snakewood Grotto."

The lizard dropped the dried sticks of meat into his lap and rubbed his hands together greedily before holding them up toward the fire. "Can't wait, can't wait."

"What 'chu goin' on 'bout over there?"

"Oy! Don't 'cha remember Barlow's plan? To capture dat girl. What's her name?" The lizard snapped his fingers in an apparent attempt to jar his memory.

"Yeah, dat girl. Barlow's all worked up over her. Think Grit will get it sorted out?"

"Ha," the lizard barked a dry coarse laugh. "Da commander always does—does everyting da boss asks. Barlow's gonna lure dat girl into his trap right good," he said, grinning. "Gonna have us a ripe 'ole party once she's done followed him to Blunder Castle. Ha!"

Valentine stared at his magical cuff sitting unprotected on the log. *I've got to get it, but how?* He tossed his head back, banging it against a wooden spoke. The pain cleared his head; he had an idea. It would work only once, but it was his only shot.

Valentine scooted across the filthy ground, inching along like a worm, forcing his face into the ground and dragging his jersey and sweatpants in the dirt. He never took his eyes off the prize perched upon the log. He was ten feet from the cuff—ten horribly long feet.

The bull stood and stretched. "Ugh!" He lazily yawned and snatched up a massive double-bladed war axe. "Gonna take a pee and check on dat boy."

"Have a go, you mug," quipped the lizard as he tore off a new piece of jerky. "'Ya gotta try this." He held his hand up in the air. The dried piece of meat he showcased slipped from his grasp and fell into the dirt. "Could use more pepper, but 'tis better than a kick up the backside."

The bull, who was now on the far side of the camp, grunted in relief. "Sure thing…can't wait to wrap my laughing gear 'round that. Gotta finish off that bag before mornin'. Don't wanna have to share our find with the rest of the crew."

Gotta move faster! Valentine wriggled in the dirt, scuttling closer to the campfire and the log. *Don't look back, don't look back,* he pleaded. Four feet away. He was so close, but how would he get the cuff around his wrist?

"Oy! 'Bout that bloke we caught."

"What about 'em,"

Valentine could barely make out the lizard over top of the log. Three feet away. He could almost touch it.

"What's the John Dory? Don't 'cha think he's a few sand-wiches short of a picnic?"

A snapping twig made Valentine flinch. His eyes snapped toward the bull. His white horns shone a creamy orange in the flicker of the fire as he made his way back toward the log. "How so?"

"'Ya'd think he'd know we'd find him. Stupid bloke."

Valentine stretched—his fingers barely scratching the golden lattice on the cuff. His heart raced worse than any game day jitters. He tried to push forward, but his bound feet kept slipping on loose topsoil. He was there. It was almost his again. Another foot closer…if he could only…

"Aaagh!" roared the bull. "What do you think you're doin'?"

Valentine caught his own scared reflection in the bull's bulging eyes. The crazed bovine lifted the axe high overhead. Valentine recoiled. The bull's wild swing barely missed him. The blade whooshed past and sunk into the log, almost hitting the leather straps to the cuff.

"Oy! What's he doin' over there?" cried the lizard as the bull struggled to free his lodged weapon.

Valentine regained his wits and wriggled wildly forward. All pretense of secrecy was out the window as he tried to scramble for the cuff. In his struggle it fell in the dirt. He stretched out his fingers. It was at the tips. Ha! He finally pinched the long leather tie straps between his fingers and tugged it into his palm.

The bull freed the axe and leapt over the log at the same time the lizard lunged for Valentine's legs. He struggled for a second, finally inching the cuff up against his rope restraints. It moved as far on as it would go. Valentine winced, bracing himself for the fatal blow as he stroked the cuff's stone with his chin. He hoped against hope it would work. A blue hue filled the campsite. Time around him nearly froze.

Valentine rolled from under the falling axe and pulled his legs away from the lizard's grasp. Propping himself on his knees, he held up his bound wrists to the edge of the lowering blade. Rubbing the knots against the razor-sharp edge, he sliced through the brown twine binding his wrists. His reflection was still caught in the glare of the bull's bulging eyes. Valentine tried to read what the bull was thinking as he half chuckled, "And you wanted to trade this cuff for a helmet—idiot!"

Rolling onto his back and holding his bound legs in the air, he carefully slid the slowly falling blade between his sneakers. With a little push, Valentine severed the knots around his ankles and was back on his feet in a flash. He halted for a moment and gathered his thoughts. With a slow grunt, the lizard collided with the bull as Valentine zipped over to his gunny sack of food and hoisted it over his shoulder.

"See 'ya, meatheads!" he exclaimed and sped off at a sub-sonic speed into the night.

Time passed slowly as Valentine made quick work traveling down the road toward Thole. The moon above hardly shifted in the sky by the time the faintest image of lights of a city appeared on the distant horizon. He stroked his cuff again and slowed to a walk. Slipping his hand into his sweatpants pocket, he pulled out the map Gilles drew. By the light of the moon, he could tell he was close. The twin dune to his left was a clear indication that Gilles' cabin was nearby. Valentine sniffed the cool night air and tasted the hint of salt. *The ocean is close.*

Another ten minutes and he'd found the small dirt trail leading through the dunes. Valentine traipsed over one knoll, then another until the trail led him through a low valley where the dunes opened up into a wide meadow filled with sprouts of desert grass. Nestled in the center where the grass was thickest was a small cabin.

A yawn caught him off guard. It didn't take him long to find the single bed. Before he knew it, Valentine's eyes closed and darkness stole away the night.

34

NEVERWANDER SWAMP

Dark flashes and broken dreams, like the skipping of a scratched movie, played through Hanna's dreams. She tossed in bed as flickering snapshots of Kambo, the King of Thieves, and the mysterious Fe'Mal played out in her mind. Her vision was scarred in ribbons of vivid colors as spells of cobalt blue, emerald green, and crimson red streaked through the air in streamers of light.

Somewhere, hidden in the shadows and just beyond view, lurked a figure Hanna knew was there but couldn't see. Through the fight of might and magic, beyond the coils of spells that wrenched the air with the stench of death, two fiery, yellow eyes pierced the darkness. Twin orbs the color of ignited magnesium split the shadows and stared directly into her soul. From the recesses of her dreams, a single name kissed her lips: Fe'Mal.

Hanna shot bolt upright in bed. Tiny droplets of sweat speckled her brow like freckles. With breaths that came in shallow bursts, she swallowed hard as reality washed over her—she was safely inside the candy cottage.

To her disappointment, there was no Kambo—to her relief, there was no Barlow. But underneath it all, beneath all the layers of emotion, another emerged. A curious itch clawed somewhere deep inside her—somewhere primal. Maybe it was because of all the mystery. Maybe it was because the threat was new. A dread more basal than anything she'd ever experienced before crept under her skin and sank into her bones. *Who was Fe'Mal?*

As dawn broke across the glen, the new morning sun glistened through the sugar-glass windows in golden fingers of light. The sun painted the inside of the cabin in warm hues of pear and peach. As her heart rate slowed, Hanna yawned and looked about the cabin.

Ashley and Paula lay in their beds, still wrapped in the throes of sleep. Hanna leaned out of her own and softly stroked the dampened hair from her sister's eyes. Ashley's brow was wet and still hot to the touch. Her broken blisters stopped oozing and the tops of the sores dried into tough cakes of yellowed crust. Was that a good thing? Did that mean her immune system was fighting off the Curdling? Hanna didn't know. She sighed in frustration. The good thing was that her sister's shallow breaths meant she was still alive.

Hanna flung the brown, patchwork quilt off her legs and quietly hopped out of bed. She was the first to wake. Hanna bent down between the beds and reached for the shallow metal cup that held the remains of Gob's serum—his elixir of rejuvenation. She cupped her hand, cradling the back of her sister's head in her palm, and lifted the sap to Ashley's dried and peeling lips.

"Drink…come on…just a little," she murmured, tipping the serum into Ashley's mouth.

Her sister coughed at first, but then the strain creasing her face smoothed out as the sap seemed to do its work. With less than a quarter of a cup left, Hanna wanted to save some for later. But first, she made her way to Paula's mattress and poured some of the liquid between her fevered lips too.

Hanna sighed quietly and crossed several sun beams to set the cup on the kitchen counter. She took a moment to peer out the front sugar-glass window still frosted with frozen dew. Hanna tensed. At the edge of the swamp, just inside the tree line, stood two foggy figures smudged by the irregularity of the glass. She knit her brow and whispered, "Is that Michael and Patrick?" But Hanna turned to find them both still fast asleep. Confused, she walked to the gingerbread door.

Stepping outside, she squinted into the chilly fog. The two figures were gone, but from somewhere still close by, their faint whispers drifted across the glen. Where were they? And better yet—who were they?

Off to her left came the crack of a stick. Hanna stepped out onto the frosted lawn and listened as the morning chill bit into her toes. A momentary ebb in the otherwise soupy mist opened. Two shadowed figures stood out against the background. A gasp slipped her lips and the strangers fled into the morning.

Hanna's mouth gaped open. *That was Hagadorn and—and that guy we saw in the Salthouse Wharf.* She took a step backward and tried to think. *What's his name?* She stepped back over to the gingerbread door and it finally came to her.

Rowan—it was Rowan. That thug who chased a man into the alley. I knew Hagadorn was up to no good. All that slinking behind us and telling us to flee to the north. I knew it. I knew it. I knew it. Wait— CRAP! One's the anvil while the other's the hammer, after all. Is Grit somewhere nearby?

Hanna whipped her head around, first looking to the left of the cabin and then to the right. She listened to the noises of the swamp in the morning. Nothing but crickets and frogs and the breeze that rustled the treetops. Nothing that smacked of an ambush, but wasn't that what ambushes were all about? Secrecy and stealth? She made a mental note to pay closer attention to what was around them as they hunted for the mushrooms. *I have to tell the others what I saw. And figure out exactly how Hagadorn fits into all of this.*

She pulled her bottom lip between her teeth and turned to cross through the still opened door. A noise inside the cabin broke her train of thought. Patrick stretched lazily and stumbled his way across the crowded floor. As she closed the front door, Hugo shuffled sleepily to the fridge.

"I'll scrounge something to eat," he said with a yawn.

Patrick scratched his messy hair and yawned, too. "How's Ashley holding up?"

Hanna shrugged. "Okay, I guess. Just wish I had the mushrooms already." Before Patrick could sit down, she reached over and grabbed him above the elbow to drag him next to Michael in the recliner.

"What the—?" Michael woke with a start.

"I've got to tell you something." In hushed whispers, she recounted what she spotted outside.

Patrick leaned in. "Are you sure it was the same guy from the wharf?"

"Positive."

Michael yawned. "And you're sure it was Hagadorn?"

"No doubt."

"If that's true," said Patrick, "then we're all in danger. Barlow *must* know we're here."

Hanna's eyes darted to the sugar-glass window behind the recliner and then back again. "That's exactly what I was thinking. We've got to get out of here. Get out of this cabin. Get out into the swamp. We need to find those mushrooms and get back before something comes that's too big for us to handle."

"That bloke's a two-faced turd muncher," quipped Michael. "I never liked him. Hagadorn's in league with the Brotherhood for sure and he's leading Barlow straight to us."

Hanna breathed in deeply and let out a curt sigh. "Ain't two ways about it!"

Patrick pursed his lips. "Are we sure we want to accuse Hagadorn of this crime? Are we absolutely sure? He did fix Ashley's arm—"

"Doesn't matter," Michael snapped. "He was just trying to butter Hanna up. Remember how he treated her afterwards? And then there's the Curdling. And now this."

Hanna shook her head. "What other explanation is there, Patrick? Rowan's with the Brotherhood. We know that. Hagadorn's cavorting with the enemy—it's treasonable at the least."

"Hey," called Hugo from the fridge. "What's with the secrecy over there?"

Hanna coughed and straightened her shirt. "I've got something to share—something I saw outside this morning. Why do you think Hagadorn would be meeting Rowan out here in the middle of nowhere?"

The professor, who'd been tending to Ashley and Paula for the past several minutes, replied, "Hagadorn? Talking with the Brotherhood? That doesn't seem right. You've got to be mistaken."

Michael threw his hands in the air. "Listen to what she's got to say."

Hanna pointed out the window. "I just saw them out there."

Dan raised up from the floorboards near the hearth. "If the Brotherhood knows we're out here, we could all be in terrible danger."

Hanna nodded. "That's exactly what we were thinking. There's no time to lose. We need to get in that swamp and back out without being seen as fast as we can. I don't want anything getting in our way of making that serum. Ashley and Paula depend on it."

"Half of the Lazy Lagoon depends on it," added the professor rubbing his chin. "Strange as it is…we don't have time to dwell on Hagadorn. The clock is not our friend right now. Hanna is right. We need to move quickly." He gazed toward the pair of beds by the hearth. "For their sake and everyone else's."

As Hanna passed by, Kimberly set a black cauldron next to the fire. It hung within a sturdy frame on tall black legs of steel suspended by a thick, dark chain. "I'm just getting things prepared for when we get back with the mushrooms."

The long table in front of the walled-off humidor was littered with recipes, rolled parchments bound with colored ribbons, and detailed, leather maps. Cups of paint brushes lined the back edge of the table and small glass bottles lay in lazy stacks to each side.

"Found anything good?" asked Dan, walking up behind Hanna.

"Nope, not yet." She glanced over several maps. "How are we gonna know which one's which? There's way more here than I thought. This desk is a total disaster."

The deputy started sifting through some papers. "It looks like this map is for finding crystals in caves." He thumbed through several maps. "This one here," he held it up, "looks like a canyon…and its by Blunder Mountain. The legend is smudged, so it's kind of hard to read, but…looks like it says Blundersteep Gorge and Blundersteep Falls."

"What about that one over there?" Hanna pointed to a far pile out of reach to her left.

Dan stretched over the table. He picked up the map in question and in doing so spilled a jar of dirty brushes to the floor. Disinterested in picking up the mess, he said, "Looks like it's for herbs and tree roots, not mushrooms. It's not for horned Calypso mushrooms, at least. See?" He pointed at a recipe written on the map's bottom lip. "This next one's for a recipe about hoarfrost berries on Kragg Mountain."

"I can't find anything about horned Calypso mushrooms," Hanna admitted with a huff. "Did he lead us here on a wild goose chase?"

Several low groans crept across the room from the beds. Hanna looked over—Kim was helping Paula drink from the remains of Gob's cup.

Lexi, now awake, rubbed her eyes and threw the covers off her legs. "What's that on the floor by those brushes?" She slid out of bed and crossed the room. Bending down on all fours made her knees crack as she crawled under the table. "Something's against the wall."

All eyes trained on Lexi, except for Hanna's. Hers drifted to an off-white parchment half-covered in clutter. She pulled it out from under the mess and examined it. It was an intricately drawn map in black ink. The parchment wasn't made of paper or animal hide like the rest, but was intricately sewn together from tiny stiff threads. Its surface was as smooth as silk. Not a crease or tear marred the map as she unfolded the squares of parchment.

Why would someone have a detailed map about their own home?

It illustrated the inside of the cottage, including the bedrooms, the humidor, the kitchen, and the back study. The map also showed the open glen surrounding the gingerbread house and several hundred feet of the southern edge of the swamp. As she backed away from the table toward the kitchen, the contents of the map shifted and were redrawn as she moved.

"Shut-the-front-door," she mumbled under her breath. "It moves—the map moves!" Hanna mouthed wordlessly as she took a few more steps toward the counter. The map redrew itself again in thick, black lines always keeping her location at its center.

He'll never miss this, she convinced herself. *I'll give it back when we return the other map. What he doesn't know won't hurt him,* she reassured herself. Even as she told herself this, a pang of guilt pulled at her gut. *What kind of example am I setting? Ugh.* She looked to see if anyone was watching. They weren't. All eyes were searching the table for the recipe. So, Hanna folded the map into a thin, neat square and stuffed it into her pocket pushing the thought of stealing from her mind.

"This is it!" Lexi shouted, tossing a painted hide onto the table. A hand-drawn illustration of a white mushroom stem with a red cap and small blue horns stared from the page. "This is the horned Calypso mushroom!" She pointed to the bottom of the worn, leather map as Hanna stepped up beside her. "There's the recipe, see?"

"Better get movin'—it'll get late before we know it," Dan said.

"Hand me the map," asked Alexander, stretching out his arm. "I'll grab everything I can from the humidor." After a few minutes, he returned, arms full of leaves and sticks of herbs from the glassed-in room. "I found everything except the mushrooms." He set the ingredients on the kitchen counter and spread them out like a fan. "I think it's best if I stay here with the girls while you all go looking for them. Someone needs to stay back and tend to Ashley and Paula."

"Aaargh! We ain't goin' nowhere," barked Pete.

The professor rolled his eyes and turned back to the rest of the group. "I know you can find the mushrooms on your own. I'll use what's in the humidor to ease their suffering until you get back. Hopefully, I'll find something to help."

Lexi rolled up the pliable, soft map like a tube. She then flattened it and stuffed it into her back pocket. It stuck out over the top of her shorts by several inches.

Hugo returned from the fridge chomping on a mouthful of jerky. He handed out strips of dried beef to Michael and Patrick. "This will do in a pinch." Hugo gulped down a handful of strips in one bite.

Hanna took a few for herself and after a few bites realized she was hungrier that she'd thought. She pressed the palm of her hand against Ashley's fevered forehead. "Sisters forever," she whispered before crossing the room for the door.

She glanced back over her shoulder. Alexander dabbed a wet washcloth against Ashley's skin. The pirate twins sat along either side of their mother cramping the professor's remaining space. Hanna took a breath and the fellowship left the comfort of Gob's cottage for the brisk chill of the early morning swamp.

The seven of them headed up the peppermint sidewalk that stretched into the Wood Troll's front lawn. They soon entered the wet foliage of the southern edge of the swamp. Lexi directed their caravan using the natural markers laid out on the map. Within two minutes, each of them was covered in mud and slop. Not a single one of them dry from the waist down.

After what seemed an hour of drudgery, Dan silently flailed his arms in a panic and pointed in the distance. Through the morning fog, a patrol of Crimson Brotherhood stalked along a raised ridge of dry dirt marching in their general direction. Hanna and the others ducked behind a fallen tree lodged in the crook of a split boulder. They waited with bated breath.

"Did they see us?" asked Lexi. Hanna shrugged.

One minute…two minutes…then three minutes passed in silence. It seemed like they were crouched there forever. Hanna's stomach knotted as a drip of sweat moistened her temple. Five minutes passed. Noisy footsteps and chatter came from the other side. She held her finger to her lips. "Shh," Hanna mouthed soundlessly.

Less than ten feet away, the band of Brotherhood stopped on the other side of the boulder. The scent of burning tobacco filled the space. Hanna peeked through the crack in the rock; three wolves and two humans passed a rolled cigarette between them. The bright, crimson glow of their cancer stick burned red hot. A trail of white smoke clung to the air like a stain.

"'Ya see that," said a guard on the far side of the boulder.

A pain lanced through Hanna's stomach as if she'd been punched. *Did they see us?*

"Yeah, I see it," said another. "It's one a dem feral-thingys from da boss."

"It's a Feraling, you idiot," snapped a third guard. "Looks like it's gonna have breakfast."

A wave of relief swept through Hanna. The guards weren't talking about them, but rather something else—some other creature. She again pressed her eye to the thin slit splitting the rock. Hanna swallowed and a hard lump pressed against the inside of her throat. Beyond the Brotherhood, something floated above the ground—some kind of long jellyfish defied gravity skirting a foot or more above the swampy muck.

Hanna shifted to the right and knelt into the slimy water to get a better view. The thing floated toward a white-spotted fawn caught in some brambles. The baby deer struggled. It kicked and bucked at the branches ensnaring its neck.

"I've never seen nothing like that before," said the first wolf.

Hanna tapped Lexi on the shoulder and indicated for each of her companions to quietly take a turn looking through the slit. By the time Hanna pressed her eye back to the gap, the deer was underneath the Feraling's tentacles.

"Look at dat. It done swallowed da deer whole," shouted the second guard.

Hanna's stomach twisted. A guard flicked the burnt stub of his cigarette into the air. It twirled end over end above the boulder and landed at Hanna's feet. The seven stared at the smoldering ash. Before the hot embers were snuffed out by the swamp, the soldiers were already on the move again. The sloppy sloshes of their marching feet quickly faded from earshot.

Dan let out a harsh breath. "That was close. I think I peed a little—not much, but a little. How about you guys?"

"Okay—and that happened," Michael said.

"Are they gone?" asked Lexi.

Hanna peeked around the lip of the tree as flakes of dead bark peeled from under her hand. "Yeah, they're out of sight." She stood and walked to the raised vein of ground that ran into the horizon to either direction. To the west, she could barely make out the distant figures of Barlow's minions. To the east, there was nothing but empty swamp.

"What's the map say?" asked Hugo.

Lexi shook off droplets of water and muck from the leather skin and unrolled it. "We're in luck. We can stay on this ridge. It moves deep into the swamp and away from those creeps."

"That was too close for comfort," Dan admitted. "I've only got so many extra pairs of underwear."

The group stared at the deputy. Patrick broke the silence. "You carry *extra* pairs of underwear?"

"Why? You don't?"

"Er—no."

"Oh." Dan shuffled his feet in the muck. "Well, you can have one of mine…if you need it."

"No thanks. You keep 'em."

Kim rolled her eyes. "What do we do now?"

"Before we go anywhere, we need to come up with a plan. We have to avoid those patrols," Hugo said.

Hanna smacked her forehead with the palm of her hand. "Man—I completely forgot."

"What?" asked Patrick.

She reached into her pocket and removed two golden pendants on long, braided, leather straps.

"What are those?" Michael asked.

"I'm an idiot," replied Hanna. "These could've saved our bacon back there. Ugh!"

"What-are-they?" Michael repeated slowly.

"They're invisibility necklaces," said Lexi.

Kim pointed to the pendants. "You knew about those?"

"I didn't think of them either," Lexi said, snatching one of the necklaces by the cabled strap.

"We got them from Felicity before leaving," added Hanna. "Touch them and you'll turn invisible."

"I've heard of stones like that. Can I carry one?" asked Hugo.

Hanna handed hers over. Hugo grabbed the talisman by the pendant and immediately disappeared. "What the—"

Lexi reached out for the space where Hugo stood and also vanished from view. "Hey. Look. If you touch someone, you disappear too!" In the next moment, she reappeared.

Kim groped the air for her invisible brother. "You mean if I touch—" She vanished before finishing her sentence. "Wow! Look. I'm gone."

"Pretty cool, right?" said Lexi.

Hanna nodded. "Now, let go of the pendant."

Both he and his sister popped back into view as the pendant swung from Hugo's thick fingers.

35

WESLEY GRIT

Although the sun hid behind a thick blanket of clouds, Hanna sensed it shifted. Her shadow puddled around her feet. She was miles from where they climbed the raised path. Her clothes were nearly dry. All except for her shoes, which were still soggy sponges.

New sounds grew from the swamp as they approached a tall shroud of thick bushes. It was like a wall that extended far in either direction. Gruff voices and the rough clanking of metal against metal traveled through the hedges.

"Who's making that noise?" whispered Kim.

"Shh!" snapped Michael. "It's got to be them. Put on the pendants."

Hanna held her breath. She grasped Lexi and Michael's hands. After everyone clasped fingers, Lexi and Hugo slipped their talismans over their necks. In the next moment, the whole group vanished from sight.

"Can we go around the noise?" whispered Patrick.

Hanna glanced left and right. "Don't know. These shrubs seem to stretch on forever."

Suddenly, the bushes directly in front of them rustled and the leaves began to part. Hanna assumed that her sister pushed herself through the greenery. "Lexi, wait. Don't go through. We—"

"We can't all fit through," demanded Hugo in panicked whispers.

Lexi either didn't hear or ignored Hugo's pleas altogether. She pushed through the small opening. Lexi pulled everyone along behind whether they wanted to come or not. The gnarled branches scraped their skin. The force of them pushing through the narrow scratchy gap almost made Hanna to lose grip of Michael's hand. Suddenly, something snagged. Was Hugo stopping?

Fear of losing Lexi's grip, Hanna had to continue. What choice did she have? Hanna inched forward until she felt something slip—as if she were playing tug-of-war and the other team let go of the rope. She tried to stop herself, but stumbled forward knocking into Lexi. Did she lose the others behind? "Michael? Patrick? You still there?" she whispered.

"Yeah."

"Yup. We lost some people," said Patrick in a hush. "I think we broke off at Hugo. Must've gotten stuck."

Hanna and her friends pushed ahead through the brambles and emptied out the other side. When she finally broke through, her eyes widened to the size of teacups. "Go back! Go back!"

Dozens of canvas tents spread out like pimples across the raised plateau. Lexi, Hanna, Michael, and Patrick stood unseen on new elevation covered in a thick blanket of dry forest. Campfires speckled the black soil and the rank stink of salted stew punctuated the air.

"What's dat rustlin' in the brush?" asked a scroungy-haired opossum from the nearest camp.

Several Brotherhood stood and investigated.

"Don't know. Can't see nothin' there," snorted a boar.

"Well, sumptin' moved dem bushes. Go figure it out!" yelled a warthog from a second campfire.

Hanna froze. She squeezed Lexi's fingers hoping she'd get

the clue to remain calm. *Please don't make a sound. Please, please, PLEASE don't make a sound.* Hanna's stomach twisted into knots at the sheer size of their mistake. There were triple—no, quadruple the number of Brotherhood in this camp than in the whole attack at Breakwater. Trickles of sweat ran down her temples stinging her eyes.

A Dire Wolf parted the line of soldiers that formed in the clearing before the hedge. Hanna gaped at the massiveness of the creature. She remembered him from Breakwater, but this time he was closer. Grit appeared larger than life. He was bigger than any wolf she'd ever seen.

Grit, who was now dressed in a light-armored chest plate and black denim leggings that stretched past his knees, stepped closer to them. Was Rowan here, too? Hanna searched the camp for Grit's counterpart, but quickly abandoned the effort.

"What do you see, Commander?" came a gruff voice from somewhere in the crowd.

A litter of obese hogs dressed in muddy, leather chest armor, spiked shoulder pads, and knee-high, leather boots fell in line behind Grit's shadow. Grit scanned the hedge for something Hanna knew he couldn't see, but could probably smell. Sure enough, he raised his muzzle in the air and sniffed.

"What is it boss?" asked one of the hogs with a snort.

Grit's black nose twitched and Hanna was positive he was looking straight through her. She nudged Lexi with her hand and they slowly scooted to the left—away from the center of attention—away from Grit. She pulled Michael and Patrick along with them and the four shuffled soundlessly out of the center of the clearing. Grit suddenly held up his hand and the four friends froze in their tracks.

The bushes to Hanna's right rustled, a movement which drew everyone's attention. She pinched her eyes tight, fearing that Hugo was making a mad scramble back into the hedges. A moment later, her nightmare was confirmed as Hugo, Kim, and Dan popped into view. Something glinted in the sun and tumbled through the hedge falling to the ground. The invisibility necklace. Hanna's heart sank into her stomach.

A roar of outrage broke across the troops. Whoops and angry cheers erupted as several Brotherhood broke from the main camp and fell upon the three like savages. More and more of the Brotherhood descended on their three new friends so, that in a moment there were so many that Hanna couldn't see them anymore. It was a mad fury of fists and feet, shouting and screaming until finally the thugs dragged Hugo, Kim, and Dan out of the hedge.

"Chain and shackle them. If we've found *them*, Hanna and her sisters can't be far behind!" Grit knelt on one knee and grabbed Hugo by the chin, squeezing the tips of his claws into the hippo's meaty jowls. "Did you think you were free? The Crimson Brotherhood is everywhere!" Grit forced Hugo's face into the dirt. "Did you think you actually snuck into my swamp? You stupid fools. You were led straight into our trap." Hugo grunted as his snout was smashed into the soil. "The Wood Troll's done his job luring Hanna to the swamps. She'll fall and her sisters will be captured. Tell me, hippo. Where's Hanna and her sisters now? Tell me and I'll make your suffering quick, but not painless."

All of Hanna's strength drained away with what remaining trust she'd had in human decency. But everyone here wasn't human, were they? Everyone here treated trust and faith like a commodity. *Gob lied to me.* The professor's warning played in Hanna's head. *Don't trust anyone. Is there even a cure for the Curdling or was this all some mad scheme in Barlow's master plan? Am I a fool for following Gob's story hook, line, and sinker? But there had to be a cure, right? The mushroom was right on the map with the recipe at the bottom.*

Grit stood and spat on Hugo's face. White froth dripped down his blue cheek. Michael tried to lurch forward, but Hanna gripped him by the arm and held him firm.

"Stay quiet!" she hissed through gritted teeth. "Or you'll get us *all* captured."

The commander stormed over to Hugo's side kicking dirt into his face. "Tell me where your friends are or I'm gonna have to hurt your little, pink girlfriend."

"She's my sis—Oomph!"

Grit launched a heavy boot into Hugo's sizable gut.

"We don't know where they are," snapped Dan.

Grit sneered. "That's a load of raw, smelly cow chips. Do you think I like cow chips, donkey?"

Hanna swallowed hard, what the professor said about the King of Thieves once again echoed through her head. *Everything Barlow touches ends in tragedy.*

"This is the last time I'm gonna ask. Where are the girls Barlow's looking for?" Kim looked to her brother, tears trickling down her face. Hugo remained silent. Grit pointed at him. "Boys, take this sorry sack outta my sight. Give him some incentive."

Two of the nearest hogs gripped Hugo under the arms and hauled him to his feet. A third punched him in the gut as hard as a steam piston. Hugo's legs buckled and he fell back into the dirt. Leaves and grass jammed between his open lips as his face slammed into the forest floor. Another two hogs clamped chains around his wrists and dragged him from the crowd.

"STOP IT!" screamed Kim, wiping tears from her snout. "YOU'RE KILLING HIM!"

"Not yet," replied Grit with a devilish smirk. "Beat the pink one in front of the others."

"NO!" Dan yelled as a pair of goons dragged him from the clearing.

"It's off to Blunder Castle for the lot of 'ya."

"Please. Please, don't. Don't do this," Kim pleaded as tears continued rolling down her plump cheeks. Dirt and muddy swamp water smeared her once pretty dress, staining her rotund belly an ugly brown. Hanna stared, trembling and speechless, unable to move, unable to reply for fear of facing the same brutal fate as her new friends. "Help! Hanna, help!" Kim cried.

Hanna squeezed Michael's hand until her knuckles ached. *There's no way I can take on this many at once.* With her back pressed against the hedges, she stared wide-eyed at the wolf and over the seemingly endless rows of tents and Brotherhood. Hanna pinched her lids shut against it all. *I'm so sorry. I'll figure out somehow to save you.*

Grit went stiff and he stared out into the hedge. "She's here. Find her!"

The crowd scrambled through the hedge. Kim's screams carried over the campsite as they hauled her off. Shaking with a mixture of horror and anger, Hanna tugged on Lexi's hand. She led her sister, Michael, and Patrick quietly toward the gap in the foliage where they first entered the campsite. Wishing they'd never entered the hedge, Hanna whispered, "We've gotta save them."

"Bloody hell, we are! How are we going to do that?" hissed Michael. "They know you're here. They're looking for us right now."

"I—don't—know," Hanna replied through gritted teeth. "But there must be a way to get the mushrooms AND save them." She stood still near the bushy hole in the brush and scanned the ground. "We gotta get the other necklace. It's somewhere over here."

"You've got to be daft. They'll find us!"

"They're looking for us out there, beyond the hedge," snapped Hanna. "Not inside their camp."

Hanna spotted the mud-speckled necklace sticking end up in the torn leaves and broken branches. So not to lose contact with her friends, she knelt and awkwardly pinched the necklace between her teeth. "Yexi," she murmured with the brown strap held in her mouth. "Fix dis. I'be got it b'tween my libs. Swide it ober my head."

It took a bit of blind but gentle prodding for her sister to get her bearings, but after Lexi's free hand finally grabbed the necklace from Hanna's mouth, they stood still for a few seconds. An eternity seemed to pass before Lexi whispered, "There, it's fixed. Tied a simple knot. Not an easy task with only one hand, but it'll hold for now." Hanna felt the thin leather cord slip around her neck. Lexi tucked the pendant under her T-shirt so that it rested against Hanna's skin. "What are we going to do now?"

"We've gotta find a way to get the mushroom *and* save our friends. So, if we're lucky, those guards might lead us right out of this swamp."

"This has all gone to pot" whispered Michael. "We gotta get that mushroom and get the heck out of Dodge. Forget them blokes. The Brotherhood's got them now. What can we do?"

"No way. We're the reason they're in this mess. We're gonna get them out! They were helping *us* and nobody leaves a friend behind."

I can't believe he's actually suggesting we abandon them! Hanna's brain whirred as she racked her mind for any good reason for his behavior. *I've known him almost all my life, but never have I seen this side of him. The Michael I know would've—would've—*

"I still think it's bonkers, mate," Michael spat. "We don't owe them. We just met them."

"What's happened to you? Think about what you're saying," she snarled under her breath.

"What's happened is that I'm mad, that's what," Michael said loudly enough that Hanna's head whipped around to see if any of the Brotherhood heard him. "What's happened to me is I don't want to be here. I didn't want to come to some stupid Smaradine. My back's killing me. Your sister is dying. And I'm thinking about how to get her better—that's what I'm thinking. So, the real question is, what's wrong with you? Where are you priorities?"

Hanna felt her jaw drop open.

"Yes. That's the better question," Michael continued. "Get your priorities straight, Hanna. Your sister's sick. That's it. That's the only thing you need to worry about. Not them. Sure, it sucks they got caught, but we gotta think about us. You, me, and Patrick. The three amigos…and your sisters, of course. We gotta get that mushroom and get outta this swamp."

Michael's arm stiffened as Hanna tried to tug everyone forward after their new friends. He wouldn't budge. She sighed and swallowed her anger. "Look, you're right. Ashley's sick. We're stuck in some strange land together. You don't want to be here—I don't want to be here. But the reality of it is that we *are* here. Together. I'm sorry your back hurts. I'm sorry our new friends are captured. I'm sorry Ashley is sick. But we have to fix these things."

"You-can't-do-everything!" Michael grunted through gritted teeth. "That's what I'm getting at. Aren't you listening?"

"We have to try!"

"Why are you so pig-headed? No, we don't."

Hanna growled in the back of her throat. "What we *have* to do is find a way to save them both—Ashley and the others."

Michael scoffed. "Fine. Fine. Whatever. You win. But don't come crying to me when this dumb idea gets us captured or worse. It's like you're trimming a hedge with a chainsaw, Hanna, and it's gonna end up messy."

"Good. Thank you for agreeing." Hanna started to pull them from the clearing.

"I ain't agreeing, mate. I'm just plain tired of fightin' 'bout it."

They snuck like thieves between the tents until they found their friends on the other side of the sprawling campsite. Two were tied-up on the ground with burlap sacks draped over their heads. The deputy was already locked in a bamboo prison cell mounted on the back of a mule-drawn cart.

Grit climbed aboard the lead wagon in a train of four. "Move out 'ya devil dogs!"

The snap of his whip split the air and the trail of caravans pulled out of the campsite. Soldiers hastily shoved Hugo and Kim inside the last two cages before the final wagon rolled out.

The prisoner train jostled forward, pulling their three new friends away.

Hanna hung her head, a knot balling up in her stomach like a sour cramp. *I failed someone again. When will I finally...finally...*She struggled to come up with the right word. *When will someone in my care not get hurt because of my shortcomings?*

The caravan rocked back and forth on the ruddy trail as it disappeared out of the campsite and around a grove of trees. An idea sprung into Hanna's mind. "I have a plan. I don't think Michael will like it, but it's our only shot," Hanna whispered. "Let's move over there. Away from everyone so we can talk." Once hidden behind a wide thicket of willow trees, Hanna pulled the invisibility necklace from her shirt.

"What are you doing?" said a startled Patrick as Hanna popped into view.

"It's okay, no one can see us right now. You can let go, Lexi." Michael and Patrick, who were already visible, stood shoulder-to-shoulder with Hanna. Lexi materialized a second later as she pulled her own pendant from under her shirt. Hanna shot a tentative glance behind them across the camp at-large, then back to her friends. "Here's my plan. Lexi, you're coming with me. Michael and Patrick can go off searching for the mushrooms. We'll do two things at once. Then, we'll meet back at Gob's—"

"What?" interrupted Lexi. "Where do you think *you're* going?"

Hanna furrowed her brow. She recognized the firm setting of Lexi's jaw. Her sister was readying herself for an argument. "I need you to come with me, to the castle, after them." She pointed in the direction of the caravan. "We need to re-arrange things—change-up our agenda. I'm sorry, but I think this is the best division of our efforts."

"You're gonna make a total cock-up of it all!" grumbled Michael. "We should just get the mushrooms and split."

"I knew you wouldn't like it. You've been on edge ever since we got to Smaradine."

"I'm on edge because of my back AND we should stay focused on Ashley."

"Don't you think I want to find the mushrooms, too? I want to get them more than anyone, but we also have a duty to help our friends. Why can't you see that?"

"Duty? Duty?! Whatever," snapped Michael. "You're blind to what our duty is."

Hanna rolled her eyes. "Okay. We'll secretly follow the prisoner caravan and save the others. Patrick and Michael will take the map and get the horned Calypso mushrooms."

"That's ridiculous," Patrick snapped. "We should stick together."

Hanna stood there, dumbfounded.

"Wait—if we're splitting up, then I should go with Hanna," said Michael.

"This is insane, Hanna," Patrick insisted.

"Seriously?" snapped Hanna. "Not you, too? I thought you'd be on *my* side."

"Look. I'm sorry Barlow's captured our friends, but we have to save your sister. I agree with Michael on this one. We should just stick together, get the mushrooms, fix Ashley. Then worry about how to help the others."

A frenzied anger bubbled in Hanna's chest. "They helped us!" Hanna almost shouted. "Hugo saved Lexi from drowning in that cave. I'm trying to save Ashley AND them—why don't any of you understand that?"

"Look, I didn't get into Mensa for nothing."

"What's that have to do with any of this?"

"Have you ever thought that you going to Blunder Castle is what Barlow's bargaining on? What if he's counting on you rushing in to save them? I mean, it's a pretty good ploy—he's smart. Why do the work when Barlow can get what he wants by luring you right to him?"

Michael twisted the corners of his mouth. "Yeah. That is a pretty *stupid* idea, taking your sister right to Barlow."

"It's *not* stupid," snapped Hanna. "I *am* protecting her. And I'm the only one who can *really* do it, remember?"

Michael scowled. "What are you saying? That we're worthless?"

An angry heat flared in Hanna's cheeks. "No, that's not—"

"You're handing Lexi right to him," protested Patrick, "and you're not the only one helping. What do you think *we're* doing?"

"Hey, I'm standing right here," spat Lexi. "I can decide for myself, you know." She eyed the three of them. "I can look after myself, AND I'm going to get the mushrooms. Plus, I think Michael and Patrick have the right of it—staying together and saving Ashley is the ONLY thing we should be worrying about right now."

"You're coming with me," insisted Hanna. "I can protect you."

"You can't *make* me do anything. Come on, Patrick." Lexi dropped her invisibility necklace back down her shirt and disappeared from view. "I'm not waiting for my know-it-all sister to finally realize what the right thing is for our family."

"Hey, wait—where are we going?" Patrick asked, glancing from where Lexi once stood to Hanna. Then Patrick vanished from sight, too.

"Ugh. I'm so *peeved* at you," Hanna said in the direction of their footsteps and the depressed leaves on the ground. She turned back to Michael. "You've got to find my sister for me before they get too far away. They're going that way—toward the mushrooms—try to follow their footsteps or voices or something. If I know my sister, I don't think Lexi will wear her invisibility necklace for long anyway." She pointed off over Michael's shoulder. "Their steps led that way." Hanna cupped her mouth with her hands and whispered loud enough, she hoped, for them to hear. "Michael's coming with you…"

"What?" Asked Michael.

"You know what she's like. She'll get herself into trouble—

and I mean *real* trouble out here." Michael glanced back, peeking around the trees. "Pay attention, Michael."

"What are you, my mum? Don't tell me what to do!"

"I need to chase after that caravan," said Hanna.

"Bloody hell, then. Do it. Do what you want. You're gonna bloody do it anyway regardless of what anyone else says. So, blimey do it already."

"I need to know—"

"Know what? You need to know what?"

"That you're headed out to find Lexi."

"Bollocks, Steele."

"Please…protect her. Can you do that for me?"

"I said it before, you can't do everything and save everyone."

"Yeah, well, I can try."

"No, you can't!" snapped Michael.

"I'll meet you back at the cabin with our friends in no time."

"So, what? The three of you get to be invisible, but I have to stomp around plain as day? Is that the deal?"

"They'd be looking for us back the other way."

"Brilliant. Just brilliant."

"Now hurry! Lexi's getting away."

"Don't know why I listen to you sometimes, Steele."

"Michael, just share her necklace when you find them. I need my necklace to rescue Hugo and the others."

"What you *need* is to work together with everyone. How long have we been telling you that? If you do this, then I should come with you."

"No. Please. You know their general direction. They won't stay invisible forever."

"Bloody hell, that's a stupid plan. Why do you gotta go alone?"

"Because I *can* go alone. I've got *this*." She held up the ring on her hand.

"Come on. That's double stupid."

Hanna smirked. "Double stupid's not a thing."

"You know what I mean," snapped Michael. "Why do you gotta go and do everything by yourself—don't *we* matter?"

"Of course, you matter!"

"Well, you don't show it."

"Because I don't need your help!" Hanna spat and immediately regretted her words, but there was no way of taking them back.

Michael's eyebrows creased and a flash of hurt crossed his face. "Okay. It's like that, huh?"

"I didn't mean—"

"Oh, I *know* what you meant," Michael cut across her. "Forget it and FORGET YOU!"

"Wait! It's not…" But it was too late. Michael stormed off in the direction of Lexi's footsteps. She'd said too much. Hanna turned around. She set off on her own toward the caravan that trapped her new friends while wondering how to make it right with her old ones.

36

A PARTING OF WAYS

Lexi pulled Patrick through the forest until the tangled mess of cots and campfires were obscured by the cover of thick trees and brush.

"What'd you go off and do that for?" Patrick demanded. "Why'd you pull us away like that? I would've come on my own, you know?"

Lexi peeled the pendant off and tucked it inside her pants pocket. They immediately popped back into view. She kicked a clump of dead leaves. "I can't take it anymore! Hanna makes me so mad. I had to get out of there, Patrick. I just had to. Ugh! Why does she act like that?"

Patrick sighed. "Don't be so hard on—"

"Oh, just shut it already. Stop—just, just stop."

"What?"

"Stop defending her, okay?"

Patrick rolled his eyes. "Okay. Fine. She can be a bit much at times."

"At times," Lexi repeated. "Did you hear her back there? Did you hear her bossing me around like I'm a kid?"

"You're not a kid."

"NO, I'M NOT! I'm fifteen—almost as old as she is," she

barked. Lexi took a deep breath and then ran at the mouth as fast as she could. "I-can-do-what-I-want-when-I-want-and-how-I-please-thank-you-very-much." Lexi took a deep breath, then another, and let the anger drain from her voice. "Ugh—Hanna's such a drama queen."

"Guess she's just trying to do what's right."

"What's right?! What's right for *her,* you mean. Hanna can do this—Hanna can do that," she said in a squeaky, mock imitation of her sister. "Hanna's the best student. Hanna's the best daughter. Hanna's got magical powers." Lexi waved her hands wildly in the air.

"She doesn't mean to be that way, I'm sure. She's under a lot of pressure."

"Pressure? You want to know what pressure is? Pressure is living under her shadow—that's what pressure is."

"I didn't know you felt like that," Patrick mumbled, diverting his eyes to the ground for a moment before looking back up into hers. "You're a good person, Lexi. You're great actually—you should know that."

What remaining anger she had trickled away as if Patrick had pulled a plug on a drain. A euphoric warmth bubbled up from her wet socks to radiate in her chest.

"You…you think so?" she prodded, stepping closer and wearing a new grin that climbed to her ears.

"Sure." Patrick started to tick off reasons on his fingers. "You're smart and pretty and assertive and—"

Lexi shuffled even closer. "Smart and pretty, huh?"

"Um, yeah?" He glanced up and stumbled a step backward.

She was on her tippy-toes, lips puckered and leaning toward him.

"Whew! " Michael trudged up to them, his chest heaving and holding a stitch in his side. "I finally found—wait, what—what are you two doing?"

Lexi's face burned. "Ugh!"

Patrick's gaze darted from Lexi to Michael. Realizing how

they must've looked, he recoiled from her. Patrick's face flushed scarlet. "Nothing! We weren't doing anything."

Lexi gawked at Patrick's response.

"This is stupid, guys. Can't you see that?" snapped Michael, still trying to catch his breath.

"What's the problem now?" asked Patrick.

"Leaving Hanna alone—that's the problem." Lexi and Patrick shared a quick glance. "You two can obviously look after yourselves."

Lexi threw her hands up. "That's what I was just saying to him."

"Look, you two find the stupid mushrooms, kay? I gotta bounce. I shouldn't have left her alone. Gonna go help Hanna." Before either of them could protest, Michael whirled around and sprinted back through the forest in the direction he came.

Patrick raised his hands to the sides of his mouth. "How do you know where to find her?"

"I'll find her! You just worry about those stupid mushrooms!"

Lexi shrugged and looked up at Patrick. "What else could go wrong?"

37

THE BEAR AND THE BOAR

Barlow paced the open throne room passing a colorful, saltwater aquarium for the twelfth time. "Do you know what I think?" he asked, leaning over to peer into the tank. He tapped the powder-blue glass with his finger. Two dozen shrimp-like Sea-Monkeys scurried for cover under a coral alcove. Two bears seated around the long table behind him shifted uncomfortably in their chairs. "One of you has failed me."

Somewhere behind them, the clink of a chain rattled and scraped as if pulled along the floor. "Do you see what happens to those who displease me?" asked Barlow, proffering a hand toward his throne. The two bears, one smaller than the other, swiveled in their seats. A naked boar sat tied up and laying prone along the floor. A thick, metal chain weighted heavily about his neck.

"Frank," whispered the smaller bear.

"I require the two sisters," Barlow sneered. "Hanna's already come of age—come into her powers. But the half-blood's nearly no use to me, except for her ring and that pendant. The younger girls' raw, untapped magic, however, that is more valuable than you could possibly imagine.

"Commander Grit, who travels here as we speak, has sent messenger of your continual failure. I must admit—if truth be told," said Barlow, more to himself than to his present company. "I underestimated my first encounter with the half-blood. Understanding my own shortcomings is one thing, but your failure is unacceptable." The smaller of the two bears nervously tugged at his misshapen ear. "Look into the corner," demanded Barlow, pointing past the aquarium. "Tell me what you see."

Rowan stood and walked behind the small, brown bear. The bear's upper lip twitched. Panic apparently gripped the smaller of the two, who looked wildly about the room. The larger one sat stiff and silent.

In a voice little more than a whine, the little bear stuttered, "I-I don't see nothing."

With a twist of his arm, Barlow pulled a floating figure from the corner with the beckoning of his hand. A delicate fairy, the size of a wood troll, hovered into view. Misshapen patches of black and green were painted across her gauntly-thin arms and bird-like legs. Sunken, sallow cheeks accentuated the shadows under her unfocused eyes.

Barlow twirled his finger and the fairy spun like a mannequin in mid-air. A pair of folded and sagging wings hung like twin cords of limp rope from her back. They draped flat against her tangerine tunic that stretched in torn ribbons to her knees.

"What's this about?" snapped the larger black bear.

"Willow is in equal company," sneered Barlow.

The bears' eyes flicked between them, the brown one continued to tug on his ear. "I'm—I'm sorry, sir—"

Barlow held up his hand and silence fell. "Willow," he said, gesturing to the fairy, "failed me, too. And misery loves company, does it not? As a member of the Fae, I've been pressuring her to divulge the coveted secret of converting raw Smaradite ore into its powerful cousin, tempered and magically potent Smaradite. But it's become painfully apparent that I've been too lenient on our guest."

He pursed his lips. "Why even tell you this? You probably don't care about Willow. I wouldn't blame you if you didn't. I surely don't. What does it matter, right? She's a disposable asset. Willow failed to perform. But what's that mean for you two? I'd like you to witness first-hand what happens to those who don't perform for me."

With a burst of wind, Barlow shot twin shafts of air, like miniature ice picks, at the helpless Fae. Willow screamed as they ripped through flesh and bone, tearing her wings from her shoulder blades. The lifeless membranes dropped to the ground in an unceremonious flop of tissue. Barlow cast the fairy across the room. She skidded on the floor in a mass of blood and tears.

"It wasn't Frank's fault!" the small bear blurted, pointing to the naked boar.

Barlow held up his hand again. "You are aware, are you not, that I require the capture of the girls before the summer solstice? You are aware, are you not, that your attempts at securing the youngest at Breakwater failed? You are aware, are you not, that your attempts at capturing the middle daughter in the swamps was a catastrophe?"

"But, Crowthorn was there and then Morgana on flying dragons—"

"Silence!" thundered Barlow, cutting off the larger, black bear. The twin rubies on his skull ring glowed like hot embers.

A cinnamon-crimson aura formed from thin air and swirled around the large bear. He opened his mouth, but nothing came out except a chortled gag. The bear's marble-like eyes bulged as if threatening to leap out of his face. He gripped at his throat and gasped for breath. The bear's tongue turned black and jut straight out of his mouth like an exclamation point.

The smaller bear jumped up in a panic. He toppled his chair behind him in an effort to get away from the ruby-red vortex enveloping his friend. He gawked, open-mouthed, and watched the fur on his partner turn from a shiny coat of black to an ashen gray in a matter of seconds. The heavy bear kicked his feet wildly against the underside of the table until, tipping backward, his legs flung up into the air.

The crimson aura slithered to the prince and enveloped him like a cocoon. As the last of the coils left its victim, the bear's eyes stared out in a blank, lifeless gaze. Sweat matted the fur along the smaller bear's face. His upper lip twitched uncontrollably as his friend lay motionless on the floor.

"Do I have your attention?" asked Barlow. "Do you think you can accomplish the simple things I've laid out before you?"

The small bear nodded vigorously as the hog in chains cowered next to Barlow's throne. A Feraling, with its large protuberant eye, drifted lazily between the closest pillar and the throne. Its arms draped along the stone floor like a limp mop, stroking the hog's back as it passed.

A witch, dressed in torn robes of filthy brown, cackled from across the hall. "Oh, do as your master wishes, you will," she crowed, parting the graying and dirty dreadlocks from her face. "Dead as the other you will find yourself if not the girls you seek are found."

Barlow pointed to the far end of the hall. "The Summer Solstice is in a matter of weeks. I want them sooner rather than later. Leave my sight and bring me the girls."

The remaining bear stumbled and tripped over his friend's corpse. He scrambled to his feet and without a word, disappeared out the great doors. Barlow then turned to Rowan.

"Send more Feralings to Devil's Drop, Winter's Edge, and Thole. I need to keep a closer eye on them. And I want you to personally deliver a bag of kaura to each city council member. Buy them with gold or pressure them through fear. Those cities will be mine before the close of the Solstice."

Rowan bowed. "It will be done, sir."

Barlow closed his eyes and images played behind his lids. A metallic eyelid on another of his rings peeled back its dome to reveal a stark, white eyeball with a blood-red iris. It stared unblinkingly up at its owner. With a mental nudge, Barlow cycled through the visions from one Feraling to the next until he found the Feraling he needed in the swamps.

"She's coming to me, Rowan," he whispered with his eyes still shut tight. "I couldn't have asked for a better plan. Hanna Steele is on her way to me as we speak."

38

SOMETHING IN THE DARK

Hanna stomped through the forest underbrush and onto the dirty, winding path taken by the carts. As she marched somewhere behind the prison caravan, she wondered what to do about Hugo and the others. After a while, her thoughts drifted from her new friends to her old ones. Any hope of a relationship with Valentine was lost when she stepped through the portal to Smaradine. But what about her other friends?

It's obvious that Michael wants some kind of relationship. And Patrick wants something, too. But do I even want that right now? And if so, with which one?

She hurried her pace as a new glimpse of the wagons disappeared around a faraway bend. Voices carried across the forest, but she couldn't make out their words. Her thoughts circled back again to Michael and Patrick.

If I were interested...how to choose? All the other girls say Michael's hot, and I guess he kind of is. A small smile parted her lips. *But what about Patrick? He's super sweet, emotional, and cute. Which is more important? Looks? Or emotions? How to choose?*

Hanna fought herself for what seemed the longest time over the idiotic idea of getting involved with either of her friends.

Suddenly, a splash yanked her from her personal dilemma. She turned, and Michael rushed past her toward the caravans.

What is he doing? Why can't he just stick with my—Ugh!

"Michael! Michael!" she shouted as quietly as possible. Hanna pulled the necklace off her head. "What are you doing? You're supposed to be with Lexi."

"There you are…finally!" He slowed down and held a stitch in his side. "I was afraid…thought I wouldn't…wait, what? Your sister? About that. I told you it was a crazy idea." He huffed as he bent over with his hands on his knees. "You need more help…than they do. They're getting some stupid mushroom… and you're raiding an enemy castle. That's what I'm talkin' 'bout…I came 'ta help my girl storm a castle."

"You're the one that's crazy, 'cause I told you I didn't need your help. Plus, I'm nobody's girl."

"I was just sayin'—" but before he could finish, he winced and pressed his hands against his back.

"What is it?"

Michael stumbled a step or two forward. "Blimey. This really hurts again." Hanna rushed to his side. "My back—it burns. 'Ya know, like—like a hot match burning me from the inside. It's never hurt this much. I think—" He buckled and fell to both knees. "It's getting worse. I think it's got something 'ta do with this place."

"Smaradine? How's that possible? That doesn't make sense."

"Dunno," he said, clenching his hands into fists. "How's you having magic powers make any *more* sense?" Michael grimaced. "Why's it gotta hurt? How am I supposed to help you like this?"

"I told you from the start, I didn't *need* any help. I wanted you to stay with Lexi."

"Yeah, but I wanted to be with you!"

Hanna's voice raised with her temper. "It's not about—"

"Shh!" He pressed a finger to his lips and pointed down the road with the other hand. "They're coming. I saw 'em through the trees."

No sooner had Michael's warning spilled from his lips, then a pair of heavily armored boars wearing chest plates appeared from between some distant grove. The pain in his back almost forgotten, Michael scrambled behind the nearest elm on the other side of the road. "They heard you yelling…told you to hush."

Hanna scurried to the side of the road, diving behind a cluster of dry, leaf-less bushes. *Dang-it, dang-it, dang-it. I've got to get back over to Michael.* She stared across the ruddy dirt road. He's thrown himself belly-first into the mud. Surely the Brotherhood would easily spot him? Hanna shoved her hand into her pocket and gripped the Invisibility Stone in her fist.

Gone from view, she bolted in the opposite direction, hooting wildly as she went. The pair of thugs followed the sound of her voice. Hollering a line of gibberish, she kept running through the leaves and sticks to pull them further away from Michael. A hundred yards in, Hanna stopped and doubled-back behind the soldiers. She left them searching for her.

They're so stupid. But when she arrived at where she left Michael by the road, he was nowhere to be found. *Where'd he go?!* She looked up the path toward the caravan and back down the trail, but he'd disappeared as if he had an Invisibility Stone of his own. "Michael! Michael!" Hanna half-shouted into the forest. There was no reply, except for the hammering of a lone woodpecker.

"Back here. I heard a voice from back this way," said one of the Brotherhood.

Still concealed by her necklace, Hanna simply waited for them to give up. Five minutes passed. Ten minutes. It felt like an eternity before they headed back for their wagons.

There was still no sign of her friend. *I hope Michael wizened up and went back to find the mushrooms with Lexi.* Hanna put the pendant away and followed the caravan east out of the forest for what seemed like forever. She used the sleeve of her T-shirt to wipe the beads of sweat from her eyes. The sun, by then, already tipped to the other side of the sky.

What am I gonna do about Michael and Patrick? How could this have happened? Not one, but both of my best friends like me. And not in that 'hey, you're my best pal' kind of way, but 'hey, I like-like you' way. Why couldn't Michael have just listened from the start? Why's he got to play the hero and come after me? I'm not some damsel in distress. Ugh, boys.

She sighed and rubbed her temples while continuing up the muddy path. *After all these years together, those two buffoons make a move. One's too forward—all hands and lips. The other one's too passive and proper about it. Ugh.* Hanna shook her fists at the sky. *How am I gonna do this? How am I gonna like 'em both—or neither— or whatever. This is impossible.*

The caravan finally came into view again. The steel and bamboo carts swayed as their wheels caught in deep ruts in the road. The wagon stopped at a rocky outcropping, shaded by shrubs and an overgrown mound. A few Brotherhood jumped from their wagons. They parted some shrubs revealing a small, hidden entrance.

What purpose could a cave have way out here on the edge of nowhere?

The caravan disappeared cart-by-cart into the dark mouth of the cave. As she waited for the last minion to follow through the shadows, her thoughts overtook her once more. This time Lexi's defiance surged in her like a swelling tide. Hanna's cheeks heated. *Why does she have to be so stubborn? Can't she see I'm doing this to protect her? Does she think this is some kind of game? Who's gonna look out for her if it isn't me?*

With the Brotherhood gone, she finally crept to the entrance and peeked through the dead shrubs. Hanna listened for a sign of ambush, but she found none. She pushed her way through the dried, leafy branches, following the creak and groan of the wagons deep in the throat of the cave. Guided by touch, she used her hand against the tunnel's walls to follow the dark curves. Hanna inched along until her eyes adjusted to the darkness. Up ahead, a series of small torches fixed to the walls gave enough light to illuminate the rough path.

How could Lexi be so irresponsible? I just wanted her to be safe. Now look what's happened. She ran away. Patrick was with her, at least. That's good. And hopefully Michael's on his way, too. Dang, my friends are infuriating. It was a good plan! How could they not understand? Lexi wasn't ready to do stuff on her own. Why did Patrick just run away with her instead of listening? Hanna thought about her choices as shadows danced along the rough cave walls. *Everyone was against me. Not one, not two, but all three of them resisted my plan. Were they right? Could I have been the one who was wrong?*

A sour ache clenched her stomach as she thought of what could happen to Lexi. She pinched her eyes closed as another wave of memories about her sister's childhood accident swam in nauseating waves behind her eyelids—then the thought of Ashley smacked her in the face like a two-by-four.

Did I make the wrong choice following the caravan? I really don't know these people—and my sister's really, really sick. Maybe I should've gone after the mushrooms with the rest of them? Hanna squinted and pushed those thoughts from her mind, swallowing some of her anger. *No...Lexi's with my friends. They can handle the mushrooms and I can save the others.*

The distant crunch of wheels on stone drew Hanna deeper and deeper into the tunnel. The air grew crisp inside the cave and the once hot sweat which peppered her skin chilled enough to give her goose bumps. Although stale and foul, the chilly cavern air was a paradise compared to the sticky heat outside.

What a horrible day. I opened a portal to another world; lost one sister, got the other one sick; got my new friends captured by some crazy tyrant; now I'm following a psychotic wolf through a tunnel to free my captured friends...Sure, what could go wrong with that? Should I have listened to Lexi and the others?

And what about my dad? He's been lying to me—keeping secrets.

Why'd he hide the box, the ring, everything from me for all this time? Why not just tell us about Smaradine from the beginning? And why does everyone call him Kambo? I've never heard that name before—never heard of a lot of things before. Could Kambo be someone different? Is he the guy I saw in my vision—the big blue one fighting with Barlow? Have I been living a lie all this time? Could the dad I know not really be my dad?

That thought rippled through her like an out-of-control truck. *Don't trust anyone. But that doesn't mean my parents, too, does it?* The professor's words rebounded in her head like a broken record. *Everything Barlow touches ends in tragedy.* Alexander's voice in her head was quickly followed by Golinveaux's. *The way forward is found within. What did that even mean?*

Hanna's hopes at catching up to the caravan ended in disappointment. Each bend revealed only more trail ahead. Every corner hid new shadows. Anxiety over losing the wagon overtook her cool reasoning and she started to run.

She rounded the next corner as dust plumed behind her sneakers. The chilled air grew colder the farther she ran, dashing wildly around one blind bend then another. Her throat and lungs burned. *How far ahead did the caravan get?*

Hanna burst from the narrow tunnel into a wide cavernous space. Darkness wrapped its cold arms around her as she strained to make sense of where she was. In a heartbeat, Hanna's eyes widened as fat as silver dollars as she skidded to a stop against the lip of a dank, open chasm. Chips of stone and dirt tumbled into the black ravine below.

"Whoa!" she screamed, tipping forward. Her voice echoed in the darkness. *Oh, my god, oh, my god, oh, my god! Lean back. LEAN BACK!* Hanna struggled to regain her balance. Tilting back on her heels, she fell onto the cold dirt. Panting, she took a moment to settle her nerves, then walked back to the tunnel to grab a torch from the wall.

Along the rocky floor where the tunnel wall met the path, she found a loose stone the size of a softball. As she bent to pick it up, something glinted in the flicker of the flame. Hanna squinted. It was a large plate on the ground outside the mouth of the tunnel. It wasn't directly in the path but off to the side, otherwise she'd have run right over it in her haste to reach the caravan. She stared for a moment at the plinth, then down to the Portal Dial clipped to her waist, and finally out into the darkness of the cave. *I don't have time to play guessing games with this thing. Don't even know if it's a portal.*

She returned to the edge of the abyss with the torch in one hand and the stone in the other. Inspecting the ledge revealed a wooden bridge off to the side swallowed in shadows. She placed one foot on the planks and, when it showed no struggle at holding her weight, she stepped fully out onto the bridge.

A stiff breeze blew through the belly of the cavern. The wind didn't travel sideways but whipped upward. Hanna stuck her outstretched arm beyond the safety of the bridge; there was a steady stream against her hand. She dropped the stone. Hanna never heard it strike the ground.

Gotta be careful —

A low rumble reverberated from the depths of the chamber. It rattled in her guts as much as she heard it. Hanna slowly swiveled in a full circle. Her torch barely dented the thick cover of darkness.

I can't see a thing!

The low, rumble shook her ribs again, but this time an accompanying throaty gurgling sent the hairs on her arms standing on end. Hanna burst into a sprint, but the trestle rocked on its foundation and she tripped, falling to her knees.

She cried in pain as the coarse wood bit into her skin. Splotches of blood blossomed like scarlet rose petals from her torn knees. The torch jerked from her fingers and tumbled out of reach, illuminating an empty patch of darkness. Sprawled out on all fours, the entire bridge rippled in spasms beneath her. Something was coming.

Hanna held her breath, her stomach twisting in knots—she

dared not blink and pressed her eyes against the gloom. A new rumble shook the planks. She darted for the torch. Hanna's sneakers squeaked as she slipped on the wood. The bridge swayed in uneven jerks and a thin squeal crept from her throat. Her mind raced for a way out. She gripped the planks and prepared to dart when something frightened all movement from her bones. A massive, gnarled tentacle slithered between her and the torch. Hanna's body locked up.

Don't move an inch.

Glowing cobalt specks painted the creature's plum skin. Ribbons of needle-sharp talons lined the pink under-side of the limb. Hanna slowly followed the tentacle with her eyes as the arm slipped back off the edge. She slid her head under the support chains and peered down into the abyss.

Holy mother of all that is righteous.

The blackness of the abyss was alive. The once midnight pool was lit like the Milky Way. An enormous leviathan loomed from the cavernous depths below the bridge. A Goliath squid was illuminated by the glow from billions of bioluminescent microorganisms. Ten massive arms sprouted from a snapping beak the size of a truck.

Oh, God, I'm gonna die.

Hanna made a frantic dash for the torch. She dove in a flying summersault, scooping it in her fingers, and sprinted almost blindly down the length of the bridge. But there was no real escape. She reached the stone ledge on other side of the gorge with no visible direction to go.

Everything Barlow touches ends in tragedy.

Seconds after pebbles crunched under her feet, a slimy, mucus-covered tentacle wrapped around her ankle. The slick, clammy arm coiled around her calf like a snake. Needle-like pain flared up her leg as razor-sharp, comma-shaped talons gouged her flesh.

With a cry, Hanna was raked off her feet. Her face crashed into the unforgiving ledge where she'd stood moments before.

Blood spurt from her chin as air was expelled from her lungs. She grappled for breath, but the wind was knocked from her.

Hanna scraped her fingernails into grooves along the dirty, stone ledge. Several nails split before she was pulled into the air. Her lungs burnt. Abandoned of air, it was as if a building sat on her chest. Hanna struggled to inhale the crisp, cold air of the cavern.

Warm blood mixed with a dirty-green syrup trickled off her thigh and dripped in splatters across her cheek. Her right leg burned. The creature hoisted her over the deep gorge and hung her high above its gaping mouth.

"NO!" she screamed at the top of her lungs.

Hanna stared at the blue glow that slicked the water at the bottom of the gorge. It washed in and out of the giant squid's snapping beak. The bioluminescent pulse of the pool stretched for hundreds of feet in every direction.

"I need a knife!" she cried, images flooding her mind of cutting the creature to ribbons.

Almost before the words slipped from her lips, the base of her neck tingled and a trickle flowed down her right arm. A thin spear of rock shot from the cave's wall, severing the beast's arm, and Hanna plummeted into the shimmery cobalt depths of the cavern.

With a splash, the frigid pool stung her skin like bees. She screamed as icy, black water filled her mouth and she was plunged deep below the surface. Hanna raked her hands through the murky pool trying to swim to the top. She kicked again and again until she finally breeched the surface, covering herself in bioluminescence. She shivered, her teeth chattering together as the biting water robbed her of any remaining heat.

Magic—of course, I'm an idiot! Why didn't I think of it before!

The leviathan snaked tentacles through the murk as she flailed in the black pitch. She wished she was back on the stone ledge high above the pit right before something hard struck her on the rump.

Hanna held her breath for the plunge under the water, but she didn't get pulled under the surface at all. Instead, she was hurled upward. She rode on a spire of rock shooting two-hundred feet into the air.

Hanna almost giggled as she brought her hands to blazing life. They shone with a glow as bright as headlamps. Bathed in her power, she clambered to her feet and cast light to illuminate fifty feet in every direction.

"How'd I make that spire? Think—think," she screamed into the belly of the cavern.

Just as the limbs of the beast reached her feet, a new stone platform shot up from the murky gorge standing five feet away. "There's another one," she exclaimed with glee at the thin shaft of rock.

As Hanna constructed her plan to escape, a row of more spires formed a dotted path down the length of the pool. She leapt with a heavy limp across their tops. Her wispy shadow danced along the sides of the great cave. She struggled with her gimp leg jumping weakly from platform to platform, tottering sideways once or twice and almost falling back in. By the grace of God, Hanna managed to stay on top and flee high above the creature.

Out of breath and near exhausted, Hanna finally reached the end of the long and winding cavernous lake. She leapt to an inclined ledge, leaving the beast far behind. She bent over with her hands on her knees and pinched a stitch in her side. "I did that—I just did that! I don't know how, but…it was amazing! I told everyone I could do this…on my own, but no one…believed me. Ha—I showed them," she practically shouted into the darkness.

Hanna tented her fingers together so the tips on her right hand met the tips of her left. Thinking of the stone spires that traced a line through the gorge, she ripped her hands apart with a quick jerk. A new roar filled the cavern as her rocky platforms exploded into millions of fragments.

"Take that, fish bait."

Impressed with herself, she stared at her glowing hands. *Golinveaux was right. My dad must be a god. Why'd dad hide all this from us? Why not show us any of his powers?* Hanna pursed her lips. *Why didn't I see any of this before now?* The GodStone ring, the Portal Cube, the dent in her locker, the voices in her head, her mysterious necklace, the strange mark on her right palm, and now her miraculous powers made her shake her head in awe. *I can't wait to tell dad I know his secret.*

Hanna doused the light from her hands. The adrenaline coursing through her veins began to fade, leaching from her muscles and leaving her shivering. She turned to face the rocky incline that led to a small patch of daylight. The caravan was nowhere to be found. Had it had already traveled out of the cave or had it somehow plunged into the depths of the murky pool far below?

She turned and tried to look back through the darkness to where things went wrong—back to where she lost the wagon and almost her life. How did the caravan get so far ahead? Had she somehow gone the wrong way? Was her fight with the leviathan that long that the carts already made it to safety?

A patch of light fell into the cave through an entrance which looked wide enough to fit a wagon. Hanna turned, scuffing her feet along the wide rocky path, and stepped toward the doorway. She didn't make it two steps before crumpling to the ground.

Her calf burned as though it were on fire. She brought an illuminated hand close to inspect it. Her skin was speckled with angry, crimson ulcers. A thick, green ooze that was sickly pungent seeped from the puckered center of each round tear.

"Ugh," she cried and gripped the meat of her leg just below the knee. "What the heck is going on? I'm not healing like before."

Forcing herself back to her feet, Hanna stumbled from the shadows and into the light, dragging her gimp leg behind. As she exited the cave, she stood on the edge of a tall cliff over-looking a perilous drop to a raging river below. A dark castle slathered in a muddy-green moss sat across the gorge, curled in shadows. A solitary tower punctured the charcoal blanket of clouds. The rest of the castle, however, was hidden behind enormous stone walls.

"Blunder Castle," she murmured. "That has to be it. Michael would've loved to see this." Hanna paused, her last interaction with him bubbling back into the forefront of her mind.

I wonder if I was too rough on him? Maybe I should've let 'em come along. Then she thought about the kiss. *Why'd he try to kiss me—why ruin the great thing we already have?* Hanna curled her bottom lip between her teeth. *Maybe it's best he went back with Lexi to find the mushrooms,* she convinced herself. *He needed to keep Lexi safe. Regardless of his kiss and the fact that my feelings are a jumbled mess, there's no denying that Michael is a good friend—he'd have done the right thing. I shouldn't be so hard on him—he's stuck in this mess, too. I'll have to remember to apologize.*

A low constant roar, like the sound of a locomotive, rumbled up the cliff. "This must be Blundersteep Gorge," Hanna whispered, thinking back to the map they found in Gob's cabin. What looked like Blundersteep Falls sat far to her right. Mist roiled into the air above the roaring mouth of the chute. *Where's the caravan?*

She traced the stone pathway from the cave down the outside of the cliff. There it was—near the bottom. She hadn't lost them at all. The wagon started across a massive stone bridge. An enormous slab of granite sat over the mouth of Blundersteep Falls, jutting out over it like an enormous tongue.

Hanna peeked over the ledge and her stomach flipped. It was a dizzying drop straight down at least three hundred feet to an angry, churning emptiness far below. By the time she made her way down the path and reached the start of the granite tongue, the prisoner wagon already climbed the last of the trail. It rolled toward the front gate of the castle.

"I can't let Grit take them inside," she said making her way to the bottom of the path. Hanna half-hobbled with her gimp leg and half-jogged across the stone tongue. Thin, red streaks from the gouges in her leg stretched from her calf to up past her knee. She bit back the stabbing pain and hobbled in a last-ditch effort to save her friends. Hanna slipped the talisman over her neck before reaching the other side of the bridge. She shook her head. *I'm too late—too late.*

The rolling, wooden cells housing her friends rounded the top of the hill. As she reached the crest, Hanna spotted Michael in the rear cage as it rolled through the front portcullis. Her ears rang with the *clickity-clack* of the large, steel chains that lowered the main gate to the ground.

"Nooo!" she yelled and collapsed to her knees in the dirt.

39

NO WHERE TO RUN

"Do you think Michael found Hanna?" asked Patrick.

Lexi sat on the gnarled roots of a needle-less pine and caught her breath. "Dunno."

"Do you think they're safe?"

She shrugged. "How should I know?"

"Well, what *do* you know?"

"I think we're close to finding the mushroom." Patrick tipped back his head and gazed lazily at the gloomy clouds. Lexi stared at him with bemused interest. "What do you think we'll find when we get there?"

"If these mushrooms are anything like fungus in Midtown Valley, they'll grow in clusters."

"Clusters, huh…how many do you think we'll need?"

"Heck, I don't know," he said, shrugging. "I guess it depends on how big they are."

"Give me your best guess. You're smart—the smartest person I know."

Patrick's face split into a small grin and a blush crept into his cheeks. "It depends on how potent they are. Based on the number of sick people, though, we'd better grab at least a dozen or so. Fungus are normally extremely potent plants, so my first guess would be that is enough." The pair trudged through the muck, making their way from one landmark to the next.

"I have a question," said Patrick, his face flushing a further shade of scarlet. He shoved his hand in his back pocket and pulled out a note. "Well, I've been thinking…" Lexi cast a sideways glance and gasped at the red heart stenciled on the front. "Do you think—"

Lexi lunged for the note. Pulling it from his fingers, she clutched the colorfully folded paper in her hands. "I thought—I mean—I thought you'd never ask." She excitedly flipped the note over to its front.

"No—it's not—it's for—" he stumbled over his words.

The corners of Lexi's mouth drooped. A sudden cascade of icy water tumbled through her insides. The vibrant spring in her voice was deadened by the words he failed say. "Oh…it's for Hanna," she mumbled, staring at the hand-drawn name.

"Yeah, well," Patrick muttered. "I mean, I was gonna ask myself, but…"

"But what? You thought it'd be easier to ask me to be your gopher?"

"Well, yes—I mean, no…that's not…"

Tears welled in Lexi's eyes and she turned away from him so he wouldn't see her cry. Pushing the heels of her hands against her face, she wiped the evidence away, and swallowed her anger.

"I—I'm sorry. I shouldn't have…I like you, I really do, but—"

"Even after I tried to kiss you back there?" She pointed behind her.

"Yeah…I wasn't sure how to…I mean that was exciting, but—"

"Forget it!" she interrupted and crumpled the folded note in her fist, shoving it into her front pocket without making eye contact. "Sure, whatever. I'll give it to her."

"Do you think you could say something on my behalf—like something encouraging?"

Lexi slapped Patrick hard across the face. "You're a jerk!"

"What?" he said, startled.

"You're probably the smartest guy I know n'all, but you've got to be the dumbest, too." Patrick's eyes bulged as he held his cheek. "Well? Say something, would you!" she hollered.

His head jerked to the side as if expecting another blow, but she didn't even raise her hand again. Patrick frowned and looked through the surrounding trees. "Shh!" He was still holding his cheek.

"Don't tell me to—"

"Shh!" he hissed again looking around. "Do you hear that?"

She stared daggers at the back of Patrick's head. "No. I hear nothing!"

"That's just it. Everything's quiet—the birds, the frogs, the chittering bugs—everything!"

A cold wind tossed Lexi's short, chestnut hair across her face. Carried on the back of the breeze was another noise—a completely new and different sound. A low, resonating groan cut through the air and sent goose bumps up her back. She spun and searched the trees. "Is that Commander Grit?"

Patrick shot quick, furtive glances over his left and right shoulders. "No, I don't think so. That's something else entirely—I think we need to hurry out of here."

"Why, what's out there?" asked Lexi.

"I...don't...know," he said slowly, surveying the area. "Remember what Gob said? Don't dawdle in the dark? Yeah, well I don't think we should dawdle in the light either. So, let's go. I don't want to find out what's out there." They jogged through muck until they were splashing waist deep in the bog. As they struggled, the low rumble echoed again. "Where's that coming from?"

A loud crack suddenly split the air like a bullet. Patrick whirled just in-time to dodge a broken tree hurling at him through the air. It crashed and splintered against a grove behind them. Patrick screamed, sending Lexi into an all-out panic.

The two bounded through the muck as if cement blocks were tied to their shoes. Too scared to turn around, Lexi ran as fast as she could, but the soupy water pulled at her legs. She splashed, half-running, half-stumbling, and completely covered in sludge from head to toe. The swamp pulled at her feet no matter how fiercely she tried to race. Patrick sloshed passed her and turned back, reaching for her hand.

Tears streamed down Lexi's cheeks as she ducked under a tipped-over tree and dared a glance over her shoulder. A beast more monstrous than anything she'd ever seen was right behind her. The only saving grace was that it, too, appeared to struggle.

"GET AWAY FROM ME!" she screamed, choking on her spit.

It was bigger than Hugo, bigger than Crowthorn, bigger than anything ought to be. Tendrils of black ooze dripped from everywhere. It had no bare skin, no fur, but was slathered in a shimmering, viscous tar that seeped off it like hot sap.

"Over here, Lexi—run over here!"

Concealed by a grove of weeping willows, Patrick sprung from behind their sunken roots, waving his arms. Lexi panicked, splashing over to Patrick's hiding spot. Still crying, she ducked for cover. Lexi hid waist-deep in the filthy sludge and gripped Patrick's waist so tight that her knuckles turned as white as paper. "What now?" she pleaded.

"Under here." Patrick pointed to a gap under the roots in the grove of trees.

Lexi tucked herself inside the mess of tangled limbs. Swamp grass twisted and knotted around her feet like wet yarn. "I think I can squeeze through—" She pushed her legs in first and struggled between the mangled roots. Lexi sucked in her belly and squeezed between the stiff wood. Halfway through the maze of tangles, she ducked under a knot and dunked her head under the murky surface. It tasted horrid.

Finally confined within the open space beneath the trees, Lexi sat submerged up to her chin. "Get in here," she shouted.

"Quick!" Lexi reached for Patrick's hand. She tried to pull him through the same maze of roots.

He squirmed halfway inside, but got stuck against his collar bone. "I'm too big—I can't—I can't get through!" His voice rose higher the more he panicked. Patrick struggled to thrust his shoulders through the tiny gap. He tore his shirt and red scrapes raked his clavicle.

"You have to try harder! Hurry, Patrick!"

Lexi's eyes widened as she stole a glance through the roots which sat like a cage above the surface of the water. She barely had enough room to breathe. The creature sloshed around the grove, trudging near the wide tangle of roots. Soupy water splashed in heavy waves of foul-tasting muck. Her gut curled as a horrible thought flashed to mind. Patrick might not survive.

Patrick squealed in pain. He was stuck neck-deep inside immovable limbs. His blue shirt, now ripped above the shoulder, hung in patches from his collar. Patrick's backpack lay half-slung off his elbow. The creature rounded the grove of willows. Patrick's mouth fell slack as tears filled his eyes. The swamp between the two friends grew warm. Had he peed himself?

"Lexi," he whispered. His lids peeled back to expose two egg-sized eyes. He stared transfixed at the beast. He no longer thrashed about. Patrick stood petrified. "Lexi," he repeated, this time louder. Then he screamed, "LEXI!"

It stretched out a long, thick arm toward Patrick's head. Tears splashed down her friend's cheeks. At the last moment before the creature's hand reached him, Patrick turned to Lexi. Their eyes met as she reached out for him. And Patrick vanished.

40

THE PROPHECY

Hanna crawled to the front portcullis and pressed her forehead against the thick, steel bars. She craned her neck, looking to the stone rampart thirty feet up and to the steel-gray sky. *All this effort—for what? To come this close and for nothing but to lose more friends?*

She climbed back to her feet on shaky legs. Her temper mounted. A wave of frustration climbed until the tips of her ears burned. Her day seemed to be nothing but failure after failure. When would she catch a break?

Hanna rubbed her injured leg. Although she couldn't see the wounds because of her invisibility necklace, her hand came away tacky and wet. Fiery pins prickled up her leg. She fell more than sat in the dirt. Hanna pressed her back against the unforgiving steel gate and stared at where her leg would be.

"What the heck—some sort of poison, I guess?" She traced the wounds with her finger following the painful trails up her leg. "Why aren't I healing like before?" She flexed the knuckles of her right hand. There was no pain from her bike accident at Midtown Valley High. A sickening weight sank in her stomach. "What if the squid's poison is too powerful? Am I dying?"

She knocked the back of her head against the portcullis. The long, rusty rivets in the gate bit into her scalp. Hanna took in a deep breath and let it out in an exasperated huff, slumping her forehead into her hands. *What in the heck am I gonna do now?*

Her head throbbed behind her eyes. But as she fluttered them closed and back open again, she caught a glimpse of a bear, two wolves, several boars, and a badger passing behind her. They disappeared behind a stone wall.

Hanna remained with her back against the bars. Before she could react, the *clackity-clack* of the portcullis sounded again and the humungous gate slowly rose off the ground. She twisted to look, but her necklaces snagged on a misshapen rivet in the gate. Hanna was hoisted into the air by her neck.

She floundered in the air, choking—strangled by the unbreakable cord of her blue pendant. Hanna gagged in dry chortles trying to free herself from her noose. As she dangled, her feet kicked and bucked above the Brotherhood as they walked below her invisible feet. Hanna struggled, grasping for any way to peel the necklace from her throat. *Not like this! It can't end like this! Magic...make it work...make...it...*

Hanna's thoughts faded as consciousness waned in and out. She couldn't summon anything. She writhed and grabbed at her neck, forcing her fingers under the tight cable. Hanna finally got her fingers around one of two necklaces, hoping against hope that it was the one to free her, and pulled with all her might. A slight give slipped around her neck, then something broke free. But her father's magic necklace kept her in place.

Her head throbbed, choked of air. She tried magic again, but it was still no use. Hanna clutched at her throat as she kicked again and again. Something dropped and hit her feet. The invisibility necklace fell into the dirt.

Struggling with the last of her strength, Hanna kicked again and fell finally feeling free air beneath her feet. She hit the ground with a crunch and gasped for breath. Hanna pushed herself up onto all fours in the dirt and filled her starved lungs with oxygen.

"What the—" cried a guard.

"Look what we have here," said a wolf in a gravelly voice.

A second wolf pat the bear on the back and said, "Go on, Chowder—have some fun."

Hanna blinked wildly, still trying to shake the blur and tears from her eyes. Barely able to stand, she staggered to her feet gulping mouthfuls of air. She looked from one soldier to the next as her vision cleared. She held her hands out in front of her and croaked, "I'm not looking for trouble."

Chowder tossed a long, metal spear back and forth between his hands as he shuffled forward. "Oh, trouble is what you found, sweetheart. You found it in spades." His long un-retractable claws *clinked* and *clicked* against the metal staff in his hands.

He towered over her. Chowder was bigger than Hugo. He barely needed armor. His thick, heavy fur was enough to protect him from almost anything. Hanna stepped back, wincing and stumbling at the burn in her gimp leg.

"Get her!" shouted a wolf.

The bear flipped his spear end over end. Hanna tried to lean back on her injured calf and nearly fell to the ground. Chowder thrust the blunt end of his spear into her diaphragm.

"Oomph," she grunted. The muscles of her gut spasmed as precious air fled her lungs again. Half-a-dozen chuckles filled her ears. Hanna buckled with her hands clutching her stomach. She held up her ringed hand and groped for breath for the second time in as many minutes. Regaining some strength, she hovered her arm at waist level, palm-down, as the laughter grew.

"Whatcha' doing, love?" asked Chowder. "Waitin' ta shake hands?"

Think. Think. How did I topple Barlow in Breakwater? Hanna tossed the feeling of magic quickly around her mind. She focused on the way it felt—the way it seemed to flow through her. The tingles in the palms of her hands and the warmth that danced like scampering mice around the nape of her neck. *Think. How did I escape from the giant squid in the cave? Do it now—do it now!*

The words echoed in her skull and the familiar tingling spread down her arms. The corners of Hanna's mouth twitched in response. She thought of a thin, stone shaft—and created one from below the soil. It shot up like a piston and landed in her hand.

Chowder's smile faded. Hanna twirled the dense staff of stone from side to side. It was something she'd done in her martial arts dojo for years. She caught the rod under her armpit and beckoned him forward.

Chowder charged in wild rage. "You're gonna find out why they call me Ch—"

Before the bear could finish, Hanna lunged forward on her good leg and thrust the end of her staff into his throat. It caught Chowder in the soft waddle of skin below his chin. He dropped his spear and clutched his neck with both hands.

Hanna pulled back and spun her staff over her head, swinging it in a long arch in-front of her. It caught Chowder in the side of the jaw. Bones splintered. Her staff's momentum clipped the next two wolves in the side of the head. All three fell to the dirt. The impact of stone on bone brought a high-pitched yelp only a canine could make. But their cries brought new attention.

From across the courtyard, a large Dire Wolf advanced. "Crap. Grit's coming."

She hobbled toward him and away from Chowder. Suddenly, an explosion of pain broke across the back of her knees, buckling her to the ground once again. An arm slipped around her throat as her stone staff tumbled to the ground.

"We've got her now," snorted a boar as he scraped a dirty hoof down the back of her bad leg. Hanna screamed. Her leg felt like liquid fire. "Take a swing, boys." She struggled against the boar's chokehold as a metal baton slammed into her gut. She coughed and curled forward, but didn't fall. So, the boar jabbed a knee into the small of her back and wrenched her backward again.

Anger twisted with the pain and her emotions exited through her hands. Her palms glowed white-hot. She reached over her head and gripped the sides of the boar just below its ears. The heat seared the pig's flesh and the smell of fried bacon filled the air. His grip slackened as he screamed, and Hanna flipped him over her shoulder. She swung a fist at the side of his head, knocking him out.

As Hanna straightened up, she looked at her hands in a moment of awe. *What else can I do?*

"Ain't seen nothin' like that before," said a third wolf as Hanna picked up her staff.

Chowder finally pushed himself back to his feet. His head swayed on his thick, stumpy neck like a bobble doll until his half-crazed eyes settled back on her. A growl resonated in the back of his throat, but his broken jaw hung loose, wobbling back and forth.

He wildly lunged forward, but Hanna hopped sideways and tripped him with her staff. The grizzly stumbled headfirst into the stone wall at Hanna's back. She spun and pointed at the wall. A pocket of hard stone melted to a puddle in the dirt. Chowder landed in the opened space. The bear turned to escape, stepping halfway out the hole, but Hanna reformed the pool of rock back into a wall of hard stone, closing it in around him.

Spinning on her heels, she yelled at the bear's friends, "You boys want some of that medicine?"

"Bravo," said Grit, slowly clapping his hands. "You're either very brave or incredibly stupid." He unraveled a twelve-foot long black whip from his hip. Grit flicked his arm. Before she could react, a piercing crack split the air and a searing burn ignited on her shoulder. The skin above her collar bone ripped open and a scarlet stain leeched across her T-shirt.

Two of the previous wolves sprinted back into place, flanking her. Hanna clenched her fingers into another fist and commanded the ground to react. The rock beneath the topsoil burst through the grass, swallowing the wolves' feet as they ran, stopping them in their tracks.

Dog barks came from somewhere within the compound. Grit raised his whip over his head again. "That's the last trick you'll—"

Hanna didn't let him finish. The ground parted below Grit's feet at her command. A six-foot hole opened below the dire wolf and he tumbled inside. Before he could jump out, Hanna flooded it with dirt up to his neck.

"You'll pay for this insolence!" he shouted.

She smashed his snout with the stone staff and his head fell limply to the side. Kneeling, Hanna placed her hand in front of his slack snout. Slow, warm breaths brushed her open palm. *I'm getting the hang of this magic stuff.*

Hanna limped into the busy courtyard. The noisy rhythm and chatter died away completely as she came into full view of the Brotherhood. She was deftly aware that all work in the quadrangle stopped as a hundred pairs of eyes followed her.

You've got this. Look what you've done. It's just me—turning Barlow's castle on end. If I've only a sliver of the power my father has, there's no end to the things I can do. I can't wait to meet him.

But a new image flooded her brain, and a pang of guilt twisted in her stomach as the image of her stepdad—or foster, or whoever the man who raised her is called—flashed across the back of her eyes.

She didn't know what to call him, but the two figures—the one of her father in Midtown Valley and the other of Kambo, the man she'd convinced herself was her real father, clashed in her mind. Another ribbon of guilt snaked down her throat as the longing to meet Kambo butted violently against the love for the man she'd called dad her whole life. Surely, with her magical abilities, her dad in Midtown Valley wasn't her real father. How could he be? He'd never shown an inkling of magic.

Hanna tried to push those thoughts away. As she moved into the courtyard, ready to release her friends, a burst of wind lifted her off the ground. "What the—" she gasped as her back crashed against the rocky courtyard floor. Stars swam across her vision as her head bounced on the ground. Hanna blinked and tried to shake the high-pitched ringing from her ears.

"Who do you think you are?" boomed a deep, familiar voice. "You're nothing but a little schoolgirl with a few new tricks." Hanna looked up. Two figures floated in the air above her. Slowly, the blurry haze merged and only one figure came into focus hanging over the courtyard. "This is my kingdom—my castle. How dare you come here, you little whelp."

Hanna pushed herself shakily to her feet. "You're a—"

"You've come here on some misguided agenda," Barlow cut across her. "You've lost your friends. You have no hope of help. And best of all, you've lost yourself."

"Shut up," she spat. "I don't—"

"You've practically gift wrapped yourself for me," he interrupted again, feigning a look of shock. "You think you can defeat me?" He laughed deep in his throat. "Just look at where you are, little girl. I defeated your father. What makes you think a half-blood like yourself stands a chance?"

Hanna glanced about the quadrangle. She passed her eyes from thug to thug across the courtyard. A curl of doubt twisted in her stomach and a whole mess of emotions knotted themselves in her mind. Confusion, anger, fear, and revenge welled up like a tangled ball of yarn.

She thought of her dad in Midtown Valley; she thought of Ashley broken and sick; she thought of her other sister running what may be a fool's errand in the depths of an unknown, dangerous swamp; she thought of Michael's back; she thought of her other new friends. Hanna trembled with uncaged rage. She flicked her eyes toward Michael in the bamboo wagon not twenty feet away.

"Your friends are mine. You'll be mine. Your sisters will be mine. This whole kingdom will be—"

A familiar tingle radiated down her arms like a hot fuse. Hanna's hands glowed white-hot once more. She wanted to hurt him. Wanted to make him pay for what he'd done—to stop this man bent on destroying everything she loved. Without being fully aware of how she did it, Hanna thrust her arms forward and flung bolts of hot plasma from her palms.

Over the crackle of electric discharge came the laugh of madness. "Energy bolts—you are indeed your father's daughter. The God of Light would've been proud to see how his little girl turned out." Barlow dodged her volley without effort. "Too bad he'll never get to see you."

Hanna dove into a rolling summersault and crouched behind a short stack of wooden crates. She lobbed a fresh series of hot plasma charges, filling the air with a static charge and the pungent smell of ozone. Barlow, still hovering above, ducked out of the way, but not before getting his good ear singed in the process.

The King of Thieves swept his hand in an arch, and Hanna was again blown backward, head over heels, past Grit and through the open portcullis. Wooden boxes and debris tumbled out the gate after her. She barrel-rolled down the dusty trail and over the crest of the slope toward the great, stone tongue.

"I underestimated you before," Barlow boomed. "But never again. Today you die."

The world spun in a dizzying swirl as she lay panting on her back. Exhausted and bruised, Hanna tried to catch her breath and stumbled to her knees. She shook the dizzying fog from her head and found her footing once again. But this time, her injured leg wouldn't take any more weight. She collapsed in the dirt.

The prince floated high over the front gate and landed on the ground a stone's throw up the slope. "You surprised me in Breakwater, but here I still would've expected more from Kambo's daughter."

She mashed her teeth together, brushed the dirt from her legs, and looked to Barlow. He carried a wand. Hagadorn carried an ivory tusk like this one, but the King of Thieves' wand wasn't smooth and white. His was dark and twisted like the spiraled cone of a seashell. Gnarled barnacles sprouted like boils from its surface.

"Anyone ever tell you the best wands are made of snakewood or from the majestic horn of a unicorn? They lied—mermaid horns are the best. Mine comes from royal lineage."

Hanna pressed the heel of her hands against her knees and stood. She limped with all her weight on her good leg. Hanna flicked a glance at the solitary GodStone fitted into her ring and the corner of her mouth curled.

She thrust her hand toward Barlow and a slender spire of rock shot from the hillside. It flew high into the air, but before reaching him, it exploded as a fork of lightning lanced it from the sky. Bits of rubble rained down across the grassy knoll.

With a quick snap of Barlow's wrist, an invisible column of air punched Hanna in the chest like a steel rod. She folded inward onto herself as she was hurled backward off the hill and rolled to the bald, wet cusp of the great stone tongue.

"Foolish girl—think I'd fall for the same trick as in Breakwater?"

Her shoulders smacked the granite lip half a breath before the back of her head slammed into the unforgiving ledge. Stars swam in her vision for the second time as oxygen was violently thrust from her lungs. Hanna clutched at her chest and gasped for breath. She rolled to her belly. The mist from the falls filled the air with a dusting of water.

She hated the prince more than anything in her life. Hanna wasn't going to let him win—wasn't going to let him hurt her sisters—not after all she'd been through. As she knelt on all fours, her leg pulsed worse than ever. The poison stretched red scratches up her thigh. Hanna grit her teeth and pushed away her pain as her hands glowed with a renewed electric light.

Hanna launched a ball of plasma at Barlow, but he levitated effortlessly above it. "Kambo couldn't beat me. What makes you think you can?"

Barlow pointed a jeweled fist at Hanna. Two crimson rubies the color of smoldering embers glowed from a ring on his right hand. Her chest arched as a new swirl of crimson light tugged at her body. It rose from her skin like gossamer fingers of steam. The reddish glow around Hanna drifted in wispy tendrils, trailing through the air to Barlow, surrounding him in a ruby haze.

"Your magic is mine. You are nothing—just like your father."

Hanna slumped in the dirt. She raised her bent head enough to watch her energy—her magic—drain into the prince. But her vision was assaulted with new images dancing in her head. Somehow, connected to Barlow through Dark Magic, inside her mind's eye there raged a battle between Kambo and the King of Thieves.

Kambo, caught in the open hall of an enormous, stone coliseum, drew plasma from the air with his outstretched hands. He formed an energy ball greater than Hanna ever had and hurled it at the prince. Barlow ducked behind a massive pillar and the fireball slammed into the column.

As if detonated by dynamite, a whole section of the pillar was obliterated in a cloud of dust and rubble. Screams of agonizing pain erupted from behind the wreckage and Barlow stumbled from the ruin with the side of his head burnt nearly to the bone.

"My face—my face!" screamed Barlow. *"You'll pay—you'll pay for what you've done!"*

Hanna was wrenched from the vision by a piercing agony of her own. Like water down a drain, her magic flowed away. Every nerve stung like a thousand needles. A crimson glow swirled around her, siphoning off her power. In that brief moment, Hanna's thoughts snapped back to Breakwater when she first met Barlow, when she'd seen the red glow before.

She grew weaker as the magic within her was pulled from her bones. Hanna threw her head back and screamed, unable to do anything. She tried to pool what remained of her power—tried to cast one last spell—to stop him from taking what was rightfully hers, but it was too late. There was nothing. No familiar tingle—no trickle at the nape of her neck. Hanna thought back to what Golinveaux told her—Don't give him the chance to steal any of your precious aura. Shame swallowed her whole.

"You've got no one to save you this time." Through her half-opened eyelids, Barlow's chest swelled as he breathed in the last of her magic. The reddish cloud, which swirled like a whirlwind around her, vanished, retreating back into prince's ring. He barked a loud, piercing laugh. "Like father, like daughter. I should've done that the moment I saw you in Breakwater."

"You'll never get away with this!" Hanna screamed slumping over in exhaustion.

"Oh, but I have gotten away with it. But don't worry, I won't rob you of *all* your power—I'll leave enough for you to remember me while you're still alive."

Hanna tried to create an energy bolt, but only a short, stubby six-inch blade of energy poked out from between her knuckles.

"Don't worry. I haven't forgotten about the pendant around your neck. I wondered where Kambo hid his powers. When I defeated him, he robbed me of my prize. His magic was already gone—vanished somehow. Now I know where and I'll peel it from your corpse."

With her eyes half-closed, Hanna clenched her fists at her side. Tapping into the magic of her GodStone ring, pillars of stone shot from the ground below the prince and clay-like hands reached to grip him. But just like before, Barlow effortlessly rose out of their grasp.

"I tire of the childish games from a lonely girl who knows nothing of herself—nothing about a kingdom she once-upon-a-time would've inherited." Hanna knit her brows together.

Barlow chuckled. "You don't even know your own story. Who you are. Where you're from."

"What?" she wheezed, crawling on all fours.

"It's a shame this couldn't have happened sooner. I tried, of course, to rob you of your powers when you and your sisters were no more than suckling babes. But someone stole that opportunity. You were kidnapped. You became a lost demigod in a place where I couldn't touch you. But that's not the case anymore. You touched my ring. Fourteen years later and I still get what I justly deserve."

Hanna sunk her head between her shoulders.

"With you gone and out of my way, your sisters will be mine by the Summer Solstice! The coming weeks will pass soon enough—by the time the sun sets on the Solstice I'll be a god. You've evaded your own death too many times—let's finish this charade."

Everything Barlow touches ends in…

The King of Thieves thrust out his open palm and in a sweeping gesture, clenched his hand closed. Hanna was gripped by the wind and dragged into the air. She snatched a fleeting glance toward the prince. Barlow whipped his arm and Hanna was hurled around like sack of flesh. The last thing she saw was the lip of the great stone tongue cast upside-down as she was catapulted over the mouth of the falls and into the gaping abyss below.

41

BLUNDERSTEEP FALLS

Hanna plummeted over the falls. Her arms and legs flailed limply like a rag doll. The deluge of water, which spilled from under the great stone tongue, soaked her to the bone. If she tried, she could've touched the stream as she tumbled down the long drop to the bottom. Her limbs went numb as she twisted through open air.

Everything Barlow touches ends in tragedy.

All the pent-up anticipation of using magic—of meeting her real dad, of finding answers from the people she'd called her parents her whole life, of finding out what Patrick's note really said—it all leaked from her mind in a single explosive collapse of her world. As she dropped, things seemed to slow in her mind, old memories flooding in.

Hanna remembered a long time ago, when she and her sisters were very young. The three played in the backyard around their enormous oak tree in Midtown Valley. They had a picnic together with their mother and father and sat on a red and white checkered tablecloth under the shade. It was a powder-blue sky on that warm, summer's day. It was the first day the family began work on building their treehouse together.

Stings of icy pain against her face brought her back to her

perilous flight over the falls. The wind was savage. She descended so quickly, it was like teeth biting into her skin. The roar of the water deafened her ears.

Everything Barlow touches ends—

She pressed her eyes tight and the cold rush of air buffeted her face as she plummeted down the throat of the falls. Her heart crashed against her ribcage. The chilly, violent wind whipped like needles against her face and limbs. It choked the breath from her throat. She could barely open her eyes as the force of the gust blurred her vision and the roar of the water drowned out the world. Hanna did everything she could to block the moment from her mind. More memories poured in to take its place.

It was the first day of middle school for the three of them. Ashley started sixth grade, Lexi seventh, and Hanna eighth. They'd made peanut butter and jelly sandwiches in the kitchen before school. One thing happened after another and before any of them had known it, a food fight broke out. Jelly smeared the walls and there was peanut butter hanging from the light fixtures. Overturned slices of bread were scattered like miniature, fluffy Frisbees across the room. But most importantly, there had been laughter. Laughter and smiles and happiness.

Frigid water blasted against her face, and Hanna was forced to again confront the worst moment of her life.

Everything Barlow touches—

She fell down, down, down. The biting air stung her eyes. It whipped her clothes. It tore at her skin. She closed her eyes tight, her mind scrambled for anything but the image of her own death.

Patrick's face filled the space behind her eyelids. A smile cracked her face as the memory of him kneeling on the classroom floor, picking up his books and things from the floor. It was then that she'd seen it—the note. It was under her knee and then it was in Patrick's hand. Although he'd tried to conceal it, she knew—she'd known what it was the moment she saw the folded paper beneath her.

What did it say? What did Patrick—her best friend in all the world—want to say to her? Could it really be that he felt that way for her? How long had that been going on? How long had he cared for her that way and she'd not noticed? Now she'd never find out.

A sour knot turned in her stomach. She'd never know. Today she'd die cold and alone and loveless. Hanna silently sobbed. Her tears whipped off her eyelashes like bullets, her cries lost in the thunder of the falls.

She fell down, down, down.

Everything Barlow—

Hanna thought of Ashley. Then she thought of the time when Lexi was almost struck by the car in the street. How she'd not been fast enough to save her, but Michael was. She remembered sitting Ashley and Lexi down to explain—to explain what needed to happen. Ashley's eyes threatened to spill tears onto her cheeks as Hanna told her that she herself needed to have an operation. That it was an operation that could possibly save someone's life—her friend's life—Michael's life. Hanna explained to her sisters why it had to be done regardless of the dangers. It's just what needed to happen. That's what you do for someone you care for, she'd told them—

The horrible truth hit her like a ton of bricks. Hanna's eyes snapped open, falling victim to the wind and water. She did care for one of her friends, but she'd never get the chance to tell him.

Everything—

42

A GIFT THAT KEEPS ON GIVING

Time was funny. It seemed to just slip into and out of place. The last Michael remembered he was in a rolling crate in the courtyard with Hugo and the others. Now…well, Michael wished he was still locked in that bamboo cell.

Bound in place with a clasp of steel around his neck, Michael crawled from behind a massive throne. He hunched over like a dog at Barlow's feet with his nose mere inches from the prince's black boots. Pools of dark dried liquid stained the floor like bruises. Could that be blood? He crawled over the stains that blemished the gray cobblestones in swaths of scarlet and crimson.

Michael balled up what little courage he had and screwed his eyes tight. "Bloody hell! What do you want with me?" He pressed his palms to his eyes. The waggle of the steel links around his neck clinked like ice cubes. Sweat trickled down his wide nose and stained the floor in tiny droplets. "Please let me go—Oh, God—c'mon—" Barlow struck Michael across the face with the back of his hand. Michael yelped holding his cheek. "Okay—I'm sorry—I'm sorry."

Why does Hanna get powers? If I only had magic. It's not fair. It's not fair. It's not —

A stringy line of red drool as thin as fishing wire dripped from his lips. Michael shakily looked around the edge of the throne and saw a ragged hag. The woman's black, tattered robe hung on her ancient frame like sagging skin. The corners of her mouth curled from behind a mop of matted, long, gray hair.

Three Feralings floated in a circle next her. Their tentacles wrapped tightly together to form a grotesque ring of flesh and sinew. Michael blinked, shifting his gaze from the hag to the carnivorous abominations. Up close, they looked even worse than in the swamp.

He recoiled as the stink of rotten flesh wafted to his nose. Michael was mesmerized by the single, large eye that topped their mop of tentacles that he had originally taken for their body. Strips of yellowish-green sinew tethered the bulbous, bowling ball-sized eye to its purple arms. Each eye stared unblinkingly into the great hall. The remaining leathery tentacles not linked together to form the inky black ring in their center hung limply toward the floor.

Could that be another portal?

The Feralings' curtain of tentacles began to violently shake. Their arms, which formed the top ring to the portal, undulated in rhythmic convulsions, at first pulsing slowly but growing in speed and intensity. Suddenly, out of the middle of the black void, a new Feraling was vomited into the hall.

I've got to get it. It's there somewhere. He didn't find it. Michael reached for his trinket slipping the tips of his fingers into his pocket. He searched for the cold, metal medallion the drunkard slipped into his pocket after Michael first entered the Salthouse Wharf.

The hag hacked up phlegm and swallowed. She pointed a craggy finger at him and when she spoke, her voice came out cracked and old. "Do what I command. Tell me your secrets…"

"Witch!" snapped Barlow, turning to the woman. "What do you see?"

Before the hag could speak again, Michael rolled to his side, gripping his back at the prince's feet. The pain crawled in spasms up the middle of his back. Pinching his eyes tight, he sucked air through his teeth and tried to conceal his discomfort, but the damage was done.

"The boy is holding secrets… He holds a raven on his arm… But there's more…"

Barlow pulled out his spiraled wand and knelt holding it in Michael's face. With slow, deliberate words, he said, "Show me your arm." Michael lifted it exposing the raven scar. "It's you I spoke to in the Wood Troll's cabin." Barlow pursed his lips and spoke again. "So, tell me. How did you get the branding of my Brotherhood? Was it a shrine?"

"No," Michael said without looking at him.

"Who are you, boy?"

"Nobody," he said through clenched teeth. "Just nobody, 'kay?" Barlow rose his arm and Michael floated up into the air on a gust of wind. "What's happening?" Michael rose belly-up until the chain around his neck was stretched tight against the throne. "W-what are you doing?!"

Barlow pressed the tip of his wand between Michael's eyes. The hard, coarse shell of the mermaid wand was cold against his skin. The witch slipped forward and pulled up the hem of his shirt until it bunched up around his chest. Barlow walked in slow, concentric circles around him.

"Very interesting," The King of Thieves said, looking at the angry streaks that wrapped around the side of Michael's back.

With the slight flick of his wrist, the prince flipped him onto his belly. Michael tried to fight against it, but he was caught in Barlow's magic and there was nothing he could do other than surrender to it. The links in the metal chain around his neck clinked. Barlow examined the streaks radiating from the small of his back underneath a three-inch scar.

Michael struggled again to peel his hands from his sides, but he couldn't move. *I've got to reach the medallion.* His pocket seemed miles away.

"How is this possible?" muttered Barlow. "How can you possess this kind of power?" Michael's breath caught in his throat. *What power?* Barlow leaned forward and spun Michael back upright so his nose almost touched Michael's sweaty face. "I'm going to ask you again. Who are you?"

"W-what do you mean?"

"Don't play stupid with me, boy. Who are you and where are you from?"

Michael stuttered, "I-I don't under—"

Barlow twirled a finger and spun a thin, cone-shaped spike of air. It hovered for a moment until he sent it piercing into Michael's bicep. "Answer me, boy!" Michael screeched as blood welled up from the wound and soiled his sleeve. "Answer—me! Who—are—you?" Barlow hollered. "Witch, if he won't talk, then find out for me."

Michael looked up at the old hag as she closed her eyes and inhaled through her long, hooked nose. A parched tongue parted her mouth and ran across cracked lips. With a final inhale, her hazel eyes snapped back open. "His name is Michael Grand."

Barlow made the smallest of nods and paused. "Mr. Grand..."

"What?" Michael whimpered. "She told you who I am."

"I know you're friends with Hanna Steele, but I'd still like you to tell me where you're from?

"I'm from—I'm—oh, my arm, man! Take it out of my arm. I'll tell 'ya whateva 'ya want."

Barlow flicked his wrist as if swatting a bug and the spike of air dissipated into vapor. Michael's head slumped forward.

"My patience is growing thin, Mr. Grand," Barlow snarled. "You want to be friends, right?"

"Yeah, mate. Whatever you say. We'll be friends—good friends."

"Good. And in order for us to be friends, we've got to work together."

"Right. Work together."

"Let's let bygones be bygones."

Beads of sweat trickled down Michael's forehead. "Sure. Bygones."

"I've got something you need and you've got something I want."

"What?" Michael wheezed. "What could I possibly need from you?"

"You've got something inside you, but before I help you, I need to know something…"

"H-help me?" Michael asked before what else Barlow said settled in. "Inside me? What the bloody hell do you mean something's in me? What's in me?"

"You first need to answer my simple question. Where—are—you—from?" Barlow repeated.

"Midtown Valley—I'm from Midtown Valley, Illinois."

"That's good. Now, how is it that you've obtained magic if you're not from Smaradine?"

"M-magic? What magic? What are you talking about?"

"I'm sure you're in great pain, boy. You seem to hide it well, but I can read the truth of it. It radiates from this spot." The prince reached around Michael and tapped the boy's back with his wand. "It's from un-tempered magic."

"Un-tempered magic? That's good, right?"

"If left untreated, it would kill you."

Michael's throat turned dry. "Can you treat it? Fix me, FIX ME!" Barlow stared silently. "PLEASE!" Michael hollered. "I DON'T WANNA DIE."

"It's not me that's causing you the pain, Mr. Grand. The magic's already inside you." The King of Thieves lowered Michael so his feet again rested safely on solid ground.

"How's that possible? I don't know nothin' about magic, I swear."

Barlow moved around Michael. "What's the scar on your back?"

"My scar? You're bonkers, mate. What's that have to do with anything?"

"No more games!" shouted Barlow. He spun a new vortex of air in preparation. "Tell me about the scar."

Michael stared wide-eyed at the spear of air. "It was a transplant—a kidney transplant."

"A kidney?"

"I went into renal failure. My kidneys were quitting, you know, shutting down—not working. I had an accident. Hanna saved me. Both of my kidneys were damaged and had to be removed. They were smashed. Hanna gave me one of hers—saved my life."

"Hanna saved you?"

"Yeah—that's what I said."

"You have one of Hanna's kidneys—inside *your* body?" Barlow repeated in a hushed whisper as he paced in slow circles around Michael's body.

"Yeah. That's how it works." He turned his head to keep the prince in view.

Barlow chuckled. He came around to face Michael and leaned uncomfortably close—so close, the curly, coppery wires of his single sideburn brushed against Michael's cheek. "Why don't I just rip it from your back?"

"It doesn't work that way!" You gotta be a match—a blood type match or you can die."

"Oh, Mr. Grand. You see, I would have no need for your magical kidney myself. I have more than enough magic to last me a dozen lifetimes."

Michael considered Barlow's words. "Then why...why would you do that? Why would you take my kidney...and...and kill me? I didn't do anything to you."

"Oh, but you're missing the bigger picture." Barlow cleared his throat. "Leverage. It's all about leverage. Let's be friends, is that okay, Michael? Say I don't kill you, but instead I help relieve the pain in your back. By tempering the magic, it would release latent abilities. For my services, however, you'd have to pledge your complete loyalty to me."

The witch, who stood somewhere behind Michael's back, cackled a high-pitched laugh.

"Loyalty? W-what do you want?"

"I want Hanna's two sisters by the Summer Solstice. It's a win-win for everyone."

"I thought you wanted Hanna's necklace. Why not just take it and leave the girls alone?"

"I do want it. I've already sent men to get it from the bottom of the Blundersteep Falls, but those sweet, innocent girls are just too tempting to pass up."

"I-I don't understand why you need them," Michael stammered, his brow creased. "Wait…did you say the bottom of the falls? What'd you do to Hanna?!"

Without a hint of emotion, Barlow shrugged. "I threw her over Blundersteep Falls."

Michael knees buckled as if his legs turned to warm licorice. "OH MY GOD! Hanna—not Hanna. Oh my god, NOT Hanna!" He screamed, his eyes swelling with water. "I ain't helping you nothin!" Michael raged, spittle and drool flew from his lips.

Barlow spun a new vortex and plunged it into his chest. "There are NO demigods here to save you, boy. It's either deal or die!"

Tears streaked Michael's anguished face as he thrashed his head back and forth, screaming. Blood spurt from the puncture above his right nipple, peppering the floor in scarlet freckles. "All right—stop—just stop! I'll tell 'ya anything."

The prince waved his fingers and the vortex in Michael's chest turned into steamy mist. "All I want is the girl's magical aura. What's that to you?" Barlow stared unblinkingly into his eyes and waited.

Michael shifted his gaze to the floor. "So, you won't hurt them?" he murmured.

"They'll be safe—enough."

"Safe how?" asked Michael, frowning.

"Their lives are meaningless to me, Mr. Grand. I'm only after their magical aura. Once I have that, you can take what's left. They'll be of no use to me. You will work for me. Bring me the girls by the end of the Summer Solstice in a few weeks' time and I'll give you your life back—and by extension grant you magic beyond your wildest imagination."

Michael pondered the offer. "So, the girls will be safe and I get magic? Real magic?"

The witch's haggard face appeared from the corner of Michael's eye. She stepped close, placing her hand against his chest. The stink of unwashed skin and musky clothes wafted into his nose. Michael curled his lip and shied his chin away from the woman as she laid her bare cheek against his blood-stained arm. She offered a toothless grin in reply, just before she plunged her finger into the fresh wound above Michael's nipple.

Michael shrieked as her finger wormed into the hole. His arms were locked to his sides. He could do nothing but scream and scream and scream. She pulled her finger out with a wet slurp. As tears ran down Michael's flushed cheeks, she stuck out her tongue and licked the fresh blood from around her fingernail.

"Circe," Barlow barked. "Do you have it?"

The witch craned her head around. "I've got da scent of 'ya now, boy," she whispered.

"Get her away from me!" Michael screamed.

Barlow waved Circe off and she backed away. "After I heal you you'll get some magic. I don't know what—presumably some of what Hanna had, since it was *her* kidney, but time will tell."

Michael paused as new rivulets of red trickled from the

wound on his chest. The magical coin weighted heavier than ever in his pocket.

Blimey, what are you thinking? You've known them your whole life —YOUR WHOLE LIFE. You just gonna give 'em up to this prat for magic powers? Yeah, no doubt magic would be cool, but we're talking about people, here. Real people. Ashley and Lexi. You can't be seriously thinkin' about this, right?

Michael fought with himself for a few moments before whispering, "I can't."

"I could use a servant on the inside," Barlow whispered back. "But not one who can't see the value of what I'm offering." With a flick of his wrist, the prince flung Michael against the wall between his throne and bookshelf with a dull thud. "I can be a patient man, Mr. Grand, but what I hate more than anything is the stupidity of the weak."

With a fresh cry on his lips, Michael thrashed against invisible restraints. "Let go of me! Put me down."

"I offered you more than most could possibly dream of. Your love for those girls has blinded you to the power I wield!"

Michael lay sprawled out spread-eagle against the wall. His eyes bulging in terror as the King of Thieves spun more vortexes from thin air. Curdling screams erupted from his throat as the cold daggers punctured the length of his arms. Blinking away tears along his lashes, his screams echoed throughout the hall as more blood dripped in pools of scarlet on the cobbled floor.

"I don't ask for much, Mr. Grand. I ask for loyalty. Bring me the girls and all your wildest dreams will come true."

"Stop. Stop. STOP!" Michael screamed. "Anything. I'll do anything! Just make it stop!"

It was over as quickly as it started. Barlow dissolved the air spikes and Michael fell unceremoniously to the floor in a heap. His chest heaved in heavy gasps. Thick rivulets of blood streaked down his wet arms. Exhausted, he wiped the tears from his face, smearing warm, damp blood across his cheek and forehead. Barely lifting his head, he whispered, "Whatever you want."

"What was that, Mr. Grand? I didn't hear you clearly."

Michael lifted his head hating himself for doing it. "I'LL DO IT!"

The prince's smile inched up only one side of his face. His tight, pink scar held his burnt cheek stiff and inflexible. Barlow touched the tip of his wand to Michael's forehead and his arms and legs went stiff; Michael's back arched upward as a gurgled scream swam up his throat. Taught muscles rippled in his neck as his whole body trembled.

Barlow then moved the wand against the scar in Michael's back and the angry stain that pulsed in his kidney melted away like honey. The magic spread like warm, slender rivers into every extremity of his body. Michael's eyes rolled to the back of his head as the heat crawled through Michael's veins, into his neck, and to the top of his head.

"It is done," Barlow said, withdrawing his wand. Michael's body fell limp. He collapsed in a heap on the gray, stone floor striking his head with a hollow thump.

43

THE HORNED CALYPSO MUSHROOMS

"Don't say a word!" Lexi whispered to Patrick through gritted teeth. Dirty water sloshed in and out of her mouth. She squat in the muck, still submerged to her chin within the tangle of thick protective roots.

Her arm was stretched through the gnarled twists holding onto Patrick's hand. Lexi gripped Patrick's arm so tightly, the knuckles of her right hand went numb. Inside the palm of her left, she clutched the Invisibility Stone.

As if looking out the slatted bars of a prison cell, Lexi peered at the swamp creature with wide eyes as it reared back and bellowed its frustration. Tendrils of thick black viscous ooze dripped from its skin. It momentarily froze, as if stuck in mid-reach. Its massive hand remained stretched out to grab Patrick.

Go away, go away, go away. Please go away.

Patrick's choppy, panicked breath danced in Lexi's ears. The creature stood, as if frozen by confusion. Then, as if hearing Lexi's silent pleas, it recoiled its outstretched arm. With a second ear-splitting roar, the beast pounded against the thick grove of trees above Lexi's head. The trunks violently shook from the beast's unleashed rage. As if granted by Lexi's wishes, the beast lumbered away in the direction it came.

Within seconds, the healthy grove started to whither, gray, and die. The coiled roots bent and shriveled, pinching her arm, and threatening to loosen her hold on Patrick. Her arm was torqued sideways, wrenching her shoulder upward. Lexi's head pressed against the low-slung trunk, twisting her neck to the side and tangling it in the contorted mesh of wooden roots. Her fingers ached and began slipping from Patrick's arm.

Hold on—just hold on a little bit longer…

The seconds ticked away in slow motion as Lexi tried to keep the creature in view. When her torqued shoulder could take no more, her fingers slipped from Patrick's elbow and he popped back into view. She breathed heavily as she pulled her arm back in and tucked the Invisibility Stone back into her pocket.

"Patrick—Patrick, are you okay?" she whispered.

"I almost died!" he cried.

"Not so loud," she pleaded.

"I almost—"

"C'mon, you didn't."

Patrick leaned against the misshapen roots of the dead willow and wretched his breakfast into the brown stew of the swamp. After a moment, he pushed himself up and turned toward Lexi. "I can't believe you remembered that necklace. Thank GOD!" He wiped his mouth with the back of his hand. "My mind just froze—I couldn't think of a thing. I-I think I peed myself."

"Pretty sure I peed, too" she said, trying to resist her own urge to spew chunks.

Patrick nodded and slouched over, panting, his hands on his knees. "I've never been so scared in my whole life!"

Lexi held her breath and leaned closer to hold his hand. "I thought you were really brave."

"Thought I was gonna—" Patrick paused and stared at her. "What?"

Lexi bit her lower lip. "I thought you were brave. You stood up to that thing, didn't you?"

"Well, I guess? Sort of."

"Sure, you did. You saved me. I wouldn't have thought of the pendant if it weren't for you. You let me hide. You saved me."

"Yeah." He drew himself up to his full height. "I suppose you're right."

"I'd kiss you if I could," she said through the gray roots. Lexi twirled strands of her short, wet hair around her fingers.

Patrick jerked his eyes toward hers. "You'd what?"

Lexi jerked a thumb over her shoulder. "Meet me on the other side of the grove and figure out a way to pull me free."

"Wait! What about that thing?"

"Heck, 'ole tall, dark, and ugly is gone. Come help me out. Let's make like diarrhea and run before it comes back."

Patrick walked to the other side of the grove. "You're disgusting!"

The corners of Lexi's mouth twisted. "I know, but 'ya still love me."

He cracked a smile and looked for a spot wide enough to pull her out. "Here's a spot," he said and pulled her through a small opening in the roots.

As Patrick hauled her up, Lexi lifted herself on her tip-toes and kissed him on the lips. She pushed her mouth onto his. A rush of emotion washed over Lexi. It felt wonderful. She pulled back for a moment and then kissed him again for what seemed like hours. The best part…he kissed back.

When they finally parted, Patrick's cheeks were pink. "Oh—um—yeah. Thanks," he stuttered. After a moment of looking into her eyes, Patrick's eyes dropped to the swampy water. She wondered what he'd say next. Would he finally tell her that he loved her? Was he going to tell her that everything he thought about Hanna was wrong? She waited with baited breath. Patrick opened his mouth and then closed it. When he opened it again, Lexi's heart tumbled out of her chest. "Pull out your map. I want to see how far we have to go."

Her brow knit together. "What? That's what you have to say? I give you my first kiss—with barf breath—"

"Your first kiss?"

"Yeah. I give you my first kiss *ever* and you ask me to pull out the map?"

Patrick's eyes darted from the water to Lexi and back to the bog. "Er—that was *my* first, too."

Butterflies danced in her belly. "Really?"

"Um—yeah," he seemed to stumble over his fat tongue. "Don't tell Hanna."

Her brief elation was ruined—dashed before she could really relish the moment. It was as if a brick fell through the bottom of her stomach. Anger swelled as she stared up at him. "Hanna? Hanna? That's what you're going with as a follow-up?"

"Er—I said thanks."

"Ugh," she groaned as she yanked the map from her pocket and slapped it against the center of his chest.

"Um…"

"What?" she snapped.

"I did like the kiss."

Lexi's cheeks grew hot. "I did too." After a heartbeat, she took the map back and unraveled it across the hump of some mossy roots. "Hey, look," she pointed at the red, white, and blue illustration of the horned Calypso mushroom. "We're close. The mushroom's gotta be right there."

Patrick followed her finger up the embankment with his eyes, then swiveled around to look over both shoulders. "So, what *was* that thing?"

She shrugged. "Beats me. Some kind of swamp monster, I guess." Lexi stuffed the map in her back pocket and waded to the north side of the grove. Patrick followed and the pair climbed a raised patch of spongey, green moss, reaching the top of the long bank.

Her jaw dropped. Everything about the bog changed up

there. The trees looked healthier, the water looked cleaner, the air somehow seemed sweeter.

"Look, over there," she exclaimed, shooting a finger to their left.

A series of turtle-shaped mounds rose from the center of a large, crystal-clear pond. Following Patrick to the edge of the pool, a dozen feet of water separated them from the mossy rises where large, colorful, and grotesque mushrooms grew.

"We've found them!" she squealed, jumping in place. "I can't believe we finally found them. My sister is saved!" Lexi sucked in a breath through her teeth, and for a moment, the pair stood rooted to the edge of the embankment. She reached over, entwined her fingers in Patrick's, and kissed him for a third time.

"Yeah," he replied, seemingly a bit embarrassed. "I suppose we did find them. I never could've done it without you."

The stout mushroom's shin-high stems glistened bone white in contrast to their dark, crimson caps. Their bulbous tops were splashed with white liver spots. Half-a-dozen blue, curved horns erupted like vulgar pimples from the crest of each crown. They sat there like fat, colorful footstools.

"You were right. We didn't just find one," she said in astonishment. "We found a garden of them!"

Lexi stepped into the pool, but instead of finding shallow water like in the bog, she sunk in over her head. There seemed to be no bottom to the pool. She splashed until Patrick pulled her back to shore.

"What happened?" he cried.

"Don't know—lost my footing." She huffed. "It's deep. Really deep."

"Can you make it across?"

"Yeah. Hand me the pack. I'll hold it above my head."

Taking the backpack from Patrick, Lexi swam to the closest island and crawled upon a mound. Still sopping wet from the pond, she grabbed a white stem and with a firm tug, plucked the mushroom from the ground. Roots and mossy-green soil clung to the bottom of the meaty shaft. A greenish mist, almost like thin tendrils of smoke, sifted into the air from the cap. She coughed on the small cloud and immediately stumbled. Her head was woozy and everything started swimming in her vision. But she pressed on ignoring the feeling and plucked several more mushrooms.

Before she ripped off the head and slipped the first of the stems into her backpack, the crack of a twig broke the silence. Lexi froze, the bag half-slung over one shoulder. The fat mushroom was still pinched between the fingers of her other hand. As Patrick pulled himself from the pool, another noise, louder than the first, made him crane his neck up toward her. The beast erupted from the undergrowth in an explosion of brush and brambles as it lunged across the pool.

"Run, Lexi!" shouted Patrick, jumping into the clear water.

In her haste to escape, she slipped and fell backward, crushing half-a-dozen mushrooms. Lexi scrambled to her knees, eyes wide with terror, as a new greenish cloud of dust plumed into the air. She scrambled to the far side of the mound. "OH MY GOD—OH MY GOD —OH MY GOD!" she screamed, half-choking on the spore dust. Her vision swam as her world began to swirl and spin.

"Not her—get me. Get me!" Patrick yelled, waving his hands wildly overhead while treading water in the middle of the pool.

Lexi's unfocused eyes flicked from the beast to the mushrooms and back. The field was torn to pieces. Broken stems and smashed horned Calypso caps lay scattered across the small island.

44

MERMAID BAY

Valentine rolled the hem of his sweatpants up to his knees and shoved his socks inside his shoes. Listening to the caw of seagulls' overhead, he closed his eyes and inhaled the briny scent of saltwater. Shielding his eyes from the bright sun, he looked out across the blue surf of a strange, new ocean. He walked barefoot across the craggy coral shore near tidal pools below the tallest waterfall he'd ever seen. White-capped waves splashed against his legs as he stepped into a shallow pool.

God, I'm hungry. Those guys last night ate most of my food.

Removing his shirt, he tied the neck of his football jersey closed using it as a makeshift gunny sack. Valentine zipped around the pool in a flash using his new magical cuff. He punched his fist into the hard shell of one crab after another, shattering its orange shell to pieces.

He tossed his lunch into his jersey and craned his neck, looking up at the roaring water. Squinting, Valentine placed his hand over his brow hiding his eyes from the sun as a small figure plummeted down the throat of the falls.

"What the—" he stammered before dropping his crab-filled jersey to the sand.

Valentine cupped his hands together and expanded them as if stretching imaginary taffy between his fingers. A large blue-hued sphere filled the base of the waterfall.

From the moment the falling body entered his hologram, it slowed its deadly descent. The figure, whose long, dark hair was tousled about her head like a rat's nest, coasted toward the plunge pool in slow motion. Valentine dialed his hands some more until she practically hung in mid-air.

He looked up and down the shore for help. As his head snapped around, a new figure in dark robes appeared across the bay, running toward the water. The newcomer waved their hands over their head wildly. Unsure if the figure could speak English, Valentine pointed, jabbing his finger toward the plunge pool. "Hey, over here! She needs help!" he yelled. "I can't swim. Can you get her?"

He advanced toward the shore when a sonic blast erupted from the water; somewhere between him and the girl. The blast of air waves struck Valentine in the chest like a linebacker plowing him onto his back. Another blast sailed mere inches above his face. He leaned up on his elbows; two fish-like humans were half-submerged in the tide.

"Holy crap! What are those—mermaids?!" he exclaimed and scrambled up the reef, staring in disbelief. One of the mermaids had a thin, spiraled horn sticking out its forehead. Valentine cupped his hands again and created a new time-shift sphere between himself and the mermaids, just as another blast pulsed toward him in slow motion. "Man, who wizzed in their corn flakes?"

He twisted his hands a third time and fled at sub-sonic speeds. Ignoring the robed figure on the opposite shore, Valentine snatched his football jersey full of crabs, along with his shoes, and sped up the coral embankment. He glanced back around, first at the mermaids, and then to the figure he suspended over the plunge pool. *I can't save everyone—I tried.* As a third sonic blast rocketed toward him, Valentine dashed up onto the endless shoreline that extended away from the bay and toward Gilles Devereaux's shack he called home.

HANNA STEELE AND THE DEMIGOD CHRONICLES

~

The Crimson Queen
Book 2

TEASER

BOOK 2: THE CRIMSON QUEEN

Mermaid Bay

Hanna Steele coughed and gagged on the salty brackish water. Warm spit and sea water vomited back onto her chin from between half-parted lips. The roar of Blundersteep Falls raged in her ears louder than a freight train carving a track through the center of her skull. The force of thousands of gallons of water a second hitting the plunge pool sucked her under as if pulled by a weight.

She struggled to remain afloat, but she would've had more luck building a fire out of wet cornflakes than fight against the undertow. Hanna struggled for air, but there was none. Not where she sank. The sky above became a murky white as the pull of the current tugged her down as if rocks were tied to her ankles.

Hanna's lungs burnt like a lit match behind her sternum. The surface seemed so far away. There was no hope—no matter how she fought her way toward daylight. She was doomed. Dead after all. Hanna gagged on a mouthful of water. With her lungs spent of oxygen and the last of her air escaping her lips in a futile bubble, she closed her eyes against the end.

Suddenly, something wrapped around her neck, an arm, maybe, and pulled her back up against the tidal flows. Hanna burst from the surface coughing and gulping for air barely aware of the blue light pulsing from the pendant around her neck. "Are you alright? Can you breathe? Hold on, I'll tug you to shore," said a stranger.

Someone, maybe a woman by the long black hair that splashed into Hanna's face, tugged Hanna in awkward thumping jerks toward the shoreline. Hanna tried to talk, but it was as if her voice was gone along with her energy—leached from her by the harrowing plunge over Blundersteep Falls. She floated on her back as if filled with straw like a Raggedy Ann doll. Hanna stared up in a dumbfounded daze at the torrents of water plummeting down the waterfall. She thought of how she fell too. *Barlow did that. He threw me off the falls like so much discarded trash. Barlow did everything.*

Everything Barlow touches ends in tragedy.

Hanna's heart thundered in her chest and she coughed again as more brackish water splashed down her throat. Worried that she'd never get to shore, Hanna kicked and suddenly—miraculously—felt sand under her feet. She twisted onto her stomach and crawled weakly up the wet and gritty shore. Sand and small broken shells lodged under her fingernails. Hanna collapsed panting with exhaustion, her right cheek, neck, and body now covered in grit. *How could I still be alive after falling so far? This woman…this woman is a magician.*

"We have to get away," said a woman's voice from somewhere behind so Hanna couldn't see. "The water isn't safe. Are you strong enough to walk? The mermaids will be angry."

Hanna opened her mouth to say thank you when she heard hurried voices, strained thick with worry and excitement. Did she hear it right? Did the woman say mermaids? Hanna pushed herself up on shaky elbows, her breath coming out in choppy heaves. She saw a woman whose arms and face were covered in bark-like skin. The hood of her dark wet cotton robe concealed most of her face. Hanna was sure she'd seen someone like that before, but she was too tired to remember.

"Luna. Luna," said another voice, this one male and deep. "C'mon. Away from the shoreline. Before they know we're here." Hanna crooked her neck to see a black bald man in a dirty brown torn tunic and tattered jeans pull the woman to her feet.

Another woman, by the sound of her high-pitched voice, tugged at Hanna's elbow. The woman looked like a tabby cat with spots of copper and brown. Her marbled fur stuck out from the sleeves of her denim blue dress. It was a stitch-work that reminded Hanna of how her grandmother sewed homemade clothes. "Stone. Go there. Up the beach," she pointed in the direction of the giant cliff. "If they come, draw them away. The girl's leg is injured. She won't make it far." She turned her attention back to Hanna; the slits of her cat eyes widened showing a brilliant emerald green. "Come with me. I'm Felix. Hurry. We haven't much time." The feline's voice came out in quick purr-like commands. "Can you stand? Run if you can. They'll be here in no time."

What was she talking about? Was Felix still talking about mermaids? They were on dry land. How was that possible? Hanna was confused. She was tired. All she wanted to do was rest her face against the sand. She could hardly catch her breath. How long had it been? It seemed like only moments ago that she fell down the waterfall for Christ's sake. Didn't Felix and Luna understand that? Why were they prodding her to move so much? What the Billy heck was the hurry? She tried to jerk her arm free, to lay on the warm sand for a little bit longer, but Felix's grip tightened on her arm. The feline's sharp nails bit into Hanna's skin almost painfully.

A question took root in Hanna's mind and began to germinate. Why would mermaids be angry? An image of The Little Mermaid cut through the fog in her mind and Hanna was sure that mermaids weren't mean or dangerous. How could they be? All they did was sing. Then Hanna remembered the old maps she'd learned about at Midtown Valley High School—of the horrible sea monsters printed in the open spaces. Eerie thoughts crept in replacing the beautiful friendly face of the redheaded mermaid with pictures from old stories by sailors on the open seas who told of dangerous encounters. Images of Greek mythology punched through her foggy mind like someone trapped behind a theatre curtain and finally bursting free. Hanna suddenly remembered how the Sirens, with their sharp teeth and welcoming voices, enchanted sailors to their doom.

A fresh wave of goosebumps coated Hanna's arms and she made to move away from the cold water, but before Hanna could get her feet underneath her, the water along the shoreline erupted sending out streamers of brackish water. An absurd scene burst from the waves knocking Hanna onto her back. A dozen giant walruses rushed from the surf barking and jiggling their brown blubber in the sunlight. Hanna scrambled to her feet digging grooves with her hands and toes into the mushy sand. The cat woman pulled at Hanna's shoulders as the two half-ran, half-stumbled up the beach away from the new danger.

The great tusked beasts came in waves of three and four at a time charging up the shell-strewn beach. Sand and grit flew from under their flippers. They advanced, snorting sea mist into the warm afternoon air. The walruses jerked their heads so that their long white tusks flashed dangerously through the air looking more like sabers than teeth. Hanna was amazed at how quickly they were on land as the beasts kind of skipped up the beach on all four flippers leaving the water far behind.

Something else scared Hanna more than the ton of blubber and muscle barking its way up the beach. Her eyes drew upward to the backs of the walruses where riders mounted saddles like sea cowboys. Before Hanna could grasp the magnitude of her danger, sonic blasts erupted from the single spiraled horn protruding from the mermaid's foreheads. The sonic waves rippled through the air like a bullet and struck the sand blasting grit and sea shells twenty feet into the air. Other pulses whizzed by so close that the change in air pressure made her eardrums pop. *Plunk.*

Hanna saw Luna waving her friends away from the beach. "Over here," she yelled. "Off the beach…to the cave."

Hanna fell backward before finally gaining her footing on legs which felt as shaky as raw biscuit dough. She suddenly felt hot as if someone turned up the heat. It was as dry as a popcorn fart. Angry at the sudden attack, Hanna thrust her hands forward like she'd done so many times before since arriving in Smaradine to conjure her magic.

There was no tingly feeling that started at the base of her head to trail down her arms like marching ants. Instead of shooting bolts of hot blue plasma from her opened hands, a pathetic six-inch nub of energy jut from between the knuckles of her right fist. Her heart seemed to tumble from her chest. A hollow pain lanced deep within her as if she'd been punched in the lung. Although her hand still hummed with a magical vibration, in the chaos, Hanna forgot that Barlow, only minutes before throwing her off Blundersteep Falls, stole the magic that made her special.

The King of Thieves left her without any of her father's magic except the useless nub of plasma. What had Barlow said before hurling Hanna to her death? "I'll leave enough of your magic to remember me by…" Her mind glazed over and suddenly she couldn't think of anything at all but rage and a deep emptiness.

Now, not one, but two pairs of hands clutched at Hanna's shirt as two women dragged her from the shoreline; Luna on the right and Felix on the left. The man whose name must've been Stone, Hanna thought, wrinkled his face in a scream giving it the appearance of a shriveled apple. He screamed at the horde of mermaids and their mounts. It gave them just enough time to get away or so Hanna thought.

A noise like that from an explosion erupted from the plunge pool spewing brackish water fifty feet high and raining down upon them in blankets. A beast larger than a Greyhound bus burst from the center of the plunge pool. It was a horse-like leviathan so gargantuan that it made the Gorgon from the cave look like a puppy. The creature looked as if it were ripped straight out of a B-rated horror film. Greenish-blue scales coated its snout, neck, and body. The thing walked on four enormous legs which ended in webbed hooves.

The ground beneath Hanna's feet quaked under the its enormous weight. Its massive tail whipped back and forth as the creature's chest climbed out of the water. Anchored to its back were thick cable-like tentacles. The beast reared its head and bellowed a roar as the walruses parted for it to pass. Hanna stared in stunned awe as Luna's voice carried over the beach from behind.

"The queen…the Crimson Queen!" screamed Luna. "Everyone, run!"

Hanna's mouth fell open as if the hinges holding it together no longer worked. She stared gobsmacked at a woman sitting atop the leviathan's back—but she wasn't really just a woman. Far from it, Hanna thought. She sprouted a tail at one end and wore a crown at the other. Her milky-white skin juxtaposed the fiery red hair which cascaded over the Crimson Queen's chest puddling around her waist. Below that was a muscular body covered in greenish scales which tapered to a fish-like tail. Something stuck out from the queen's forehead like the start of a horn or the stunted end of a broken one.

Hanna tried to flee with Stone and Felix, but couldn't. Her legs didn't feel like her own. Hanna felt as if she were standing on wooden stilts rather than legs. Before she could move two steps, a slimy, wet tentacle stretched out groping with its suckers and talons. Hanna dropped to the ground and the tentacle ensnared Felix instead.

"No…NO…NOOOOO!" screamed Felix, her voice turning

into cat-like hisses and growls. Felix tried to claw her way in the sand back to freedom, but it was done and over quicker'n a hiccup. The beast lifted Felix from the sand as she kicked and hit and clawed in the air toward certain death. Hanna reached up jumping in the air to catch Felix's leg or maybe a toe, but the woman was too far out of reach.

"Girl," stormed the Crimson Queen, her voice somehow echoing across the open sand. "I know your kin...I know your kind." Hanna scrambled out from under the shadow of the queen's mount, her injured leg aching with every step. Horrorstruck, she limped up the beach ignoring the salty taste of brine and grit between her teeth. She reached for Stone, but he was with Luna much too far away to be of any help. Hanna was alone so, she turned back to face the abomination.

"Your kin," said the Crimson Queen as she spat a wad of phlegm at Hanna. "The great savior of Smaradine, murdered my husband. Kambo treated my husband's life as if it were nothing." The queen raised herself even higher in her saddle and pointed a milky-white finger at Hanna. "You, girl, kin of Kambo, will pay for the sins of your father. I will avenge my husband's death and you shall perish at my hand."

A chorus flowed from the surrounding mermaids on their mounts. "It has been said. Make it so."

Hanna opened her mouth to reply, but before she could respond the monstrous leviathan, which towered over the beach-front, lunged forward snapping its jagged jaws. The Crimson Queen thrust herself forward as her beast raked its great claws into the sand. It lashed out with its cord-like tail. Hanna screamed and dove face-first into the sand. She could feel the tentacle pass just over her back.

"Let me down! Let me down!" panicked Felix who dangled high above the plunge pool.

"Who are you?" screamed Hanna. "I've done nothing to you. Nothing!"

As if she didn't hear or ignored Hanna's words altogether,

the Crimson Queen barked a new command. "Surrender, demigod, or your friends will pay the price for your arrogance."

I can't surrender, Hanna said to herself. *I can't just quit. I have to save Ashley. I have to save my friends. I didn't come all this way—go through all this to give up—to throw in the towel to her.* She took a few steps backward.

"You have been marked, girl," said the Crimson Queen.

"It has been said. Make it so," echoed the mermaids a second time as they flanked their queen.

Hanna inched backward. The sand gripped the heel of her gimp leg as if it wanted her to stay, but she forced herself back dragging it more than stepping with it up to where the sand was dry. Hanna flicked her eyes toward Felix and mouthed the words 'I can't—I can't. I'm sorry'. She shook her head slowly and then backpedaled turning an awkward limp into a type of skipping sprint.

"Your cowardice will be your friend's demise!"

Hanna heard a loud splash and when she turned around Felix was gone. Water filled the edges of Hanna's eyes and blurred her vision into a kaleidoscope of shapes. She blinked away the tears and limped the rest of the way up the beach toward Luna who stood shell-shocked and silent.

"There is no place to hide, kin of Kambo," screeched the Queen from across the beach. "You will die."

Hanna pushed past Luna working herself through the fissure. She had to get away and somehow put the visions of Felix out of her mind. While Hanna did all she could to get away from the monsters that lurked outside, she couldn't rid herself of the monsters that lurked in her head. *You're not good enough. You could've saved her. You could've done something more. You let her die.* She felt a ripple of wind as a sonic blast erupted at the mouth of the cave behind her. Bits of rock and rubble spewed into the air and peppered the back of her chestnut hair. Pressed between the two halves of rock mid-way through the crevice, Hanna looked back into the daylight.

Hanna looked back to see Luna following her as the leviathan and the mermaid horde disappeared into the bay. *How did the Crimson Queen know about me? How did she know who I was?* It was at that point that she remembered the pendant around her neck and its blue pulsing light while she was in the water. So much of this new world was a mystery to Hanna, the pendant appeared to be a beacon for the Crimson Queen. How? Why? She thought for a moment and then realized that she may never know the answers. She may not live long enough. Hanna was trapped in a cave. The Crimson Queen lurked below the surface of the water and Barlow with his Brotherhood hid somewhere high above her in Blunder Castle. Saving her sisters and friends seemed like an impossible task, now more than ever.

ABOUT THE AUTHOR

Alex Dove was born November 25, 1970 in Detroit, Michigan. He spent his formative years moving between schools from the east coast to the Midwest with his parents. Before graduating from a small rural high school in 1989, he made the winning basketball shot during the Turkey Tournament on his eighteenth birthday.

He graduated four years later from Indiana University. Several years afterward, Alex earned a second bachelor's degree from DeVry University graduating Summa Cum Laude. He continued on to earn a third degree, a master's in history, from Eastern Illinois University.

After teaching history as an adjunct professor, Alex strived to make even more of an impact and shifted his focus to writing. That is when he authored his first manuscript, THE LOST DEMIGOD, in the six-book series, HANNA STEELE AND THE DEMIGOD CHRONICLES. Since his debut manuscript, Alex has authored seventeen additional manuscripts.

MORE BOOKS BY ALEX DOVE

More of Hanna Steele and the Demigod Chronicles coming soon…

The Crimson Queen #2

The Royal Thief #3

The Shadow King #4

The Gate Keepers #5

The Last Godstone #6

∼

Other books coming soon…

Stolen

Jack Must Die

∼

Join Alex Dove on social media. Follow his newsletter for exciting information. Visit www.AlexDove.com to learn more.

www.ingramcontent.com/pod-product-compliance
Lightning Source LLC
Chambersburg PA
CBHW061238120726
48001CB00001B/24